CLOSE TO ME

WITHDRAWN

Amanda Reynolds has taught creative writing in Cheltenham for the last five years. She currently lives in the Cotswolds with her husband, two children and two furry retrievers. *Close To Me* is her first novel.

Follow her on Twitter: @amandareynoldsj

Praise for *Close to Me*:

'Gripping, claustrophobic and often deeply unsettling, *Close to Me* exerts a magnetic pull from its first pages' – Kate Riordan, author of *The Girl in the Photograph*

'Amanda Reynolds . . . masterfully peels away the layers to keep the reader turning the pages. [L]yrical prose . . . adds to the wonderful experience of reading this accomplished debut' – Kathryn Hughes, author of *The Letter*

'*Close to Me* keeps you guessing, and then just when you think you know, you find another twist in the road. Gripping and suspenseful' – Michelle Adams, author of *My Sister*

CLOSE TO ME

AMANDA REYNOLDS

WILDFIRE

First published in 2017 by WILDFIRE
An imprint of HEADLINE PUBLISHING GROUP

1

Cataloguing in Publication Data is available from the British Library

ISBN 978 1 4722 4513 7

Typeset in Dante MT by Palimpsest Book Production Limited,
Falkirk, Stirlingshire

Printed and bound in Great Britain by
Clays Ltd, St Ives plc

Headline's policy is to use papers that are natural, renewable
and recyclable products and made from wood grown in sustainable forests.
The logging and manufacturing processes are expected to conform to the
environmental regulations of the country of origin.

HEADLINE PUBLISHING GROUP
An Hachette UK Company
Carmelite House
50 Victoria Embankment
London EC4Y 0DZ

www.headline.co.uk
www.hachette.co.uk

For Chris, Beth and Dan

Twenty-One Days After The Fall

I turn away from my husband, shifting my weight on to my side, as far from him as the bed will allow. The movement is instinctive, dulled by the fact I'm only half awake, in the place between reality and unreality. I shiver, close my eyes tighter. Outside, the blanket of deepest night is unrelenting, the wind charging its way between the tall trees which edge the drive. I listen to the rain hitting the tiles as it pummels the roof and stone walls of our converted barn; a lone parapet at the top of the hill. I imagine the water tracking its way down the huge windows, swamping our garden and then soaking into the ground beneath.

My husband's slow steady breaths and the familiar night-time noises within the house find my ear. I pull the duvet around me and allow my subconscious to take over, unlatching from the present, an almost physical letting-go. As I succumb to sleep the memories come, but I know they are unreliable; broken and unpredictable. The harder I search the further they retreat, but then something breaks through, at once unbidden and yet desperately wanted. As much as I crave the past, I fear it too.

He lunges, his right arm raised, slamming me hard against the wall; the force of his body holding me there. In his eyes I recognise passion, but of what nature and from what emotion it's derived I cannot tell. I reach out again to the memory, my hand touching his face, turning him towards me to read something in his expression, to look into his eyes, begging him to stop. He pushes me away, grasping my wrist to dig his fingers hard into the pale skin and then the veins beneath, his rapid breaths hot against my neck. Insistent and urgent he holds me there, pinned to the wall. I fought him, of that I'm certain; my nails deep in his skin until he cried out.

I open my eyes; traces of early morning sunlight warming the room, creating patterns on the ceiling. I watch the rise and fall of my husband's chest; the gentle sound of his breathing. Then he wakes too, turns to me and smiles, an easy smile, no trace of deceit; as though the last year had never happened.

1

The Day of The Fall

Cold and smooth, the flagstones of our hallway are reassuringly solid beneath me, each one a raised bump, the mortar crevices like emery boards to my touch, segmenting the repeating pattern. There's no part of me I can move except for my left hand, and yet I feel I'm floating free.

'Jo, can you hear me?' my husband whispers, his skin damp to the touch as his top lip brushes my cheek. 'Jo, answer me,' Rob insists. 'For god's sake, Jo. Are you okay? Just answer me!'

A loud sound echoes down the hallway, thuds so imperative they pierce the darkness, pulling me up to the surface gasping. There's someone at the door, shouting to be let in, but Rob ignores them, asking me over and over what's wrong. I don't reply, the words forming, then gone. The door is opened, a chill blast of air rushing towards me as a woman's voice draws near, calm and measured. Then at last blissful

3

sleep, like a cool blanket enfolding me; releasing the tight fist of pain.

Consciousness arrives piecemeal; elements returning one by one, although I resist them. First there's the light beyond my closed eyelids, then sounds and movement around me. I may have been lying here a while, or no time at all. I try to recall what happened, my fingers worrying at the stones beneath me, their cool touch comforting. I was on the landing, I know that much, and Rob was behind me, too close, his long strides outpacing me. 'No!'

'Jo, it's okay, you passed out again, but I'm here to help.' She smells sharp and astringent, her breath warm. 'Please try to stay still so I can help you.'

I shiver, the cold air funnelling in through the open door, the wind whipping around the barn, relentless as always. I'd thought we could tame the elements, lay down roots, but, fifteen years on, the constant battering of the wind still disturbs me. Nothing fragile survives up here, stringy shoots plucked from tender soil, saplings bent then snapped, gates snatched from hands, car doors wrenched open and slammed closed, tearing fingernails and bruising shins. 'We live at the top of a hill, what do you expect?' Not this. Not every day.

'Jo, do you remember what happened?' Rob asks. 'You fell, Jo. You fell down the stairs. Lost your footing. You were coming down in front of me. I tried to save you, Jo. I tried to save you.' He keeps saying it, as if that will make me remember.

A pinch to my finger, a cuff to my arm, sensors stuck to my skin. I try to sit up, but Rob tells me to stay still, his palms under my armpits, hoisting me on to his knees, the bones of

4

them angular beneath my back. I loll against my husband, too weak to struggle, his long limbs now encircling me, but his hold on me is too tight, I can't breathe.

'Jo, can you answer some questions?' the calm voice asks.

'She's barely conscious!' Rob shouts, his words slicing through me. 'Can't it wait?'

The reply is firm. 'Rob, you need to move back, let Jo speak.'

I open my eyes to the bright light, the stairs stretching up and over me, dizzying. 'I don't want him,' I say. Rob's hands are hot on my skin, his fingers stroking my neck, my shoulder, pressing in. 'Tell him to let me go!' I struggle and cry out in pain, but she insists I stay still.

'Can you move away, Rob? You need to let us do our job,' she says, then she leans over me, her face above mine, asking me so many questions and I try to answer, to tell her where it hurts, how I am. 'Can you remember what you were doing before you fell, Jo?'

I look up the stairs to Fin's door. 'I was sad,' I tell her. 'Because of Fin.'

'Fin?' the stranger echoes, her eyes kind.

'It's our son,' Rob says, his hand now squeezing mine.

Pain shoots through my wrist and Rob drops my hand; says he's sorry. He keeps repeating how sorry he is, and all I can think is, I don't want him this close to me.

'Just give us some space, Rob,' the stranger tells him, taking my other wrist in her hand. 'I'm giving you something for the pain, Jo.'

'I don't want him,' I say. 'Get him off me!' The throbbing

in my head takes over, a searing heat beneath my skull. I close my eyes, their voices slipping away.

Different lights when I open my eyes, brighter than before, and movement. We're winding down the hill away from the barn, and there's no siren, but speed, and so many wires, so many questions and Rob is beside me again, but I can't get away from him because I'm tethered to the bed, strapped down, and now I don't remember why I'd wanted to escape, although the urge hasn't left me and when he touches me I flinch.

'How old is your wife, Rob?' the stranger asks, her face now in focus; younger than I'd imagined.

'Jo's fifty-five,' Rob replies, his voice choked with emotion. He never cries; why now?

'No,' I whisper, my voice barely there. 'Not yet.'

'What did you say, Jo?' Rob's voice closer now.

I turn away, close my eyes, try to sleep, but I'm jolted awake by a thought. 'The kids, do they know?'

'I'll ring them once we get to the hospital,' Rob replies.

He shouldn't worry them, I tell him. Especially Fin, he's got enough to cope with on his first day.

'*First day?*' Rob asks. 'Jo, what are you talking about?'

I close my eyes again, too tired to reply. My skull feels loose beneath my scalp, each bump and bend in the road spinning my head like a gyroscope. I imagine my brain sloshing around in liquid, like a foetus in the womb, its legs and arms kicking and punching from within. The need to sleep is overwhelming, but the pain keeps me awake, my lucidity only in thought, not speech. Why would Rob tell them I'm fifty-five? He's normally such a stickler for detail. It's two months until my birthday.

We turn a sharp corner and all I can hear is Rob's voice, saying again that I fell, then he leans over me, his mouth almost touching mine and he whispers, 'You'll be fine, Jo. I promise.'

And I whisper back, 'Don't make me any more promises, you bastard.'

2

The Day After The Fall

'*If you were going to kill me, how would you do it?*' *I ask, turning to Rob in the darkness, my hands seeking him out across the bed.* '*I've already thought about how I'd kill you,*' *I say.* '*I'd stab you with a kitchen knife.*' *I laugh and move closer, draping my arm across his bare chest.*

'*Well I haven't thought about it at all,*' *he says, lifting my hand to his lips, peppering the palm with kisses. I shriek with laughter as he pulls me to him, skin on skin, familiar, safe—*

'I bet you gave yourself a fright!' the nurse says, her voice loud enough to rouse me from sleep. She pulls back the curtains and the weak sunlight lifts my lids. I shade my eyes with the back of my left hand, the right too painful to move, watching as she crosses the room, her blonde curls coming into focus, sandy tufts pulled into a top-knot, her movements perky, like her tone.

'The doctor's started his rounds, so let's get you sitting up.' She removes a remote control from my slack grasp, untangling the corkscrewed flex with her other hand as she presses a button to raise the head of the bed. 'Better?' she asks, considering my seated position.

'Yes, thank you.' I smile, but a sharp pain is shooting from one side of my head to the other. 'Do you know if my husband's brought my phone in? I'm lost without it.'

She laughs. 'You ladies and your phones. No, not yet, but I think he's on his way in.' She smooths the covers. 'He was so worried about you last night. Kept saying you fell, like he couldn't believe what had happened. It's the shock, isn't it?' She's at the end of the bed now, reading the beige folder of notes she brought in with her. 'Shook you both up like a bottle of fizz!' She laughs, and I must wince because she asks, 'Is the pain bad, Jo? Where does it hurt?'

'My head,' I reply, tears in my eyes as I squint against the agony of it, a pang of fear accompanying the awful beat of my headache. I open my eyes and tell her, 'I can't remember what happened, everyone keeps saying I fell. But I don't know what happened. Do you know?'

She's beside me again, casting her eyes down to the beige folder. 'Let's have a look, shall we?'

I look down too, at the hospital gown and bedding covering me, only my forearms exposed. There's a bruise spreading either side of the tight support bandage which stretches from the fingers to elbow of my right arm, and two of the nails are torn, as though I'd reached out, clawed at something to save myself.

'18:02 the paramedic attended you, that's what it says in here,' she tells me, very matter-of-fact. 'Took a tumble down the stairs. You don't remember, sweetie?'

I shake my head and the pain worsens. 'I remember I was at the bottom of the stairs and then I must have blacked out. Do you know what time Rob went home last night?' I start crying again, the nurse's kindness releasing more emotion. 'I can't remember much at all of what happened after we got here. When did my husband leave? Do you know?'

'Oh, Jo. Don't upset yourself, sweetie. I'll ask the doctor to give you something stronger for the pain. You lie still for now.' She's wheeling the blood pressure monitor around to the other side of the bed. 'You got any kids?' she asks me, wrapping a cuff around my upper arm.

'Two. Sash and Fin. Fin's just gone to university.'

She smiles. 'You must be very proud. Your daughter going to go too?'

'She's finished her degree; got a job and her own flat.'

The nurse laughs loudly. 'Nooo! You're not old enough.'

There's a tap on the door and, as the nurse rushes to open it, the tension on my arm builds until I think the Velcro fastening is sure to pull apart. As the cuff slowly deflates a young man with dark brown eyes enters the room.

'Well, Mrs Harding, you're looking a bit brighter this morning,' he says in heavily accented English. He turns to the nurse and asks her about my blood pressure, which had apparently been a concern last night.

'BP back to normal, I'm pleased to say', the nurse tells him, rewarding me with a smile, although her eyebrows are raised as if I have finally decided to behave.

I smile back and ask her if she'll stay with me a while. She laughs, tells me I'm a funny one, but I mean it; I want her here when Rob arrives. Every time I think of him all I can see is his angry expression at the top of the stairs, although my recollections are incomplete. *Were we arguing? Is that why I stumbled? Was I trying to get away from him?*

'Good,' the doctor says, studying the notes the nurse has handed him, reading as he nods. 'Very good. And the headache, Jo?' He regards me from the end of the bed, his manner detached.

The nurse answers for me. 'She still has a headache; we've had a few tears.'

'Okay, I can prescribe something for the pain. No dizziness, nausea?'

'No, not really,' I reply.

His dark eyes rove over me like a scan. 'You seem to have passed all our tests with flying colours. I think you can go home, if you would like?' I hesitate, but he's already saying, 'Good, good. I'll arrange for some painkillers to take with you and the leaflets we talked about, do you remember?'

'I don't—'. I begin, interrupted by the door opening.

'You look a bit better, darling,' Rob says, my overnight bag in his hand, stepping aside to allow the nurse to leave. He drops the bag to the floor and leans down to kiss me. I turn my head away and he frowns, asks how I'm feeling.

'Mr Harding.' The doctor extends a small hand to my husband's much larger one. 'I'm Mr Agrawal, we briefly spoke late last night as you were leaving. Your wife seems to be recovering well; a nasty sprain to her right wrist, some bruising, but of course our primary concern is still the head injury. She took a nasty knock and was unconscious for several minutes, I understand.'

Was I? I think back, recalling again Rob's anger, then lying on the hallway floor, but nothing in between. There was an ambulance ride, followed by endless waits for scans and X-rays, and then another delay as a bed was found – Rob's insistence I must have a private room slowing down the process. I'd wanted to sleep above everything else, even the kids had dropped out of my mind, a thought which brings panic as it returns. 'Are Sash and Fin okay?' I ask Rob, cutting across his conversation with Mr Agrawal.

'. . . she was out for maybe one or two minutes, I'm not sure.' Rob sits down in the chair next to the bed, his right hand balling into a fist on the blue waffle blanket. 'They're both absolutely fine. Worried about you, of course, but they're fine.'

The doctor tells me I can see them soon, clearly assuming our children are younger, still living at home and waiting for our return.

'*Home?*' Rob asks, standing up. 'You mean now?'

I listen to the doctor's instruction that I mustn't be left alone for the next twenty-four to forty-eight hours, but yes, I'm well enough to be discharged. Rob protests, says surely I need to stay longer, but the doctor tells him as long as he's there to keep an eye on me I'm fine to go home. Rob explains how he needs to make arrangements; he has work to think of; other commitments. He finally remembers me, glances over and says of course he'll sort it out, he just needs to make some calls. Shame he didn't say that first, I think, looking away from his false smile.

'Good, good.' The doctor is writing now, his pen quick across the pages of notes. 'The memory loss is most troubling, of course.' He pauses. 'It's relatively common with this type of injury, but it's unusual for it to be so protracted. I was just reminding your wife of the—'

'I don't understand.' I look from the doctor to my husband. 'What does he mean?'

My husband sits beside me again, lowering himself into the armchair. 'Last night, after you'd fallen, the paramedic asked what was the last thing you could remember. Do you know what you said?'

I think back to yesterday, the ambulance that brought me here, the tests which followed, the drug-induced sleep. 'I remember the ambulance, then here—'

'No, before all that.' He glances at the doctor then back to me. 'You said something about Fin, that you were sad, then in the ambulance you said—'

The doctor interrupts now. 'Anything you like, Jo, just tell us what your most recent recollections are.'

I know I woke up on the hall floor, the stones cold beneath me, the wind howling through the open door. I try to recall what happened before that, the details much harder to work back to. 'I think I remember you and I on the landing,' I say to Rob. 'What were we doing?'

'We were just coming down the stairs when your foot slipped. You don't remember?'

'Try not to prompt your wife, Mr Harding,' the doctor says, moving closer. 'Let her be the one to speak.'

'Sorry.' Rob stands and walks to the window, his back to us both.

'I don't remember how I fell,' I say. 'Just that I was at the bottom of the stairs.'

'What about before the fall, Jo?' the doctor asks. 'Anything at all . . .'

I take a moment, digging deeper this time, although it's hard to concentrate with the pain in my head. I can't be certain Rob and I argued, but I do recall our day. 'We'd just got back from dropping our son at university,' I tell him, then I speak to Rob, who has turned to face me, his left hand covering his mouth. 'I don't want Fin's first few days disrupted. Tell him not to worry, he mustn't come home just for me.'

'Oh god, Jo. Is that really the last thing you remember?' Rob sits down in the armchair by my bed. 'Last night, you were so disorientated, I thought by this morning you might have . . .'

'What?' I ask him, trying to pull myself up, my right wrist sore when I try to use it.

'I know you don't remember falling, but—' He looks away, glancing at the doctor.

'What's wrong? Are the kids okay? Rob, tell me!'

'I've told you, Sash and Fin are both fine.' He sighs and takes my good hand in his, staring at our entwined fingers for far too long before he speaks, the feel of his palm against mine unnatural. 'But that wasn't yesterday, Jo. You're talking about something that happened a year ago.'

'You must be mixed up.' I pull my hand away.

'I'm not, Jo. Fin went to university this time last September.'

The doctor is explaining episodic and semantic memory, telling us I will most likely remember the everyday matters of my life even though the events of the last twelve months are currently eluding me. I can hear his words, but I'm not listening. It must be a mistake. The memory is so clear to me: dropping

Fin at university, coming home to an empty house, the smell of his sheets as I gathered them around me. It feels as if it were yesterday; surely it must be so? I can't have lost a whole year just because I banged my head at the bottom of the stairs. I'm here, I'm fine, just a few bumps and bruises. This must be a mistake. But even as I explain away the frightening facts, I sense their truth. It may feel like Fin left for university only yesterday, but somewhere deep within I know that, between that moment in Fin's empty bedroom and my fall down the stairs, there's a huge hole; an immense gap in my understanding.

'Rob?' I whisper, looking up at him. He's on his feet now, pacing the room, filling it with his tall presence. 'I don't understand, Rob. You're frightening me. What have I missed? Tell me what I've missed!'

But Rob isn't listening to me, he's addressing the doctor, his voice raised to him, looking down at least a foot to the slight man he's asked to clarify *exactly* what I will and won't remember.

'It's like I was trying to explain to your wife last night, the events immediately prior to Jo's fall may never come back,' the doctor replies. 'The brain may not have had time to encode them properly before the trauma, but everything else should return, given time. There are support groups, and counsellors, and I will keep in touch, see Jo in a few days, to check how she's progressing. The good news is that there's no permanent damage, the scans showed nothing untoward internally.'

'*Is that it?*' Rob roars. 'That's what I pay a bloody fortune for, so we can have the best care, and you're telling me to take her home and hope for the best?'

'If you could try to remain calm, Mr Harding?'

'Rob, please,' I say. 'I need you to explain to me what's going on.'

Rob sits beside me again, gently resting his hands on the bed, but avoiding any direct contact, as though I might break if he should touch any part of me. He tells me everything will be fine, promises in fact. I sob, pushing Rob away when he tries to comfort me.

'You can help your wife, Mr Harding . . .' the doctor says '. . . guide her through this difficult time, but it will require patience. And you will need to be patient too, Jo,' he tells me. 'Of course, if you require any help, we will do everything we can, but rest at home is the best thing, where you will be surrounded by familiarity.'

'And you still think this is likely to be temporary?' Rob asks.

I say nothing, the sobs all-consuming now. None of it makes sense; the doctor's words unreal, as if it were someone else he and Rob were discussing. He tells us it will take time and, when I do remember things, it will probably be like pieces of a jigsaw puzzle falling into place, a bit here, a bit there. The doctor is leaving now, telling us he'll ask the nurse to bring us some leaflets – support groups, that kind of thing. 'If you need anything at all, please contact my secretary.'

Rob waits until the door is closed, then stands to vent his fury. 'That's it? You've got a brain injury and they expect us to cope on our own?'

'Please don't shout,' I tell him, wiping away my tears with my palm. 'My head hurts so much.'

All I want is for this to go away; for yesterday to be yesterday and Rob to be the husband I remember, but when I look at him I feel nothing but unease. I reach up to touch the sore spot on my head, a soft squashy egg on my scalp, too tender to explore further.

Rob turns away and walks to the window again, staring out at the uninspiring view over the hospital car park. I glanced out on my first excursion to the bathroom, late last night after Rob had left. I felt sore and disorientated, but nothing like this and I don't recall the doctor telling me about the memory loss. How can I have lost a whole year? What has happened in that year? Fear and panic grip me and I sob again. Rob is at my side instantly, telling me the kids are fine, we're fine, there's nothing important that I've missed, I just need to rest, to get better. I have him. He will look after me. Just him and me. We'll be fine, he promises.

So we wait, Rob returning to the view, the silence slowly eating up the minutes as I try to find my way back to the events that brought me here. I know I was ferried to this room in the early hours, although time had become elastic, as if the night would never end. I was in a wheelchair, the young porter teasing me that I was off to the Ritz. 'That's what we call the private wing,' he'd said, and I'd felt the need to apologise for my good fortune, then wondered why. It's only now, as I recall fragments of a conversation between Rob and me, a memory from that lost year, presumably, that I begin to make the connection. I must have remembered the feeling it invoked last night, then lost the thread of the memory on our arrival in this room, overtaken by my desperate need to sleep. I think of it again now, something to do with a holiday we took, just the two of us, the same feeling of disquiet accompanying my recollections, but this time I hear Rob's words more clearly: '*They need our money, Jo. It's what keeps their economy alive.*' I look up at him, his focus still beyond the window, his shoulders up, hands in his trouser pockets.

'We were planning a holiday, just you and me,' I say, triumphant at the retrieval of a lost memory, and so quickly, as if the rest will follow, an avalanche displaced by a shout echoing through the expanse of white. The hope of it all-important.

He turns, his expression anxious. 'You've remembered something?'

'Maybe,' I reply. 'Did we go away?'

'Yes,' he says. 'The Caribbean; last October.'

'What else?' I ask. 'What have I missed?'

'Nothing much,' he says. 'I'll tell you everything when you're home, but there's nothing to worry about, I promise. Try to rest.'

I turn my head to the pillow and close my eyes on the pain, too tired to argue with him.

'Hey,' Rob says as I open my eyes. 'You've been asleep almost an hour. How you feeling?'

He's seated beside me and I can smell his cologne and the washing powder in his fresh shirt. 'I'm okay,' I tell him, looking towards the door. 'Do you think it will be much longer now? Perhaps I should get dressed?'

'I want you to come home, of course I do,' Rob says, leaning closer. I wonder if he's been beside me the whole time I was asleep, watching me. He smiles, then sighs, his breath glancing my cheek. 'But this memory loss, Jo. We've no idea what we're dealing with. Maybe if you stay another night or two—'

The door opens and the nurse arrives, all bustle and business, tablets to explain, leaflets to pass on, then she's gone again, telling us we need to get ready to leave. Rob unzips the bag he brought with him and helps me to sit, then stand, the wooziness each movement brings making my progress from lying to standing much slower than I'd like. I lean on him, the necessary contact unnatural to me, as though my hand in his were the last thing I want. The feeling is strong, but I have no idea why. I look at him and he smiles again, helping me to dress in the clothes he's selected. Getting into jeans is awkward; my head pounds as I lean over to insert one leg, then the other. I tell him he chose badly, expecting him to react, but he surprises me and agrees, then apologises. He's overly attentive, his constant fussing and questions tiring, and I tell him so. Again I think he'll say something retaliatory, I don't usually speak to him like that, but he doesn't, just repacks the bag with the nightclothes I don't now need, then he answers the door to the nurse, who's returned with a porter and a wheelchair.

'Ready to roll?' the young man asks. I'm not certain if it's the porter from last night, or someone similar, but either way his breezy attitude is welcome.

'I'm sure I don't need a wheelchair,' I tell him, feeling weak as I stand again.

'It's hospital policy,' the nurse informs me, helping me to climb in. 'I'll walk with you to the door whilst you bring the car around, Mr Harding. Just avoid the ambulance route, okay?'

The nurse waits with me at the sliding doors, the ambulances coming and going, patients stretchered or walking, some with obvious injuries, the last one inert. I wonder if that patient, their identity concealed in a rush of activity, is already dead. The trolley disappears through the double doors to our left as the nurse is saying how kind my husband is, how handsome. 'How many years have you been married?' she asks.

'Twenty-three,' I tell her, then realise it must be twenty-four, although I don't bother to correct myself. It doesn't really matter.

When Rob's car pulls up beside us I hesitate, struck by the thought I may not want to go home after all. The nurse asks me if I'm okay, I look so pale. Then Rob is helping me into the passenger side, strapping me in.

The nurse raises her hand to wave us off, her blonde curls turning back towards the doors. I want to call out to her, to keep her with me. I place my good hand to the window and allow the tears to fall, turning away from Rob as he reaches across to me.

September – Last Year

'He didn't mean it,' Rob says. 'I'm sure he'll be back for a visit before then.'

'I know he didn't mean it, of course he didn't,' I reply, picking up my pace so I'm slightly ahead of him, although I've no hope of maintaining my lead, with Rob's long legs taking one stride to my two.

Fin's parting words, *'I'll see you at Christmas'*, were clearly meant to lighten the mood, but I can feel the swell of my tears, a hard lump in my throat as I march towards Rob's car, parked at the opposite end of the campus to Fin's accommodation block. The realisation that all the closer car parks were full had finally stretched Rob's tolerance beyond breaking point on our arrival and he'd argued with the jobsworth parking attendant, pointing to Fin's belongings, which were stuffed into every inch of the car. It had already been a long morning, but Fin's quiet words, 'Dad, don't', had silenced him, and he'd driven into the packed car park without further complaint.

'Come on, Jo. Don't cry.' Rob catches me up and grabs my hand. 'I thought you'd be okay today; second time around and all that.'

He's right, but it's actually much harder this time because we're going back to an empty house. I glance at Rob and he grins back, squeezing my hand. Everything is so simple for him, emotions dismissed with reason and logic. He wants to solve my problem, always has, but I'm really not in the mood. I'd prefer to lick my wounds than be consoled or cajoled.

'Anyway, you've still got me,' Rob observes. 'God help you!' He laughs, swinging our clasped hands between us and I smile back, but the tears fall too. 'Come on, Jo. You and me. It'll be fun!'

I pull my sunglasses from the top of my head and we walk on, past concrete sixties accommodation blocks identical to the one where we've just left Fin; right-angled buildings with square windows which afford brief glimpses of student life: empty beer bottles and pizza boxes, stacks of textbooks, and posters of films and bands I've never heard of. We drop hands to crush ourselves against a wall, past unloading cars, each one a repetition of much the same scene; teens disassociating themselves from their parents, ready to become something other than a child. I smile at a woman who, like me, is losing her battle with threatening tears, her cheeks damp as she cradles a box of belongings to her, hugging them tight. She smiles back; a moment shared.

The drive home passes slowly, each mile extending the distance between me and my boy. And he is still a boy. I saw it in his eyes as we left; the throwaway comment to mask his emotion, his fragility as he allowed me to hold him and then shaken his father's hand. I check my phone again, resisting the urge to send Fin another message, the first unanswered.

'You okay?' Rob taps my knee as he changes gear.

I'm looking out of the window at the lorry we're overtaking, the solidity of it then replaced with the blur of the endless grass verge. 'I'm fine,' I reply. 'Just tired.'

'Have a sleep if you like,' Rob says, turning down the sound of the tennis match on the radio.

'You think he'll be okay?' I ask, glancing at Rob's profile against the fading light. 'I mean, after what happened at school. He's never really settled well, and—'

'That was years ago,' Rob says, patting my knee more firmly this time. 'This will be the making of him. He'll love it, promise.'

I close my eyes, but although I'm exhausted, my mind is not. I see Fin in his student room, the accommodation so basic and lacking in home comforts, despite the posters we Blu-Tacked to the wall and the bright bedding I'd chosen. 'You sure you'll be okay?' I asked Fin, hugging him one last time; taller than me, but still a boy.

'I'll be fine,' he said. 'Don't worry about me, Mum.' Then he lowered his head and flicked his fringe back, not in an ostentatious way, because that's not Fin's style, but because it helps him cope with those moments in life that overwhelm him. He looked so alone, waving us off at the door, his attempt at bravado slipping as soon as we'd walked away, his vulnerability caught in his expression as I glanced back.

'You asleep?' Rob asks and I shake my head, then close my eyes tighter, allowing the movement of the car to lull me into a fitful sleep.

The barn feels bigger, the silence echoing around us, between us, from us. I leave Rob to bring in the emptied boxes and suitcases and go upstairs to change, pausing outside Fin's room. The tidiness within is unsettling. *'He hasn't died,'* Sash said when I rang her from the car. *'He's just gone to university.'* I pull the duvet from its cover, strip the sheet from the mattress and the pillowcases from the pillows and, although I'd intended to throw the washing straight in the laundry basket, I sit down on the empty bed, gathering the musty bedding around me to inhale Fin's scent.

'He hasn't died, Jo,' Rob says, finding me there. He's carrying a suitcase, now lightened of its load, just a few hours ago filled with the shirts and jeans I'd ironed.

'That was Sash's line,' I say, sitting up. 'You two are so alike.'

Rob lays a hand on my shoulder, the fingers reaching my collar bone, gently pressing in. I stand and hold him for a moment, his long arms wrapping around me, his head resting on top of mine. 'Come on,' he says. 'We're both tired.'

We make love, the day edging away as we comfort one another. Afterwards, Rob rolls away from me and I know he will fall asleep immediately, so I nudge his back. He turns over to face me, but I can see little of his expression; the bedroom is almost entirely devoid of light, just the green glow of the numbers on his alarm clock telling me it's almost midnight. 'What is it?' he asks.

'Do you remember how we used to play that silly word game, before the kids were born?'

'What game?' he replies, his words slurred with impending sleep.

'If you had a superpower, what would it be?' I say through the darkness. 'Or if you were going to kill me, how would you do it?'

'And you've thought about this already?' he asks, the moonlight seeping around the corners of the blind to pick out his creased eyes, a faint smile.

I tell him my superpower would be time travel and he says he has no idea what his would be, although he's clearly enjoying the game.

'And you've decided how you're going to kill me?' he asks, his interest piqued.

'I'd stab you.' I laugh, reaching out to him, laying my hand on his bare chest. 'With a kitchen knife.'

'Yes, that's good.' He laughs too and squeezes my stabbing hand. 'Hopefully death would be instantaneous, and we already have a knife block, so no preparation required.'

'How would you kill me?' I ask, leaning up on one elbow to wait for his response.

He hesitates, then says, 'I guess I'd strangle you with my bare hands.' Then he grabs me and pulls me to him, both of us laughing.

3

The Day After The Fall

The first thing I notice when we arrive home from the hospital is the head-shaped hole at the bottom of the stairs. The plasterboard to the right of the tread is caved in, a hollow bowl-shaped impression, presumably made by my skull, which took the brunt of the impact. Rob sees it too and, although I try not to, I flinch when he reaches out to comfort me, my hands instinctively covering my bruised scalp. I look up and imagine the drop, maybe eight or nine stairs missed as I fell. *If I fell*. I pause, the thought shocking. I glance across at Rob, watching as he pokes the toe of his brogue into the crumbling plaster.

'The whole staircase will have to be repainted. And some plastering I guess.'

I tell him not yet; I don't want the mess or the noise.

'No, of course not yet,' he says, taking his jacket, slung across my shoulders as he'd helped me from the car. He drapes

26

the soft tweed over the bannister and tells me to go up, he'll stick the kettle on.

I tackle the stairs slowly, framed portraits accompanying my climb, a mixture of school photos of the kids and snaps of family holidays. They're all familiar, but I look at them with fresh eyes, searching each one as I pass, perhaps afraid there will be one I don't know. I'm relieved to find there isn't. Sash was always so blonde, with a mane of almost-white hair against olive skin. She tans at the merest hint of sun, her skin colouring just like Rob's. But her hair was always mine, the sleekness of it. Fin is the image of the grandfather he was named after and can now barely remember, the shock of dark hair and pale gentle features so reminiscent of my father's. I stop to touch the children's faces through the glass, but the sharp pain returns, my injured hand reaching up to cradle the side of my head. I sink down to the stair beneath me, my head now in both my hands, my eyes closed. With the pain comes a memory, indistinct and hazy, but persistent, and despite the waves of agony I concentrate, in the hope it will form more clearly. *There are flashes of two people, Rob and me. There's a struggle, at the very top of the stairs. We were definitely arguing, but more than that, Rob was holding on to me.* I open my eyes to see Rob, his hand outstretched to me as he runs up the stairs. 'Jo? What's wrong?'

The pain intensifies, stabbing behind my eyes so I'm forced to close them again. *The image is still there; Rob holding on to me.*

I open my eyes to ask him what happened between us before I fell, but something holds me back. He's two stairs below me, looking up, and in his eyes I see a note of caution.

'Take my hand,' he says, reaching out.

'I can manage,' I tell him, standing and walking up the stairs, then past three empty bedrooms until I reach our room.

The bed's unmade, a wet towel on the floor of the ensuite. Rob apologises for the mess, rushing past me to pick up the towel. He then pulls back the duvet and straightens the sheet, gesturing me towards the bed, a hand cupping the back of my head to guide me down towards the pillows.

'How's that feel?' he asks, casting me entirely in shadow so I can't see anything but him.

'Better,' I reply, lifting myself up so I'm seated, the pillows at my back.

'Good.' He walks out and returns with my overnight bag, placing it beside me. 'I'll be back with a cup of tea.'

I hear him run downstairs and go into the kitchen as I unzip my bag in search of the painkillers, calling down to Rob that I'll need a glass of water too, although I can't find the prescription as I rummage amongst yesterday's clothes. I check the side pocket and see my passport is in there; I toss it on to the bed and then watch it slide to the floor as I get up. Staggering to the bathroom I splash my face with water, studying the bruises on my face then peeling away my clothes to inspect my body. I hold up my right hand first and look at the compression bandage, noticing how swollen my wrist is and shocked again by the dark purple stain creeping out from under the bandage, but also by something else I hadn't spotted at the hospital. On my inner wrist, nestling amongst the bruises, there is a curious set of tiny cuts, semicircles, which look to be healing over now, as though they are an older injury. I rub at them, then look up

28

at my face again in the mirror, running my fingers over the swollen and puffy skin, two black eyes to complete the picture, the right one much worse than the left. Finally, I look down at my naked body; the lost year's wear and tear is not particularly evident, although I think I am thinner and I also have a rainbow of bruises on my knees and thighs.

Rob knocks on the door. 'You okay in there? I've got your tea.'

I take my robe from the hook and open the door. 'Inspecting the damage,' I tell him, and he looks away as I cover myself.

'Must have been quite a fall,' I say, climbing into the bed again.

Rob leans over me to tuck me under the duvet, my tea placed at my side on the bedside cabinet, the painkillers next to them, which he tells me we left in the car.

'You forgot my water. And my handbag,' I tell him, trying to find a comfortable position for my right arm.

Rob bends down to pick up my passport from the floor. 'Why's this out?' he asks, holding it up.

I shrug, tell him it was in the overnight bag which he's now unpacking for me. He looks unsure, as if he's working something out, then he says, 'Must be from when we went away last October.' He looks over and asks if I remember much about the trip. I shake my head, immediately wishing I hadn't and wondering how many more times he's going to ask me if I remember things and I'll have to say, *No, I don't.* 'Anything else you need?' he asks.

I tell him just my handbag, thinking my phone will be in there. He runs downstairs and I hear him taking the stairs back up, two at a time. He holds out a handbag to me I don't recognise, a beautiful soft leather, my favourite designer label, telling me it was my birthday present. I take it with my left hand, searching around inside for the reassuring solidity of my phone. Frustrated, I tip the contents out on to the bed, but it's clear it isn't there. Rob watches me, asking what I'm looking for, then commenting that I don't need to text the kids, he's spoken to them; they're coming over later. 'Fin's on his way home from uni?' I ask.

'I told you, he'll be here later,' Rob says, turning away. 'So try to relax now. You don't need to—'

'That's not the point!' I shout, holding the side of my head, as if that will steady the rocking inside.

Rob looks startled at my outburst, as am I, but he says nothing.

'I need my phone, Rob. I need it.' I'm crying, although I'm angry with him, not upset.

He sits on the bed and tells me to calm down, returning the tipped-out contents to the opened bag. I stare at him, daring him to ignore me when I'm so weak, so battered. 'Where's my phone?' I ask again. 'I need it.'

He sighs, 'I told you, Jo.'

'Told me what?'

'Jesus! That your phone broke when you fell. You dropped it and it smashed on the hall tiles. I'll order you a new one today.'

I don't recall that conversation, but everything's so confused and my head hurts so much. I demand to know where my phone is, my belligerence surprising us both it would seem, but I need my phone, it's important to me, not just to text the kids, but to reconnect to my old self, the one before the fall.

'If I order it now, it should be here tomorrow, Monday at the latest,' he says, creasing his forehead as he folds my clean nightclothes into my bedside drawer. 'I'm guessing you want the same one as before.'

'No, not the new one!' I shout, the pain exploding inside my head with each syllable. 'My broken phone, where is that?'

Rob takes a deep breath, as though I'm the one being unreasonable, and tells me it's in the dustbin, he threw it away this morning, then he corrects himself and says actually, it's gone, the bins were emptied while we were at the hospital. He sits on the bed again and tries to manoeuvre me back on to the pillows, but I resist, arguing that if he'd removed the SIM card we might have an old handset it could go in. But of course he didn't, commenting that 'strangely enough' he was thinking about me at the time, not a broken phone.

'But you found time to throw it away and to take the dustbin out?' I ask him, not quite ready to give up the fight.

'I was tidying up. What is wrong with you, Jo? This isn't like you at all. Do you need the doctor; shall I call Mr Agrawal?'

'I need my phone,' I say, sinking back into the pillows. 'Why won't you let me have it?'

Rob sighs and walks out. I hear him downstairs and then the sound of a laptop starting up, followed by the soft repetitive tones of emails downloading and his fingers tapping the keys. The familiarity is soporific, as if life were normal: Rob seated at the kitchen island catching up on work as I potter around the house, Fin on his computer or playing his guitar. He will have been at university for a whole year now, his life there established. But it's not just Fin's absence that's bothering me, I want my phone, and not having it makes it seem all the more important. I live by my phone, my umbilical cord to the kids, the outside world, a life beyond the stone walls of our converted barn; the elements battering us at the top of the hill, miles from our nearest neighbour.

I try to calm myself with the thought that I'll sit at my laptop later, check on my emails. Maybe that will provide me with some connection to the missing months, bring back some memories. I close my eyes and succumb to the exhaustion, but with sleep comes a different connection to the past, loose and undefined, but still insistent and demanding. The images tumble back and forth, twisting and changing, some clear, some not. My body writhes, the duvet kicked off, my skin prickling with heat, then damp with sweat.

His face is turned from me; in shadow. I reach out to touch him, recall him to me, he feels so far away. I'm desperate to find him, but then Rob's face appears and I'm screaming at him to let me go.

It's dark when I wake, the duvet tucked around me again, presumably by Rob. The blind is still open, but there's only blackness beyond. It reminds me of the first night we were here, how Fin had needed a night light and Sash had pretended she'd fallen asleep whilst reading so she could leave on her bedside lamp. We'd stood outside, Rob and I, the kids finally asleep, a glass of wine in hand, looking up. *'It's perfect,'* Rob had said, admiring our new home, the dark curve of the sky above us and only the brightness of the stars to punctuate the inky canvas. *'No light pollution,'* he'd said. *'And no one but us up here.'* I'd taken more convincing, as had the kids. Fin was eventually bribed with the promise of a telescope, but Sash never really settled.

I walk to the bedroom window and look out at the black hills in the distance and then down to the gravel drive and the lane beyond. Someone is driving up the hill, the hedges illuminated by a car's headlights. The familiar bubble-shaped car takes the sharp right turn into our drive and parks next to my Mini. The passenger door opens and Fin emerges, accompanied by a burst of loud music, then Sash gets out and slams the driver-side door. They both look up at the barn, but with no lights on in the bedroom they mustn't see me as they don't return my wave, their bodies bent against the wind and rain as they walk towards the front door.

I pull on my cardigan over my robe, an extra layer over the flimsy silk, shivering now I'm out of bed. Then I carefully take the stairs one at a time, my left palm to the bannister for support. I follow their voices into the kitchen, a low urgent thread of conversation, Fin, then Rob, now Sash, my name mentioned, then a shush from Rob as I join them.

'Talking about me?' I ask.

'Of course,' Rob answers. 'How are you feeling?'

'I still have a headache, but maybe a bit better.'

'You gave us such a fright, Mum,' Sash says, moving towards me, her arms outstretched, but the shock of her appearance is too much, as if it were a stranger reaching out to me, not my own child. Her hallmark long hair is all but gone, shorn into a severe cut that ends at her chin, and her make-up is harsh, smoky eyes and stained lips, her clothes shapeless and

33

unfeminine. She asks if I'm okay, how am I feeling? I say nothing and return her embrace as best I can, but I notice that she is also restrained.

'I couldn't believe it when Dad rang and said you'd fallen,' she says, stepping back to take in my injuries. 'You look like Dad beat you up!'

'And you look so different,' I say to her. 'It takes a bit of getting used to.'

'I guess you'll need time to adjust to a lot of things,' she says, looking at her father.

'Have you told them about the memory loss?' I ask Rob, and he nods.

I'd been trying to be brave for the children, but my composure leaves me now, Sash looking around for a tissue, Fin standing awkwardly by the kitchen door as though he'd rather not be here. Rob is protective, his arm around my shoulders. I fight the urge to shake him off, not wanting to cause a scene in front of the kids, and rationalising that my defensiveness is my body's way of healing, an armour to cushion me from further harm, but it doesn't feel like that. It's almost as if—

'Jo!' I jump at Rob's imperative tone. 'I said let's get you into the sitting room.'

He guides me across the hallway and down on to the sofa. Sash sits next to me, her hand reaching for mine. Her fingers are covered in chunky rings embellished with skulls and serpents, the wide bands cutting into the fleshy pads between each knuckle so I'm afraid to squeeze them too hard; they don't even look like Sash's hands. I look up at her face and search for familiarity behind the thickly kohled eyes. 'You look well,' I say. 'When did you have your hair cut?'

'Months ago.' Her hand moves from mine to her bare neck, where she pats the blunt edges of the longest layers and tilts her head to bend the thick cleat of hair in her palm. 'I'm not sure you liked it at the time. It's so strange you don't remember. You sure there's nothing coming back to you since Fin went to uni?' She glances across to Rob and Fin. 'Not my birthday, or your holiday? Christmas?' She stops herself, her eyes darting towards Rob again.

'Even stranger for me,' I tell her. 'Like waking up after a year's worth of sleep.' I look across at Fin and Rob, seated on the other sofa, their long legs stretched out in front of them to reach the rug, neither of them looking at the other. 'Did we have a nice Christmas?' I ask Fin.

He smiles at me. 'You had three trees.'

'Oh my, sounds like me.' I smile at him. 'I bet I loved having you home, but you needn't have rushed back to see me now. I'm fine.'

Fin smiles back, his appearance relatively unchanged, although he's lost weight and he wears the last year heavily, his narrow shoulders more drooped, his eyes darting from me to his lap as though he can't bear to look at me and also can't look away. 'I wanted to see you, see how you are. It must be really weird, losing your memory.'

'There are bits I remember,' I say. 'Just fragments, more a feeling.'

'What kind of feeling?' Rob asks, leaning forward.

'A feeling that things have changed, I suppose,' I reply. 'As though I'm missing something, which I suppose I am. Lots of things.' I stare at Rob until he looks away, then I smile at Fin. 'You don't have to worry, darling. I'm sure it will all come back. You can get back to university and by the time you next come home I'll be right as rain.'

Rob stands up. 'Did you say you'd brought something for dinner, Sash?'

'Oh my goodness, a lot has changed!' I say, as brightly as I can.

Sash unpacks the contents of a cool-bag on to the kitchen island. Despite Rob's objections I've insisted I'll be fine perched on one of the high stools watching her preparations. 'I didn't even know you could cook,' I say. 'And you have a cool-bag, you're very grown-up.'

Sash smiles. 'Nice to return the favour.'

Fin and Rob are upstairs tidying, at Sash's insistence. She seems to have taken charge, shouting instructions up the stairs every now and then. 'And bring the washing down with you!' she calls up to them now, pushing up the sleeves of her jumper as she rejoins me in the kitchen. It looks like she's borrowed the shapeless garment from a male friend. I keep looking at her, hoping I'll get used to the new Sash, but silently mourning the version I remember; girlish and softer. She grasps the onion she was expertly chopping, her eyes streaming as she picks up the knife, dark rivulets of eyeliner tracking the contours of her face.

'What are you making?' I ask.

'Pasta with peppers and mushrooms,' she replies, wiping her

36

eyes with the back of her hands so they too are streaked with black. 'And there's salad and bread.'

'Mmm, sounds wonderful, darling. Can I help?' I slide down from the stool, but Sash rushes round to stop me.

'You stay there; you're doing nothing until you're better. When Dad's back at work Fin can take over. About time he did something useful with himself.' Sash looks up at me with alarm.

'What do you mean?' I ask, repositioning myself on the stool, using my good hand for support. 'Fin needs to get back to university.' I look across at her. 'Doesn't he?'

Fin walks into the kitchen with armfuls of bedding and towels and asks Sash where she wants them, Rob at his shoulder.

'Why aren't you at university?' I ask my son.

Sash looks at her father, her eyes widening. 'I didn't tell her, Dad. Honestly.'

'Oh for god's sake, Sash!' Rob shouts. 'I leave you alone with your mother for ten minutes . . .'

'Rob, calm down,' I say, frowning at him. 'You're overreacting. Sash didn't say anything. I guessed.'

I look at Sash and smile, but she's still staring at her father, her eyes locked on his, as if she's daring him to challenge her. 'I said I didn't tell her, okay?'

'Well someone did, and you were the only one here,' Rob replies.

'Fin?' I ask, ignoring Sash and Rob's argument. 'Why aren't you at university?'

He's looking at Rob as though his father's reaction were more important than mine, the washing falling from my son's skinny arms. 'It wasn't for me, Mum,' he replies, flicking his fringe back and then looking down at his feet, covered by the dropped laundry.

'You've left your course?'

'I'm really sorry.'

I tell him he doesn't need to apologise, but it's hard to conceal my shock. Maybe there's more to it than I know; a better plan. I just don't understand why no one said anything. I challenge Rob, who mutters something about not wanting to worry me, pushing past Sash to pick up the discarded washing.

'Well you *are* worrying me.' I stand up from the stool to look at Fin, whose head is still bowed, his eyes to the floor. 'So where did you stay last night?'

Fin looks at his father, then to me. 'With a friend.'

I ask him which friend and he says he's called Ryan, and no, I don't know him.

'Are you home tonight?' I ask, the thought of Fin sleeping just a few doors away from me a comforting one.

'I don't live here any more, Mum,' Fin says, again glancing at his father.

My head is filled with lead. I'm unable to process the fact he's left university, let alone left home, which I guess proves Rob's point that I'm not up to all this, although I'm not ready to give up on the truth quite yet. Fin shrugs when I press him further, but says nothing.

'Ask Dad.' Sash answers for him. 'He's the one pulling the strings, telling us what we can and can't say.'

'What does that mean?' I ask Rob. 'Is there something else I should know?'

'No, nothing.' He glares at Sash. 'Like I said, I didn't want to worry you.' He smiles at me, throws the washing into the utility room and comes back to give me a hug which I accept because the children are watching, then he guides me towards the dining table. 'Just try to relax. We're all fine and we're all together, okay?'

But it's not okay. I don't understand what's going on; all the looks, all the secrets.

We eat in relative silence, every topic a sticky one, and I find I have no appetite for the food, only the lost information. I ask questions, but every answer is guarded, passed through the filter of Rob's approval; the kids both looking to their father for his blessing when they tell me anything of their lives since last September. I glean some facts: Sash has moved out of the grotty bedsit she'd rented after she came back from university. She's somewhere much nicer she says, which is a relief, and she's seeing someone called Thomas, the name provoking a beat of silence at the table. Fin is happy, he says, living with a friend and playing guitar in a band.

They leave because I'm tired, but more so because Rob insists. He sees them out and when he comes back to sit beside me on the sofa, his arm along the back of the cushion, fingers almost touching my shoulder, I ask the question that encompasses everything I've wanted to ask all evening. 'What is it you're hiding, Rob?'

He tips his head back and looks up at the ceiling, taking an audible intake of breath. 'I'm not hiding anything, Jo.'

'Start with the kids. Tell me everything,' I say, folding my arms and ignoring his excuses until he begins to unravel the past, or at least his edited version of it.

Fin had stayed at university until the end of the first semester, Rob tells me. Rob and I went on holiday, redecorated a bit, had my birthday meal, which was nice, then it was almost Christmas. I ask how Fin had seemed when he came home at Christmas, trying to work out how we could have neglected him for a whole semester, three months of ignoring the signs whilst we went on holiday and redecorated, celebrating my birthday without him. What was I thinking? Fin's always been a loner, bullied at school, retreating into himself at home.

'He was . . .' Rob pauses, then says, 'He was definitely quiet. But that's Fin, isn't it?' He rubs his face then supports his chin with fingertips dug into his square jaw as he tells me more. 'It was the New Year when he told us. We were starting to pack up his stuff to take him back when he announced he wasn't going, had decided it wasn't worth it.'

'He must have said more than that,' I say, sitting up to fend off the tiredness which is threatening to engulf me. 'Was there a problem; friendship issues? The course?'

Rob tells me Fin just kept repeating how it wasn't for him. It had seemed ridiculous to abandon his studies with no other plans, not even a job lined up, but he'd been adamant. I concede that I can't imagine a scenario where either of us would have allowed Fin to leave university without a fight and Rob says we both tried our best.

'You really don't remember?' Rob studies me again, as if I'm lying to him and might give myself away if he watches me carefully enough.

'No, Rob. I *really* don't remember.'

'There's no need to speak to me like that,' he says, standing up to collect our glasses from the floor, water for me and another glass of wine for him. 'I'm only telling you what happened. Don't make me accountable for it all over again.'

He walks to the kitchen and I can hear him loading the dishwasher. When he returns he reaches out his hand to cup my face and tells me he's sorry, and I allow him that contact because I want him to start talking again. He glances the pad of his thumb across my cheek and I curl my feet beneath me on the sofa, resisting an involuntary shiver at his touch, looking away as he insists again that he will look after me; I'm not to worry. I'm so tired, but I force myself to stay awake and ask him how we could have missed the signs with Fin.

'You had your suspicions,' Rob tells me. 'You'd noticed how there was barely any contact from him after we'd dropped him at university. I told you to give him more space, time to adjust, but you were right. He struggled from the start, never really took to student life.'

'Poor Fin,' I say, more to myself than Rob.

I look over at Rob, imagining how he'd suppressed my concerns, told me not to fuss, to give Fin some space. But I'd been right. Our son was miserable. I swallow my recriminations and ask, 'So why did he decide to leave home? Surely he would have been happier living here?'

Rob clears his throat; tells me he wasn't there when Fin left home the next morning.

'*The next morning?* I assumed he'd only recently moved out.'

Rob scratches his arm. 'I lost my temper with him, Jo. He wouldn't see sense.' He looks over at me. 'It was so frustrating to see him throw everything away like that.'

'*You hit him?*'

'Why on earth would you say that?' Rob asks, his voice raised, his body turned to face me, his face full of obvious hurt. 'You always have to think the worst of me.'

'Sorry, I thought—'

'You've only lost the last year, Jo. It's like you don't know me at all. You honestly think I'd hit our son?'

'No, of course not,' I tell him, and I *do* know that, because Rob would never ever hurt the kids, he idolises them both. That's what makes his frustration so understandable, and I feel it too. I may not remember it, but I can imagine the impossible position we were in, witnessing our fantastically bright son throw away everything he'd worked for, and knowing there was nothing we could do to make him change his mind.

'So what happened?' I ask, and when Rob doesn't respond, his face turned away from me in protest, I add, 'I'm sorry, I didn't mean it. Please tell me what happened.'

Rob looks back at me and sighs. 'What happened was I gave Fin a lecture about making choices that could affect the rest of his life, how he was too young to know his own mind.' Rob arches his neck, looks up at the ceiling with his eyes half closed. 'I wish I could undo it, but then again . . . If I hadn't said those things, maybe I'd be kicking myself for not trying.' He catches my eye and says, 'Sometimes you just have to be the grown-up, unpopular as that is.'

'Do we know this boy Ryan he's staying with?'

Rob shakes his head. 'You met him the day Fin moved out. He came here to pick Fin up. You said he seemed nice, a bit older. Fin's very vague on the details, doesn't want us involved.'

'But he's not found a job?'

'A day here and there, nothing permanent. He and Ryan helped at a festival in the summer, and he went to a fruit-picking farm in Devon for a week.' Rob raises his eyebrows as he tells me. 'It's disappointing, to say the least.'

'Oh god.' I look away from him, trying to process everything he's told me. There's an unreality to it, which cushions the blow, but only a little. 'How does he manage? Do we help him?' Rob tells me he sends him rent money, but it's best not to mention it to him.

I nod. 'He's always been so independent, must be killing him to take your handouts.'

Rob rubs his hands over his face. 'It's a mess.' He glances at me. 'Are you tired?'

'No, not really. Tell me about Sash.'

Rob sighs, asks again if I'm sure I'm up to this. I tell him I need to know. He shifts his position, angles himself towards me on the sofa, one knee raised up to rest beside me. 'You remember her flat? The grotty bedsit.'

'Unfortunately I do; she was there before I . . . I mean it was over a year ago when she moved in.'

'She only stayed a few months in the end,' Rob says, grimacing when I say, 'That's good, isn't it?' He looks like he's going to tell me something, but isn't certain how to word it; a few false starts before he says, 'It's complicated. She met this guy called Thomas.'

I nod, recalling the atmosphere at the table when his name had come up.

'Do I know this Thomas?' I ask, looking at Rob.

'We've met him a couple of times.' He sighs, as though the effort of telling me is almost too much. 'He works in a wine bar in town, manages it in fact, but only because his friend owns the bar and the flat above. Thomas is one of those liberal posh boys, the kind who think they're going to save the world from the likes of us because they joined the Labour party and turned vegan.'

'You don't like him?'

'Neither of us do, Jo. He's a nightmare.'

'And Sash is living with him?'

'Unfortunately, yes.' Robs rubs his eyes.

I think of our daughter's appearance, so altered. Her hair shorn into a roughly cropped style, her clothes unfeminine, her lipstick red and dark. I'd told her I liked it, but I hadn't, not really. I ask Rob how they met and he says at the bar, maybe, he's not sure.

'When did she cut her hair?'

'Don't know,' Rob replies, still deep in thought.

'You must have noticed; it's so different.'

Rob shrugs. 'We didn't see her for a while. At least, you did, but she was angry with me. I told her I didn't approve.'

'Of this boy, Thomas?'

He sighs. 'She brought him here, I told him off. He was a complete idiot. It's been a huge compromise, but at least Sash is back in our lives. I suppose for a while you blamed me, and it's true, I shouldn't have . . . Jo?'

The painkillers I took at dinner must be wearing off; my head feels heavy, the weight of it too much to bear. I lean against the back of the sofa and close my eyes for a second. 'It's all such a mess,' I whisper.

'Jo.' Rob pats my knee with his hand, the force of it causing me to open my eyes. 'I'm sorry it's not better news,' he says. 'But the important thing is we're all still in each other's lives. The kids will get past this; *we'll* get past this.'

'Will we?'

Rob smiles at me. 'Of course we will.' He leans across and kisses me on the cheek. 'I promise.'

I recoil from his touch, the pain in my head obliterating everything else, even the questions which remain unanswered. They can wait. For now, my headache throbs so hard it's all I can do to stagger up the stairs, Rob worrying at my side until I crawl into bed, the sheets cool and soothing as he leaves me to rest.

Rob joins me much later. I turn away from him, protecting my wrist perhaps, although it's more a feeling I can't stand to have him anywhere near me.

September – Last Year

'So you still like your job?' I ask my daughter, smiling at her across the café table, the tea things laid out between us, although Sash has chosen, as always, her favourite marshmallow-topped hot chocolate. Her long hair falls across her face as she leans forward to pick up the end of the long-handled spoon. Then she looks up from her drink, her lips pressed tightly together in that determined way she has when she's asserting her right to independence. I first saw that expression when she was a one-year-old trying to walk, her frustration arriving in angry bursts as she struggled to move around on her own, batting away my helping hand.

'It's okay,' is her considered response. She licks cream from her top lip. 'Just a job.'

'Not a career?' I pour the loose-leaf tea into my cup, the strainer balanced across it, catching the delicate dried leaves.

'I don't know, Mum.' She raises her eyebrows at me. 'Maybe

I'll jack it all in and work in a bar or something. It would pay more!'

I reach across the table to pat her hand, the rings which cover each of her fingers catching the light from the small window. It's a dark café, small and expensive; I'm not sure why we always come here, it's not even particularly near her work.

'You need to give it a year or two, then you'll be doing more interesting stuff; you said so yourself. Bar work won't offer you any progression.'

'It might.' Sash slurps her drink from the spoon. 'How's Dad?'

I tell her he's fine, thinking how much easier it's been for Rob to adjust to our empty nest, his career filling up the spaces the children have left behind. He's also thriving on the extra attention he gets from me, says it's like we're newly-weds again, although I decide not to share this nugget with our daughter, imagining her reaction.

'And you?' Sash asks, looking up.

'I'm okay.' I smile back at her. 'It's quiet without you and your brother.'

She asks how Fin's coped with freshers' week – '*Hardly little bro's sort of thing*' – and I tell her she's right, her brother is very different from her. She'd loved the whole experience of university, throwing herself into it from the start, gathering friends like the badges she pinned to her rucksack, the same one she still uses, although I've offered to buy her something better. I suppose it reminds her of student life and the friends she made; I can only hope Fin finds his tribe as easily as she did.

'I couldn't tell you if he's enjoying it,' I reply. 'You know what he's like; not a lot of communication.'

'Oh, for god's sake!' Sash discards the spoon, dropping it into her drink. 'I told him you'd worry if he went all quiet on you. Why doesn't he listen?' Sash lifts her hair from her neck, a ribbon of silk that almost reaches her waist as she leans back in her chair. 'So what are you doing with yourself, now you don't have to tidy up his mess all the time?'

'Oh you know, generally lying around, painting my nails, that kind of thing.' I curl my fingers in and blow on imaginary wet polish. 'I have nothing else to do, after all. No purpose in life . . .' I smile at her.

'You know what I mean.' She rolls her eyes at me. 'You must have more time on your hands.'

I tell her how we're thinking of redecorating her room, turning it into a guest bedroom so Rob can have the smallest room as his study. 'It's a project for me, really—'

She pounces on my words. 'What if I want to stay the night?'

'You never stay the night, but it would still be your room whenever you wanted it,' I tell her. 'You know that.'

Sash prods at the melting marshmallows with her spoon, scooping them into her mouth as she ignores me. I offer to help with her flat, give it a spruce-up at the same time, suggesting I could even get our decorators to take a look, see what they can do with the place, but she tells me there's no point, she probably won't be there that long. For a moment it sparks a hope that she's finally seen sense and, far from redecorating her room, we may soon be moving her back into it, but she says she's looking for somewhere else, maybe to share; a disappointment to me, but anywhere would be an improvement on her bedsit, or as Sash likes to refer to it, her 'studio apartment'. It's the kind of hovel I'd thought no longer existed; acrid damp spores stick to my clothes long after I've been there, not that we're often invited. The two visits we've made since she moved in have both been fraught occasions; Rob clock-watching, concerned about the dodgy neighbours who might take a fancy to his expensive car, and me trying to find something positive to comment on, but failing miserably. I tell Sash I'm pleased she's moving on, and if she needs a bit of a loan from us she's only to ask. She rolls her eyes again, but doesn't refuse outright.

The waitress arrives with our order: one tuna, one cheese. We split the sandwiches between us, and Sash says, 'Ooh, I know what I was going to say to you: voluntary work.'

I listen, although resistant to the idea. Not a laudable reaction, but I've never really fancied the coal-face of charity work, preferring to ease my conscience with a generous direct debit. But Sash manages to capture my attention with her personal account of helping at a drop-in centre next to her office. 'Don't look so surprised,' she says. 'I've only been once, but hopefully I'll go back. There's a food bank and an advice centre. I just handed out leaflets and washed up, but it was good fun.' She glances up at me. 'Met some nice people.'

'What does it involve, this drop-in centre?' I ask, trying to imagine Sash in such an unlikely scenario.

'You have to get a background check, make sure you're not a raving paedo. Work sponsored mine, but I'm sure the centre would help you with that. Then it's just a case of turning up and pitching in with anything you can do to help.' She bites her sandwich. 'I feel a bit guilty that I haven't been back after they went to all that trouble.'

'What sort of people go to this drop-in centre?' I ask, pushing away my plate.

'Anyone who's vulnerable and needs help.' Sash picks up my uneaten crusts and nibbles them.

I imagine drug users and homeless people, and scratch at my scalp. 'I don't like the sound of this, Sash. Who's in charge? How are you safeguarded?'

'*Safeguarded?* These people are all around us, Mum. All the time. That's our society.'

I look around us at the café clientele; mostly silver-haired apart from us and the ladies-who-lunch seated by the door, boutique shopping bags propped up at the sides of their chairs. Sash sighs and concedes that okay, maybe they don't pop in here for their three-quid latte, but they're part of society and they need our help. I resist the temptation to point out she's drinking a three-quid hot chocolate and most likely I will be the one paying for it. Her principles are perhaps no better than mine, the badges on her jacket about as committed as she'd become at university, the realities of charity work as unappealing to her back then as they are to me now; which makes her stance all the more surprising.

'Think about it, Mum. Helping others would give you a purpose.'

'So now you've moved out and Fin is at university, I have no purpose. Is that what you're saying?'

'You actually said that yourself.'

'I was joking!'

50

'You know what I mean.' Sash drops a crust back on my plate. 'You need something new to focus on, or you'll end up depressed. Something just for you.'

I laugh at her dramatics, chiding her for suggesting my main aim in life was to tidy up after her and her brother. 'I do things,' I tell her, struggling to come up with anything that doesn't involve the home or her father. 'I have purpose.'

'I need to get back to work,' she tells me, picking up her rucksack. 'How much do I owe you?'

'No, nothing. My treat.' I stand up to kiss her goodbye, then watch as she leaves, her white-blonde hair catching the breeze as she walks away, back to her work, a purposeful occupation, even if she doesn't see it that way.

I'm paying the waitress when Sash's text arrives.

It's fine with me if you want to change my room. Thanks for lunch. S xxx PS Think about what I said. Love you!

4

Two Days After The Fall

*H*is face is turned from me; in shadow. I reach out to touch him, recall him to me, he feels so far away. His body is naked, the skin smooth, contours highlighted by the weak light. My fingers run over his back, encircling him. His body is warm against mine. He touches me and I cry out, the desire palpable. I need to see his face; to know who he is. And even with my husband sleeping beside me, I don't want to leave this man, to open my eyes and be apart from him. He's touching me now, pulling me to him, and I can feel the tension between us. This is illicit, forbidden even, and dangerous. This is not my husband. What was this? An affair, a fantasy? What am I remembering?

'Jo, are you awake?' Rob's face is close to mine. 'Do you need your tablets?'

'No, it's fine,' I tell him. 'Go back to sleep.'

I lift myself up on to the pillows, forgetting the sprain in my right wrist until it's too late. I take a deep breath, holding in the moan that threatens. Rob has shifted on to his side, right arm above him, his eyes closed. I look across at him, his head a dark oval on the white pillow, full of things I have lost. I wish I could cleave it open like a coconut, scrape out the bits I need and discard the rest. The revolting idea both appals and fascinates me. I wonder at my own thoughts; so twisted, so random, and I wonder at the images, what they mean. I'm a wife, a mother, faithful, monogamous; *aren't I?* I leave our bed, Rob asleep again now, and close the door gently behind me.

The landing is dark, a sliver of moonlight illuminating my way, delivered to me from the window at the far end; the only one we decided shouldn't have a blind because of the unobstructed view down the valley, green slopes and black hills beyond, as though we were the last people on earth. The thought of our splendid isolation feels bleaker at this unearthly hour; but everything does when you're the only person awake. I walk past the smallest bedroom, then with a hand to the wall to guide myself I switch on the light and walk into the room which I still think of as my daughter's. Sash's double bed is now in the middle of the wall facing me, not pushed into the corner as I remember it, and the floral bedding has been replaced with a muted green, topped with a throw and scatter cushions in the same grey as the freshly painted walls. Her desk is gone, as are the posters and photos, and there's a new light fitting. I open the wardrobe and find it empty, the winter clothes she'd left behind in the heat of summer now gone.

The night after we'd dropped Fin at university I'd woken early too, or maybe it was not long after I'd fallen asleep. I remember going into Fin's room in the darkness. Rob was exhausted, he'd worked hard packing up the car and driving us there and back. He'd slept soundly after we'd made love. The thought of the closeness we'd shared, maybe even taken for granted, is a shock to me, as though we were never capable of such tender moments. I push aside that feeling and go back to that night, recalling how I'd stared at the angular digits picked out on Rob's clock radio, sleep eluding me. Fin was on my mind, a dip in my stomach each time I'd thought of him alone. He'd messaged me just one letter in response to my numerous texts: **K**. Despite the melancholy of that time I smile at the memory, or perhaps at the fact I've recalled something new, even if it is only a few hours reclaimed from a whole year of loss. I switch off the light as I leave, the insistent pounding in my head reminding me I need more painkillers.

Downstairs, the kitchen echoes with the loneliness of the hour. I open the blind to retrieve my tablets from the sill. The window fills with nothing but blackness, but then, as my eyes adjust, I can make out the silhouetted trees which edge the drive. They've stilled. The wind must have dropped a little, and the rain has gone, allowing a glimmer of dawn beyond the hills, etching their outline.

I flick on the lights, the glare from the recessed down-lighters above the kitchen island causing me to screw my eyes tight for a moment, then I push a glass against the dispenser on the front of the fridge, swallowing down two painkillers and refilling my glass with ice-cold water. My thirst is hard to slake, the dehydration of the hospital clinging to me like the antiseptic smell on my skin. I sip the second glass more slowly, my eyes drawn to the familiar ephemera attached to the fridge: photos and cards trapped by an eclectic collection of magnets. I began collecting them when we first moved to the barn. The huge bulk of the American-style fridge freezer needed softening, I felt; the colourful souvenirs relaxed its harsh lines. Maybe it wasn't just the fridge. Every line in the barn is angular, with huge open spaces to be filled, but the fridge was my focus, its brooding presence somehow symbolic. It had been a big move for all of us: leaving behind the estate house where we'd returned with our newborns to come up here, to the top of the hill, distancing ourselves from the other families with whom we'd shared the children's formative years. Rob had wanted clean lines to match the newly converted barn; minimalistic. It hadn't felt compatible with family life, the Italian leather sofas and smoked-glass tables, the charcoal-grey blinds instead of curtains, but Rob had convinced me, as he always did, his clarity of thought over-riding my half-formed objections. It wasn't as though I minded, at least not much. But the gaudy fridge magnets became my battle ground, and I won. Everywhere we went I would buy another one, cheap mementos of trips we took, places we'd visited. I run my fingers over them now: an apple from New York, a dolphin emblazoned with a glittery 'Florida' sign, the leaning Tower of Pisa picked out in technicolour. Their familiarity is comforting to me, each card and photo they secure well known. The children are so much younger, their expressions open and without guile, their home-made birthday messages and Mother's Day cards written in the spidery hand of many years ago. I'm not remembering anything new, but familiarity is good, and there have been flashes, snippets coming back.

'Jo? You okay?' Rob has placed his hand on my back, finding the square of exposed flesh between the straps of my nightdress. I turn to face him, the heat of his palm on my skin startling me. He's naked except for a pair of boxer shorts, his face slack with tiredness.

'You frightened me,' I tell him. 'I told you to go back to sleep.' I push past him to lean against the kitchen island for support, the exhaustion and my headache returning and redoubling their onslaught.

'Do you remember all these?' he asks, looking at the magnets. 'The holidays, I mean.' He touches the dolphin and it twists in his large hand, the bond broken by his clumsiness. The magnet falls, his quick reflexes only just saving it from the hard floor.

I take it from him as he stands up, his touch feeling strange to me so I pull back and almost drop the magnet again. I replace it on the side of the fridge, finding it awkward with my left hand, but refusing Rob's offer of help.

'Of course I remember them,' I tell him, my fingers tracing each one again: Florida, Italy, New York; then my hand hovers over the only one I don't recognise. 'Except this one.'

The magnet is of a white sand beach, blue ocean and palm trees. Rob points to the messy lettering, tiny at the bottom of the magnet, his broad shoulder touching mine as he leans forward. I look more closely, struggling to read the small writing without my glasses, but also so I can disconnect myself from him. 'Dominican Republic?' I ask, having no recollection of going there. 'I'm guessing that's the holiday you mentioned.'

'You don't remember?' he says, his chin digging into my shoulder now.

'That hurts,' I say, shrugging him off. 'And, no, I don't remember, Rob. How many times are you going to ask me that question?'

I push past him to pull out a stool at the kitchen island, unsteady on my feet, my hands trembling as I try to hoist myself up on to it. Rob rushes to my side, helping me up, and I allow him to because there is no way I can manage by myself. Then I rest my head on the cold granite surface and allow myself to cry, the tears falling freely until Rob begs me to stop.

'I can't stop! I'm frightened! Don't you get it?' I say, looking up at him, his expression not angry, as I'd imagined, but crumpled with pity.

'You don't have to be frightened. I can tell you whatever you want to know,' he says, his hand hovering next to mine, then withdrawn. 'I can't bear to see you like this.'

I watch as he walks to the other end of the open-plan kitchen, past the dining table, retrieving a photo frame from the windowsill behind. 'Maybe this will help,' he says, propping it up in front of me on the granite.

The silver frame has two apertures, both landscape, one above the other. The top photo is of a similar view to the one depicted on the magnet: sand, sea, palms. Below it is a picture of Rob and me. We're close to the lens, the picture taken with a camera phone I presume, a *selfie* as Sash and Fin would say. Our heads are touching, an orange-and-pink sunset behind us, and we're smiling.

'That was taken on the terrace after dinner, we'd had a great night,' Rob says, smiling now. 'You don't—' He stops himself and apologises.

I wipe my eyes and look again, then shake my head. We do look happy, but so does every smiling face placed in a frame. Maybe we were, but it could just as easily be a lie, a moment of 'making the best of it'. Again I wonder at my train of thought since the fall, why Rob's attentiveness and our previous happiness leaves me cold.

Rob picks up the frame and looks at it. 'It was such a good holiday,' he says. 'Like a second honeymoon.'

'*Was it?*' I ask, the words sounding harsher than I'd expected.

'Is that so hard to believe?' Rob returns the frame then looks at me for some kind of reaction as he walks back, shrugging his shoulders to reinforce his point. His hair is sticking up from his forehead where he's grown hot in his sleep, his naked torso causing me to look away, a vulnerability to it that's at odds with my defensiveness in his company.

'You were lost without Fin and Sash,' he says, yawning. 'I booked it as a surprise, to cheer you up.' He smiles at me.

'I wasn't sure,' I say, the words formed as if by someone else, although once I've spoken them I know they make sense and that bolsters my resolve. 'I'm right, aren't I? I wasn't sure about going, because of Fin.'

'Come on, let's try to get some more sleep,' Rob says. 'You need your rest.'

He helps me down from the high stool and through to the hall and I'm so exhausted I lean on him and allow him to take my hand. It's when he turns to help me up the stairs, his other hand outstretched, that an image returns.

He'd reached out to me at the top of the stairs, but I was trying to do something, quickly, before he could stop me.

'Jo!' Rob has stopped two stairs up. 'You coming?' He takes a step down. 'You're exhausted, Jo. Let's go to bed.'

'I'll manage on my own,' I reply, batting away his hand.

October – Last Year

'And you didn't think to ask me first?' I say, switching the phone to speaker and propping it up against an emptied jar of passata.

'I thought you'd be pleased,' Rob says, the click of an indicator switched on and then off accompanying his words. 'It's five star, Jo. On a private island off the coast of the Dominican Republic. Cocktail hour all day; just the two of us. Come on, we barely celebrated my birthday last month and it won't be long until it's yours. Let's call this a joint splurge for the two of us.'

I stir the bubbling vat of Bolognese sauce, a displacement activity whilst I process what he's just told me. It's not so much that he's booked a holiday without consulting me which peeves, more the lack of empathy it displays. He's adjusted to our childlessness, embraced it in fact, and therefore I must too. But I'm not ready to travel thousands of miles away from the kids, especially Fin. Not yet.

'I'm not sure, Rob,' I reply, estimating I have enough pasta sauce to freeze at least two portions for later use, my habit of cooking for twice as many people also hard to shake off. 'Can we talk about this later?'

'There's not much to talk about as I've already booked it,' Rob says, the loud sound of his car horn taking over. 'Why can't people learn to drive their bloody cars?'

'You can't cancel?' I ask, moving the phone further away as I add salt and a touch of sugar to the tomato sauce.

'Pick a bloody lane!' He curses under his breath. 'No, I don't think so. Anyway, I don't want to. Jo? You still there?'

'Yes, sorry. It's just a surprise, that's all. So we're away for my birthday?'

'No, back before then. We leave on the fourteenth, so we need to get some jabs, organise malaria tablets. Can you give the surgery a ring tomorrow, see if we can go in over the weekend?'

I put the wooden spoon down and tap a button to switch the sound back to the handset as I tell Rob it's a lovely thought, and I really appreciate the gesture, but—

'But what?'

'You could have asked me.'

'It was a surprise! You said we should make more of this time, travel together. Have some fun!'

He's technically correct, but it was spoken as a theoretical ambition, a glass of wine in my hand and from the comfort of our sofa, and I hadn't meant for us to go so soon. I pick up the spoon and taste the sauce with the tip of my tongue, almost dropping the phone into the pan as I juggle the two implements; my heart beating a little faster at the near-miss.

'We'll talk about it when I get home, okay?' Rob says, hanging up.

I put the phone down and then the spoon, Rob's words repeating in my head. He's right, of course, we should spend this time together as a couple, embrace the new status quo. Our lives have changed, we need to reconnect, learn how to be together without the daily exchanges required to raise two children. We've kept them alive into adulthood, made sure they had a good start; now it's our time. It's only one week away, an entirely feasible proposition. One which I should find attractive. Rob had meant well and I've sucked all the joy out of the surprise. I pick up the phone to call him back, then think better of it. He'd been preoccupied with the rush-hour traffic and his signal was breaking up. It will be better to have the conversation once he's home, as he suggested.

I leave the sauce to reduce down, another hour or so until the meat is soft and the flavour concentrated. Spag Bol was the kids' favourite, not so much Rob's, but he'll eat it. I walk through to the den, sitting down at the glass desk which was intended for Rob's new study upstairs but was too big for the small room. Rob was annoyed at his mistake, but I'm pleased I inherited it; it makes the den feels even more like my domain. It's a pleasant spot to sit at my laptop; beneath the window and with a view over the back garden. I think this is my favourite room, the only one in the barn that feels cosy, the proportions less grand. It was meant for the kids and their friends, an addition we added to give them their own space, or maybe as a sweetener to extend the allure of living at home, which it clearly didn't do, although I'm hoping Fin will come back for a year or two after university. I open up my laptop and type in 'Dominican Republic – Five Star', distracted by a robin in the garden as I wait for the intermittent Wi-Fi signal to catch up. The light is fading now, I should close the blind, but as is so often the case these days, inertia slides over me, pinning me to the chair as I stare straight ahead.

I find the website of the resort relatively easily – it's the only one on a private island. Five star, as Rob had said. The reviews look amazing, the guest photos like an advert for paradise. It's just a week; what can go wrong in a week? But even as I talk myself into it, I can feel the swell of panic rising; all those thousands of miles between us and the kids. And I know they're not technically children, but they're not adults either. Sash still needs us for this and that, mainly to sort out problems with her grotty rented flat, and Fin hasn't even left home properly. He's only been at university for a couple of weeks and although he says he's fine, who's to say he really is? We haven't seen him, and his messages are brief and infrequent. He could be depressed. Or on drugs. 'He just needs to find his tribe,' according to Rob, and on the whole I allow myself to be persuaded by this argument, but Fin's always been a quiet soul, sensitive and insular. We wouldn't necessarily know if something was wrong.

I still my thoughts, walking back into the kitchen to stir the simmering sauce. I'll feel better once Rob's home; he'll talk me round, he always does. And anyway, it's hardly a problem, being taken to a five-star island paradise. I can almost hear my daughter saying, 'First World problems, Mum.'

5

Three Days After The Fall

I abandon sleep and open my eyes to the darkness, a cast of faces still before me; the players in a lost year, some known, some not. I look across at Rob, his breathing slow and almost silent, then I close my eyes again. There are two distinct faces amongst the many, a man and a woman, both equally transfixing, both strangers. I need to separate them out, examine each one carefully. I'm drawn to the man first. He's younger than me, not handsome as such, but he has presence, and confidence, a smile emerging from the shadowy features.

Afraid I may betray myself, even in the dense blackness, I force the image of him away, my breaths shallow as I glance across at Rob once more, his prone figure a dark mass; inert.

I look for the woman now and she stares straight back at me, her stance at first defiant, her face unknown, hidden beneath the layers of memory which elude me, but then she changes, her whole body contorted with emotion, her hands covering her eyes, then reaching out to me. I don't want her, she repulses me, although I pity her too.

She's pulled apart by terror, or perhaps grief; all-consuming. I need to sleep, but even as I feel myself unlatch from the world, they both follow me into the hinterland of my subconscious, walking at my side, tugging on my thoughts, demanding I remember them.

The morning arrives with a blinding headache and the sense I may not have slept for more than one continuous hour, the disturbing images prompting even more alarming questions now I'm awake; as though I were assessing a stranger's actions over the last year, not my own. I pull myself up to a seated position, then lean back to rest my aching head against the pillow as Rob bangs around in the bathroom next door. He frowns with concern as he walks out of the ensuite, his continual assessment of my every move exhausting. 'I'd like my laptop, please,' I say.

'You need to rest,' Rob says, tucking the duvet around me. 'And if you won't, then I'll simply have to work from home again today. There's some toast and juice there when you're ready.' He points to a plate on my bedside cabinet.

I tell him to stop fussing, I'm much better, but he's insistent I mustn't do anything but stay in bed today. I fall silent, thinking I can do what I like once he's gone; watching him as he walks across to his wardrobe, pulling open a drawer to select a pair of grey balled-up socks. I must have paired those, I think, probably in the last few days; a simple task, not noteworthy, but another memory gone.

'That's what your consultant said when he rang,' Rob says, glancing at me over his shoulder. 'Rest is the most important thing.'

'When? I didn't hear the phone.'

'You were still asleep,' he tells me, closing the wardrobe door. 'I told him you were feeling much better and he said that's great, but not to overdo it.'

'I'll be fine,' I reply, smarting at his high-handed attitude.

'Sorry, I don't agree,' Rob says, sitting next to me on the bed. 'The doctor said you need complete rest. Maybe I should stay at home today . . .' He smiles. 'Keep an eye on you.'

I've already endured two days of his constant surveillance, losing count of how many times he's asked how I'm feeling. 'No, I'll rest. I promise,' I tell him, adding a smile.

'Great,' he says, standing up again and passing me my new phone, which he tells me arrived early this morning. 'Everything's on there: email accounts, contact details; no need to go down-stairs.'

'Thanks, but I could have done all that,' I reply, taking the new handset and clicking on the Mail icon, surprised at the anticipation I feel.

'I checked your mail just now,' Rob tells me, looking over his shoulder and smiling as he tosses the balled-up socks in the air. 'Nothing exciting I'm afraid.'

'I'd have rather checked that myself,' I reply, scrolling through the recent emails.

He's right, they are dull: an overdue refund to our account for two over-ripe avocados in a supermarket delivery, a few discount codes for chain restaurants, and a dental appointment missed. I discard the phone on to the bed beside me.

Rob's seated at the end of the bed with his back to me, shoulders hunched over his knees as he pulls on his socks. His long thin legs are bare beneath the tails of his crisp work shirt, his bony feet raised, one then the other, the skeletal outline visible beneath the skin. I watch him, his head bent forward over the task, the tanned skin above his collar picked out by the neat line of his haircut. He stands to place one socked foot, then the other, into his suit trousers, then he walks over and plants a kiss on the top of my head before he stretches up to his full height. I wait silently for him to make a move, but he just smiles at me and then regards me again, as if he's still weighing up the pros and cons of leaving me on my own all day.

'Go!' I shout. 'Just go to work!' I want to say more: how I can't bear another day of his micro-management; every word, every movement analysed. It's like I'm his science experiment, to be prodded and managed, surveyed and inspected. I can't breathe for his concern. But I don't, for I see the hurt and shock in his eyes.

Rob steps back and looks at me, his face now filled with regret, not the animosity I'd expected. He says he's sorry, he had no idea he was upsetting me. 'Look, I know I might seem . . .' He looks away. 'I'm sorry. I'll back off a bit, okay?'

His apology reminds me of how he has been in the past after a major row. Not the daily squabbles of normal married life, but the big blow-outs we've had; so infrequent I could probably count them on one hand. Those quarrels had been about money, or kids, or the barn; his anger often followed by a period of over-compensation. I wonder what the row was about at the top of the stairs which has prompted this contrition, but my memory of it is so unclear. What might he be atoning for?

'You need to get back to work,' I tell him matter-of-factly. 'You're driving me crazy.'

'Charming,' Rob replies, affecting amusement. 'I know when I'm not wanted.'

He opens up the wardrobe again and picks out a tie, standing in front of the mirror in the ensuite to fasten the knot. I wait for him to speak, unsure what I'm expected to say; it's the truth after all: he's not wanted.

'You have to promise me you won't drive,' he calls through. 'Or leave the house. Or do anything other than lie in bed.'

'I promise,' I say, as he walks back into the bedroom, rewarding him with another smile which I hope will settle him this time.

'Text me every hour.' He gives me a stern look. 'Or I'm driving straight home.'

I pick up the shiny new handset again and hold it up. 'Every hour,' I tell him. 'Promise.'

'I was hoping Sash would pop over in her lunch hour to check on you,' he says, pulling on his jacket. 'Apparently she's too busy today, and I can't get hold of Fin. I can make you a sandwich for your lunch if you'd like?'

'I'll be fine,' I tell him again. 'I wish you'd just go!'

Rob looks at me, pausing as though he might say something this time, but instead he walks away, his tall frame filling the bedroom doorway, then he turns back and says, 'I worry about you on the stairs.'

I hesitate, wonder if it's a dare, to see if I've remembered anything of what happened before my fall, but I don't, not properly. I tell him I'll be very careful, probably won't even go downstairs, which finally prompts his departure. I watch him from our bedroom window, his laptop case tucked under his arm as he looks up at me, raising his free hand to wave goodbye before the heavy rain forces him to run to his car.

Even when he's gone I stare after him as though he might think better of leaving, his car turning full circle at the end of the lane to come home. I wonder if I want him to come back – a perversity prompted only by the emptiness I feel now I'm finally alone. I place my good hand flat against the glass, tracing a line to follow the tracks of the raindrops with my forefinger. Then I rest my sore brow on the cold pane.

I used to have a routine when the children were here. It went some time ago, I understand that, at least on an intellectual level, but knowing Fin went a year ago doesn't mean it feels that way. To me, it's as if he's just left, Sash too, her move only just preceding her brother's departure to university. When they were younger those drives to and from school had felt without end. I'd wanted those days to pass more quickly, had cursed the fact I had no time for myself, not a moment to think, but the years have flipped over, one after the other, lost to the very routine which was sustaining me. And now, in a cruel twist, the year in which I should have adjusted to a new routine has been stolen from me by memory loss. In the weeks before Fin left for university I'd tried to imagine carving out a new life, a life beyond my children, a life that would be different, but just as good. I wonder if I did. I wonder if I found something to replace the losses, something which took over my life. Something dangerous and illicit. The thought appalls me; the possibility I may have risked my marriage too awful to entertain.

I tear myself away from the bedroom window, my feet taking me past unoccupied rooms, the changes disorientating, as if someone is playing a spiteful trick on me. The spare room, now Rob's study, is filled with masculine furniture which I can't possibly have chosen, and Sash's room, fully revealed in the daylight, has had all the personality stripped from it, the effect being one of a luxury hotel room, pristine but impersonal. I can see that it's been executed with taste, and concede I may have had a hand in its transformation, but why bother? Who do we ever have to stay? Sash, perhaps? But the room appears untouched. Fin's room is much as I remember it, but that's even more disturbing – as though he's still away at university, rather than permanently moved out. I reach the top of the stairs but then double back, unsure of my destination until I'm in our ensuite. I turn on the shower, inspecting my bruises again as I undress. Some are fading, some darker in colour. I remove the elasticated bandage from my wrist and step into the cubicle. The tiny cuts on my inner wrist catch my eye again, but then I'm distracted as the scalding beads of water locate the tender squashy bump on my scalp. Wincing with the pain I steady myself against the tiles, but the exhilaration of washing my hair for the first time since my fall takes over. Afterwards I sink down on the closed toilet seat, my hair wrapped in a towel, my robe damp from the moisture on my skin. I'm faint with exhaustion and shivering with cold, the porcelain hard against my back as I lean against it, resting there until I'm recovered enough to replace the bandage on my wrist, reassuringly tight against my skin.

The rain is still falling as I pass the bedroom window, the outside world cold and unforgiving, a slate-grey sky sending down hard drops which the wind lashes against the glass. I make a pillow of my towel to protect the bedding from my wet hair and lower myself on to the bed. At first I try to rest, but when I close my eyes the questions return. Giving up on sleep, I pick up my new phone, squinting to see the screen until I retrieve my glasses from the bedside cabinet. Rob has indeed copied across the kids' mobile numbers, as well as all his contact numbers at work, home and the office, but there were more names on my old phone; I'm certain of it. I try to recall who may be missing, willing myself to remember the missing contacts. But there's something else which preoccupies me instead, something that lurks between Rob and me, unexpressed and yet a barrier between us; both of us guarded. He's my husband, he loves me, would do anything for me, and yet his love feels cloying, his attention claustrophobic. Something must have happened in the last twelve months which has changed us both. Something no one is ready to tell me. I felt it more keenly than ever this morning, at times the unspoken words palpable between us, the flashes of those moments before I fell tantalising me. I close my eyes and this time the images are bidden more easily, but it's not my husband I see.

I can't see his face, but I can see his entire body, reclined. The beauty of it catches my breath in my throat, sending a thrill of desire through me. I reach out to touch him, my hand finding the curve of his waist, then the muscles in his back and thighs. The skin is taut, younger than Rob's.

This cannot be me with another man. I've always been a faithful wife, never once strayed. I need to rest, to push these thoughts away. I turn to feel the cool of the pillow against my cheek as I slide the towel from beneath my head, ignoring for now my tangled hair; the thought of dragging a comb through it, the teeth finding the soft lump on my scalp, causing me to shudder.

Sleep settles on me some time later; black and blank, no faces, no memories except a recollection of that scene in the holiday photograph Rob showed me. It's probably just a replication of that image rather than a true memory, but I feel again a sense of unease at our smiling faces. Then that image fades too, leaving only a thickening in my head, a soupy mess of nothingness which I cannot shake off, even when I hear the landline ringing.

October – Last Year

I look beyond the white tablecloths of the empty adjoining tables to the grouped holidaymakers by the bar, their laughter drifting through to us as they take their first cocktail of the evening. It's our third night here and the second time we've declined an invitation to join them, Rob preferring our own company to those of our fellow Brits. My gaze travels from their bonhomie to the bewildering and eclectic choice of something akin to European cuisine comprising the buffet. I have to hand it to the chefs, the appearance of the dishes is a neat deception, promising flavours which are rarely delivered. Nevertheless, the exotically displayed platters attract a steady stream of grazers, their appetites undiminished by the rather odd combinations we are presented with. I look down at my plate and disregard almost everything on it except a small piece of steak; surprisingly tender.

'It doesn't bother you?' I ask Rob. 'Look!'

He follows my eyeline to the queue of wristbanded guests, their length of stay indicated by the deepness of their suntan; every one of them European or American, although I did meet a very nice Canadian lady in the lift.

He frowns at me. 'What am I supposed to object to?'

I lower my voice. 'White privilege.'

'Don't be ridiculous,' Rob replies, spearing a piece of salmon. 'We're in the Caribbean, of course the staff will be locals.'

'Yes, I know that, but not one guest, Rob. Not one.'

'Why would the locals holiday here?' Rob asks, entirely missing my point.

It had initially struck me when I'd leant over our balcony on our first morning here; the magnificence of the tiny island spread out beneath me. We'd arrived late the previous evening, exhausted by our epic journey. The nine-hour flight had been followed by a life-threatening four-hour private transfer, our driver having perfected the art of the last-minute overtake, but only just. I'd wondered if it would be worse if I were killed, or Rob. I was tired. I wasn't thinking straight; the journey was interminable. Finally, when I'd thought we'd never arrive, we'd boarded the resort's boat for a choppy ten-minute crossing from the mainland, the woman seated opposite us growing ever greyer with seasickness. Our arrival after dark had denied us the view from our suite, its spectacular beauty revealed the next morning: the whitewashed colonial-style villas, manicured gardens surrounding them, then the beach beyond, and at the resort's centre the blue expanse of the swimming pool, circled by cushioned sun loungers and curtained cabanas (always draped with towels before breakfast). I'd called Rob and he'd looped his arm around my waist, said he knew I'd like it, before turning back to the room in search of his Kindle for by the pool. 'Yes, it's lovely,' I'd told him. 'Sorry if I was bit unenthusiastic at first.' And he'd smiled, told me I'd been fine, only a trace of irony in his tone, more of a good-natured tease than a jibe at my expense.

That's when I'd spotted the golf cart, its meandering journey drawing my attention as it navigated the ups and downs of the landscaped roads which linked the villas to the restaurants and bars. It was ferrying a large tourist sporting a very small pair of swimming trunks, the slender young Dominican driver smiling happily to himself as he hauled his overweight cargo towards their next visit to the buffet. I'd turned away, the scene I'd witnessed at odds with my middle-class principles, but I was also aware of the double standard it highlighted in me. The corpulent passenger below was no different to us, the ubiquitous all-inclusive wristbands bearing constant testament to that.

'I'm not saying the locals would come here for a holiday,' I tell Rob, swallowing the last morsel of steak. I look around me, lowering my voice. 'It just struck me as quite a stark image that no one in that queue is anything other than white.'

'You're being silly,' he replies, his eyes returning from the buffet to me, the lids slightly narrowed, eyebrows knotted.

'Don't patronise me!' I drop my fork on to my plate and sip my wine. 'You know what I mean.'

I look away, towards the doors which lead out from the restaurant to a wide patio, and beyond that the sun setting over the beach. I can just make out the silhouette of a young man raking the sand to a smooth till, the cooler evening breeze returning the scents of the salty waves which crash in at the shoreline. 'At least I have a conscience about it,' I mutter to myself.

'The inference being that I don't?' Rob asks, still chewing.

'No, I'm not saying that, but doesn't it make you feel awkward? It's like we're the Raj or something; cocktails brought to us on trays as we lie on sun loungers. Is this what our retirement will be like, getting fat and drunk?'

'No,' he says, raising an eyebrow. 'But we've worked hard for this; why not enjoy it? Besides, it supports the local economy, brings in dollars.' He butters another bread roll, then adds, 'It's not like they're oppressed, we're just their guests.' He refuses the waitress who offers him a water jug, a shake of his head as he chews. 'It's a business transaction.'

'Yes, I know.' I accept a top-up to my water glass with repeated thanks to the heavily pregnant girl. 'Maybe it's because I haven't worked in years, not really. Maybe I feel a bit . . . undeserving?'

Rob tells me off in a good-natured way, saying how I had the hardest job of all, bringing up the kids. 'You did a great job. We both did.'

I shrug and look away. 'Maybe.'

'What do you want to do tomorrow?' Rob asks, finishing his meal, the plate pushed away from his waistline, which is still surprisingly lithe despite the amount of food he's consumed in the last few days, although maybe the shirt buttons are straining a little.

'I guess we could get up early, grab a cabana by the pool?' I suggest. 'Or there's a dancing lesson at eleven. Salsa.'

Rob wrinkles his nose at the idea. 'The cabana sounds good,' he says. 'And maybe we can plan a different kind of holiday next time, a bit less participative.' I catch a hint of irritation in his tone. 'You know how I hate organised fun.'

'Not for a while,' I say, sipping my water.

'You still worried about leaving the kids? You know, if you allowed yourself to relax and stopped worrying about home . . .'

'You're right.' I glance at my phone on the table beside me and smile back. 'But . . .'

'Fin?' he asks, leaning back in his chair.

'Don't you think he's been overly quiet?' I ask. 'I know that's not unusual for him, but even so . . .'

Rob launches into his usual speech about allowing our son to settle into university life, and how Fin's probably trying to give me some space too.

'I sometimes wonder if it's our fault Fin finds it hard to make friends,' I say, but Rob tells me of course it isn't, his tone dismissive. 'I'm not blaming you,' I say. 'I love the barn, you know that, but the kids were so young when we moved.'

'Do you?' he replies. 'Love the barn, I mean?'

It's well-worn territory, although we haven't touched this subject in years. When we do, it always begins with Rob seeking my assurances that the move he pushed for was the right one. 'It was a joint decision,' I reply, smiling at him. 'Live the dream!'

'And was it the dream?' he asks, his tanned face creased with concern.

'Yes, I think so.' I twist my glass by the stem as I consider my response. 'But maybe now it's just us—'

'Not when Fin's home in the holidays,' Rob replies.

'No, not then. But I'm sure we could manage with somewhere a bit smaller, maybe nearer town and your work. You could cycle, keep fit. I could walk to town, meet Sash, and we'd be more central for Fin when he does come back in the holidays.'

'I think we'll still need the extra space,' Rob replies. 'All it takes is for Fin to get a girlfriend, then we'll have to accommodate her too. And Sash is bound to find someone to tempt her out of that filthy flat, then she'll have lots of babies and the house will be filled with visitors; little ones again.' He smiles and takes my hand across the table. 'Let's wait a year or two, see how the barn suits us then?'

'I'm not quite ready to be a grandmother, but I take your point,' I reply, although his easy dismissal of my idea has left me out of sorts again.

'And I'm not quite ready to be sleeping with one,' he says, squeezing my hand. 'Come on, let's go and find that cocktail waiter, the one at the beach bar who actually knows how to mix a drink, Mr Ex-ce-len-tay,' he says, mimicking the charming young waiter's inflection.

We walk via the terrace, drawn by the exquisite view of the sunset. 'Let's take a selfie,' Rob says, pulling me towards the balustrade and holding his phone above us. I smile at the obvious reference to the kids' vernacular, Rob holding me tightly by my waist so we're close together, but he fiddles with the camera settings for too long and my smile becomes set.

Rob finally takes the picture, passing me his phone so I can see the result. The smile I'd managed to hold is surprisingly convincing, our happy faces looking back at me. 'It's perfect,' I tell him, handing back his phone.

'We make a great couple, Jo,' he says, still looking at the image. 'Always have, always will.'

6

Three Days After The Fall

I reach out to touch his naked back. His skin is taut but soft, a sheen of sweat polishing the contours. I run my fingers along the curve of his thigh, the dip of his waist, the breadth of his shoulders; and I shiver in anticipation.

Startled awake, I sit up, shaking my aching head as though that will free me of the man I'd dreamt of. The tangled bedding constricts my movements as I turn on to my side to glance at Rob's alarm clock. It's later than I'd expected, almost evening, the hours endless and yet truncated by sleep so they've passed unnoticed. The afternoon has evaporated into nothingness, my confused thoughts constantly disturbing me, whilst Rob's movements downstairs have travelled to me through the barn's ancient timbers, filling up the empty spaces between us. He hadn't even lasted a day back at work. I'd barely been alone for two hours when his call had woken me, his tone at first concerned, then abrupt. He'd called me a dozen times on my new phone, he'd said, angry when I'd told him it was switched to silent so I could sleep. By the time the landline had woken me he was already on his way home and I couldn't persuade him otherwise.

I kick the duvet away, images of the naked man still tormenting me, although I tell myself it was only a dream, not a memory. I have no reason to doubt myself, not really, but my head feels heavy as I lie back, bile in my throat. I thought the memories would have formed more clearly by now, but they've tantalised and teased, darting in front of me then receding again. I sit up and check my phone, then lie back and force myself to think back to my fall, collating the facts as I know them.

It was 18:02, the nurse had told me. I'd woken on the floor in the hallway, banged my head on the wall, the damaged plaster a testament to that. I run a finger over the lump and find it's a little less swollen, less painful to touch. I'd clearly tried to save myself as I fell, reaching out with my right hand, but for what: the bannister, the wall, Rob? Then I'd blacked out. I turn over and try to find a comfortable position so I can focus properly. *Concentrate, Jo. Think!* Rob and I were definitely on the landing, arguing, but I think the argument had started in our bedroom. I remember him out-striding me and catching up with me at the top of the stairs. Rob says I slipped, lost my footing, but I have no recollection of the fall itself.

The image of the naked man reappears and with it a stab of guilt. Maybe it would be better not to know what I've missed in the last year. Rob clearly feels that way, choreographing what the kids should say and sketchy with the details when I press him to fill in the blanks.

I sit up in bed and listen intently for my husband, catching the sound of a microwave *ping* downstairs and the scent of reheated food, the thought of joining him for dinner filling me with dread. What is it I'm afraid of? His devotion to me has been absolute, not only in the last few days, but throughout our marriage.

I negotiate the stairs with care, joining Rob in the kitchen as he's spooning the contents of a plastic tray on to two plates, any anticipation the smell had created immediately dispelled by the food's gelatinous appearance. He looks up at me, a flicker of surprise on his face, then a half-smile. 'I thought you were asleep; I was going to bring this up to you.'

'No need,' I reply. 'I'm quite capable.'

I open a drawer to take out the place mats, but Rob stops me with a hand to mine, ushering me towards a dining chair, his palm on my back, his other hand supporting me under the elbow of my left arm.

'I told you; I can manage,' I say, freeing myself from his grasp.

He lays the mats out, then puts a plate of food in front of me and a glass of water and two painkillers beside it. I concentrate on chewing, the microwaved pasta thick and tasteless in my mouth. Rob eats too, the space between us much greater than the width of the table, the silence stretching out. I wonder at how we've cancelled out the previous twenty-three years of marriage in a single year; become strangers to one another, distrustful ones at that. I look up at him and find he's regarding me with a look of deep concentration, as if he's working me out as I try to do the same with him.

'I'll go food shopping tomorrow, get something better for dinner,' he says. 'I just called in at the village shop for this, but there's never much choice in there.'

I look beyond Rob to the window behind, the blind still open. It's almost dark, the rain tapping out a staggered beat. It seems odd that he rushed home – leaving a meeting, he'd said – and yet he'd stopped at the shop to buy pasta. I remark on this and Rob looks up from his food and tells me of course he was worried, but we need to eat; and besides, he'd spoken to me on the phone by then, he knew I was okay. He frowns, then stabs a tube of pasta with his fork. 'I feel like I always have to explain myself.'

'You do,' I say, then before he can reply I change the subject and ask, 'Wasn't there anything in the freezer?' An image of bags of frozen Bolognese sauce is in my mind, decanted from a bubbling pan into two-person portions.

Rob gets up and opens the freezer door, holding up two solidified bags, their contents reddish brown. I nod, swallowing down one of the painkillers. 'They'll do for another day.'

Rob returns them to the freezer; telling me they're dated months ago as he sits back down.

'They'll still be okay,' I reply, but he says he hadn't meant that, pointing out how I've remembered something pre-fall; the frozen Spag Bol.

'I've always batch-cooked,' I tell him, dismissing his smile. 'That's a general memory, nothing specific.'

'You remembered anything else?' Rob asks, reaching across towards my hand.

'No.' I lean away from him, tired of the question. If I'd

remembered something important then I would have told him, although maybe I wouldn't. The idea Rob is concealing something, maybe many things, and that perhaps I too have secrets, has begun to inform what I share with him. 'Where are the kids?' I ask.

'I told them not to visit tonight.' He smiles at me. 'You need the rest.'

'I didn't mean that.' I sip my water. 'I mean where exactly are they living?'

I need to collate the facts, they're Rob's currency and it's ridiculous I don't know where my own children live.

Rob looks up from his food. 'I told you, Fin is sharing a house with a friend called Ryan and unfortunately Sash lives with Thomas.'

I ignore the impulse to ask more about Sash and Thomas, because if I allow myself to become diverted I will forget what I had meant to ask. Since my fall I've noticed I'm easily sidetracked, which makes recovering information even more difficult, especially when Rob is so evasive. Perhaps I should write everything down, the connection between pen and paper more reliable, but then I'd have to hide my notes and remember where I'd hidden them; more secrets.

'I'll need their addresses,' I tell him, wishing I'd brought my new phone down with me so I could input the details straight away.

'Is this important right now, Jo?' he asks. 'We're trying to eat.'

I tell him, yes, it's important to me; I've lost a year and he seems to want to make it as difficult as possible for me to catch up. I stare at him, waiting for his reply.

Rob sighs. 'That's just not true.'

'Then tell me where they live,' I say. 'So I can imagine them being there.'

Sash apparently moved out of her bedsit and in with Thomas quite quickly – an unlikely scenario for our somewhat pampered eldest child, sharing a flat above a bar. Although maybe it's an improvement on the damp bedsit. I try to picture The Limes, where Rob tells me Thomas works, and have a vague recollection of once standing on the other side of the road, looking across at it, but Rob says we've never been there so I decide not to share that with him. He confirms my initial thoughts by telling me Sash hated living above a bar. It was noisy and cramped, so he's helping her with the rent on a flat overlooking the park, one of the newish ones. I nod to indicate I know which ones he means; they're impressive and, I imagine, hideously expensive. 'How much is that costing?' I ask.

'You don't want to know,' he replies.

'Can we afford it?'

'Just about,' Rob says, rubbing his eyes so they make a squeaking noise which goes right through me.

Our son's new home is not so nice apparently. Rob tells me the road name and, although at first I don't recognise it, I do know the area. It's in the roughest part of town, row upon row of tired terraced homes, trainers suspended from the telephone lines which criss-cross the narrow streets to indicate the availability of drugs, or so I've heard. We haven't been invited round there, Rob says, but we've been to Sash's flat.

I ignore his comments about them both growing up, how it's natural, because to me Fin is still a boy, and Sash is living with Thomas, which is clearly a bad thing, because Thomas is, to quote Rob, 'a nightmare'. I take the second painkiller, adjusting my focus away from Rob's enquiring stare, my attention falling on the framed photos behind him, the ones he showed me last night, of a holiday I don't recall.

Rob looks over his shoulder to see what has caught my attention. 'Do you remember it at all?' he asks, standing to retrieve the frame, his back to me as he looks at our smiling faces.

'Not really,' I say, coughing, the tablet now lodged in my throat. I sip the water to help the bitterness on its way. 'Maybe a faint recollection, but I think it's only because you showed me the photo.'

Rob stares at the sunset and our smiling faces. I can't see his expression, but his hand is clutching the frame tightly, as though he doesn't want to let go, then he looks back to me and says, 'That's a shame; we were so happy.' He holds up the picture to me again. 'Perfect couple.'

He looks at me for a response, but there's such an intensity to his stare that I look away, coughing again, the tablet still there, acrid on the back of my tongue.

I leave him to clear up the dishes, pulling myself slowly up the stairs with my good hand. He told me Sash's address, and Fin's – clearly no secret, and why would they be? But as I reach the top I realise I've already forgotten the details. They're my children, so precious, every movement monitored, and now I can't even remember how to find them.

November – Last Year

Despite Sash's poor choice of venue for our lunch date – 'The park in November, are you sure, Sash?' – I'm pleased we're here together. I suspect her insistence is more to do with finances than preference, although I'd insisted I was happy to pay.

'Good holiday?' Sash asks, kicking up the fallen leaves with her chunky knee-high boots.

I haven't seen the boots before and I can't say I care for them much; they're deeply unfeminine, even on her gamine frame. They look strange against the softness of her long hair, as though she's one of those composites in a child's picture book; the top and bottom halves swapped to make nonsense characters. Fin used to love mixing pirates and ballerinas, farmers and sheep, his giggles filling me up with the joy only a child's happiness can bring. His pre-school days were perhaps his happiest, which is such a sad thought I almost forget to answer Sash.

'Feels like ages ago we were away,' I tell her, trying to recall the warm days we'd spent in the Caribbean, the disquiet I feel at the recollection unsettling my previous good humour. I'd been so looking forward to seeing Sash, and now I'm sabotaging our time together. I smile and add, 'Almost two weeks we've been back.'

'Is that a dig?' she asks, kicking the leaves even higher in protest. 'It's not that I don't want to see you; I'm just so busy.'

I assure her it's merely a statement of fact, which strikes me as a very Rob-like comment, but she seems content with it. I pull my coat around me as the chill wind sweeps across the empty park, as though it's followed me from the top of the hill, its restless grip ever-present.

'But it *would* be nice to see more of you,' I tell her. 'I want to show you the changes we've made to the barn.'

'I'll come over soon, Mum.' Her tone is defensive, dismissive even, but there's also a smugness to it, as though she's holding a secret to her that warms her despite the icy day, something she clearly feels no need to share with her mother. 'Like I say, I've been busy.'

'Busy doing what?' I tease, eager to eke out some kind of confidence. I link my arm through hers, enjoying again the pleasurable feeling of closeness and the rustle of burnished leaves beneath our feet. 'Are you seeing someone?' I ask, the thought only just occurring. She drops my arm and moves on, but I notice a smile on her lips, a sly grin which she cannot suppress.

We sit down, huddling together on a bench in the most sheltered spot we can find, the bare limbs of a tree above us. It's been over a month since we've been in one another's company, our return from holiday followed by a fortnight when Sash was far too busy to arrange anything. I've spent the time trailing after the decorators with a cloth or the Hoover, and making them endless cups of tea. They'd promised they would be finished before we returned from our holiday, but they've only just left. There's also been the debacle with the too-big desk, and then the new blinds to be fitted, but we're getting there. It's odd, but I've felt little enthusiasm for the project, Rob taking the lead as far as the new colour-scheme for Sash's room, and the overtly masculine furniture for his new study. My main aim is to have everything tidy by my birthday in two weeks' time.

Sash lifts her khaki rucksack from the ground and unfastens it to remove a Tupperware container which she opens up with the edges of her nails under the rim of the blue lid, releasing a stale odour with a puff of trapped air from within. Sash informs me it's vegan, a concoction of lentils and beans, although the aroma is redolent of tinned sardines.

'What's in those?' she asks, looking tempted as I unwrap a foil parcel of thick-cut sandwiches.

'Your favourite: tuna on ciabatta,' I say, holding them out to her. 'I'm trying to persuade your father to lose a bit of weight post-holiday, so we're cutting down on meat.'

'I'm trying to avoid meat *and* fish,' she replies, taking one and grinning at me, the contents of the Tupperware inverted over the bin at her side.

'Is your new boyfriend a vegetarian?' I ask, biting into a sandwich too, earmarking the rest for Sash, who looks like she needs feeding up. If she has met someone then she's clearly still in the skinny-infatuated phase, the comfortable weight-gain phase yet to come.

'I don't know what you mean,' she says through a mouthful of food. Then she smiles and says, 'He's vegan, actually.'

'And do we get to meet him?'

'Uh-uh,' she says, shaking her head whilst chewing, her hand covering her mouth. 'He's not your type and you're definitely not his.'

'What's that supposed to mean?' I ask, dropping my half-eaten sandwich back into the foil.

Sash apologises, but then reiterates her assertion that it's true, we just won't 'get' him. It's seems unfair to be condemned for something I haven't actually done, but I swallow down my comment and tell her I'm sure I'll like him if she does, and I hope he'll like me and her father too.

'He'll probably charm you,' Sash says, contemplating her sandwich as she adds, 'Not so sure about Dad.'

'Why not?' I ask, wiping a smudge of mayonnaise from her cold cheek.

'He's very political,' Sash says, the words delivered with pride, as though they were daubed on a placard she's waving in my face. 'And not *your* kind of politics.' She flicks her hair from her face.

I ask what she means by *our* politics and she says I know what she means, 'Yours and Dad's kind of politics', as if that's supposed to illuminate her point. I consider her opinion, wonder at the gap in my understanding. When did my daughter become so disdainful of us? So apart? 'Will we ever get to meet him, this . . . ?' I ask.

'Thomas,' Sash replies, helping herself to another sandwich, the mention of his name bringing back her secretive smile. 'Let's see how it goes; early days yet.' She looks across at me, a sideways glance. 'He's a bit older than me.'

After her previous comments I hear myself saying that it doesn't matter how old he is as long as he's nice to her. I also resist the obvious question, 'Exactly how much older?' She smiles and says she'll think about maybe bringing him over one Sunday for lunch. *Maybe.*

'You know we'll make him welcome,' I say.

I look at my daughter who appears to be considering the veracity of that statement, as am I. Rob and I have found ourselves to be almost entirely friendless, those acquaintances we'd gained along the way proving to be transient, suitable for purpose at the time, but nothing more. Maybe that was due to them, not us, but we were the common denominator. Rob's never been a mixer, preferring it to be 'just us', but now that's only me and him and sometimes two people isn't enough. He has his work colleagues and I had the children. It was neglectful of us and I'm not sure how to remedy the situation; any suggestions I've made about widening our net a little have always been dismissed by Rob as unnecessary. I envy him his surety that I'm all he needs or will ever need, even if at times I find that dependence too much of a responsibility.

'We get on with most people, don't we?' I ask her.

'You get on with *your* people,' Sash says.

'Is that what you think?' I'm stung by her words, and more so because there's some truth to them. I've always thought of myself as generous, altruistic, moral even, but perhaps I do need to consider my rather narrowed choices in recent years. I don't spend every waking moment with Rob. I have a lot of free time, especially now Fin is at university.

'I should get back,' Sash announces, standing up.

I want to point out that we've only just got here. Surely she must have an hour for lunch? I haven't even had a chance to show her the photos of our holiday. But she's already striding out. I run to catch her up, then slow my pace to hers, savouring the precious minutes I have in my daughter's company, ridiculously grateful for them. When she waves goodbye I'm surprised at the lump which forms in my throat, forcing me to walk away at speed. It's only once I'm sure Sash must have disappeared inside her office building that I allow myself to look back, wiping away the ridiculous tears which have fallen. I wish I'd hugged her, tried to secure our next meeting, insisted she come over for lunch one Sunday soon. She hadn't even asked about her brother, or mentioned anything about my birthday plans. I stare at the revolving door which took her away, watching the office workers who come in and out, speculating whether they know my daughter better than I do; are privy to the secrets she keeps from me. Then something else draws my eye.

Hidden amongst the alcoves and pillars of the next building I spot a recessed door with a sign propped up next to it: 'Drop-in Centre – Please Come In!' I must have passed it before, perhaps many times, but I don't recall ever noticing it. It was of no interest to me, but now it reminds me of Sash's suggestion that I try my hand at voluntary work. My previous discomfort at my cloistered middle-class existence pricks again at my conscience. I used to have a stronger moral compass, a wider view of life; now all I have are holidays and redecorating to occupy me. I still waver, caught between the impulse to find something meaningful to fill my days and the imprudence of such a snap decision, but something compels me to walk towards the drop-in-centre, just to take a look.

I'm struggling with the door, my coat pocket somehow hooked on the outside handle, when I hear someone approach, the kind of shuffling sound only associated with the bearing of an elderly person. I untangle myself and turn to face a white-haired lady who looks more befuddled than I do.

'I'll get Rose,' she says, and shuffles away.

The room she slowly traverses reminds me of a village hall, much like the one where I used to take Sash and Fin to toddler group: dusty parquet flooring, pin-boards and posters on the walls; although here they carry more serious messages, shouting warnings of the dangers of drug use and the hazards of smoking. On a table beside me are piles of leaflets entitled 'Making Healthy Lifestyle Choices' and 'Your Benefits, Your Rights'. I pick up a tri-fold pamphlet and flick it open, distracted from the contents by a generously proportioned woman walking towards me; presumably Rose.

'After some advice?' she asks, hands planted on her wide hips, pinning back a long, misshapen cardigan. She nods in the direction of my reading material.

I glance at the pamphlet I'd quickly discarded, the cover depicting a woman's face covered in bruises, the word 'No!' emblazoned across her raised palm. 'Oh no, not that,' I say, appalled at the misunderstanding. 'Sorry, no. I just picked that up; didn't even read it.' I push the pamphlet further from me on the table to emphasise my distance from its message.

'Are you sure?' Rose asks. 'Lots of people come in with—'

'No, sorry. That's not it,' I reply. 'Sorry, can we start again?' I smile at her. 'My daughter said you needed volunteers, but that was a while ago, I'm not sure if—'

'We always need volunteers,' she replies, flashing me a wide smile, her upper gums exposed, pink and glistening. 'I'm Rose, by the way.'

I tell her my name is Joanne. 'Call me Jo.'

I follow her past wipe-clean tables and plastic chairs, our path impeded by the haphazard layout of the large room. She says it's a quiet day, pausing to pick up a discarded crisp packet from the floor, but apparently some days it's heaving in here; 'You just never know.' The food bank is always busy, she says, but that's on a Saturday morning; for the working parents. I look down at my designer handbag and think of the shopping list on my phone: avocados and salmon fillets, bottles of wine and ciabatta. We squeeze around two sides of a table crowded with young lads discussing last night's game, and then another table with just two occupants, the white-haired lady who first greeted me and a young woman at her side, the former squinting through thick lenses as they pore over the small print on a complicated-looking form.

'You okay, Sue?' Rose asks, looking back at me to raise her eyebrows, as if I know what she's implying about her older colleague.

'It's an open-door policy here, which can throw up a few challenges, as you can imagine,' Rose says, smiling back at me as we walk on.

I feel myself carried along by something I was at best undecided about, my impetuousness in pushing open the door rewarded with her earnest expectation the other side, politeness precluding an early exit. 'I'm not sure there's much I can offer,' I reply as I continue to follow her, a clear image in my head of Rob's expression as I tell him where I've been today.

We reach a door, the wood silvery grey beneath a thin coat of varnish. 'This is Nick's office,' she announces, holding the handle. 'He's not in today, but you'll like him. He's quite an extraordinary man, really. Totally not what you would first imagine.'

The office is cluttered, an old-fashioned desk piled high with cardboard folders, stacks of them covering every surface and more papers piled on the floor, the only light leaking in through a high window behind the desk, the glass etched so there's no view, just a blurred collection of colours, all dark. Rose offers me a seat and I look at the low armchair, upholstered in imitation leather, also covered in files.

'Sorry,' she says, rushing to clear the chair for me. 'One day we'll catch up with the rest of the world and go paperless!' She dumps the files on the floor. 'Okay, Jo. Welcome! Let me just find the right form and then we can get started.' She sits down in the chair behind the desk and begins rooting through the drawers at her side. 'You said your daughter's a volunteer here?'

'Yes. No. Not exactly. Sash works in the office block next door, but she's only been here once.' I think of Sash, poorly paid, but hopefully on a fast-track to better things. It's not really the kind of work she'd hoped for, although I'm not sure what that might have been. Her interpretation of the ideal career has always been skewed in favour of *something fun*, but it was the first job she applied for and the only one she'd needed to in the end. I don't think it suits her, corporate life, chained to a desk and phone, but at least it's a graduate-level scheme with prospects.

'She was probably part of the Lunch Time Club,' Rose replies, pulling out more folders to pile them on the ones already stacked on the top of the desk. 'I don't recall a Sash, but there were a few of them came round from there. I think they've tired of us. Faddy, some young people.'

I want to defend my daughter, but unfortunately Rose is right. I watch her sort through another drawer of folders and then she declares, 'Ah-ha! Here they are. I'm assuming you don't have a current DBS certificate?'

'I'm sorry?'

'Disclosure and Barring Service Certificate. It's a background check to make sure you don't pose any risk to the vulnerable people you'll be working with.'

I hadn't thought about the threat I might pose to the patrons of the drop-in centre, more the other way around, but I recall Sash mentioned something about a check. 'No, I don't have one,' I reply. 'But if it's a problem, please don't worry, I wasn't actually—'

'It's very straightforward, but it does take a few weeks to come through, and until you've got clearance we can't offer you a place as a volunteer.'

'Oh, I see.' I'm surprised to find I'm disappointed.

'Everyone assumes they can walk in here and we'll fall over

ourselves to recruit them.' Rose's words, although startlingly honest, are spoken with a disarming smile. 'But we have to protect everyone who uses the centre. I actually think it's better this way; a good test of your commitment.'

'Yes, I suppose it is,' I reply, sensing in her a perceptiveness I hadn't immediately recognised.

'Let's get the form-filling done, then I can show you around. Had you thought how many hours a week you might spare, Jo?'

I tell her I hadn't, but maybe a couple. She replies that anything is good, they're so stretched, but consistency is important, so there's a rota. I hadn't expected it to be so formal, imagining a couple of older ladies, much like the white-haired lady who'd greeted me, doling out tea and biscuits to a queue of unsavoury characters.

Apparently Nick, the much-lauded boss, is an ex Community Development Officer, and before that he was in corporate finance, so he's got loads of experience.

'If you ever need any advice, he's your man,' Rose informs me.

There's training provided, but that's mainly on the job, she says. She blames funding issues and I nod as if I have knowledge of this myself. The last time I worked in any capacity, paid or unpaid, was before Sash was born, typing up dictation and filling in carbon memos. It would seem times have changed. It's daunting, but there's a stronger emotion too; I feel I've opened up a raft of opportunities outside my immediate experience, my mind skipping ahead to where it might lead. It's scary, but aren't you supposed to scare yourself every now and then?

'Of course you can come to me at any time,' Rose says. 'I'm always here, practically my second home.'

I pull my chair closer to the desk as Rose places a pen in front of me, searching in my bag for my glasses.

'We'll need some ID: driving licence, that kind of thing,' she says. 'Did you have any thoughts as to what skills you might bring?'

'I can make tea,' I reply, looking up from the form.

'That's a good start,' Rose says, smiling at me. 'But I'm sure you're up to more than making tea. How are you with computers?'

'Not too bad,' I reply, returning her smile. 'I have a laptop at home.'

'Then that's settled,' she says, grinning at me now; the disproportionate amount of gum somehow less alarming this time, as if I've already got used to it.

7

Four Days After The Fall

After last night's discussion with Rob, when he told me everything about Sash and Fin's new living arrangements, I should perhaps be feeling a little better; if not about the kids then at least about my husband. He seemed open, told me I could ask him anything I liked, but inside me the constant struggle to separate out the past, real and imagined, goes on. I look at Rob now as he smiles across the breakfast table, his expression all care and concern, but his face morphs before me, becomes contorted with anger as I relive how we'd argued before my fall. *If I fell.* And then I see the naked man in my dreams, and feel again my desire, shameful in its intensity. Rob stands up, placing a hand on my shoulder as he passes my chair. The clatter of his bowl in the sink causes me to jump and he looks back at me and frowns, then says again he's not sure he should go to work, although he's already heading towards the door.

'Honestly, I'm much better today,' I insist, following him into the hallway, the wind rushing in through the front door as he opens it. It's already taken several attempts to persuade him back to work after yesterday's abortive attempt; I don't want him to change his mind now he's finally agreed to leave. I need some time alone, to order my thoughts, maybe even search for some tangible evidence of the past.

'My headache's almost completely gone,' I lie, adding a smile to convince him further, squinting into the early morning light.

'*Almost?*' he asks, turning back. 'What does that mean?'

I shield my eyes from the sun with my left hand, although my sprained wrist has improved enough for me to remove the bandage permanently this morning. 'My headache is much better, and my wrist,' I say, holding up my unfettered arm to prove my point. He seems unsure, but I tell him I'm positive I'm well enough to be left alone, trying to keep my voice light, no trace of the annoyance I feel at his reluctance to leave me unsupervised.

He looks down at his feet, the gravel beneath them dusting the toes of his polished shoes. 'Doesn't feel right,' he says, straightening up and taking a step towards me.

'No!' I say, standing in the door to bar the way. 'Don't come back in!'

'What is wrong with you?' He steps back and throws his laptop case on to the gravel drive. 'All I'm trying to do is look after you; why won't you let me do that?'

'Losing your temper doesn't help,' I say, looking at the laptop case.

He takes a deep breath and closes his eyes. I expect him to

lose control again, but instead he picks up the case and pulls open the Velcro flap to inspect the laptop inside. I ask him if it's okay and he tells me of course it is, but he's calmer when he says, 'Promise you'll keep in touch today; I worry about you.'

'Go!' I say, leaning away from his goodbye kiss. 'You'll get caught in the school traffic.'

He backs away, raising his hand in surrender. 'I mean it, Jo. I want an hourly text. Or an email – no excuses. Okay?'

'Okay – unless I'm asleep,' I reply, closing the door.

I watch from the kitchen window as he manoeuvres his car; the gravel carved into deep grooves where our tyres have worn paths in and out. My Mini is parked on the far side of the drive and I wonder when I last drove it and where I'd been. It's as I turn from the window that the image returns. *A naked back, the face featureless, in shadow, except now it turns to me and I can make out a generous mouth, a wide smile.* The smile draws me in, sucks the breath from my lungs so I'm forced to lean against the sink for support. Who is he? What had he meant to me that even the thought of him leaves me breathless? Maybe I'd been with him the last time I drove my car; a liaison, reaching out to touch him as I do in my memory, to pull him to me, the smile closing in. I can feel that same pull, the desire to be with him, my breaths shortened as I struggle against the feeling, so strong, until I say aloud, 'No!' The word echoing around the empty house.

I run the kitchen tap and splash my burning face with cold water, again and again, until the image retreats and I'm able to look up at the view of the drive and my car. I'd probably been out shopping, or to visit one of the kids, something normal, routine. Maybe I'd seen Sash, although she's apparently besotted with her new love Thomas, and I have no recollection of him at all. I imagine instead that I'd driven to Fin's new home, in a rough part of town, in a street whose name I don't recall, fallen out of my memory like everything else. If only I could remember, perhaps I could save myself the shame, the doubt, the fear. Maybe all this angst is needless.

The coffee machine grinds and pops, then a slow trickle of dark froth emerges. I take my cup through to the den and look across at the squashy sofa, recalling Sash sitting there with her friends not long after she'd finished university. It must be over a year ago now, although it feels much more recent to me. Sash had moved out a month after her graduation, the job and the bedsit secured as easily as everything else in her life, arriving as soon as she'd decided it was what she wanted. I look around me at the den; another dead space now, except that beneath the window there's a glass desk, new to me, but appealing; especially as my laptop graces its surface.

Rob told me this morning the desk was meant for his new study upstairs, but it was too big. He'd noticed me looking from the breakfast table towards the den and began to ask me if I'd remembered the new desk when he stopped himself, setting his bowl and glass down in the place opposite me and apologising instead.

'So that was when exactly?' I asked, ignoring his ridiculous question and curious to mark the lost months with memorable landmarks. 'The redecorating upstairs, I mean.'

'After our holiday. I told you that last night. You'd wanted it all sorted for your birthday; the study and Sash's room,' he said, smiling at me. 'But the trades were still here when we got home from holiday. It must have been mid-November before it was all done.'

I imagined my concern, anxious the disruption was over so Sash and Fin could sleep in their old rooms on the night of my birthday, but apparently Fin hadn't come home from university for my birthday. 'It must have been lovely having Sash here again,' I said to Rob, but he shook his head, swallowed his mouthful of cereal and told me Sash hadn't been well.

'Neither of them came to my birthday meal?' I asked.

Rob chewed on his daily vitamin tablet, an interminable wait, then explained how it was a difficult time for all of us, but we'd had a nice evening anyway, gone out for dinner, just the two of us.

'What's happened to this family?' I asked. 'I don't recall any birthday when we haven't been together; all four of us.'

'Well, they weren't there for mine either,' he said, staring at me. 'And anyway, just because you don't remember the last year doesn't mean you weren't involved.'

I asked him what that was supposed to mean, but he seemed confrontational, daring me to say that yes, I knew I was also to blame, and the shame burned deeply into my cheeks then too, although I didn't know why; not really.

'I'm sorry,' he said. 'It's just that this isn't easy for me either.'

Rob continued to talk, something about carrying the burden, feeling as though he had to justify every bump in the road to me, but I stared at the desk and the laptop resting on its glass surface, wondering why it felt like the great hope.

'Do we use it much?' I asked. 'The desk in the den, I mean.'

'*You* do,' Rob said, grabbing his spoon again, drops of milk on his chin as he finished his muesli. 'You said the laptop keeps you company; window on the world.'

I found his comment unsettling in so many ways, as if I'd been remarking on the lamentable life of a stranger; when the object of pity was actually me; and this is still my reality, a lonely woman on her computer, tapping her way into the outside world.

I sip my coffee, and I open the lid of the laptop, watching as the screen lights up, although what I hope to find I'm uncertain. *Think, Jo! What are you looking for?* I need to be methodical if I'm to recover the past, forensic like a detective. There's no hurry, I have all day, but at the same time Rob could change his mind and come back at any moment, as he did yesterday. I'm not doing anything wrong, but when he's with me I seem to have less clarity of purpose, as though he's in control of what I do and think, and although I'm not sure what I hope to find, surely something of the last year must be lying amongst the hundreds of saved emails; clues to the minutiae of all those lost days? Maybe even a hint about the naked man, his face in shadow, just a smile visible as he turns to me. The thought causes me to hesitate, fearful now of remembering, but also desperate to know the truth. Yes, there was a smile. A dangerous, secretive smile. Just for me.

Scrolling back through the emails on my computer I'm able to quickly dismiss the more recent ones I've already read on my phone, but I take more time as I go further back, searching for anything unusual, something that catches my eye. Every now and then Rob's email address crops up, standard exchanges of a shared life: meal times, errands run, a leaving party we'd both been invited to by someone I knew over twenty years ago who still worked with Rob, but the sight of Rob's name always raises my hopes there will be something of more significance buried amongst the banality of a married couple's messages to one another. There's the odd comment about Fin or Sash, but even they disappoint, pointers to facts I already know; Sash had moved in with Thomas above the bar, and we'd both clearly disapproved, united on that front, then references to the much nicer flat overlooking the park, which we'd visited. I read one email in which I tell Rob I'm pleased about the new flat, despite Thomas's continuing presence, but it would seem there was some resentment on my part at Rob's decision as I refer more than once to the '*huge expense*' of it and the fact it hadn't worked out '*at all as intended*'. The email ends with an oblique sign-off by me, '*Sash needs us both, you're right; we'll get through this together. Jo xxx*'

I sit back and consider those words. I'd written them, but they mean nothing to me. I assume the problem I was referring to was Thomas, but perhaps there's more to it than that.

After that the pattern of our correspondence doesn't make sense, as if some of our emails are missing. I imagine the interim conversations were conducted in person or by phone, maybe a rushed text here and there, but without my old phone I'm unable to check. The obvious, but unbelievable, thought is that the missing emails were deliberately removed by Rob.

I lean back in my chair as I allow myself, just for a moment, to follow this train of thought. It would have been easy enough for Rob to access my email account on the web; he knows my password, it's the same one I always use, a combination of the kids' birthdays. And I'd slept a lot when I first came home from the hospital so he'd have had ample opportunity.

I sit up and take a deep breath, lifting my chin as I suck in air through my nostrils, then exhaling as I dismiss the idea as complete paranoia. He's still Rob; the man I've been married to for twenty-four years. Even if I can't recall the last of those years I can't discount the previous twenty-three. I know him better than anyone else in the world. He's my husband, he loves me, of that I'm certain. He wouldn't be so calculating as to deliberately tamper with my correspondence, and to what end? What could possibly be lurking there that he doesn't want me to see? I have no proof he's hiding anything at all, let alone going to such extreme lengths to curate what I see of the past. I wonder again if the paranoia is a symptom of my brain injury and begin researching head traumas on the internet, typing in 'Head injuries, memory loss' and finding my way to forums and chat rooms. It's scary stuff and I have to force myself to close down the horror stories and pretend I haven't read them; I'm finally distracted from my searches when my phone emits a single tone, a message from Rob. I tap in the beginnings of a reply, preoccupied still by the troubling research and the vexing issue of our sporadic emails.

The last email from Rob was three weeks ago; something about another late night at work, and no response from me in my Sent mail. Why didn't I reply? Was I deliberately ignoring him? Maybe, as I previously hypothesised, I'd sent a text-message reply instead, but it seems unlikely. Why would I have swapped to a different means of correspondence when I'd clearly read Rob's email? Was I angry because he was going to be late, a dinner ruined? Or more fundamentally aggrieved that the kids had both left home and blaming him? Although why delay my reaction until months after the event? I'd sounded supportive in July, as though we'd worked our way through those issues together, so what happened after that? Was it his fault or, as I fear, something I had done? We'd gone on holiday in October, celebrated my birthday in November; Rob said we were happy back then. I mark August in my head as a question mark then return to my partially composed text message to reassure Rob and keep him at work. But then I'm distracted once more, this time by the arrival of a new email, the tone of it immediately troubling.

Jo, Please, please, please reply to this! I wouldn't normally email you, but I'm at my wits' end. I must have called you a thousand times and sent you a dozen texts in the last week. What's going on? Are you okay? Where are you, Jo? Please get in touch!!!! You know I'm here for you, whatever you need. No judgements, just help, okay? Rose xxx

November – Last Year

'Had a nice birthday?' Rob asks as he drives us towards home.

The town centre lights are blurred by the heavy rain, the wipers hypnotic as they sweep arcs of clarity across the windscreen, revealing the way ahead a moment at a time, now-you-see-it, now-you-don't. I tell him it was lovely, although we both know it was a compromise; Fin 'swamped with coursework', and Sash due to join us until the last moment when she'd made her excuses. Our tradition, a family meal for the four of us, either at home or at our favourite Italian restaurant, replaced by a meal for two at the bistro we normally reserve for wedding anniversary celebrations.

'I think that place is going downhill,' Rob is saying. 'My steak was okay, but nothing amazing. How was your fish?'

'Very good,' I reply, my focus remaining on the blurred view. I turn to look at him; the profile familiar, although it has changed over the years. He hasn't gained weight, or grown or lost a beard, nothing that dramatic, but the chin is less defined, the nose a little longer. 'Just a shame the kids couldn't be with us,' I say.

Rob glances across at me and frowns.

'Sorry,' I tell him, not really meaning the apology. 'But you know I wanted them there; it is my birthday and fifty-five is kind of a big deal.'

'So you can refer to your age, but if I do . . .' He smiles. 'Just remember I'm almost at the end of that decade.'

'You take it all in your stride,' I say, smiling back. 'Yesterday, I could say "I'm closer to fifty than sixty," and now I can't.'

'We're all one day older, Jo,' he observes, throwing his car around the bends of the one-way system, the speedometer creeping above the thirty-limit. 'Better than the alternative.'

I stare out of the rain-soaked window at the bars and clubs; the girls with their arms around one another as they stagger along the pavements in heels and skimpy dresses, bags held above their heads to protect them from the rain; groups of boys, some even younger than Fin, cat-calling after them. We stop at a red light, the only car at a pedestrian crossing packed with revellers. They drift in front of us, their eyes meeting ours for a moment, unfocused and disinterested. We must look so old to them; on our way home before their night has begun. The lights change and Rob presses hard on the accelerator. Then I spot her, running in front of us, a lone figure emerging from the shadows. '*Rob!*'

He slams on the brakes, the car skidding on the slick surface, unable to find enough traction on the wet road. The girl appears oblivious to her fate, her face half turned away from us, a smile to her friends on the other side, as though there were a bubble of sound-proofed invincibility around her. She's impervious to everything except her aim to cross the road, but the distance between us is being devoured by Rob's monstrously heavy car. My mouth opens to release a scream, my hands reaching up to cover my eyes as the car finally stops, a spray of water from a huge puddle breaking across the windscreen.

'Oh my god!' I say, my palm clasped to my chest. 'We almost—'

'I saw her, Jo,' Rob says, hanging on the horn and shouting at the girl, 'Bloody hell, watch where you're going!' But she's not looking at him, running to catch up with her friends on the other side of the road; her high heels spindly, her legs bare gooseflesh.

'You could have hit her,' I say, my words almost swallowed as I recover my breath, pulling the locked seatbelt from my chest, its tightness claustrophobic against the rapid beat of my heart.

'Well I didn't,' Rob replies as he restarts the stalled engine. 'Like I said, I saw her.'

He appears much less shaken than me, commenting on the fact that we have German engineering on our side and his reflexes are still sharp, although I note a defensiveness to his tone. I think of the bottle of wine we'd shared, at least two large glasses each, and I thank god it didn't end in a different way; an image of the girl hitting the bonnet, then the wind-screen, vivid before me as the wipers execute their smooth paths. It could have been our daughter. It wasn't of course, but that girl is someone else's precious child, and she seemed familiar. I wipe the condensation from the glass beside me and watch as she runs to her friends. She must have been frightened by such a near-miss, however drunk she may be.

I'm still drawn to her as we pull away, fascinated by the developing scene, her friends holding out their arms in a group hug, enfolding her and laughing as if they're all untouchable. Then I spot something at the centre of the group, a flash of white-blonde hair, almost waist-length. 'Stop the car, Rob! Stop the car!'

'What now?' He frowns across at me.

'It's Sash, she's at the crossing. It was her friend who ran across. I knew I recognised her.'

Rob indicates left and pulls in, waiting for Sash and her friends to draw level. He watches in his driver mirror, me in the door mirror, both of us identifying Sash at the centre of the group as they walk along the pavement towards us.

'Looks like there's a boy with her,' Rob says.

I look closer, sliding on my glasses, studying the lone boy amongst the group of giggling girls, a tall, handsome boy, a man in fact; a man who is holding our daughter's hand.

'Drive off!' I tell Rob, glancing across at him. 'Quickly, before she sees us.'

'No, I want to speak to her,' Rob says, remaining inert. 'She can explain herself to you.'

'Rob, no! Not now.'

'Why not?' he asks, opening his window to wave the traffic past us.

111

'Because I don't want to humiliate her in front of her friends.'

'I won't,' Rob says, pressing the button to lower my window. 'I'll just have a word.'

I lean back from the rain as it finds its way into the car and ask Rob again if we can please go home, but he shakes his head, tells me he won't lose his temper, he just wants to have a quick chat with her. Sash is near enough now that I can see the smile on her face. She'll notice us soon, recognise the car and be embarrassed we've stopped, caught out in a lie and shamed in front of her friends. We need to go, whilst we still can. I look across at Rob, who seems oblivious to my panic. He won't care about the embarrassment of a confrontation; it's of little consequence to him if he feels he's in the right. I glance back to the mirror, Sash my focus again, praying she doesn't notice us and relieved to see she's still looking up at the tall man, his dark hair flopping down as he bends towards her in a kiss.

'She lied to you,' Rob says, looking at me now.

'I'm well aware of that, but this isn't the time or the place.'

'It's your bloody birthday. She should make more of an effort.' He leans across me and calls out her name through the open window. 'Sash! Sash! Over here!'

'Oh god, Rob, please,' I say, but it's too late.

The man notices us first, then Sash too, her smile fading as the lights of the passing cars flash us interrupted images of her startled expression. She whispers something to her companion, and he hangs back from the rest of the group, who are pushing past our car now, peering in at me through the open window. The girl from the crossing laughs as she unsteadily negotiates the pavement beside us and mutters under her breath, 'Hello Mrs Harding.'

I smile back, but my attention is immediately drawn again to Sash and the man, his face in shadow as he watches her approach our car.

'I thought you were ill,' Rob says, leaning across me so he can address our daughter.

'I was,' Sash says. 'I had a headache.'

'Are you okay now?' I ask her.

'Of course she is,' Rob answers for her. 'She always was.'

'Mum, I'm sorry if—'

'Pretty horrible thing to do, Sash,' Rob replies on my behalf. 'Lie to us so you can get out of seeing your mother on her birthday.'

'It wasn't like that,' Sash tells him, glancing over her shoulder to the dark-haired man. 'Can we please do this another time? You're embarrassing me in front of my friends.'

'Embarrassing you?' Rob taunts. 'Oh no, we can't have that!'

'Rob, let's just go. We can talk to Sash tomorrow,' I say, but my words are lost as Sash retaliates, telling him to be quiet for fuck's sake.

'Oh, nice language, Sasha Harding,' Rob says as they continue to argue, but my focus switches to the dark-haired man, who is now lighting a cigarette. The flame skitters, extinguished by the heavy rain, then flares again to illuminate a wide mouth, traces of a smile, then dark eyes as he looks straight at me, the smile spreading wider. I look away, brought back to the escalating row being conducted across my lap.

'Well if you don't want to believe me—' Sash is telling her

113

father, her words cut off by the rising window, Rob's thumb pressed hard to the button beside him.

'That was rude of you,' I say, thrown back in my seat as Rob pulls away at speed. 'Sash was still speaking.'

'I'm the one you're blaming?' Rob replies, his foot heavy on the pedal. 'What about her? You should have told her it's not on, she needs to bloody grow up.' He slams the car into fifth gear as we exit the ring road. 'You always let her get away with it.'

'If she doesn't want to be with me on my birthday, then—' I turn away from him, a hard lump in my throat. 'I don't want her there just because she feels she has to be.'

'Of course she bloody has to be,' Rob replies. 'That's what kids do for their parents, whether they want to or not!'

We're leaving town now, the roads wider and straighter, but darker too, the shadows concealing my anger as I stare at my monochrome reflection in the window beside me.

'Come on, Jo. Don't let this spoil your birthday,' Rob says, glancing across at me.

'Oh, I think that ship has truly sailed,' I reply.

'Thanks a lot,' he says, swerving to avoid an unlit cyclist.

I tell him I don't mean to sound ungrateful, I know he went to a lot of trouble and I love the present he bought me – I smooth the soft leather of my new bag, the exact one I would have picked out for myself – but the scene with Sash was awful, and he shouldn't have humiliated her in that way.

'Someone has to tell her, Jo. If she wants to be a grown-up, then she needs to act like one.'

'She's not though, is she? She's still a child in many ways.'

'I know it's hard for you to accept . . .' Rob says. 'But you knew this was going to happen; kids grow up.'

'Like we all know we're going to die?' I reply, holding on to the side of my seat. 'Quite soon if you don't slow down a bit.' Rob frowns and reduces his speed with a tap on the brake.

'Just for once try and understand how hard this is for me,' I continue. 'It's not about my birthday. Every day is hard for me, *every day*.'

Rob sighs audibly. 'You need to find something else to fill the time; look on it as a positive thing.'

We continue our journey in silence, the traffic lights and partygoers of the town centre behind us. Past the new flats by the park, then the larger estates which have sprung up in recent years, filling the pockets of land which once edged the town, then the village which signals our journey is almost done; just the narrow climb up the hill to the barn.

'Actually,' I say, sitting up straight in my seat, 'I have already.'

Rob glances across at me as we twist our way up the long narrow track, his expression obscured, only the reflected light from the car's headlamps to illuminate our discussion. 'Already what?' he asks.

I'd wanted to tell Rob about my decision to volunteer straight away, but I'd decided to wait, in case it didn't happen. It's been a couple of weeks since I filled in the forms at the drop-in centre and in that time I'd set aside my expectations of the place, vacillating between relief at not hearing anything from Rose, then disappointment that I may not. But this morning she'd rung me to say my clearance had come through and to invite me in for 'a cup of tea and a quick chat'.

Maybe I should have said something to Rob over our meal this evening, but the chance hadn't really arisen. Although, if I'm honest, it was more the thought of his reaction which has held me back. I think of Rose, how she'd welcomed me with such enthusiasm when I'd called by this afternoon, and how her boss Nick had taken me aside, laid his hand on my arm and thanked me for giving up my time, 'a rare thing these days'.

'I've volunteered at a drop-in centre,' I say, holding my breath.

Rob doesn't reply, distracted perhaps by the demands of the country lane, the incline building, as is the force of the rain.

'It's in town, next door to Sash's work,' I continue, filling the silence, just the elements providing a soundtrack. 'She's helped out there herself, with her work colleagues.'

'*Sash* did?' Rob asks, the difficult driving conditions demanding his concentration, the road up to the barn temporarily obliterated by the heavy downpour.

'A while ago. Just the once. That's not the point. I'm trying to tell you I've volunteered.'

We've reached the obscured entrance to our drive, marked by a stone painted white which is now lit up by the headlights. Rob locks the car as I run across the drive, the door key ready in my hand, although we're both soaked through by the time we're inside.

'Good grief!' I say, shaking out my jacket to place it on the back of a dining chair. 'That rain is vile.' I turn on the coffee machine and smooth down my hair. It had felt as though the wind might rip it from my scalp on my way from the car. 'Coffee?'

Rob is drying his hair on the towel he's taken from the downstairs cloakroom. 'Yes, thanks. Then you can tell me what on earth you've been up to.' He pulls the towel from his face to reveal a smile. 'I'm teasing you! Come on, I'm interested.'

Twenty-three years of marriage creates patterns of behaviour, some helpful, some not. We've learnt how to placate one another, and how to deliberately antagonise. There's also a level of candour which can be helpful or destructive; both of us able to speak with blistering honesty. In the fight-or-flight analogy, I am neither. I'm a hedgehog curled into a ball in the corner, Rob the determined predator poking at my spines until I respond. He sits with his feet stretched out under the dining table so they almost reach mine on the other side, both our coffees finished, the discussion far from over. I try to deal with Rob's questions in a measured manner, but as I field each of his concerns I can feel the rage swelling inside me. His prejudices against the kind of people I want to help are uncensored. He warns me of the threats they present: I could be attacked, robbed, abused. And why do I want to give my time away to 'dossers' who don't even try to get work, begging on the streets for drug money? I remain silent, hot anger boiling inside me; although I know he's voicing some of the fears which were mine until recently. Then I met Rose and Nick; felt the warmth of their generous spirits, admired the aims of a place which offers hope to people who have been dealt a rough hand. It isn't always their fault, Rose told me, and I agree.

'We have so much,' I tell Rob. 'Shouldn't we do more? These people shouldn't be defined by their problems; it could just as easily be us, or the kids. No one is immune. They need to be listened to, supported.' *And I want to feel needed again, Rob.* Although I don't share this last thought with him, for I know he would tell me that he needs me and isn't that enough?

'You sound like—' he says, stopping himself.

'Like what?' I ask, worn out by his narrow-mindedness.

'A *therapist*,' he replies.

Rob has no time for 'talking therapies', and he always provides air quotes to accompany his criticism. As a deeply logical and pragmatic man, he subscribes to the least-said-soonest-mended mantra, and it's taken many years of persuasion and sometimes frank discussions for him to even partially accept that not every problem requires a solution; sometimes you just need to be heard and acknowledged.

'Well clearly I'm not a therapist, Rob, but you don't have to have any special skills to volunteer. You just have to be calm and friendly.' The bottle of Prosecco we shared at dinner appears to have loosened my usual reserve. 'Rose, she works there . . .' I explain, for some reason choosing not to mention Nick. 'Rose says the people who come in have a lot to say, but they're rarely heard; just listening is often enough. I know this might seem sudden, but I've realised lately that I've become too self-involved, that I don't always like the choices I've made, they're selfish.'

'Look, I get it,' Rob says. 'You're trying to help. But not like this, Jo.'

'Why not?' I ask, pushing my chair back from the table. 'You said yourself I need something else to focus on now the kids are gone.'

Rob is warming to his subject, telling me it's not like we don't give to charity, but this, putting myself on the front line;

he just doesn't think it's safe. I explain, as evenly as I can, that I won't be on my own, I'll be part of a bank of volunteers. I can do as little or as much as suits. I've signed up for two hours a week, that's all. If he's worried his dinner won't be on the table—

'Don't be ridiculous! That's not what I'm saying at all.' He clasps his hands together and breathes in through his nose, his eyes raised to stare at the kitchen ceiling. 'Why do you always have to turn this into me being some kind of . . .' He sighs, looks at me. 'Tell me what you'll be doing for your two hours? Please, I'm interested.'

'Helping at the Job Search group,' I tell him. 'They come in for advice on their CVs, applying for jobs, to use the computers . . .' I trail off, unsure how to continue. I'd felt secure when Rose had suggested it, convincing me I could easily cope with the duties.

Rob sits up and, to my surprise, his tired face relaxes, then breaks into a weary smile. 'I'm sorry,' he says. 'I'm not being fair to you.' He stands up and walks around the table to kiss me on the top of my head. Then he gathers up our empty coffee cups and holds them in one hand. 'It wouldn't be my choice, but evidently you're a much nicer person than I am.'

'Really?'

'You don't need my permission, Jo.' He reaches out to help me up from the chair, pulling me to him with his free hand and kissing me on the lips. 'Come on, you!' he says, putting the cups back down on the table and leading me out of the kitchen towards the stairs. 'I've never had sex with a fifty-five-year-old.'

And although I'm yet to catch up with his sudden about-turn, I smile back at him, allowing us to slip back into the manufactured happiness of my birthday celebration, because Rob's love and loyalty are two things I never have to worry about.

8

Four Days After The Fall

At first glance I assumed Rose's message must have been sent to me by mistake. I finished my reply to Rob's text, reassuring him I was fine, and re-read the email, the undercurrent of alarm, or was it excitement I felt, undiminished as I absorbed the words and their possible meaning for a second time.

Jo, Please, please, please reply to this! I wouldn't normally email you, but I'm at my wits' end. I must have called you a thousand times and sent you a dozen texts in the last week. What's going on? Are you okay? Where are you, Jo? Please get in touch!!!! You know I'm here for you, whatever you need. No judgements, just help, okay? Rose xxx

Maybe we were newish friends, and Rose was someone prone to the dramatic who I was trying to shake off. I'd probably missed a lunch or coffee date with her; but deep down I knew there was more to it, and my attempts at calm analysis were little more than camouflage for my true response. There had been no previous emails from her – I double-checked – but maybe she could provide some clue to my state of mind before my fall. I've never been one to seek out a confidante, someone to share the intimate details of my marriage with over a cock-tail or a coffee, but I might have inadvertently given something away. I considered the merits of responding and decided to reply; as I'd always known I would.

Rushing to get ready for our 'catch-up' had been exhausting; every ounce of regained strength wrung out of me. By the time I heard the taxi's tyres skidding to a halt on the gravel I was already feeling overwhelmed. Halfway down the hill I'd shouted at the driver to stop, the motion of his fast decent and his unsavoury body odour causing me to lean out of the door, gasping for air. Fortunately, I'd rallied enough to assure him we should continue, accepting his warnings I'd have to pay for the clean if I, as he called it, 'hurled my guts up'. I'd cracked the window and lifted my perfumed wrist to my nose, willing away the rest of the journey.

'You sure you're alright, love?' the driver asks me again, watching me climb out on to the pavement. 'You still look peaky.'

'I'm fine, thanks,' I tell him, pressing a twenty into his hand. 'Sorry about before.'

'No need to apologise; I've had much worse.'

I move away before he can furnish me with the details of his *much worse* fares, glancing across at the office building where

Sash works as I walk past. She must have been working there over a year, although it still feels relatively new to me. 'Just think of all the taxi fares you'll save when I go out drinking,' she'd said, knowing I'd have gladly paid them ten times over if it would have changed her mind about moving into that awful bedsit. She'd taken the first job she was offered, the independence it promised too alluring. The thought of my daughter holding down a full-time job, even one for which she clearly has no real commitment, is something I'm yet to fully assimilate. I watch the revolving door, but it remains still. It's mid-morning. Everyone is inside, doing whatever it is they do in there.

Beyond Sash's office block I notice a recessed door and a sign propped up beside it; 'Drop-in Centre – Please Come In!' I pause in my step, recalling something familiar about it and also that the bar where Thomas works and Sash briefly lived is quite near here. *The Limes.* An image drops into my mind's eye. I was standing opposite the bar, looking up at the flat above. I hesitate, wondering why I feel unsettled by the return of that memory, forcing myself to focus on the reason I'm here: to meet Rose.

The coffee shop is just past the drop-in-centre sign, exactly as Rose had described it. She'd seemed confused when I'd told her I didn't know where she meant, another quick exchange of emails establishing where and when we should meet, the directions eventually given although she'd clearly wondered why I needed them. 'It's literally next to the drop-in centre, Jo.'

I'd assumed Rose would be about my age, maybe older, but as I look around the half-dozen or so tables an unkempt woman in her mid-to late thirties looks over, her hand shooting in the air. She's seated at the front of the café, next to the wide bay window.

'Oh my god, Jo,' she says, standing up to greet me and almost knocking over her coffee in the process. 'I thought . . . when you didn't reply . . . well let's not go there. Thank god you're alright.' She looks me up and down, reaching out to lay a hand on my arm. 'You *are* alright?'

The bruises on my face have faded, a touch of concealer taking care of the remnants of a black smudge under my right eye, and the bump to my head is covered by my hair. My wrist is also improved, no longer bandaged, the bruises hidden beneath my jacket, although it is still tender to the touch. There are no obvious signs of my injuries, but I know I must look pale, my movements laboured.

'Why wouldn't I be alright?' I ask, removing myself from her touch as we sit down, her concern even greater in person than by email.

'I was so relieved to finally hear from you,' Rose is saying, ignoring my question. 'I know you said you needed some time away from the drop-in centre, but when I didn't hear from you . . . and then I kept trying to—'

'*The drop-in centre?*' I ask.

Rose looks at me and laughs nervously. 'Of course. It's not been the same without our best volunteer. I didn't know where you might have gone. You said you were . . . Jo, you sure you're okay?'

Rose reaches across to pat my arm again, but manages to knock her coffee, the contents spilling across the table. She fusses with napkins, cleaning up the mess as I take the chance to look out of the window to the street outside, considering the implications of her comments. I came here in search of clues to my new life, wondering what or whom I may have found to plug the gap left by the kids, in many ways dreading the answer, but it would appear at least some of my time was spent in a laudable manner. I was a volunteer at a drop-in centre, a regular by the sound of things. Although Rob hasn't mentioned it, which now feels very deliberate.

'So, how have you been?' Rose asks, scrunching the sodden napkins into a heap before her.

I'm unsure how to respond. I could play it safe, tell her nothing of my fall, but already I've learnt something by taking a chance on meeting her, and her interest in me seems genuine.

'I was in hospital,' I tell her, her eyes widening as she asks me what happened. Clearly she had no idea. I reassure her that I'm much better now, the effects of my fall already wearing off.

'*A fall?*' She grips my arm again; fortunately the left one this time. 'What kind of fall?'

'A slip, down the stairs. Quite a few stairs in fact.'

'Oh my god, are you hurt?' She removes her hand from my arm.

I tell her I'm much better now but I would like to get myself a coffee, realising if I'm to get through this, my first outing since leaving hospital, I'll need something in my stomach. I look at her latte glass, now half empty. 'Would you like another?'

'Oh my goodness, I'm so sorry. I'll get it.' She stands, the table swaying as she squeezes past, the remains of her latte sloshing from side to side in the tall glass. I mop at it with the pile of damp serviettes. 'How about you, black as usual?' she asks, turning back.

'No, I'll have the same as you.' I smile up at her. 'Thank you.'

She grins at me, her gums pink and glistening, and for a second something tweaks in my brain, as if a file has been opened up, then snapped shut again. 'Coming right up! Don't you move!' she instructs me. 'I'll be right back.'

My coffee, thick with caramel syrup and full-fat milk, is bringing the colour back to my cheeks, or so Rose tells me. Her close scrutiny reminds me of Rob's searching glances and the thought prompts me to check my phone. I retrieve it from the bottom of my bag and, sure enough, the screen is full of notifications; all of them messages from my husband.

'Sorry, I should . . .' I say, tapping in a reply.

'Is that Rob?' she asks, her head tilted to the side.

I send the message and then glance up at Rose. 'You know my husband?'

She smiles, perhaps misinterpreting my question as a statement. Her expression is kind, but it's unfamiliar, and her intimate knowledge of me is unnerving. It's why I'm here, but it's still disconcerting to be at such a disadvantage. 'He worries about me,' I say.

'You don't have to stay with him, Jo,' she says. 'Just because you—'

'*Excuse me?*' I ask, interrupting her. 'Why on earth would you say that?'

She leans forward, points to my right eye. 'Did he do that to you, Jo?'

I'm shocked by her directness, about to challenge her on it, but then an image of Rob and me arguing on the stairs comes back to me. I need Rose to stop her persistent questioning, to look away just for a second so I can think; to define the expression on Rob's face, the words I've spoken which have angered him so much, but the memory slips from my grasp, Rose's insistence recalling me to her.

'Jo? Are you okay?' Her hand is on my arm again, the concerned smile accompanying it. 'You know you can tell me anything.'

'Can you stop touching me,' I say. 'I don't like it.'

She snatches her hand back and I can see the hurt in her eyes, although she rallies immediately. 'You really don't seem yourself today.'

'I'm fine.' I sip the sweet drink, reviving me now. 'I'm sorry, I didn't mean to sound rude.'

'You're upset; I can understand that.'

'I should probably explain,' I say. 'You see, since my fall I find it difficult to remember things. I have memory loss. A whole year in fact.'

It's not that Rose is unsympathetic as I explain, not at all, but her reaction is also detached; almost professional, which comes as a relief. As she listens it occurs to me she may be a trained counsellor rather than a volunteer as I'd assumed, and then another, more alarming thought occurs: maybe I'd been to the drop-in centre seeking as well as offering help. But I have no time to consider this, as Rose asks me lots of questions in quick succession and then listens as I explain how the bruising to my head, yes, from the fall, has caused a persistent headache and, more troubling, the memory loss. Maybe it's Rose's encouraging smile, or the pink gums, or the floral scent of her, but I have an image in my head of her turning to me as I walk into a large room. It's filled with activity, people at tables, the low hum of voices. It's a place I go to often, where I feel in control, and for a second that thought is all-encompassing, a flicker of something positive amongst all the terrible things which seem to have happened in the last year.

'I think I remember you,' I tell her, smiling now. 'And the drop-in centre. I liked it there.'

'You do, and you're such a great volunteer, Jo.' She smiles too. 'A real asset.' But then her expression becomes serious and she says, 'Jo, I'm very worried by this fall.'

I assure her I'm feeling much better, although in truth I'm struggling at the moment, my head pounding and exhaustion threatening. Rose says she's very pleased to hear I'm improving after such a horrible incident, but it wasn't exactly what she'd meant.

'The last time I saw you, you said you needed some time away from volunteering.' She looks me directly in the eye. 'Because you were leaving your husband.'

'What?'

'You told me you were leaving Rob.' When I say nothing, too taken aback by her words to form an immediate response, she squeezes my arm and says, 'Do you think he might have reacted badly?' She runs a finger gently over my bruised wrist. 'When you told him?'

I snatch my hand away and then hear myself defending my marriage to a stranger. She must be wrong, Rob and I have

128

been married for – I think carefully – twenty-four years. *I would never leave him.*

'I don't need to hear this,' I tell her. 'I'm not strong enough. And you're wrong!' I stand up, but Rose does too, asks me to stay a minute, please. We need to talk. 'I have no idea why you're saying these things to me,' I tell her, ignoring the stares of the other customers. 'I don't even know you.'

'We were friends, Jo. We'd become close. Please stay.'

I sit, but when she reaches out to take my hand I draw it back. 'Start from the beginning,' I tell her.

Rose says we first met last November when I came into the drop-in centre to volunteer. I'd told her my daughter had been there one time herself. She hesitates, then says, 'At least, you said you'd come in to volunteer, which of course you did – still will I hope – but I think there was another reason which prompted that first visit.'

'What do you mean?' I ask, trying to process all this new information.

'You've never said what really brought you to the drop-in centre, not as such, but I normally have a pretty good instinct with these things.'

'What things?' I ask her, leaning forward now. 'Tell me!'

Rose looks startled by my tone, asks me if I'm okay and I tell her I'm fine, impatient for her to continue.

'You'd picked up a leaflet,' she says, still frowning. 'You were reading it as I came over. I assumed that was why you'd come in, but you were insistent—'

'What leaflet?' I ask, interrupting her.

She places her hand on my arm again, and this time I let

her because her eyes are kind and full of pity. 'It was for women like you, Jo,' Rose says. 'Advice for victims of domestic violence.'

I withdraw from her contact, resisting her advances when she tries to soothe me, telling her she's got a bloody cheek, making accusations about my husband like that. She doesn't even know him, *does she?* She says they've never met, but I've talked about how we've argued about the kids leaving home.

'There are all kinds of abuse, Jo. Physical, verbal, mental abuse. A controlling partner can—'

'I'm sorry, but I can't let you insinuate that my husband . . . Rob's not like that.'

I stand up to go, but Rose again pleads with me to stay. I sit, but then turn away, allowing myself a moment to think, to come up with arguments against her mistaken assumptions. She doesn't know Rob. And she certainly doesn't know me. She may think she does, but I know what I'm like, I would have kept personal things to myself, I always do. The trouble is, her account does resonate with one aspect of my recent recollections. Rob and I were arguing just before I fell. But I can't believe he would have deliberately pushed me. Or that I was leaving him. We were happy. He said so. I try to trace a path back to the truth, seeing Rob and me at the top of stairs, arguing with one another, his grasp of my wrist tightening as his anger spills over. I wince with pain and rub at my right arm and Rose asks me if I'm okay, but I ignore her, instead staring out of the window; the street scene out of focus, blurred by the turmoil of my thoughts. Rob has always been a loving husband, devoted to the kids and me. What could have happened between us to drive him to such anger, such naked aggression? My thoughts run on, my feelings towards Rob since the fall so negative, my distrust of him always there, but why?

Then something outside diverts my attention. *Someone*, in fact. There's something familiar about him, something that flips my stomach over and makes my heart beat faster. I am drawn to his confident walk, the overcoat, the thick hair which almost covers his face, but the feeling of familiarity I experience isn't comforting or reassuring; it's disturbing. And yet I'm trans-fixed by him, fascinated by his long strides which cover the pavement so quickly, his huge coat billowing around his strong frame. I only have a second or two to take in his appearance as he passes by. He's tall like Rob, maybe even taller than my husband, and at first I wonder if that's what caught my eye, something resonant in his gait, or his demeanour perhaps, but this man is much younger than Rob, closer to Sash's age, although maybe he's older than that, his clothes giving him a more youthful appearance. And he's self-assured, his dark hair thrown back as he lifts his head, his eyes turned to me, and as he does so he smiles, a wide smile which precipitates a memory, the images and reality fusing.

A naked back, the face featureless, in shadow, except now it turns to me and I can make out a generous mouth, a wide smile. It pulls me in, sucks the breath from my lungs as I'm reaching out to touch him, the smile closing in.

'I need to leave,' I say, snapping back to Rose and the café.

Rose, who was still talking, stands up as I do. 'Jo, don't leave like this. I've upset you.'

'No, not really, it's just I have to go. I've remembered, there's somewhere I need to be. Sash, I'm meeting her.' I'm frantic now, desperate to leave, but it takes ages, my escape only facilitated by Rose's eagerness to pay for our coffees. By the time I run out into the street those long strides have taken him away from me. My disappointment is too much to bear and I turn my face from Sash's offices in case she should look out and see her mother outside, a crumpled mess.

He'd just smiled and walked on, a young man I have probably never seen before, but that smile had felt like a secret travelling between us; as if the images of the naked shadowy-featured man in my head had materialised before me, his face at last revealed. But now he's gone and I have no idea how to follow him. I dab at my eyes with a tissue from my coat pocket and wonder if I'm losing my mind, visions of those awful internet searches of brain trauma victims returning to haunt me. I look up and down the street, then walk a few halting paces in the direction he was heading, but exhaustion breaks over me like an ice-cold wave, deadening my senses. It's all I can do to put one foot in front of the other as I walk towards the taxi rank on the corner, glancing back for Rose and relieved to see she's not there.

The journey home seems longer, my mind and body drained. It's all I can do to reply to Rob's latest message, assuring him again that I'm fine. I pay the driver and hold the keys in my weak grasp to let myself into the barn.

Dragging myself up the stairs, I lie down on the bed, hoping sleep is not too far away, but my thoughts will not settle. I close my eyes, anticipating a vision of the naked man, his face turned to me to reveal the same smile I'd seen outside the café;

hoping the revelation he's flesh and blood, not just a fantasy, will cause a more distinct memory to return. The truth, however awful, is still preferable to this perennial soul-searching and doubt. But a flash of something else returns instead; Rob's face, mocking, dismissing my work at the drop-in-centre, telling me they're druggies, I shouldn't waste my time on them. I turn on to my side, closing my eyes tighter and hugging the pillow to me.

Why didn't he tell me about Rose and the drop-in-centre? Perhaps he'd forgotten I'd been a volunteer, although that seems unlikely. Or he never knew – but why would I have kept such a huge part of my life a secret from my husband?

I shift my weight from one side to the other, trying to find a comfortable position, turning back from Rob's side of the bed to face the window again. The sky is grey and listless to match my mood, the cloud heavy and static.

I need to go back to the drop-in centre, see what it brings forth – hopefully some memories – and to ask Rose what she can remember that I cannot. I need an ally and I need to find the man who walked past the café, whoever he is, because he's back again now, his face no longer in shadow, turning to me, smiling, my desire also returning as I reach out to touch him, to kiss that mouth. I close my eyes once more, shutting out the thoughts which I'm also trying to connect up. Have I somehow forced them to meld as I attempt to make sense of the past? All I know is that I have to find out who that tall young man is, his smile so familiar.

December – Last Year

Our untraditional Sunday lunch limps on, the conversation stuttering once more. I smile at Sash, but find myself distracted, my gaze moving to Thomas, seated at her side. There's something charming about him which, despite my many misgivings, leaves me conflicted about our daughter's new love. Rob, on the other hand, clearly despises him and has done so from the moment they arrived. I can only hope he keeps his unfavourable opinion to himself until after they've gone. I mutter something about it being warm in here and Rob taps my elbow and frowns at me, asking if it's a hot flush. 'Don't say that!' I tell him, mortified he would say a thing like that in front of Thomas, and then doubly so when I realise how much I care. This first meeting is not going at all as hoped.

I was thrilled when Sash rang to suggest they come over for Sunday lunch; her call, late on Friday evening, interrupting

Rob and me mid-row. Rob's been particularly irritable of late, exhausted by the demands of his job, which seems to take up more and more of his time. I'd been tired too, my new routine of helping at the drop-in centre taking it out of me; the two hours a week I'd initially offered already stretching to many more as Rose is 'truly desperate' for my help. I could easily say no, but I like the work; and Rose too. I also enjoy the company of Nick, the manager of the drop-in-centre, my chats with him less frequent than the ones with Rose, but no less welcome. Nick is earnest, caring, endlessly generous with his time with me and those who come into the centre looking for help. A very different attitude to Rob's, who just before the phone call had, as usual, been grumbling about the time I spend volunteering when really all people need is a kick up the—

I dived for the phone, so rare for the landline to ring that I assumed, catastrophist that I am, something was dreadfully wrong. The kids always text if they have good news; so it could only be bad.

'Who is it?' Rob whispered as I listened to Sash's excitable request. I mouthed back, 'It's Sash – she wants us to meet him.'

'Who?' he asked, as if he hadn't listened to anything I'd told him about Sash's mysterious new man. 'The guy we saw her with on your birthday?'

'No, it's fine, darling. Of course I don't mind,' I told her, shushing Rob as I tried to concentrate on my conversation with Sash. 'I'll adapt my lasagne, make a vegetable one.' I glanced across in time to catch Rob's expression of horror. 'No, Dad

135

can go meat-free for once, won't hurt any of us. What time will you get here?'

Sash had made the arrangements quickly, eager to get off the phone and back to Thomas, whose voice I could hear in the background as she said her goodbyes.

Rob had been full of questions about him. Would we like him? What was his job? Mindful of Sash's lecture about us only liking 'our type of people', I'd told Rob I'd never met Thomas, so I didn't know, but from what Sash had told me so far he sounded fine. I suppose I wanted to give Thomas a fighting chance, but I suspected we would very much *not* like him, every indicator pointing to his unsuitability. All I knew at that point were the snippets I'd already gleaned from Sash, who'd told me he worked in a bar and lived in the flat above. She said they met at the drop-in centre because he was a volunteer like her, but she also commented it was so good I was giving up my time to help 'people like Thomas's. I hadn't picked her up on it at the time as she'd clearly given away more than she'd intended to, and I hadn't want to stop the flow of information, but my gut feeling is Thomas may have been there seeking rather than offering help. Perhaps, I'd thought hopefully, he was after careers advice, but having now met him, he appears without ambition; the manager of his friend's bar at the age of what, thirty-five?

Rob, seated across the dining table from Sash and picking at the vegetables in his lasagne, bristles at every word Thomas says. He took an instant dislike to him the moment Thomas swaggered through our front door, a long arm around our daughter, looking at least a decade older than her. He's an inch taller than Rob too, an advantage my husband usually enjoys. Thomas, an over-confident smile on his face, immediately dropped a complimentary but inappropriate comment about my relatively low-cut dress. I blushed deeply, Rob grimacing behind Thomas's back as he'd picked up the moth-balled coat our guest had deposited on the hall table. I don't blame Rob for feeling put out, Thomas is being deliberately provocative, but we have to accept he's Sash's choice of boyfriend and as such it is up to us to make the effort until hopefully she tires of him or, perhaps more likely, he moves on to someone else. Parenting is full of injustices, the inequalities always falling in favour of the child. Sometimes, we have to swallow our opinions and make the best of it.

'Sash tells us you manage a wine bar in town,' I say to Thomas.

He's seated opposite me at the dining table, Sash's arm linked through his, her eyes only for Thomas, or perhaps she's simply avoiding the pointed stares of her father. I glance sideways at Rob to check he's behaving himself. His jaw is set, brow furrowed, but at least he's keeping quiet.

Thomas lifts his chin and regards me from under his long fringe; there is a protracted silence before he responds. 'Yes, The Limes. Do you know it?'

'I think so – it's in the centre of town?' I'm recalling a run-down establishment which has changed its name many times over the years; the kind of place Rob and I would never frequent; full of hardened drinkers who stand outside to smoke.

'Yeah, you should come in some time, have a drink.' He

smiles at me; that self-assured, almost daring grin, then he looks across the table at Rob. 'Both of you.'

I pick up my wine glass, nudging Rob at my side. 'We'd like that, wouldn't we?'

'Must be unsocial hours,' Rob mutters. 'Bar work.'

'Yes,' Thomas replies. 'But I live in the flat above, so long lie-ins.'

He smiles at Sash and she colours a little, not something I recall ever seeing her do before. I also notice the return of her smug smile, the one I'd first seen in the park, a twitch at the corner of her dark red lips. She's sleeping with him, that's obvious. They constantly find ways to touch one another: hands held under the table, arms linked. But sex means nothing. It's transient. I look at Rob, trying to recall how we were at that stage in our relationship, but it's too long ago, layers and layers of life obscuring my view of the past. A stab of something akin to jealousy surfaces, then I look at my daughter, her face so young, so innocent, despite the heavy make-up. I want to ask her, 'Do you love him?' because I know he's handsome in an unconventional kind of way, and charming, and older than her, confident, which is always attractive. But he's also no good. *You must see that, Sash.*

'Mum.' Sash recalls me to the conversation. 'I asked how are you enjoying your work at the drop-in centre?'

'It's early days, but I like it.' I return her smile, avoiding Rob's expression, which I can imagine. 'I'm already quite involved.'

I think of Nick and Rose, how they've both become such firm friends in a short period of time; and how at times I've found myself thinking of Nick when I'm away from him, smiling at his obvious regard for me.

'The place next to Sash's work?' Thomas asks, helping himself to salad.

'Yes, I understand you two met there?' I say, avoiding his gaze and looking at my daughter instead.

I notice Sash's discomfort as she says yes, although she doesn't elaborate further; no romantic tale of how their eyes met across the washing-up. It's obvious Thomas has a past, and it's therefore not too much of a leap to work out why he was really at the drop-in centre; certainly not as a volunteer. I look across at Rob, his jaw clenched even tighter, and I send him a silent plea to suppress his opinion. He already disapproves of my voluntary work, and now he has another reason to despise the place as it has brought Thomas into our lives. I notice Sash is looking at her father too, her smile fixed and unnatural.

'Do you still volunteer?' I ask Thomas, offering him focaccia, although my line of questioning is devious, not the kind to break bread over. 'I don't think I've ever seen you there.'

'It saw me through some dark days,' he replies, enigmatically.

He's clearly unfazed by my excavation of his personal history, or concerned by Sash's obvious embarrassment, her cheeks flaming as she looks down at her food.

'What's that supposed to mean?' Rob asks. '*Dark days.*'

Thomas ignores Rob and tells me he hasn't been to the drop-in centre for a while as he's been *crazy-busy* at work. He looks at Sash, his face moving closer to hers. 'And this one keeps me busy at home.'

'Thomas, don't!' Sash laughs, but I can tell she's uncomfortable.

Thomas looks across at me. 'But well done, Jo. Gotta give something back.' He looks around the room – a designer kitchen at one end and our bacchanalian feast at the other – his steady gaze then falling on Rob. 'We all have so much. It's immoral, don't you think?'

'Any news of baby bro?' Sash asks, before her father has time to reply.

'Not much,' I tell her. 'You heard anything from him?'

'Of course not! Fin doesn't message me,' Sash replies, using the tone she reserves for any mention of her brother. 'But I told him to keep in touch with you.'

'Maybe there's a girl involved,' I reply, smiling at Sash. Fin's always been too shy to ask anyone out, but I know he's had plenty of admirers.

'A *partner*,' Thomas corrects me, the smile temporarily gone, his expression serious. 'It's important to allow your son the freedom to explore his sexuality.'

'What the—' Rob says, sitting up straight in his chair, but Sash interrupts him again. 'Ooh, Mum! I almost forgot your present.' She reaches down to the rucksack by her feet. 'Sorry about, you know, missing your meal.'

'It's fine,' I reply, looking away from her.

I've tried over the last two weeks to rationalise her deceit, but there's really no excuse for telling me she was too ill to join us for my birthday meal when she'd clearly had a better offer. I haven't challenged her on it since, despite Rob's suggestion that I should if it's still upsetting me. It's true, with no card or present forthcoming the hurt has remained, but there seemed little point in pursuing it; the damage was done. I suppose I'd hoped she would be the one to make amends. I take the gift bag Sash is holding out and peek inside. 'A book?'

'Not just any book,' she replies, her face full of anticipation. 'An *amazing* book.'

She tells me to read the gift tag and I remark on how it's from both of them, the longed-for acknowledgement of my missed birthday already losing its shine. Thomas smiles, then shakes his head and leans in to kiss my daughter again. I look away from them; the continuing displays of affection are becoming tiresome. Rob and I exchange a look of mutual exasperation.

'It's a self-help book,' I say, removing the book from the gift bag and turning it over to read the back cover.

'Thomas lent me his copy and I read it in one sitting, Mum,' Sash explains, pulling away from Thomas's continuing advances. 'It makes you think in an entirely different way. It's so empowering. You should read it too, Dad.' She looks at her father who is now tapping away on his phone, probably sending a message judging by the rapid movement of his thumb across the keys. I'd asked him not to bring his phone to the table, his work becoming more intrusive of late, but if it keeps the peace I'm prepared to put up with it for now.

'What's it about?' Rob asks, switching off his phone to take the book from me. 'Feminist clap-trap by the looks of it.'

'Not a feminist, Rob?' Thomas leans towards Rob, his palm supporting his chin, looking up at him from under his dark fringe. 'Because I'm proud to say that I am.'

'I bet you are,' Rob replies, leaning forward too.

'More vegetarian lasagne anyone?' I ask, my voice unnaturally high. 'There's plenty.'

'No thanks,' Thomas replies, relaxing back in his seat, his foot almost touching mine under the table, so I snatch mine back, tucking my bare toes under my chair. 'I think I'm done here,' he says, clearly amused by my reaction.

'Dessert then,' I say, standing up. 'I've made a tropical fruit salad. Hope that's okay with everyone?'

'Fine with me,' Sash replies, helping me clear the table.

'Tell Dad to go easy on him,' Sash hisses as she passes me the dirty plates to stack in the dishwasher, our heads bent over the task as we mouth our conversation to one another. 'He's being really difficult; as usual.'

I look down the room at Rob, his back to me, then take a quick glance at Thomas, both of them silent at the table, the long open-plan kitchen-diner crackling with tension. 'Thomas is provoking him,' I whisper back.

Sash rolls her eyes, then tells me, in that *you're-being-so-annoying* tone she has, that Thomas is being fine; lovely in fact. This is a big ask for him, apparently. He doesn't normally do the parent thing, but he knows it's important to her that we like him. I look at Sash's face, still so young, the disappointment obvious in her eyes.

'I'm sorry,' I reply, touching the side of her cheek with my hand. 'I'll try harder.'

'It's not you,' she says. 'Although you are being a bit weird.' She stares at the back of her father's head. 'It's him.'

'Dessert anyone?' I ask, carrying the crystal bowl to the table.

'Sash, can you grab the pot of crème fraîche from the fridge please, darling?'

'No cream for me,' Thomas says. 'Unless you have any coconut, or soy?'

'I'm sorry, I don't think I do,' I reply, looking at Sash.

'Sorry,' she tells Thomas, plonking the tub down in front of her father, so heavily I look across at him to make sure he's not spattered with dollops of thick cream.

'What?' Rob asks, and I shake my head, telling him it's nothing.

'The milk and cheese in the lasagne weren't vegan either,' Sash is saying to Thomas. 'Thanks for eating it, babe.' She smiles at him as if he's made a huge sacrifice on her behalf.

'You seemed to enjoy it,' Rob points out.

'I was being polite,' Thomas replies.

'Oh there's nothing polite about you, is there Thomas?' Rob says, locking eyes with him.

'Rob, don't!' I say, giving him a warning look, but Rob isn't done.

'You flirt with my wife, drink my wine and sleep with my daughter, but you turn your nose up at our food? *Bloody priceless.*' He slumps back in his chair and folds his arms, his eyes almost closed.

'Dad!' Sash says, looking mortified.

'Fruit salad anyone?' I ask, the words sounding ridiculous as I say them, Thomas the only one even looking at me as Sash stares at her father.

'Sorry, Mum. I think we should go,' Sash announces, standing up. 'We've clearly outstayed our welcome.'

'But you haven't seen what we've done with your bedroom,'

I say, pleading with her to stay, but she avoids catching my eye, head down as she walks out of the room.

Thomas shrugs and stands too, his movements languorous as though his long limbs need to be stretched and unfurled. His display is all for me as Rob is still in the same position, arms crossed, eyes all but closed, his only movement a slight tap of his foot against the table leg.

'It was a lovely meal, Jo,' Thomas says as he follows Sash out of the dining room. 'Hopefully see you soon.'

I hear him pick up his coat from the end of the bannister where Rob hung it, the large buttons clattering against the newel post, then he mumbles something to Sash who has opened the front door, the cold air now reaching Rob and me in the dining room. There's a moment's silence, then a loud slam as the heavy door shuts behind them.

'Rob, do something!' I tell him. 'We can't let them go like this.'

At first I think he won't move, his arms still folded tightly across his chest, chin down, then he jumps up and runs out of the kitchen. Instantly I regret encouraging him to go after them. I run too, calling for him to stop, that he'll make it worse, but he throws open the just-slammed door and is outside before I can reach him.

I hear Rob shout, 'Leave my daughter alone; you're a bloody waste of space!' Then I'm at the open door, watching the scene unfold before me, my bare feet hugging the icy step as though to venture on to the frost-covered gravel would show I'd taken Rob's side. I glance at Sash, who is sitting behind the wheel of her car, watching her father and boyfriend as they square up to one another. Rob reaches up to grasp the lapel of Thomas's moth-eaten coat in one hand, the other clenched in a fist at his side. Thomas is smiling back at my husband, daring him to throw the first punch.

'What is it you're after?' Rob asks, spittle thickening his words, his face an inch from Thomas's maddening grin. 'Money is it? How much do you want?'

'Dad, don't!' Sash is out of her car now, running towards them as she screams at her father. 'Get off him! I hate you for this! I hate you!'

I'm shouting too. 'Don't, Sash! Leave them! You'll get hurt!' I dash towards her across the painful spiky gravel as she tries to prise her father's hand from Thomas's coat.

Thomas easily pushes Rob away and then encircles Sash to protect her with his enfolding arms, her face to his chest, his hands buried in her hair which is lifted from her neck to wrap around them both, long tendrils of blonde, like ropes of silk which bind them together, white against the black of his enormous coat. She's crying now, wracking sobs into Thomas's chest; no need for me or her father. Rob backs away, his hands still clenched at his sides, and when he turns to me I see that he's entirely defeated.

'Come inside,' I say, stepping forward to touch his arm. 'We can mend this later. Just go inside, it's freezing out here.'

He looks at me and I can see my words have penetrated his despair, then his expression falls into one of further humiliation as he shrugs me off and walks back into the house.

'Sash, darling.' I walk towards her, but Thomas is holding her so tightly I'm afraid she won't hear me. Then she turns from him, looks straight through me and walks to her car, her head down as she climbs inside. Thomas gets into the passenger seat, his knees almost up to his chin in the small space, and they leave, the blue Fiat pulling away at speed. The last glimpse I have of them is Thomas's face at the window, his sly smile spreading into a wide grin.

9

Five Days After The Fall

I'd almost forgotten Sash was coming to visit me until I hear her car arrive; a little faster than I would like, the tyres sliding on the gravel, then loud music expelled as she opens the driver door. Rob had mentioned something about her popping in to check on me during her lunch break, but it had been so early when he'd left for work this morning that his words had barely registered, especially as I'd dragged the duvet over my head to shut them out. I was exhausted, yes, but since I met Rose yesterday my feelings of distrust towards Rob have intensified, my retreat into myself even greater. I suppose I could have asked him outright why he hadn't said anything to me about the drop-in-centre, but I had no idea how to frame an accusation about which I'm still so uncertain. Either Rob had known I was a volunteer there and had deliberately concealed it from me, or he hadn't known anything about it at all, which means I'd kept it secret from him. I've decided it's best I work out which scenario is correct before I tackle him. There is so much to be sorted out in my head. I need to deal with one problem at a time, not least the troubling issue of the man I saw through the café window.

I hear a key in the door, then Sash calls up to me, 'Mum? You decent?'

'I'm still in bed,' I reply. 'Come on up.'

I smooth my bed-hair down with my palms and run my tongue over my un-brushed teeth, dismayed as I look at the neon numbers on Rob's alarm clock to see it's already afternoon.

'Lazy-bones, did you forget I was coming?' Sash asks, her heavy boots pounding out her progress across the room as she moves past the bed towards the window.

Sash's appearance is still a shock to me, my recollection and the reality of it so different. I miss the long silky strands of hair that would fall through my fingers and the make-up-free face, her own colouring infinitely preferable to the harsh shades she now applies. She's filled out, too; more of a woman than a girl. But I don't mind her taking charge; it's a novelty having her fuss over me.

'I have a brain injury; I'm allowed to forget things,' I reply, lifting myself up in bed as I smile at my daughter; observing to myself how she's still *my girl*, despite the rebellious attempts to cover up her natural beauty. 'And I'm allowed to be lazy.' I squint into the bright sunlight as Sash opens the blind. 'I'm recuperating.'

'I don't have long,' she tells me. 'Food or shower first?'

'You didn't need to check on me; I'm fine.' I smile at her. 'Did your dad bully you into coming?'

'What do you mean by that?' she asks, straightening the bed as I get out of it. Her eyes are cast down to the pillow she's plumping, but I note the tension in her voice.

I tell her it meant nothing, I'm just pleased she's here. 'Tell me about your flat,' I say, slipping on my robe over my nightdress. 'I hear it's quite something.'

She's now picking up my clothes, last night's cast-offs strewn across the floor. 'Dad told you about my new flat?' she replies, looking up.

'Yes, of course. Why wouldn't he?'

She shrugs. 'No reason. Yeah it's lovely. You'll have to come and visit us again soon.'

I hesitate at the use of the word *us*, sensing, as Rob said, our resistance to her new boyfriend; or maybe it's just the feeling of exclusion the word prompts in me.

'I need to meet Thomas too,' I say and Sash pauses, her hand reaching down to the floor to retrieve a shoe of mine. 'I know we didn't approve of him at first,' I say, as she looks up. 'But that's all in the past now, isn't it?'

Sash sits on the edge of the bed. 'You have met him, a couple of times in fact.' She slides her rucksack from her back, taking out her phone and scrolling through the photos. 'This is him,' she says, handing it to me. 'Jog any memories?'

The image on the screen is of a laughing couple, Sash and Thomas, him tall behind her, his chin resting on top of her short hair, the position causing her to stoop a little. His mouth is formed in a wide smile beneath a thick dark fringe which is almost covering his eyes, one arm wrapped tight around Sash's shoulders, the other raised out of the shot, presumably to take the snap.

'It's not a great photo, I'm afraid,' Sash tells me. 'But Thomas isn't one for having his picture taken. I had to beg him to take that one for me and then he was messing around. Well, you can see.'

I look again. I'd only seen him for a matter of seconds and he'd been beyond the café window, walking fast. But that smile. *Oh my god, that smile.* I close my eyes and open them again, hoping I'm mistaken, but the man in the photo is definitely the man I saw outside the café.

'Do you remember him?' she asks, taking the phone from me.

I want to snatch it back, look again, see someone different, but it's already gone, returned to her rucksack. I look down at my hands, empty now; as if the image had never been there. But it was. I can't unsee what I now know.

'Mum?' Sash waves a hand in front of my face. 'Hello, anybody in there?'

I shake my head, not trusting myself to speak. My memories are fragmented, all over the place, connecting up in strange ways: the photo, then the man outside the café, then the images in my dreams of a naked man turning to me, that same smile on his lips. I tell myself it means nothing, it's just a photo of a man I don't know, a man I clearly remember because he's Sash's boyfriend, but the feeling of dread, even fear, is worse now than ever. Sash is talking again, asking me about my check-up last night at the hospital, her father's told her it went well, my consultant was happy with me. She stands up, still chattering on as she collects more mess from the floor, my tights and blouse in her hand as she turns back. 'Mum? What's wrong?'

'I'm fine, honestly,' I say, composing myself a little as she sinks down on to the bed beside me. I take her hand and run my thumb across her palm.

'Is there something you're not telling me? Something your consultant said?'

I look across at her, her face so full of concern. 'No, of course not, it's just . . .'

'Mum, you're scaring me, what is it?'

'It's nothing.' I look away. 'I just wish I could remember more. Everything's so jumbled up.'

'Did you speak to the doctor about this?' she asks, her hand still in mine, although I sense her resistance and, sure enough, she pulls away.

'He said it's perfectly normal to feel a bit, you know . . .' I look up at her and smile. 'Lost.'

She asks if the doctor offered us any advice; things we can do to help the memories come back. 'Just time,' I tell her, but my answer is somewhat economical as the consultant gave us a few alternatives to explore, all of which Rob dismissed out of hand.

I'd known he would be resistant to the idea of me talking over our problems with strangers, his aversion to the *talking therapies* always accompanied by air-quotes and the assertion that we will cope *just the two of us*; a phrase I find increasingly irritating, the words almost physical in their constraint. It feels like he would prefer me to struggle on like this forever, as though the loss of memory were to him inconsequential, a mere detail in my recovery now I'm recuperating well physically. I'd told him that and he'd replied that he didn't much like the attitude I'd adopted post-fall, quickly following up with an apology. Neither of us had spoken much after that, the drive home from the hospital almost silent; every conversation loaded with hidden meaning.

'And you still don't remember anything since the day Fin left for uni?' Sash asks.

I tell her how I've remembered taking my coffee into the den and using the laptop in there. Oh, and that I had some pasta sauce in the freezer. Then I hesitate, trying to recall if there's anything else I can share, and deciding there isn't.

Sash smiles. 'All the useful stuff, then! So there's literally nothing to do but wait?'

Astute as ever, Sash has skewered my vagueness. 'There's counselling. Or support groups,' I reply, recalling again Rob's negative reaction to these suggestions. 'The consultant gave me the details for a brain-injury group who meet once a week in the village; this afternoon in fact.'

'What time?' Sash asks, glancing at her watch again. 'I could take you there if you don't mind getting a taxi back?'

I knew the time last night, the consultant told us, but the information has gone again now, my frustration brimming over as I try to remember. Sash tells me not to worry, she can look it up on her phone; they're bound to have a website. 'It's fine,' I tell her. 'I'm not even sure I want to go.'

'It's not until half two,' she says, looking at her phone. 'You'll have to get a taxi both ways I'm afraid, but that's fine. As long as you're up to it?' She smiles at me as if it were settled. She's so much like her father at times; everything a matter of logistics.

'I'm not sure, Sash. Your dad thinks it's a waste of time,' I say, finding it much easier to blame my reticence on Rob's disapproval than acknowledge my own fears, the images from my internet searches populating the support group with a grotesque collection of fictional victims.

'For fuck's sake, Mum!' She stands up from the bed and paces around the room, her boots thudding across the wooden floor. 'Stand up for yourself for once! If you want to go to the support group, then go! Fuck what he thinks!'

'Don't shout, darling,' I say, my headache returning with her rant. 'And don't swear.'

Sash appears to ignore my comments, but when she speaks it is a little less volubly than before and the swear words are gone. 'Maybe you'll hate it, but you won't know unless you try.' She smiles at me, but in a tilted-head, poor-old-you kind of way. 'You need to do something, Mum. I think you're getting depressed.'

'Oh Sash, you're always so dramatic.' I smile back at her, but she's serious.

'I mean it, Mum. Lying in bed all day is a very bad sign. So food or shower first?'

After Sash's visit I do feel a little better in myself, although my sense of well-being is only pleasing when I can push the image of Thomas's photo from my mind. At least my headache's not as bad now, dulled by the painkillers Sash brought me before she rushed back to work. She also insisted I ate the sandwich she'd made, and that I get up and take a shower, laying out some clean clothes on the bed for my return. I enjoyed her take-charge attitude which seemed to come from a different place than Rob's over-attentiveness. Reminded of his vigilance, I send a text to tell him I'm fine, but tired after Sash's visit; he mustn't panic if he doesn't hear from me for a couple of hours, I'll probably be asleep for the rest of the afternoon. I thought I'd feel worse than I do, deliberately lying to him, but maybe self-preservation comes before conscience, and now that I've decided to be brave and go to the support group I need to make sure he doesn't try and stop me.

I'd promised Sash I'd call for a taxi, but it seems silly when my car is right there, waiting for me on the drive. As Sash had said, I need to stand up for myself, and after Rob's intransigence last night I feel entirely vindicated in my defiance of his rules. Besides, every time I close my eyes I see that photo of Thomas and a million questions ensue. I need something to distract me, something positive and proactive.

I pick up my keys and lock the house, reassured by the sound my car makes as I press the blip-key and it unlocks. The interior smells familiar, new upholstery and a trace of my favourite perfume, offering up my first taste of real independence since my fall. I listen to the engine start up first time, despite the days it's been left idle, as I glance around for anything that may offer clues to the past, but the car is immaculate as always. I imagine myself screwing up parking receipts and dropping them in the dustbin on the drive, much as Rob must have dropped my broken phone in there after my fall. I release the handbrake and manoeuvre the car slowly across the drive; every action feeling unnatural, although it's probably only been a matter of days since I last drove. The panic which swells in my throat is sudden and unexpected, causing me to cough. I apply the handbrake, taking a moment to compose myself, but fear grips me once more. What if I can't do this? I think of the ambulance which took me away from here on the night of my fall, and the taxi I had to call to take me to town to meet Rose. I'm a prisoner up here if I can't drive; beholden to others, especially Rob. I need to do this. I take a deep breath and try to think back to the last time I may have been in my car. It was 18:02 when I fell. That would have been around the time Rob arrived home from work, or not long after. Maybe I'd driven that day, perhaps visited the drop-in centre, or . . . I close my eyes, breathe deeply and push away the images of a naked back, a smile, a kiss . . . I have to concentrate. I can do this.

It's not an easy drive away from the barn, a single-track lane winding down the hill. There are passing places, but it's best not to meet anyone on the way as reversing up the narrow incline is always tricky. Relieved to reach the intersection at the bottom, I release my tight grip on the steering wheel and indicate left to join the main road to the village. It's a turn I've negotiated thousands of times, but the longer I wait, the more my head pounds and the less certain I am of my own judgement. I watch the traffic, car following on after car, lorries too. How much time do I need? I hesitate for too long, and when I do go, it's with a lurch in both the suspension and my stomach, more a leap of faith than a calculated decision. The van driver comes out of nowhere, flashing his lights at me, but not slowing down at all. I raise my hand and drive on as fast as I can, but he speeds up behind me, his naked aggression caught in my rear-view mirror; he's so close behind. I increase my speed as the decline steepens, although I'm already at the speed limit. I can see a turning to my right, not the one I need, and it will be a close thing, but I think I can make it. I skid around the corner, bumping the kerb and then slamming on my brakes as I pull into the side of the road, a final blast of a horn behind me now dying away.

Leaning my head forward and still gripping the steering wheel, I try to control my panic. Rob was right, I shouldn't have driven. I lift my head and look around me, my hands trembling, but I'm in one piece and the car is undamaged. The van driver was in the wrong, not me. He should have backed off, allowed me the space I needed. The village hall is just around the corner. I can do this. I take a deep breath, wipe my eyes and drive on.

The support group is already underway by the time I arrive. I can see them inside, but the double doors are firmly locked and my light tap on the glass goes unnoticed. I wait, unsure whether to interrupt, or leave before my presence is noted, but a young man who appears to be directing proceedings looks across at me now, a smile and a wave as he walks towards me.

'Hi,' he says, opening the door. His attire is casual, jeans and tee shirt, his smile welcoming. 'Can I help you?'

'I'm not sure; my consultant, Mr . . .' I trail off, trying to recall the doctor's name. 'Sorry, it's unusual, Indian I think.'

'Mr Agrawal?' he prompts and I tell him, yes, I think so,

imagining he must have to finish a fair few sentences in his line of work. He says Mr Agrawal is a great supporter of the group, then introduces himself as Matt.

'And you are?' he asks, still smiling, his hands thrust deep into his jeans pockets forcing his narrow shoulders up, his foot in the door to keep it open.

'Oh, I'm sorry. I'm Joanne Harding, Jo.'

'Hi, Jo.' Matt smiles at me. 'Well done for coming, that's the hard bit. Come in and meet the others, there's nothing scary here, I promise.'

Matt jokes with them as we approach, asking them to confirm they are all friendly – well, most of them – bantering with a couple of lads who are next to one another at the far end of the semi-circle of seated participants. The chairs are reshuffled, an extra one added for me; not at one end as I'd expected, but in the middle, next to Matt. There's respect and warmth extended towards me in the interactions which accomplish this task, and obvious affection between Matt and the assembled group. Matt introduces me and asks me to explain what brought me here today, just a few words, nothing to worry about, then all eyes turn to me.

'Hello.' I clear my throat, which is suddenly dry. 'Well, I'm not really sure what to expect, I don't even know if I qualify—'

Matt interrupts me with a raised hand, the fingers spread, non-threatening. 'Just tell us why you're here, Jo. As much or as little as you want to share.'

'I'm Jo.' I cough again. 'I suffered a head injury when I fell down the stairs.'

Matt leans forward. 'How long ago was this, Jo?'

'A week.' I pause, trying to work it out exactly. 'I think . . . maybe less . . . about five days.'

'Very recently,' he offers. 'Well done on your recovery so far.'

'Thanks.' I smile, his composure reassuring.

'And how are you feeling today?' Matt asks.

'Better, in myself, but I've lost a whole year. I have no memory of it at all – well, hardly any.'

'That must be terrible,' observes the older lady seated at the other end of the chairs to the two lads. 'I'm forgetful; but a whole year!'

'Yes, it is terrible,' I reply, turning to smile at her. 'Everyone tells me it will all come back, trying to reassure me, I suppose; as though it doesn't matter now I'm physically getting better.'

Matt nods. 'It's a common problem, I'm afraid. If people can't see what you're dealing with it's much harder for them to empathise, but it is still very early days for you.'

'My girlfriend left me,' the leather-clad biker to my right tells me, his sidekick laughing when he adds, 'She said I was a nut-job.'

'That's 'cos the accident turned you into a horny bastard,' the sidekick says, and everyone laughs except the older lady, who whispers to the blonde woman beside her, 'What did he say?'

'Okay, guys,' Matt says. 'This is Jo's time. Just tell us how you're doing, Jo.'

And so I do, everything tumbling out in a few short sentences, the fear, the confusion, the pain, and it's all greeted with knowing nods and words of support and, although I cry, I feel better than I have since it happened. Then I listen as they talk, and again, for the first time since I woke up in hospital, I feel fortunate by comparison. I'm exhausted, my head pounding, but for those few minutes at least, I've found a real understanding of what I'm going through. We gather in the kitchen, standing around a table laid out with cups of tea and plates of plain biscuits, both of which I accept gratefully. Now the tension has been released from my body, I'm shaky and light-headed. I think of Rose and the sweet coffee and spoon another sugar into my tea.

'You alright, love?' asks the older lady who'd sympathised when I'd first spoken of my memory loss. She'd shared her own concerns after I'd finished, telling us all of her increasing forgetfulness. *I don't know if it's the brain trauma, or just old age.*

'I'm fine, thanks,' I tell her, trotting out my standard reply, but then I think better of it and say, 'Actually, it's been quite an effort; it's the first time I've driven since my fall and I gave myself a bit of a fright on the way here.'

'You've done really well,' she says. 'Really well.'

'Thanks; you too,' I say, then I watch as she says her good-byes, zips up her pink anorak and pushes open the double doors.

'What did you think?' Matt asks, joining me. 'Will you come again?'

'It was good,' I reply, taking another biscuit from the plate next to my cup of tea. 'You're all very welcoming.'

'Nice to find some company; people going through the same kind of problems?' he suggests.

'Yes, definitely, although I still feel a bit of a fraud taking up their time.'

I'd listened to stories of comas which had lasted weeks or even months, battles to walk again, talk again. Tales of jobs gone, partners lost, money troubles, drastic side effects of medication, every aspect of daily life affected by their injuries. My problems seem unimportant in comparison. I don't have to fight an employer for compensation, or learn how to write my name, or post notes around my kitchen reminding me how to make a cup of tea.

Matt's expression has changed to one of professionalism. 'It's not about who deserves more sympathy, or has the worst deal. You're all going through a period of prolonged recovery and you face different challenges, but there's common ground. It's important not to trivialise your concerns. We're here to listen and support one another. After my brain injury—'

'Oh, I assumed you were the counsellor . . .' I say, covering my mouth with my hand as I chew my third biscuit.

'I am,' he says, turning his head to show me a white scar which runs from behind his ear up into his hairline. 'Skiing accident, wasn't wearing a helmet when I collided with a tree, had to have an emergency operation to remove a clot. I couldn't walk for six months. I was a driving instructor who couldn't drive, so I retrained.'

'Wow, that's incredible,' I say, swallowing. 'I never would have known.'

'That's the point, Jo. Our injuries fade, become almost invisible to everyone but ourselves. That's why we need to find somewhere like this, where people understand what it's really like.'

He walks towards the bantering lads who've taken to throwing biscuits at one another, his scar more noticeable now he's pointed it out to me, and a limp I hadn't picked up on either.

'Matt's great, isn't he?' someone says behind me.

The voice is familiar from her story to the group, the words spoken slowly and deliberately, a slight slurring of one into another, although I can't match a face to them until I turn around. Then I place her immediately; the bubbly blonde who dived into a swimming pool at the shallow end, shattering several vertebrae as well as her skull.

'Yes, he seems very capable,' I reply, glancing again at Matt. 'I hadn't realised he was a victim too.'

'You wouldn't know except for that scar, would you?' She looks over to Matt, who turns and smiles in our direction. 'He's amazing really.' She adjusts herself to lean against the kitchen worktop, balancing her crutches beside her.

'*And you*,' I say, then looking around the room I add, 'All of you.'

'You liked us, then?' she asks, sipping her tea. 'You'll come back?'

'Maybe,' I reply, asking myself the same question and finding the answer to be different from what I'd imagined. I'm glad I came, a couple of hours' distraction from my own difficulties, a sense of perspective gained perhaps, as well as some independence, but I think I've already decided it's not for me. I have too much else that requires my attention, but maybe one day, if I still need it. The thought is at once discouraging, the hope that my memory will quickly return evaporating with the realisation these things can take a long time. 'Hopefully I won't need to,' I say, then looking up from my tea and still mid-thought, I realise how tactless I must sound. 'Sorry, I didn't mean—'

'It's frustrating at first, you imagine everything will snap back into place,' she says, apparently unfazed by my comment, or the slurring of her words as she struggles to form them correctly. She'd told the group, me in particular, that it gets much worse when she's tired. 'I used to think I'd wake up one day . . .' she pauses to place her cup neatly on the saucer '. . . and everything would be like it was before, but it takes time.' She cleans her top teeth with her tongue, mindful I suppose, of the bright shade of lipstick transferring to them, as it has the white cup. 'You have to be patient,' she says. 'I think I've remembered everything, then something happens and I get another bit back, another piece of the puzzle.'

'You suffered memory loss too?'

'Three months for me,' she replies. 'I thought it was Christmas Day and it was almost Easter.' She laughs, her smile infectious.

They'd been in South Africa, she'd told us all, although I'm sure everyone except me had heard the story before. Her repatriation had been a terrible ordeal, which had apparently cost the insurance company 'gawd knows how much!'

'But your memory did come back?' I ask. 'In time?'

'Mostly, but you can't force it, you have to wait for the triggers.' I must look confused because she explains how a song, a place, a smell, a chance remark, can suddenly remind you of something. 'Those are the things that trigger real memories. Force them and you won't know if you're reinventing the past,' she says, licking her pink lips again. 'At least, that's what I think.' She laughs to herself. 'My husband showed me a photo of the hotel in Jo'burg where I'd had the accident. I hadn't a clue, not a clue! Then he took me back there and I remembered it all.' She leans on one of her crutches and snaps her fingers. 'Just like that!'

I want to hug her for being the first person to actually give me some hope. I need to push away the images from my past and rely on the facts as I know them, instead of tormenting myself with what may or may not have happened.

The drive home is much less eventful. I allow my mind to drift, at first turning over the blonde woman's advice about recovering lost memories, how I mustn't force them, and then ignoring it again as I scratch at the past, one memory in particular feeling tantalisingly close.

His face is turned from me as I trace the curve of his naked back with my fingertips, my body filled with desire as I touch his skin. Then he turns over, his face still obscured in shadow.

I drive on, concentrating on the road ahead, but he's still there, watching me.

His hair is thick and dark as it falls over his eyes, his features undefined except for the generous mouth; wide and welcoming, a smile spreading across it as he leans in closer . . .

I hardly notice my drive up the hill, my mind filled with questions. Could I really have found solace elsewhere? Even contemplated leaving my marriage? I thought I knew myself; a wife, a mother. Faithful, reliable. Defined. The dissonance between the life I thought I was living and the one I am now faced with is impossible to comprehend. Rob and I are so different with one another, detached, wary. Something must have happened to break the trust between us, something terrible enough to wipe away everything we had previously shared and replace it with this distrust and deceit.

December – Last Year

'Rob, Fin, is that you?' I rush down the stairs in time to see them come through the front door, both of them loaded up with bags and boxes which they drop at their feet. Rob back-heels the door, shutting out the filthy night. The wind is wailing around the barn, trying to find a way in, the rain battering the roof and hurling itself at the windows. The storms have been with us all week and show no sign of abating.

'Hey, Mum,' Fin says, accepting my hug.

'Let me see you,' I reply, holding him at arm's length. 'You're so thin!' He's wearing the parka I bought him for university, but filling out the shoulders much less than when we dropped him off, his cheeks hollowed out too. 'You need to eat more, look after yourself.'

'That's what *I* told him,' Rob says, dragging a bulging bin bag past us. 'This is all his washing; where do you want it?'

'Take it straight through to the utility room, please,' I reply, still looking at Fin, who is staring down at his trainers, the laces undone. 'Please don't lose any more weight, Fin,' I tell him.

'I'm fine, Mum,' he says, looking up at me and smiling. 'Honestly, I'm fine.'

I smile too, but the memory of Fin's tiny arms and legs, so thin you could almost circle them with one hand, still haunt me. He was only nine, picked on by older boys at school for reasons he never properly divulged, his response to throw away his packed lunch each day and pick at his dinner in the evening.

'Christmas tree looks nice in there,' he says, pointing towards the den.

Rob shouts through to Fin from the kitchen, 'I told you, she's gone completely over the top this year – three trees!'

'Where are the other two?' asks Fin, looking around him.

I take him into the sitting room to admire the tall evergreen to the right of the fireplace which fills the room with the sharp scent of pine needles, then I pull back the curtains to reveal a potted fir tree on the patio, smothered in lights. I've spent days preparing for his return, filling the food cupboards and fridge with his favourites, decorating the house with not just the trees, but every other Christmas ornament I can sneak past Rob. The drop-in centre has had to manage without me, because my boy is coming home. And now he's here, at last, but my excitement is tempered by my misgivings. I had a gut feeling something was wrong which has only been confirmed further by his diminished appearance.

'House looks nice,' he says. 'What's for dinner?'

'Your favourite of course.' I hug him again, but this time he pulls away. 'Can't believe you're home; a whole month!' I say, noticing something in his eyes, something withheld. I think he's going to change his mind, share the thought, but then he closes his mouth and walks out, his tread light and quick on the stairs.

'Have a look at Dad's new study, and Sash's room,' I call up, but he closes his bedroom door behind him.

I stand there for a moment, looking up the empty stairs, before I walk past the piles of Fin's belongings dumped in the hall and join Rob in the kitchen. 'Does he seem okay to you?' I ask, competing with the noise my husband is creating as he roots around in a drawer.

'Fin?' Rob asks.

'Yes, of course, Fin,' I tell him, opening the oven to check on the roast beef. 'What are you looking for?' He holds up his beer bottle. 'Top drawer, where it always is,' I say, pointing to the correct drawer.

'He's fine,' Rob says, rummaging noisily through the jumble of cutlery and utensils until he finds the bottle opener. 'Hungover probably.' There's a hiss as he levers the metal top away from the bottle. 'Typical student.' He takes a swig and then asks me, as he has done every day since Sunday, whether I've heard anything from Sash today.

'Nope, nothing,' I reply, closing the oven and turning the temperature down a little. 'It's starting to annoy me now; it's like she doesn't even consider how this makes us feel.'

Rob sighs. 'She's stubborn.'

'Wonder where she gets that from?' I ask, raising my eyebrows at him. 'You don't think she'll keep this up over Christmas, do you?' The awful prospect only just occurring to me.

Rob pulls out a stool from beneath the kitchen island and sits down, his beer in front of him, the bottle twisting in his long fingers. 'I've tried, Jo. It's up to her now.'

It's true, Rob has reached out to her, but every one of his texts has been ignored, every call rejected. The moment Rob grabbed at Thomas's lapel he lost her, and so did I. I've had the odd word of reply to my numerous messages, but nothing in her short responses gives me any hope. She doesn't want to see her father, that much is clear.

'Did you say anything to Fin?' I ask Rob as I lean against the worktop, the oven gloves still in my hand.

'No, I thought I'd wait.' He lifts his beer to his lips, then pauses and adds, 'There's still two weeks until Christmas; lots can happen between now and then.'

I go into the utility room, distractedly pulling fetid clothes from the torn bin bag filled with Fin's dirty washing, fingertip searching the pockets of jeans and joggers for forgotten earphones or coins, sorting the mouldering piles of clothing, bedding and towels into darks and lights. But the worry of losing Sash, not only for Christmas but maybe beyond, preoccupies me, so when I look down at the piles they are still muddled. I don't even notice Rob standing behind me, his emptied beer bottle in his hand.

'You want the recycling bin?' I ask, standing up to let him through.

Rob tosses the glass bottle into the bin where it clatters noisily to the bottom. 'I'll sort the situation with Sash,' he says. 'Whatever it takes. I'll even apologise to Thomas if I have to. I promise.'

I hold him then, and he kisses me on the mouth, a kiss that tells me he means what he says. He's always been the fixer, the one to sort everything out when I panicked over disasters yet to materialise.

'We can't let Thomas cause a permanent rift,' I reply. 'Whatever we have to do it will be worth it,' I tell him.

The damp spores from the piles of dirty washing fill the confined space and the dull thud of Fin's music drifts down through the ceiling as Rob holds me tight, promising me again he will sort everything out, whatever it takes.

10

Five Days After The Fall

The landline is ringing as I walk through the front door, the shrill sound resonating in the empty hallway. I suppose I should be mindful of the fact that it's almost certainly Rob demanding to know where I've been, but it seems to take me longer these days to move from one task to another, my mind still filled with my time at the support group.

Rob's tone is abrupt when I eventually pick up. 'You're not dead, then!'

I drop my keys on to the hall table and transfer the phone to my other ear. 'What?'

'I've been out of my mind, Jo. Sash isn't answering her phone either. I tracked your mobile to home, but—'

'*You tracked my phone?*'

'Yes, our mobiles are paired so we can track them, don't you remember?'

I tell him I don't and he dismisses my questions with

matter-of-fact and somewhat terse replies about how we'd paired them in case either of us ever lost a phone or had it stolen.

'I was worried, Jo. You've been missing for hours.'

'I went outside,' I reply, the story formulating as I speak. 'To my car.'

'To your car? I told you not to drive!'

'No, you're not listening.' I close the front door, which is still wide open, the wind taking it and bending it back on creaking hinges. 'I didn't drive, I just started up the engine to make sure the battery wasn't flat.' It surprises me how easily the unprepared lie comes.

There's silence then he says, 'You can't have been outside for the last two hours.'

'I took a pill,' I reply. 'Must have knocked me out.' I walk quickly up the stairs to our bedroom, the home phone to my ear.

'Are you feeling unwell?' Rob asks. 'You sound out of breath.'

'I'm fine except for you and your constant questions!'

I hang up and throw myself on the bed, reaching for my mobile phone on the bedside cabinet, deleting all his messages with a jabbing motion of my finger as I berate myself for forgetting to take it with me. Perhaps it's a symptom of my brain injury, this forgetfulness, but it's more that the replacement phone feels meaningless to me, as if it isn't mine. I stare at the blank notifications screen, then click on the Find My Friends app, the first time I can recall seeing it, let alone using it to trace Rob's whereabouts. The landline rings again and I snatch it up and shout, 'Go away, Rob!'

'Mum, it's me.' There's a pause, then Sash asks, 'Is everything okay?'

'Of course it is.' I sit up on the bed. 'Your father's been stalking me; that's all. Hang on . . .' I throw a couple of pain-killers back with some dust-filmed water and pick up the phone again. 'Sorry about that, you okay?'

'Stalking you?' Sash laughs, but she sounds hesitant, and I'm distracted too, looking at my mobile again. The app is still trying to locate Rob's mobile, then it notifies me the Wi-Fi signal has been lost; unreliable as always in the barn.

'Mum? You still there? I rang to ask you how the support group went.'

'It was good, definitely worth going.'

'But?'

'No but.'

'Look, Mum . . .' There's another long pause. 'If it's Dad's opinion you're worrying about, then don't. I won't say anything.'

And there it is, the thing I first noticed the day I came home from the hospital. Rob and Sash are different with one another, there's a gulf between them that wasn't there before, something unspoken and wrong. They still have that bond, excluding at times, but since my fall I've noticed small but significant changes in their relationship. Rob was so cross when she let slip about Fin leaving university, his temper quick, as though it had been there all along, waiting to resurface at the slightest provocation. Sash's mistake was a genuine one, but that did little to quell his obvious anger. And she did accuse him of 'pulling the strings, telling us what we can and can't say'.

172

'Is there a problem between you and your dad?' I ask her, sitting up straighter on the bed, trying to ignore my headache so I can concentrate on her reply. 'Something you're not telling me?'

Sash hesitates for so long I wonder if she's still there, but I can hear her breathing, slow and steady. 'No, of course not,' she says. 'Why do you ask that?'

'Sash, please. If there's something I should know . . .'

Again, she pauses before she replies, 'I'm sorry, Mum. I promised Dad.'

'Promised him what?'

'I'm at work, Mum. This isn't a great time.'

I lean back against the pillows, my head pounding. I should let her go, but I can't. 'I'd like you to tell me now, Sash.'

I think she's going to use work as her excuse again, but then she replies, her words rushed out so I need to rewind them in my head to gather the full meaning, 'Dad told Fin and me we're not to tell you anything that's happened since your memory loss, he said he'll tell you when the time is right, when you're strong enough, he said the last year was so awful that . . .' She stops abruptly.

'What, Sash? Tell me!'

'Mum, I can't. This isn't fair, Dad means well. I'm sure he does.'

'What does *that* mean?'

'Maybe I got it wrong, maybe I misunderstood.' She hesitates again.

'I mean it, Sash. You need to tell me. I have a right to know.'

'Okay, but only if you promise not to tell Dad.'

I tell her of course I won't, then she clears her throat and says, 'I'm only telling you this because I want you to get better as soon as you can and because I don't agree with him, you do have a right to know.'

'Are you saying your father doesn't want me to get better?'

'No, of course not. It's just . . .'

'What did he say to you Sash, tell me!'

'He said maybe it's better if you never remember.'

As soon as the words are out Sash is justifying them, telling me again she's sure her father means well; he's just being over-protective; she shouldn't have said anything. Please don't tell him. Then she backtracks further, says she's probably got the wrong idea, she's sure she has in fact, she's sorry; she didn't mean to upset me. Just forget what she's told me. She should go, her boss is coming. I plead with her to explain, but then she hangs up.

I stare at the phone, contemplating calling her back, but it's not fair to pressurise her in that way. Besides, it's Rob I'm angry with, not her, the confirmation that he's deliberately with-holding information from me galvanising my thoughts. I make my way down the stairs as quickly as I am able, fearful Rob will arrive home from work before I have time to do what I now feel I must.

In the den I open up my laptop and search the myriad websites brought up by my search. I only want a cheap handset, something simple, untraceable, but in the end I choose the same phone I already have, only selecting a different colour – metallic pink, not the muted silver Rob chose – so I won't mix them up. I tap in my order, choosing next-day delivery and taking a chance on it arriving after Rob has left for work. I can always act confused if not, hardly a stretch at the moment. It's only when I reach the check-out that it occurs to me I have no independent means of payment. Everything is in joint names: bank account, credit cards; I've always been the additional card holder, and Rob vigilantly checks our statements. But even as this thought forms another supersedes it: *I took out a new card, just in my name, quite recently*. I grab my purse and search through, immediately doubting my recollection: the cards are all well worn, slid neatly into the slits in the expensive leather. But then, in a zippered section at the back, I find the new card, not even signed; shiny red and black. I can't recall how or why I acquired this new card, but I'm certain it's just mine. I use it to make my purchase, setting up the verification process for the first time and signing the back before I slide it into my purse, checking the phone Rob provided me with for new messages. I even look over my shoulder, half expecting him to be standing there, silently observing me.

Afterwards, the adrenaline still coursing through me, I glance towards the stairs, imagining this time that I was pushed, Rob's hand at my back. He was angry, and he'd wanted me to forget something, something he's still hiding from me now. It no longer feels as impossible as it once did to imagine his anger tipping him over the edge. I shudder, turning back to my laptop to delete my browser history. I lower the lid, the harsh sound of metal on metal causing me to jump as it snaps shut.

Rob and I were fine when we dropped Fin at university, and Rob said we were happy on holiday, so what happened after that to start the domino fall? I close my eyes and try to imagine what could have precipitated so much change in just a year, maybe less. But like everything since my fall, I find no answers, only more confusion.

January – This Year

Rob's voice comes first, raised in frustration, the tone of it causing me to involuntarily shrink from the bottom of the stairs and move back towards the kitchen as Fin's response, barely audible, follows. I look up at the kitchen ceiling; a towel in my hands, still warm from the dryer. I want to bury my face in it, pretend this isn't happening. I want Rob to be kind to our son, to talk and to listen, but then I hear him shout again as his heavy footfall paces around Fin's room once more.

I blame myself. I'd noticed how Fin was more withdrawn than usual, thinner, holding something back, but I was trying to make the best of it, to enjoy the festive season in any case. I ignored what I knew in my heart, and it was all pointless anyway. It's been, without exception, the worst Christmas I can remember, including the ones spent with ailing parents. I glance at the fading tree in the den, loose needles shimmering from the branches at the slightest touch. I wish we could go back to before Christmas, do it all differently, although what could we change? Fin had come home with this news; he just chose to keep it until today, the day he's due to return to university.

The silence is unnerving now. I look up again, imagining the conversation between Fin and his father, their relationship now built on the kind of back-slapping male bonding that Fin finds difficult and Rob adopts as a defence mechanism. Rob's never had any trouble declaring his love for me, or for Sash, for that matter, but with Fin it's been left to assumptions: 'Of course he knows how I feel.' Not that Rob's more obvious devotion to his daughter has made any difference; she still refuses to see her father. Fin and I met her at a restaurant of her choice the day before Christmas Eve, exchanging presents and cards over aubergine bake. It was a lame affair, perhaps worse than not seeing her at all. Although I'd had to, the dull ache inside me growing daily as she ignored most of my texts and spoke little during our calls. The only consolation of that compromise of a lunch was that for once my children enjoyed each other's company, talking to one another as adults. I'd wished Rob could have seen them, appreciating each other, laughing and listening, genuinely interested, but part of me thought it was right he should miss out, the rift predominantly his fault.

I place the folded towel on top of the pile on the kitchen counter and walk into the hall, listening again for voices behind Fin's closed door. Rob asked me to let him deal with it and I'd reluctantly agreed, but I warned him not to lose his temper, it wouldn't help. Still silence. They should have left hours ago, it's almost dark. I move away, walking into the sitting room to begin the task I'd scheduled for after their departure, switching on the light to look at the tree, this one still green and fragrant, as if, like me, it wishes Christmas were ahead of us; full of possibility and expectation.

Right up to the day itself I'd hoped Sash would relent and join us for Christmas lunch, but Rob hadn't persuaded her home. Even his apology to Thomas was snubbed, and that had cost him dearly. I'd wanted to comfort Rob, tell him it wasn't his fault, but the words never came. By then we'd learned Sash had moved in with Thomas, sharing the flat above the bar he manages. I'd stood opposite The Limes on Boxing Day, the rain pouring down, Christmas lights punctuating the gloom of the dark afternoon as I watched the drinkers come and go. Rob's photo had appeared on my phone again and again as he tried to heal the row I'd stormed out of, but I wasn't ready to forgive him and I hadn't crossed the road to Thomas's bar either. But I'd felt closer to Sash there, staring up at the tatty curtains until the thought of her with Thomas, the other man who'd taken her away from me, had soured any comfort I may have temporarily felt, drunks tipping out on to the pavement and calling across to me as I turned and walked slowly away. They couldn't do anything to me; I was already broken.

I look down at the sofa, covered in the tangle of lights and decorations I've distractedly removed from the tree, several of them veterans of many Christmases past, and I mourn the loss of not just this Christmas, but all the ones to come. It's all such a mess.

Just a few months ago I'd cried as we'd left Fin at university and now I'm desperate for him to change his mind and go back; to fulfil his potential, to have a purpose. That's all we ever wanted for our kids. I wouldn't care so much if I thought Fin could find happiness elsewhere, if there were some great plan he has for a better future, but there isn't. I'd asked him as he'd stood before me and Rob in the kitchen, the news just delivered, and he'd simply shrugged his bony shoulders and turned away. I sit down next to the debris on the sofa, a coloured bauble rolling away to bounce on to the rug. I watch but without moving to retrieve it, an unpleasant thought now troubling me. Maybe I've been the one holding Fin back, the real reason he's struggling to adjust? He's always been my ally. Maybe he sensed my loneliness.

I abandon the tree and stand at the bottom of the stairs; listening for movement or voices again, but all is still quiet. Then, without warning, the door is flung open and Rob emerges.

'Well?' I say as he comes down the stairs, his eyebrows raised in answer to my question.

'I can't get any sense out of him.' He brushes past me on his way to the kitchen. 'You try!'

Fin is seated on the edge of his bed, his hands in his lap, head down. He looks up and says, 'Hi, Mum. You okay?'

'I'm fine, love. Just worried about you.'

He slides along the bed to make room for me and we sit side by side, silent at first, until Fin asks me what his father has told me.

'I'd like *you* to explain what's going on,' I tell him, resisting the urge to comfort him as I know he won't want me to.

'So you can try to change my mind?' Fin replies, moving further away, his size-twelve trainers negotiating a half-packed suitcase open on the floor in front of him. 'I'm not going back, Mum; you can't make me.'

'Of course I can't make you. Neither of us can.'

'Tell Dad that!' he replies, his eyes filling with tears.

'Fin, we both want to understand, to help.'

Fin fiddles with the wristbands circling his painfully narrow wrists. I'd admired the colourful bracelets when he'd first arrived home, asked what they all meant and he'd talked me through each one, explained the cause they support or the significance of the slogan. The thought of that time, before Christmas, when Fin's future had felt secure and Sash's estrangement temporary, now defeats me. I can't help but cry, the act involuntary.

'Don't, Mum,' Fin says, edging towards me, his arm awkwardly around my shoulders. 'It'll be okay.'

'Will it?' I ask, looking up at my shy diffident boy. 'How?'

He shrugs, leans away from me then lies down. 'I'm tired, Mum. Can you leave me alone now?'

I'm washing up the breakfast things, the dishwasher still full from last night, neither Rob or I having remembered to switch it on or communicate that or much else to one another, when I hear a car pull into the drive, the icy gravel sliding beneath the tyres. At first I think it might be Rob, back from work for some reason. I frown at the thought, still angry with him for his pronouncement last night to Fin that he's taking him back to university tonight, like it or not. Rob's edict had sent our son back to his room moments after having been coaxed out for dinner. But it isn't Rob's shiny black car that's pulled into the drive, but an old rusty one; startling orange. The driver gets out and looks up at the barn, squinting into the bright light. I don't recognise him, but I'm guessing he's one of Fin's friends judging by his collar-length hair and casual attire. I open the front door and call across, 'Hi, can I help you?'

'Nice place.' He smiles and approaches me, his face breaking into a wide smile. He's broader than Fin now he's up close, and a little older too, maybe early twenties, his breaths visible in the cold air as he says: 'You must be Fin's mum. Hi, I'm Ryan.'

'Fin's still asleep. Sorry, I don't . . . have we met before?'

But he doesn't answer, looking past me to nod and say, 'You all set?'

I turn around to see Fin standing in the hall, an enormous rucksack slung over his back. At that moment the wind takes the door in its grip and Ryan steps forward to stop it slamming. Fin is beside me now, turning sideways to squeeze past, his smile for Ryan not me, his eyes averted from mine.

'Fin, what's going on?' I ask, taking the weight of the door. 'Where are you going?'

Fin turns back. 'Sorry, Mum.'

I follow him out, standing in the doorway to watch Ryan take the rucksack from Fin and place it in the boot of his rusting car. 'We said we'd talk,' I call across. 'When your dad gets home from work. We all agreed.'

Fin walks over to kiss me on the cheek. 'There's no point, Mum. I'll be in touch.'

'Don't be silly,' I say, following him back to the car, the gravel painful under my bare feet, the cold wind knocking the breath from me. 'We can sort this out, just come inside for a minute.'

Fin ignores me and climbs into the car anyway, opening the window to say, 'I'll call you, okay?'

'Fin, don't! I don't even know where you're going. Have you got your coat?' Fin is ignoring me, but Ryan smiles then waves, clearly embarrassed as he slowly edges the car across the drive. 'How long will you be gone?' I call after them, but Fin is staring straight ahead of him as the rattling car turns out of the drive, exhaust fumes all that's left behind.

'Don't go!' I say, but no one hears.

I go back into the house, collecting my mobile phone from the hall table before I walk up the stairs and past the empty bedrooms until I reach ours, where I sit on the tiled floor of the ensuite, the furthest point in the house I can go. Only then do I release the sobs I knew were there all along.

I'm still sobbing as I type a message to Fin, asking him to please come back, or at least tell me where he's going and how long he'll be away. Then I look at the screen of my phone for a long time, willing him to reply. In a matter of weeks both our children have cut us out of their lives, and although I know Rob will be as devastated as I am by Fin's departure, right now I'm so angry I can't even bring myself to tell him what's happened.

11

Eight Days After The Fall

Sash's words have danced around my head continually since our phone call the other day: 'He said maybe it's better if you never remember.' Their meaning has shifted and changed in my mind as I've applied them first to Rob, then me, wondering what he, or I, have done that is so terrible it needs to be concealed at all costs. Or worse, are there a myriad of landmines to negotiate in the missing year? In calmer moments I've tried to rationalise the comment, attributing it to my daughter's propensity for the dramatic, but it didn't feel like that. I had to prise the information out of her.

My metallic pink mobile phone was delivered yesterday, a day later than I expected, the van arriving only ten minutes after Rob had left for work. I held it in my palm and wondered why I'd wanted it in the first place, doubts and confusion clouding over whatever clarity of thought I'd had at the time of ordering. Then Rob's early return from work in the afternoon brought further confusion as he announced something had come up; a conference. He knew it was terrible timing, but did I think I be okay if he went away for the weekend? It struck me as decidedly odd, on more than one count. Rob has always been a nine-to-five man, and although his hours are undoubtedly longer these days, a weekend away was unprecedented; *wasn't it?* Plus, he's held me in such a vice-like grip since my fall that two nights away feels like a massive about-turn. I voiced a version of these thoughts and he gave me one of those sideways glances he's adopted, as though I'm the crazy one, and told me that networking had become part of his job, but he could say easily say no, although he'd already begun packing his overnight bag, promising he'd keep in touch. 'Should I be worried?' I joked and he laughed, said something about me acting strangely since I'd seen Sash and I let it go because whatever Rob and I may have done to one another over the last twelve months, I find it impossible to imagine him with someone else. His love for me is all-consuming, always has been. I closed the front door behind him and began my weekend alone, alternately relieved by the unexpected solitude and then wary of it. The barn has always felt alive with life: Rob and the kids, their big personalities filling the place, even Fin in his quiet way, strumming away at his guitar behind a closed bedroom door, the comfort of him being here now gone. It was this evening as I dozed on the sofa in the den, Saturday-night television for company on my second evening alone, that the images returned. *His face is turned from me as I trace the curve of his naked back with my fingertips, my body filled with desire as I reach out to touch his skin. He turns over, his face still obscured in shadow, but then he smiles, a wide smile, not generous, but complicit, a secret behind those lips.* And I knew what I must do.

The darkness makes the task I've set myself even more intimidating, the lateness of the hour filling the town centre with a different crowd, not *my kind* of people. The phrase feels familiar, and there's an accusation in there somewhere, I just can't recall from whom. I turn my face from the passing strangers and attempt to avoid the worst of the weather; the wind and rain making it impossible to use my umbrella without it turning inside out. As I walk I search for my phone in my bag, hoping to find a text from Sash or Fin to fend off the loneliness and sense of disquiet. They've both kept in touch in their father's absence, no doubt warned to do so, but when I look at the shiny pink handset it reminds me that no one knows this number. The phone situation is confusing, something else I have to juggle. Perhaps I should hide this one away until I need it. *If I need it.* I think of Rob, sharing a hotel meal with his colleagues, or maybe in his room, calling the home phone right now, wondering where I am. I sent him a text message just before I left telling him I was going to sleep, but I wasn't surprised by the lack of response. He'd warned me he'd have to switch his phone off and check it between seminars. In fact, it's suited me that his texts have been less frequent, a reassurance as I'd tucked the mobile phone he'd bought me into my bedside drawer and pocketed this one instead. I place it back in my bag and look across at the bar. The street lamps are reflecting off the damp pavements, illuminating the lettering picked out in green above the door: *The Limes*. I try to cross, but the car tyres are noisy on the slick tarmac between us, a constant stream of traffic. I watch the door instead, the heavy rain partially obscuring my view, my glasses wet. The wind tugs at my raincoat until I surrender to the elements, my hair damp and windswept as I see a space between the endless cars and run across the road.

'You alright there, love?'

A boy, not much older than Fin, a cigarette in his hand, is sheltering under a flapping canopy as he smokes. His companion, also smoking, bare arms covered in tattoos, laughs loudly.

'Need any help with that?' he asks, pointing to my broken umbrella, still in my hand despite its lack of use.

I'm only a few yards from the door, but the smokers stand between me and the entrance to the bar; both drunk, pint glasses in their hands. I consider turning back, but my car's parked down a side street; to walk away might encourage them to follow.

'I'm fine thank you,' I reply. 'Waiting for someone.' I take a step back into the shadows, sheltering in the recessed entrance of the shop next door.

'Man of your dreams?' the tattooed man calls out. He's older, maybe late thirties, his voice deeper.

'No, my husband,' I reply, happy with the indifference my lie infers.

The thought of Rob causes me to shudder, or perhaps it's just the raindrops running from my wet hair and finding their way inside my collar.

The tattooed man laughs, then coughs loudly, spitting on to the ground in front of him. Maybe it's that which proves too much. The spittle is washed away by the rain as I stare at the place it once was, appalled to find myself here. I'll have to take a long detour to circumnavigate them, but I decide I need to get back to my car; this was clearly a terrible idea. I pull my coat around me and take a step forwards, but then the door to the bar opens and a tall man with dark hair is silhouetted in the doorway, his features in shadow, the mouth illuminated for a second or two whilst he lights a cigarette, his lips curled into a confident smile as he banters with his smoking clientele.

Perhaps I make a sound, the breath sucked from me at the sight of him, for he looks over, his long fringe obscuring his eyes. Then he smiles, a wide smile, but to himself, as though there were a joke at my expense which only he can enjoy. I take a few steps back, my breathing too fast now, the darkness no longer the threat, something much more tangible at play. He starts towards me, his long strides eating up the short distance between us; my head feeling light as though it might float free. I grip my handbag to my chest, the rain running down my fringe and into my eyes, but when I close them, it's much worse, for in my head I see that smile again and I want to escape my own body, my own thoughts, be the person I thought I was; or at least I hoped I still was, Jo: mother, wife, steady, reliable. Faithful. Trusting. Trusted.

'Jo? You alright?'

I open my eyes and he's there, right in front of me, and when he smiles there's no doubt in my mind this is the man I saw through the café window; the same man I'd recognised at once in Sash's beloved photo. And again I tell myself it means nothing, the subconscious is unreliable, it can play tricks. Just because I have some half-formed recollection of him, an image that has woken me from sleep, troubled me in my waking thoughts too, doesn't mean anything actually happened between us. Maybe on a subconscious level I had desired my daughter's unsuitable older boyfriend, but surely I would never have acted on those desires? No, it must have been a suppressed longing, nothing more, but my reaction had been so strong, as if—

'Jo,' Thomas says, 'I said we're getting soaked. Come inside.'

I walk behind him as we negotiate the smokers once more, ignoring their lewd comments, although they're no worse than my own silent admonishments, just more crudely wrought. He holds the door for me and then points to a barstool, offering to help me up, but I refuse, careful to avoid his touch. I look away, taking in the bar, wondering if the unease I feel is a memory of this place, or purely a reaction to Thomas. The bar is deserted, just a couple of drunk girls in the corner, one telling the other, 'He's not worth it, babe'; even the smokers have abandoned us, their empty pint glasses left on an outside table where they're filling up with rain. I watch Thomas as he pours me a drink I haven't asked for. I study his movements, his features, everything about him, but there's no equivocation in my mind; he's the man I saw through the café window. Perhaps I should be pleased I remember him, another slit in the veil of my lost year, but I feel my skin burn with shame and I look away, no shred of comfort in the fact I've found something real; something I have remembered all by myself and in spite of Rob; because *this*, whatever it may be, I sense I would rather forget.

Thomas places a brandy in front of me, and walks from the other side of the bar to sit on the stool beside me, a beer in his hand. The neat alcohol burns my throat, but it feels good as it slides down, emboldening.

'Wasn't sure you'd remember me,' he says. 'Sash told me about . . .' He taps a finger against his head. 'You know who I am, right? I'm Thomas, Sash's boyfriend.'

'Yes,' I tell him, clearing my throat. 'She showed me a photo of you on her phone.'

He frowns, then seems to recall the photo and smiles. 'Yeah, I guess you wouldn't be here otherwise.' He's still swallowing another mouthful of beer when he asks, 'No permanent damage from your fall, other than . . . ?' He taps the side of his head in the same maddening gesture to indicate, I guess, my memory loss. 'You remember this place?' he asks, looking around, then shakes his head and laughs to himself.

I look around too, searching for anything familiar, but there's nothing specific, more a feeling; an imprint from my past placing an indelible marker within these shabby walls. I shake my head and take another reviving sip of alcohol and look at him, just for a moment, avoiding those knowing eyes, wondering whether I should ask him now, just come out with it, face my demons head-on. He's tumbling his hair from side to side, rainwater spraying us both. He stops and smiles at me again, a daring confident grin. I have a vision of him seated across a table from me, our dining table in fact. He's asking me here for a drink, and Rob is there, and Sash. I want to ask him about that, and so much more, but I don't know where to begin and I don't even know if I want to know the truth of what I may have become, so far removed from who I thought I was. He stretches out a long leg and his knee almost touches mine. I pull back, tucking my feet on to the base of the stool.

'I saw you in the café the other day,' he says, and when I nod he smiles and says he thought I'd seen him.

'I came here before—' I begin, but then there's a noise behind us, shouts, one of the drunk girls is staggering towards the door, her friend supporting her. Thomas jumps to his feet and locks the door behind them and when he turns back to face me, I realise we are entirely alone.

He sits beside me again, his head heavy on his neck so he stoops a little, regarding me from under his fringe as he says, 'You were saying?'

His voice is low and insistent, and his words seem loaded with hidden meaning, but I'm not clear-headed enough to decode them. 'Yes, I was trying to remember why I was here,' I tell him, unable to meet his eye. 'Was it to see Sash?'

'You do know she doesn't live here any more?' he asks.

I tell him of course I know, adjusting myself to sit securely on the high stool. 'Where is she now?' I ask, panicked by the thought she may be close by, about to walk in at any moment. It hadn't even occurred to me before.

'She's at the flat, never goes out these days.' He frowns then looks back at me and asks, 'You know about that, the new flat? The fact Rob pays?'

'Yes, of course.'

He smiles. 'Where is the delightful Rob tonight?'

'At a conference,' I reply.

'*A conference*,' Thomas repeats. 'Bit weird for a Saturday night.'

'No, not really,' I tell him.

'So what does he think of you coming here?' He's thrown his gangly body over the bar, his long legs following as he retrieves his second beer in almost as many minutes. 'Bet he's *thrilled*, or haven't you told him?' he asks, bouncing back down on to the stool.

'Of course I have,' I say, looking away from that smile.

Thomas laughs and it strikes me how he's wrong for Sash in so many ways – his age, his occupation, his flirtatious manner. I can imagine Rob's disapproval, see his disgust at Sash's appalling choice, and I feel it too. She would never use the words *delightful*, or *thrilled*, they belong to a different generation, one that came way before hers. Thomas is trying to hold on to his youth, to prove that someone as bright and beautiful as Sash would find him desirable. I can almost understand that, if not forgive it, but then it hits me hard, a jolt through my body so I have to steady myself with a hand to the bar. *Maybe I am guilty of the same thing.*

'So when I was here before . . . ?' I ask, stricken by the image that's returned. The memory is indistinct, but I know it was a very similar night to this and we were alone, as we are now. *I'd pushed open the door, the bar was empty, but I think Thomas was here.* I feel sick and my head swims, more than the brandy muddling my thoughts.

'Whoa, you okay?' Thomas asks, reaching out to grab me, then throwing his hands up when I block him. 'Only trying to help.'

'I need to know what happened when I was here,' I say,

righting myself on the stool, but I'm interrupted by loud thumps against the glass.

The girls are banging on the door, demanding they be let back in, 'It's only half-past fucking ten!'

'Nice language ladies,' Thomas says, springing up and walking to the door to tell them the bar's closed.

'Bit early for closing time,' I say, watching as they stagger away. 'Weird, on a Saturday night.'

Thomas slides his long limbs back on to the stool beside me, clearly amused by my comment. 'You know, I like you, Jo. Always have. I'm glad you came by.'

I turn away from his smile, it disturbs me too much, but then he stands up again and announces he should probably get home. He walks to the door and unlocks it, turning back to tell me, 'Sash gets anxious; thinks I'm up to no good.'

I press myself against the door frame to avoid his touch, but he grazes my hand with his as he reaches out for me.

'Are you?' I ask as I pull away and look up to see the wide smile is back. 'Up to no good?'

'Always,' he replies, pulling the door closed behind him.

I wait as he locks up, the street deserted, the rain lighter, the wind dropped.

'Do you love her?' I ask when he turns to face me.

'Sure,' he replies, passing the bunched keys from hand to hand, his shoulders hunched.

'*Sure?*' I repeat. 'What does that mean?'

'Sure, I love her,' he replies.

'She's precious, Thomas,' I say, stepping forward to see his face better in the darkness.

He laughs. 'That's rich, coming from you.'

My stomach lurches. 'What's that supposed to mean?'

He throws one hand in the air, releasing the keys, then snatching them out of the darkness between us. 'I should get back to your daughter, don't you think?'

I watch as he walks away, his long strides echoing into the darkness until I can no longer make him out through the rain, his shadow turning into the blackness of the night; all-consuming. I look around me, still desperate for answers. Why had I come here before? What had driven me to the bar? Was I looking for Sash, or Thomas? Then a flicker of something returns; the drop-in centre in darkness, the door slamming shut behind me as I ran out.

February – This Year

The drop-in centre is particularly crowded today, the buzz of the place such a contrast to the emptiness of the barn. I find the noise comforting, as though it will eat up the gnawing silence I've left behind, waiting at the top of hill for my reluctant return.

Rose pounces on me as soon as I walk in. 'Jo, thank goodness you're early. Busy one today, they've laid off over a hundred at Anderson's.'

'Anderson's?'

'Yes, you know, the family firm, far side of town. All hands to the pump, quick as you can!'

'Okay, let me get my coat off,' I tell her, walking towards Nick's office. 'Is there any coffee on?'

'I just made some,' Rose replies. 'And tell Nick I need more printer paper.'

I open the office door and smile at Nick, although he's

partially obscured by the teetering piles of clutter on his desk. He looks up at me and grins back, his glasses tipped forward on his nose, his hair, as always, spiked up; a failed attempt to look younger than his forty-seven years. When I first met him I found his affectations bewildering, the 'Hey's and 'Cool's jarring, but now I like them, they're part of his unlikely transition from City boy to community worker and I've found myself increasingly drawn to him as I have been to Rose, their values aspirational to me, their friendship given unconditionally. This place is my escape; a bubble of other people's problems to temporarily distract me from my own, although Nick and Rose always enquire about the kids, how things are.

'You're looking very lovely today, Jo,' Nick says, removing his glasses.

'Am I?' I ask, pouring myself a coffee from the pot on the filing cabinet. 'I don't feel it.'

'Hey,' he says, putting the file he was reading back down on the ever-growing pile beside him. 'If there's a problem, let's talk.'

'No, I'm fine. Nothing new.' I pick up my mug of black coffee and take a sip; not too awful as it's freshly brewed. 'Anyway, too much to do.'

'Cool,' Nick replies. 'Catch up later?'

'Yes, definitely,' I say, smiling to myself as I close the door behind me again.

Rose is organising the queue, allocating numbered squares of card to the agitated throng and instructing them to wait patiently until it's their turn, her voice carrying over the many others. Somehow she always manages to stay calm, whatever the provocation. I collect a stack of blank CVs and a handful of pencils from the trays she's laid out and smile at the smartly dressed gentleman who occupies the nearest computer terminal, his formal white shirt and blue striped tie indicative of a different generation to that of our normal clientele.

'May I join you?' I ask, pulling up a chair beside him and introducing myself; the confused expression I'd noted as he'd stared at the screen now transformed to one of relief as he accepts my offer to take over. He concentrates, eyes screwed tight shut, then wistful when he recounts his working life; forty-plus years of which he tells me he spent at Anderson's.

'So, you think that's it?' I ask, typing up the last line then saving the document. 'Nothing else you want to add?'

'I don't think so.' He rubs his eyes with a handkerchief from his trouser pocket. 'I'd been at Anderson's over forty years; did I tell you?'

'Yes, you did,' I say, moving the mouse past his hand and clicking on the Print icon. He was a cook at Anderson's Electronics until the staff canteen closed yesterday; 'part of the furniture,' he told me. Everyone knew him, said he'd never retire, they'd have to carry him out in a box. 'You don't feel ready for a change of pace?'

He smiles at me, then shakes his head. He's actually a bit older than I'd thought; seventy-two, and a widower. He has no hobbies other than 'cooking', 'walking' and 'watching films', and no formal qualifications since he left school at sixteen.

'I need a routine,' he tells me again. 'Something to get up for. You know what I mean, Jo?'

'Absolutely,' I say, stapling together the printed curriculum vitae. 'Now if you want some help setting up an email account, just let me know, okay?'

'I know I should get myself on the email,' he says, fiddling with his tie.

'Yes, just let me know.' I glance at the ever-growing queue, a disgruntled mob hovering next to the occupied computer terminals: five basic laptops and three old-fashioned desktop computers, although Nick's trying to secure funding for a couple of newer ones. He told me the other day he's planning a trip later in the year to his old stomping ground in the City; 'to shake some money out of those tight-fisted bastards'. I'd laughed and he'd asked me if I was teasing him, then laughed too.

'I knew what I was doing at work, but everything's changing,' my gentleman says, fiddling with his striped tie again.

'I know exactly what you mean,' I reply. 'I was a stay-at-home mum, and when my kids both left home recently—'

'Like my wife, he tells me, his eyes lighting up. 'She never worked a day after we got married, not a day. Three kids we've got, two girls and a boy. My boy's in Australia now, family of his own, and the girls are in London; fancy careers. Grandkids are almost grown-up too, got their own lives.'

'You must be very proud of them,' I say, trying to ignore the queue, which is growing increasingly restless.

'I'd like to see more of them,' he says, his rheumy eyes misting over. 'Specially now.'

'Have you told them you've been made redundant?' I ask.

He shakes his head. 'No one wants to be a burden to their kids.'

'No,' I say, patting his hand. 'But if they love you, which I'm sure they do, then they'd want to help.'

'You're a lovely girl,' he says, taking my hand and squeezing it between his palms. 'I hope your husband appreciates you.'

'Oh, I don't know about that,' I reply, looking up at Nick who is standing in the doorway of his office watching me, a smile spreading across his mouth then up to his eyes when I smile back and free my hand to raise it a little, feeling awkward as I lower it again. 'I should probably sort out that queue, excuse me.'

It all happens very quickly, so at first I'm not even certain of what is going on. I know I was almost at the queue when someone fell, a lad, in jeans and a hooded sweatshirt. I'm not sure if was an accident or if someone deliberately shoved him towards me, but it was too fast for me to avoid the impact. It was when I was on the floor, a bit shaken but nothing more, that I became aware of Nick behind me – I thought he was there to help me up, but instead I see him grab the lad by the back of his sweatshirt and wrench him from the floor, the slight frame of the lad no match for Nick's stout grasp. By the time I'm back on my feet, Nick's got him up against the wall, one hand holding him there, the other drawn back to swing a punch.

'Nick! No!' I shout across. 'It was an accident!'

I run at them, almost taking the impact of Nick's fist as it sweeps towards the startled lad's jaw. Nick spins around, his face contorted with anger until he registers who has pulled at the collar of his jacket. He steps back, a beat before he can shake off the previous moment and say, 'Jo, I'm sorry, I—'

The lad is shouting obscenities at him now, threatening to report him to 'the authorities'.

'Okay, okay,' Nick says, raising his palms in surrender. 'No harm done. Let's just forget it.' He looks at the lad again. 'Okay?'

The lad walks off, looking back at Nick once he's joined the queue again, exchanging a few words with someone who has made space in the line for him, perhaps the person who first shoved him out of the way.

'You okay?' Nick asks, his usual demeanour now completely recovered. 'Not hurt?'

'Fine,' I reply. 'You didn't need to do that. I'm sure it was an accident.'

'Not everyone's as nice as you, Jo.' Nick smiles and adjusts his jacket collar. 'Just looking out for you.'

He turns back to his office and walks towards the door, smiling at me over his shoulder before he closes the door behind him.

12

Ten Days After The Fall

'Rose, hi.' I transfer the phone to my other ear, my hair dripping on to my bare shoulders as I lean away from the already damp handset. 'No, you haven't woken me, I was in the shower, hang on!' I throw a towel around myself and switch off the running water, padding back into the bedroom, wet footprints littering the wooden floor.

'Sorry about that,' I say, sitting on the edge of the bed and using a corner of the towel to dry my face. 'I've been meaning to get in touch after rushing out of the café like that.'

'No, *I'm* sorry,' Rose replies. 'I didn't realise I'd be dragging you out the shower. And I apologise for calling you at home, but I tried your mobile and it's still going straight to voicemail.'

I think about the broken phone, smashed to pieces on the tiled hall floor, perhaps in landfill by now, the voicemail message somehow preserved.

'Jo, are you still there?'

'Yes, sorry.' I glance at the clock radio on Rob's bedside cabinet and see it's almost lunchtime; another morning lost. 'I went for a run,' I say, although I have no idea why I feel the need to excuse my late start.

The truth is, I hardly slept last night, or the night before, thoughts of my troubling conversation with Thomas keeping me awake until the early hours. At least with Rob away I've had time to analyse my visit to the bar, although I haven't gained any clarity, not really, waking late again this morning and with no more certainty of what may have happened between Thomas and me than before. Perhaps I've had too much time to think; Fin and Sash have both been too busy to come over, a situation that has angered Rob so much I was tempted to hang up on our five-minute conversation late last night, one of the few we managed all weekend.

'Jo?' Rose's voice jolts me back to our call. 'I said, you must be feeling a lot better if you've been for a run.'

'Oh, yes. I am thanks,' I reply, using my foot to wipe the towel through the puddled footprints between me and the shower.

'Great,' Rose replies. 'Because I'm after a big favour. The thing is, and I know this is probably a bit of a cheek as you're still recovering from your . . .' there's a pause '. . . but we're so short-staffed today. Sue's had one of her turns, not that she's either use or ornament most days anyway, but it's the Jobs Seekers group. I know you don't remember it, but you really were very good with people.'

'You want me to help at the drop-in centre?' I ask, my foot stilling. 'Today?'

'Only if you're up to it, but it would be great if you could. Nick's going to be completely stressed out when he comes in. He was off all last week, up in London trying to raise some funds for the new computers, and I know he'll have loads of paperwork to catch up on, so—'

'*Nick?*'

'You don't remember him?' Rose chatters on about her boss, how he's been away, trying to persuade his old colleagues in the City to donate to the drop-in centre, but she knows he'll be really pleased to see me, he's kept asking Rose if she'd heard from me and she hasn't had a chance to tell him she's finally tracked me down.

It's odd, listening to her relay the concern of a stranger, but it's comforting in a way to know that there are people out there, beyond my immediate family, who are invested in my well-being.

'I had a really bad night, Rose. Two in fact,' I say, thinking if I could just sort things out in my head a bit first, then I'd actually quite like to go back to the drop-in centre, see if I have any recollection of my time there; but not as a volunteer and certainly not today. 'Maybe another day?'

'I'll keep you topped up with strong black coffee, just the way you like it.'

I tell her even if I did come in I wouldn't know what to do, but she counters my objections by saying she can show me the ropes, and anyway, I'm sure to remember it once I'm there.

'Please, Jo. I wouldn't ask if I wasn't desperate.'

The idea of triggering some memories – the slurred words of the blonde woman at the support group come back to me again – is certainly appealing. And Rob is due back this evening so this is my last day of freedom.

'Okay, give me an hour,' I tell Rose, dismissing her extended gratitude.

My small car slots easily into the last free space across the road from The Limes; my Mini found its own way there, as though I'd allowed my subconscious to guide it. I cross the road and look in through the glass door, but the unlit interior is empty other than a barman with overly distended earlobes, enlarged by piercings I can see daylight through as he walks towards me. I retreat before he reaches the door, walking briskly away.

A wall of sound hits me as soon as I enter the drop-in centre. I take in the scene and experience a moment of euphoria as I realise I know this place, especially the line of computer terminals where I would sit next to one person after another, tapping in a potted history of their professional achievements. But then, on the far side of the room, a closed door causes me to stumble in my thoughts. I stare at the old-fashioned wooden door, waiting for the memory which has caused such a shift in my mood, my gaze dropping to the sticky carpet tiles. Nothing concrete forms, just a feeling of dread which falls like wet sand to the base of my stomach. I force myself to look at the door again, more carefully this time, and now I can see myself on the other side, in an office I think, talking to someone, a man. There's no definition to him, just a sense that we were in there together.

'Jo!' Rose stands up from a computer terminal, the woman who was beside her still attacking a keyboard with sharp clicks of her long nails as Rose walks towards me. 'I'm so pleased you came.' She places a hand on my arm. 'Are you sure you're feeling up to this?' Then before I can answer she says, 'If you can take over here whilst I try to restore some semblance of order in the queue?' She moves closer and whispers, 'Let me know if you're struggling. Just sit and listen, help where you can, and don't take any nonsense, okay?'

I look over her shoulder towards maybe a dozen people waiting for the next available terminal. At the front of the line an argument is brimming over between two lads, both of them certain the other has pushed in, their feelings vented with increasing volume and shoulder barges.

'You go,' I tell her, removing my coat and placing it on the table beside me, my handbag on top. 'I think I remember what to do, and if not I'll ask.'

'I'll put those in Nick's office for you,' Rose says, picking up my belongings. 'Best not to leave them lying around.'

I watch as she walks towards the closed door, opening it and going inside, affording me the briefest of glimpses into a cluttered dark room dominated by a desk. She smiles at me as she emerges again, pointing towards the chair she's vacated.

The woman Rose had been helping doesn't need much input from me, just a sympathetic ear as she types up her curriculum vitae, printing it out with a hard taps of her nails on the keyboard. 'Not much point in this,' she tells me. 'Not at my age.'

She only looks about forty, but her date of birth informs me she's even younger; thirty-five. 'You're hardly on the scrap-heap,' I say, stapling together two copies. 'I've got almost twenty years on you, in fact—'

She glances up and assesses me from head to toe. 'I've got three kids under five.' She takes the documents I'm holding out to her. 'Anderson's used to be flexible about child-care, not many employers are.'

I think back to my attempts at rejoining the workplace; the term-time part-time jobs I'd considered had paid little, but which were like gold dust. We hadn't needed the money so the appeal of getting out of the house had waned quickly, something always cropping up which sabotaged my efforts. 'I hope it works out for you,' I tell her, and she flashes me a half-hearted smile.

The next in line is one of the young men involved in the tussle for first place. He sits down and tells me he doesn't need my help, thanks very much. I watch as he types in the URL of a games website, one of Fin's favourites; at least it used to be. I wonder if I should challenge him, deciding instead to check on the other computer users and make sure they're happy. Then I smile at those who are still waiting, walking up and down the queue to sympathise with them, telling them we hope to get more computers soon, sharing the information from Rose, and pleased all over again to have found so much has come back to me. I look over at the games player, who this time returns my smile and then, to my surprise, gives me a cheeky thumbs-up. I look away, laughing to myself at his audacity, but then I catch sight of the office door, still closed, and my stomach flips over.

'You okay, Jo?' Rose calls across to me.

I nod, surprised she'd noticed me falter. I'd thought her to be deep in conversation with the scruffy man standing beside her. He carries his world on his back and a folded cardboard box under his arm, his face puckered in an earnest expression of deep concentration.

'I'm fine, thanks,' I call back.

'If you need a coffee, go into Nick's office,' she tells me. 'It's in there.' She points at the closed door.

'Jo knows where Nick's office is,' says her companion, his mouth spreading into a toothless grin, his dreadlocks swishing back and forth as he looks first at me, then back at Rose as she resumes their intense discussion.

'I'll be back in a minute,' I announce to the queue, a shuffling disgruntled murmur at my back as I walk towards the closed door.

I knock and wait, then tentatively open the door an inch or two. The unoccupied room is small and dimly lit, with a desk under the tiny window and a chair behind it. Another lower chair is angled away a little, its back to me, facing the messy desk. Every surface is piled with papers and folders, the dust catching in my throat as the air is disturbed by my entry; an undernote of stewed coffee cutting through the stale atmosphere. There's nothing about the room which triggers a memory, good or bad, but the persistent sense of unease remains. I spot the coffee pot resting on its warming plate, both unsteadily balanced on a tall filing cabinet.

'You found it then.' Rose apologises for making me jump, her face full of concern as I almost spill the coffee I'm pouring. 'Just came in for one myself,' she says, pointing to the pot. 'And to check on you. How's it going? You coping alright?'

'Fine,' I reply, stepping aside to allow her through. 'I'm actually remembering a lot.' I look out at the crowded room beyond the door, alive with activity.

'I told you it would come back to you,' she says, splashing a thimble-sized pot of UHT milk into her coffee. 'Must be a relief,' she says, stirring in two sugars.

'It is.' I smile at her, resting my mug down on the desk where it leans precariously against a pile of folders. 'Nice to feel useful again.'

Rose grins, exposing pink gums. 'How's things at home?'

'Fine,' I reply, taken aback by her blunt question. 'Everything's great in fact. Why do you ask?'

Rose places her coffee next to mine then she closes the door and walks past me to sit down behind the desk. 'That lot can wait,' she says, pointing me towards the low chair then waiting until I'm seated, a space cleared for my feet, before she says, 'I know you don't believe me, Jo, but you told me you were leaving your husband. Next thing you've fallen down the stairs, and then everything's hunky-dory between you two again.'

'What were my exact words?' I ask, hoping there may have been some kind of misunderstanding. 'When I told you I was leaving Rob, what did I say?'

'Oh gosh, Jo. I'm not sure. It was over two weeks ago now; the last time you were here, in fact.' Rose looks around her. 'We might have been in this room. You don't remember?'

I tell her no, but then I wonder if that's why the office door felt so significant. Maybe Rose and I had talked, my confession the discomfiting scene I'd recalled. But it feels wrong, not a good fit at all. I'd remembered a man and me, not Rose.

She sips her milky coffee. 'You don't remember us talking . . . but you remember where we keep the pencils.' She smiles at me. 'Sorry, it just seems—'

'I'm not in control of this; it controls me,' I tell her, not finding the comparison at all funny. I'd thought she understood.

'Of course, it must be so frustrating for you.' Rose dips her head and looks up again with wild eyes, as though she's recalled something significant.

'Yes?' I ask, leaning towards her.

'We weren't in here. It was a quiet day, we'd sat at a table out there, the corner one.' She points towards the room beyond the closed door. 'Or maybe we were in here. I'm not sure, Jo. Sorry.'

'Oh,' I say, slumping back into my seat.

'I'm sorry, but like I said, you didn't tell me much, just that things had changed between you and Rob since the kids had left home.' She sighs. 'I was worried about you, it seemed like you were keeping something back.'

'Like what?' I ask, sitting up again in my chair.

'I don't know.' She hesitates. 'What's your feeling?'

Rose's practised technique is maddening. I understand she's trying to draw me out, but I want answers, not more questions. 'Oh this is useless,' I say, standing up. 'You're not my counsellor, Rose. I'm asking you as a friend. We were friends, I assume?'

'Yes, of course we were. Still are, I hope.' She picks her way around the desk to place a hand on my arm. 'Let's start over, shall we?'

I sit down again, waiting for her to speak, my right leg bouncing up and down. Like before, I'm reminded of a meal, Rob and me at our dining table, his foot tapping out a similar beat. Thomas was there, and Sash. Thomas had leaned towards me, his foot touching mine. I move mine back now, tucking them beneath the chair.

Rose sits down behind the desk again. 'You didn't always confide in me,' she says. 'Not everything, and that was okay, I didn't expect you to. But I was worried about you. There were signs, things you said.'

'How do you mean?' I ask, recognising myself in her appraisal. I wouldn't have told her everything, but maybe there were signs, as she says.

'I'd thought you were unhappy for a long time before you told me you were leaving Rob,' she replies. 'I think you blamed Rob for your son leaving home. And you didn't like your daughter's boyfriend, Thomas. Your husband had reacted particularly badly to him; caused a rift.' I nod, her account so far sounding spot on. 'But I think the main problem was . . . at least I got the impression there was . . . there may have been someone else involved.' She smiles at me apologetically, the gums covered by her closed lips. 'I'm sorry, Jo. I don't know for sure. It was just a feeling, but it felt like the logical conclusion.'

Someone else? Thomas? Or another someone else? The man I remember in this office?

'Do you have any idea who?' I ask her, not sure what answer I'm hoping for.

But before Rose can reply, the door is flung open and a man throws himself through it, his eyes ablaze behind his glasses, his hair unnaturally spiked up. He doesn't acknowledge me, my back to the door, the low chair obscuring me from his view, addressing Rose as he discards his leather jacket on to the floor. 'It's chaos out there; what's going on?'

'Nick, there's something you need to—' Rose says, standing up, but her words are lost to his.

'There's no one supervising,' he tells her, his tone abrupt. 'And two guys are brawling on the floor.' He ushers her out of his way and sits down. That's when his eyes widen as he sees me at last. 'Jo!' he says, standing up again.

'That's what I was trying to tell you, Nick,' Rose says, her hand on my shoulder as she stands behind my chair. 'Jo's back.'

I look up at the man who has just burst into the office, all bluster and noise, but who now stands still, looking down at me, his eyes not moving from mine. I scan his features for anything that resonates from the past, a gesture, a nuance, the grey-blue eyes so penetrating, the spiky hair more suited to a younger man. He clearly knows me, the intensity of his gaze causing me to look away, but I don't know him at all. Not one bit. Except . . . the sight of him has caused that same sense of dread, as though I should run away from him, out of this office, and when I half-close my eyes an image replaces his hard stare. *The drop-in centre in darkness, the door behind me slamming shut as I'd run out, away from here. Away from him.*

'Can you give us a minute, Rose?' he says.

Rose looks at me for my approval and I nod. 'I'll be fine,' I tell her.

'Are you sure you're okay? If you need me to stay . . .' She still looks unsure.

'Why would she need you?' Nick asks, not waiting for the answer. 'Close the door after you.'

He waits until her heavy footfall dies away, absorbed into the general background noise of the room beyond, then he leans forward across his desk and says, 'Where the fuck have you been, Jo?'

'*What?*' I stand up, backing away from him, but he stops me before I reach the door, his hold strong on my wrist, using the weight of his upper body to push me up against the wall.

'Let go of me!' I shout, struggling against his clumsy advances, his face so close to mine I can smell the aftershave on his stubbly chin. 'What do you think you're doing?'

'I've been out of my mind, Jo.' He stares at me again, then releases me and backs off, his hands raised. 'I'm sorry, but it's been over two weeks. You run out of here, after—'

'After what?' *I'd run out, away from here. Away from him.*

'Look, what happened that night . . .' He hesitates, looks at me for his cue, but I say nothing. 'If you'd have given me the chance to explain—'

'*Explain what?*' I ask, a hand to the wall, steadying myself.

'Okay, that's fair enough, but you do know what happened was just as much down to you as me. I've been getting a lot of mixed messages from you since . . .'

'What happened?' I ask, edging my way towards my exit, my path impeded by the small space and the clutter it contains.

'I suppose I deserve that.' He sits down behind his desk and looks across at me, my hand behind my back, now grasping the door handle. 'Where have you been, Jo? Why didn't you answer my calls? I thought I might never see you again. I thought—'

'You didn't call me,' I tell him. 'Unless . . .' I think about the phone that was thrown away, the one that smashed on the tiles in the hallway. 'My phone broke.'

Nick has closed his eyes to compose himself. 'What's going on, Jo?'

He stands up and I flatten myself to the door, turning the handle towards me.

'Wait!' he says, taking a step back and almost falling over a pile of folders. 'Don't run out again, please. Sit down. Let's talk about what happened.'

'I can't,' I tell him, my voice raised. 'I don't remember what happened. Nothing. Not you. Not this.' I look around the room. 'Nothing.'

'I don't understand what you mean,' he says.

I feel the door handle in my grasp, the cold metal reassuring. 'I had a fall, down the stairs.'

'My god,' he says, moving towards me to ask, 'Are you okay? Are you hurt?'

'No, except . . .' My hand falls from the handle. 'I have no memory of the last year.'

I move to sit down before my legs give way, refusing Nick's offers of help and sinking down into the low chair as he takes the chair behind his desk. He's far enough away from me now that I feel able to answer his questions, the solid desk a barrier between us. I hadn't thought I'd tell him so much, but once I've begun it all comes out: the fall, my smashed phone, the hospital, my memory loss. I only stop when his hand reaches across his desk towards me. I warn him not to, the thought of his previous grasp on my wrist causing me to flinch. He apologises, says he won't touch me again, he promises.

'What do you think Rob did with your phone?' Nick asks.

'I told you, it smashed when I fell. Rob threw it away, bought me a new one.'

Nick raises an eyebrow. 'I suppose he deleted my emails and

messages as well as disposing of your phone.' He pauses, then almost to himself he asks, 'Oh god, do you think he read them first?'

'I don't understand.' I can feel my headache returning, the confusion pounding through my skull, disorientating me. 'You're saying Rob has deliberately kept me away from here?'

'From *me*,' Nick replies, a comment which he savours, delivers with aplomb.

'Are you saying you and I . . . ?' I can't finish the thought, can't verbalise something that feels so impossible, and yet has been consuming me for days now. Could I really have cheated on my husband? It feels wrong, entirely out of character, and yet—

'You really don't remember?' he asks.

I shake my head and he tells me there have been a couple of 'incidents', a few months apart. He looks at me again and apologises for embarrassing me.

I stare at Nick, trying to keep my voice steady. 'I need you to be more specific.'

'Jo, please . . .'

'When?' I ask.

He tells me the first time was in February. We were in here, just the two of us, drinking, late one evening. Rose had gone home; I was upset about the situation at home. I kissed him. He tried to resist my advances, not because he didn't want to, but we were drunk, he didn't want to take advantage. It was something we'd both wanted for some time.

'Just a kiss?' I ask and he shakes his head.

'Were we naked?' I ask.

'What?'

'It's important. Please.'

'I think I took my shirt off, undid my trousers.' He looks down at his desk, moves some papers around before looking at me again. 'Jo, do we really have to talk about it like this? What happened between us, it meant more than that.'

His body is naked, the skin smooth, contours highlighted by the weak light, my fingers reaching out to touch him, desire coursing through me.

'We had sex?' I ask.

'No, you stopped it, just before.' He looks away again, towards the wall next to the desk. 'God, this makes it sound so sordid.'

'And there was a second time?' I ask. 'When was that?'

'A couple of weeks ago, the last time I saw you, but it was nothing. A misunderstanding. I kissed you, but it wasn't what you wanted. Nothing happened.'

'*Nothing?*'

'No, not nothing, but we didn't . . .' He smiles at me. 'I got the wrong end of the stick.'

'What does that mean?' I ask.

'You only wanted us to be friends. At least, that's what you said.' He pauses. 'Look, I think you were conflicted, feeling guilty. You ran out. I tried to contact you, but . . .' He looks straight at me. 'How did you find your way back here?'

'Rose emailed me, we met up the other day.' My tone is abrupt as I try to make sense of what he's told me. I need him to be quiet for a moment. *I was unfaithful to my husband; kissed another man and we almost had sex. And it was me that initiated it the first time. Oh my god, what have I become? Who the hell am I?*

'Jo?' He leans forward, agitated. 'I asked you why Rose didn't say anything; she knew I was desperate to speak to you.'

'She said you were stressed, maybe she was trying to—'

'Don't you defend her!' he says, his hands tapping out a rhythm on the nearest pile of files. 'She should have told me straight away.' He's silent for a moment, then he looks back at me and says, 'Why did you fall?'

'I just slipped,' I say, but an image of Rob and me has been conjured by Nick's words. *We're at the top of the stairs, Rob's anger spilling over. He's screaming at me . . .*

'And you don't remember me?' Nick asks, his eyes boring into mine, a trace of sadness in them, and an intensity I find unbearable. 'Not at all?'

'No,' I reply. 'Except . . .'

'Yes?' The drumming fingers are stilled.

I look around me, trying to find the right words. 'It's hard to explain,' I say. 'I just know something happened in here.' I look at him again, his staring eyes, the passion with which he watches me, as though he wants to split open my head and see what's really inside, and I think of Rob, how I'd wanted to do that to him, to release the endless secrets he keeps, but maybe those secrets were all mine. 'I don't remember anything; not really,' I tell him.

Nick smiles at me, the tension falling away from his features. 'A whole year lost,' he says, shaking his head. 'I can't believe it.' He switches on his desk lamp, the weak sun through the small window not bright enough to illuminate the room, and for a second the pool of yellow light is comforting. 'Must be horrendous.'

I tell him I should go, standing up from the chair and collecting my coat and bag from the corner where Rose had stowed them for me.

Nick watches me, then says, 'I guess you need some time to process this.'

I open the door, allowing in the noise from the room beyond, feeling the protection it instantly brings, then I close the door behind me and walk across the crowded room, ignoring Rose's calls, desperate to get outside, to breathe in fresh air. I don't even look across at Thomas's bar as I drive away, my mind filled with Nick's words, still trying to make sense of them, searching for something recognisable as I relive his account of our affair.

February – This Year

The debrief with Nick and Rose has to be quick, the Job Seekers group running way over time today, and Rose has a bus to catch, she informs us, stuffing a pile of paperwork into her bag-for-life. Nick and I exchange a smile as we both stand to watch her go, her sturdy legs trotting across the empty room, cardigan billowing at her back, the door slamming shut behind her.

'I imagine her sometimes, in her flat, eating alone, a pile of forms on her lap,' Nick says, his short arms folded across his barrel chest. 'You think she's happy?'

'Yes, I do,' I say, smiling at him. 'Probably more than most.'

Nick frowns at me then laughs, a deep sound that has become as familiar to me as Rose's gummy smile. I walk out of his office but Nick calls after me. 'Time for a coffee and a chat? It's been a heck of a day.'

'I should probably get home,' I reply, turning back to see he's holding up a bottle of whiskey.

'Rob due home soon?' Nick asks, an almost imperceptible upwards inflection in his voice. 'Or have you got ten minutes?'

The office has grown dark around us as we've talked, late afternoon turning into early evening, one 'coffee' following another, just the weak light of the Anglepoise lamp to illuminate the chaotic room. The single pool of yellow light has lent the room an intimate feel, and I've kicked off my shoes, stockinged feet resting on the edge of Nick's desk, my legs lifted up from the low chair where I currently lounge, a mug of coffee laced with whisky, my third, in my hand. I drink it back, the coffee cold, but the alcohol still burning my throat.

'I don't even like whisky,' I say, laughing to myself.

'You seem to be managing,' Nick says, his eyes creasing into a benevolent, possibly admiring, gaze.

'How am I going to get home now?' I shake my finger at him, noticing the way the blue flecks in his grey eyes catch the low light, as does the hint of blond that passes through his mousy-brown spiked-up hair. 'You're a very bad influence. I thought you were a moral man.' I pause. 'Come to think of it; I thought I was a moral woman.'

'There's no way you're driving home,' Nick says, standing up from his chair to pour me another. 'May as well finish this.' He pauses, bottle poised. 'Unless you're expected somewhere?'

I laugh, raising my mug for him to fill. 'By Rob? I doubt he's even home.'

'Bad as that?' Nick asks, topping up his mug too then perching on the edge of his desk. 'Guy's an idiot, neglecting you.' I notice he glances down at my legs, my skirt ridden up to my thighs, but I make no attempt to readjust it, enjoying the confidence his appraisal arouses within me. 'Wanna talk about it?' he asks.

'Not much to say,' I tell him, but I do, everything spilling out of me as the coffee sloshes around my mug.

'So Fin's still living with a friend called Ryan . . .' I say. Nick raises an eyebrow. 'No, nothing like that,' I tell him, but he smiles. 'It isn't!' I repeat. 'And Sash is living with Thomas . . .' I point in the general direction of the bar. 'And my husband, who is at least partially responsible for all this, spends every waking hour at work.'

Nick steps forward and takes the mug from my slack grip. 'Yeah, maybe you've had enough.'

He helps me up from the low chair, then puts my feet back into my shoes and my arms into my coat as I laugh at the ridiculous way my limbs seem to be misbehaving.

'There!' he says, still holding me up. 'Respectable again.'

I lean towards him, our faces almost touching. 'I never noticed your eyes before,' I say, laughing at the cheesy comment, then I lift my hand to touch the side of his face, the roughness of his chin catching the soft skin of my palm. 'You know, Nick . . .'

'Jo . . .' Nick steps back, regards me for a moment, his expression confused. 'I'm not sure we should—'

'Shush . . .' I place my finger to my lips, then press the same finger to his mouth. 'Don't say anything.'

We kiss, his mouth covering mine, an urgent, desirous kiss. He holds me to him, tighter and tighter, then he pushes me back towards the wall, his hands all over me, working their way under my skirt, then my tights, his fingers exploring my skin now. I try to think of Rob, our home, our marriage; but I want to escape all that, to be me again: Jo, who is desired for who I am, not some trophy for Rob to admire, the perfect wife who cooks his dinner and waits for him at home. He says I'm everything to him, but he's never there, and although we still make love some nights, I don't ever feel like I do right now; abandoned and desired. As I give in to that thought I begin to act rather than think, Nick's passion arousing my own until I almost convince myself it's him I want. My breaths come short and sharp, and soon it will be too late to stop.

'No!' I draw back, gasping for air, pushing him away. 'This is wrong. I shouldn't. It's not fair to Rob. He's never cheated on me. It's—'

We look at one another, then Nick nods, turns away and pulls on his shirt. 'You can't drive,' he says, turning back as he fastens his trouser belt.

I retrieve my shoe from under his desk, buttoning my blouse as I stand up. 'I'll find a taxi outside,' I say, pulling on my coat and slinging my bag over my shoulder.

'Can we talk about what just happened?' he asks.

I shake my head and walk towards the door, but he follows, grabs my wrist. I look down at his hand, and he lets go, stepping aside. I leave his office, closing the door behind me.

The room beyond is empty, only the light from the computer screens to guide me around the tables and chairs. I'm disorientated, the darkness and the effects of the alcohol combining to confuse me, but I walk fast. Then the door behind me is thrown open again, the weak yellow light spilling across the carpet towards me. 'Wait!' Nick calls after me. 'Jo, please. Let's discuss what's just happened.'

'I'm sorry,' I call back as I stumble, banging into a chair, my shin throbbing from the impact, but I don't look back.

'Jo!' Nick calls after me. 'Don't leave like this. We need to talk about it. Jo, please!'

I pull open the door to the street, the intake of cold air in my lungs beginning to sober me up, although my head still spins, the view of the artificially lit street tilted on a twisted axis. I shake my head to clear it and hurry on, past the closed shops and empty offices, even faster now, the throbbing pain in my shin causing me to limp, a dampness between my legs I try to ignore. I don't look back until I've turned the corner. Then, glancing back to see no one is behind me, I stop and rub my shin, although the pain is good. *Real. Appropriate.* I slump against a wall, almost falling, reaching out a hand to steady myself as a couple with a small dog look over at me with obvious disapproval.

Disorientated by my flight, the direction of which seems irrelevant, I move on, away from their stares, on and on in a state of panic until I finally must stop, my lungs screaming at me, my leg throbbing with pain. I look around me, noticing a rough-looking bar across the busy road: The Limes. Thomas's bar. The curtains in the flat above are half closed, but there's a light on behind them. If I could see Sash, drink some coffee, sober up enough to drive home, I might be able to face Rob. I try her mobile, but it goes straight to voicemail, her chirpy greeting bringing more tears and renewed determination to find her. I cross the road, a hand raised in apology to the driver who brakes then swerves his car around me. I reach the door to the bar and pause to gather myself, rehearsing my excuse to Sash; a friend who was poorly and had to go home, a meal abandoned, a long queue for taxis, a few too many drinks. When I peer through the glass door, the interior looks deserted. I almost turn back without trying the door, but when I do I find it's unlocked.

Inside, the bar is empty. The door swings closed behind me cutting out any outside light. I stumble across the room, a chair leg tripping me up, the heavy mahogany of the bar hitting me as I turn the corner too early into a dimly lit corridor at the back. There are so many doors: a cupboard, a stock room, the stinking gents' toilet. Then I spot a flight of stairs, a sliver of light at the top from an open door. *She's still awake. Thank god.* I trip again as I climb, crying out then lifting the palm which saved me from the dusty step to cover my mouth. I look up at the door above me, hoping Sash will have heard me and come out. It's so careless, leaving the place unlocked, typical Sash, and Thomas by the looks of it. Anyone could have wandered in, just as I did. At the very least I need to tell her that. I dust myself down, shaking my head to try to clear it. Listening for sounds of life, I almost lose my resolve again, but the light is on and I'm so close now. I just need to get to Sash and I'll be fine. I'll ask her if we can go somewhere, get a coffee. The door is ajar; I just need to call her name. If no one's there I can leave the way I came. I push open the door to reveal one room, a bed at the centre. I hadn't expected that, assuming there would be a hallway, or the sitting room first, but I'm already in the room and someone is stirring, turning over in their sleep to see who has walked in. At first I fear I may have walked in on them both, joined as one in an embrace, or worse, but as my eyes adjust to the light I can only make out Thomas, his back turned. I shrink back into the shadows, still looking around for Sash, but she's not here. I should run out the way I've come, back to the safety of the dark street, but I don't. Maybe it's the alcohol, dulling my senses, or the shock of what I've run from, or what I've run to, but I'm transfixed by the beauty of that naked body. Oh the exquisiteness of it, a smooth curve of taut skin, the muscles beneath defined, moving slowly, flexing as Thomas turns to me.

'Jo?' He sounds half asleep, his expression hard to read in the shadows.

'I was looking for Sash.' The words are slurred, I hear it and so does he, commenting on how I'm wasted. Then he laughs and throws the covers back, inviting me in.

13

Ten Days After The Fall

Walking back to my car I go over the conversation in Nick's office, imprinting his words on my memory in case I should lose their sense. It's possible, I suppose, to imagine myself led astray by Nick, but I find it harder to accept that it was me who initiated our first liaison. I've never cheated on Rob, never even contemplated it and, if Nick's to be believed, it wasn't a one-off; it had recently happened again, although he admitted he'd misread the situation the second time. I unlock my car and climb inside, too preoccupied to look across at the bar as I drive away. Thomas is now the least of my concerns.

The ring road is relatively quiet, not quite rush hour yet, and with my confidence in my driving ability safely restored, I allow my thoughts to return to my conversation with Nick, running it in my head again and again. Since my fall, the process of memory has become more precious and I've realised I'd taken for granted something that is infinitely more delicate than I'd previously understood. I can almost feel the memories securing themselves in my brain, like running an ink roller back and forth across a printing block; every detail revealed.

I'd certainly experienced no physical attraction for Nick this afternoon, I hadn't even remembered him, but if what he said is true then I must have felt something. Maybe it was an intellectual attraction, or perhaps I'd turned to Nick because he represented a change of direction; towards altruism and social conscience? He's certainly a very different man to Rob. Could I have used Nick as an antidote to my husband? Nick was convinced Rob has deliberately kept me away from the drop-in centre, deleting emails and lying about my phone, which suggests Rob knew I was unfaithful. But an affair would require a degree of capitulation on my part, and longing, attraction, desire, none of which I now feel. Had my marriage really deteriorated to such a degree that I would turn to someone else? I shudder, shutting out the endless questions as I stop at a set of traffic lights, waiting as the pedestrians cross; an image of a lone girl dashing in front of the car flitting in and out of my thoughts. I press my foot harder to the brake pedal, although the car is already stationary. *It was a rainy night. My birthday? Was Sash the girl at the crossing?* I close my eyes and lean forwards on to the steering wheel, willing away the flashes of memory and the confused thoughts ploughing furrows into my psyche and lines across my forehead; begging them silently for a moment of peace. There's a loud blast of a car horn and when I look up the lights have changed. I raise my hand in apology and drive on, away from the town centre, certain only of my desire to be home.

The barn is quiet as I walk in; even the wind has dropped to a whisper, as if we have both been hushed by this afternoon's revelations. I make tea and take a couple of painkillers for my headache, then I retrieve my mobile phone from my desk in the den and send Rob a message. His conference concludes today; a day of boring presentations he'd informed me in this morning's message. I text him to ask what time he'll be home, then with my phone still in my hand I tackle the stairs slowly, pushing away the images of Rob and me arguing at the top.

It's getting dark when I wake up, the room grey with shadows. There's a message from Rob saying it's been a tough few days, he can't wait to see me, but it might be late before he's home. I put down my phone and lift myself up in bed. I feel awful, my head thick with sleep and confusion. I need some water, maybe more painkillers, although I can't remember how many I've taken today. It's as I make my way downstairs, both hands gripping the bannister, that the images of Rob and me return.

We were arguing, I was telling him something, screaming it at him, but he wouldn't let me go, he was holding on to me, and he was distraught, begging me to stay.

I stop, my foot paused mid-air, looking down at the hole in the wall, just about visible in the semi-gloom. Is it really possible he deliberately pushed me? I take another step down and look at the photos of the children, our family that was; the changes from one year to the next, chronicled in reverse as I slowly descend. Would I turn the clock back if I could? Almost certainly the last year, which strikes me as ironic given the trick my mind has played on me to achieve that very same thing. But maybe

227

it's the kindest, not cruellest, of tricks. Perhaps I'm being saved from the worst year of my life.

In the kitchen I switch on the lights, the glare burning my eyes, adding to my headache. I place my hand on the kitchen island to steady myself, wondering again how many painkillers I've taken today. I decide not to risk taking any more, walking past the dining table to pick up the photo frame from the windowsill behind. Outside the blackness is descending, a stark contrast to the beautiful sunset in the photo. Our laughing sun-kissed faces look back at me. We were happy then, October I think, or maybe November? Rob had said it was just before my birthday; a surprise trip which had been wonderful; a second honeymoon. We certainly look like a couple making the most of the next phase in our lives. Yes, Fin was miserable at university and Sash was living in a cramped bedsit, but that's real life, difficult and complicated. Children grow up and make their own choices; not always good ones. Every family has its own troubles. I look at the photos: sun, sea and palms in the top print, and below a snap of Rob and me in front of a balustrade, a terrace maybe, the ocean behind us as the sun slips out of view. There's something familiar in there, just a glimmer, although I can't be sure it's not my imagination filling in the gaps. *I see Rob's face across a table for two, a conversation, my frustration with him as he tells me not to be silly.*

The landline rings and I rush to answer it. 'How long will you be?' I ask.

'I'll drive quickly,' he says. 'Be home soon, okay?'

I listen for the sound of traffic, clues to his journey. 'Where are you?' I ask. 'It sounds quiet.'

'I'm not far away,' he says. 'Can't wait! I've missed you so much, Jo.'

I replace the receiver and look down at the photo frame still in my hand, resisting the urge to throw it against the wall.

February – This Year

'How's your head this morning?' Rob asks as he rolls off me and grabs his glasses to look at the time.

I think of the coffees laced with whisky Nick poured last night, and the ache in my head and the guilt settling in the pit of my stomach both intensify. 'I told you, it was Rose who was drunk, not me.' I turn on to my side, away from my husband, and swallow the rising bile in my throat.

'I should go; I'll be late for work.' He gets up and walks to the bathroom.

Rob was much less perturbed by my late return than I expected. He'd only just beaten me home, he said, readily accepting my excuses that a quick pizza with Rose had turned into a drunken night out. 'She was a mess,' I told him. 'I couldn't leave her like that.' The pang of remorse I experienced using Rose as my excuse was chastening, but more than eclipsed by my guilt at the dreadful deceits which had forced my hand.

Rob hadn't appeared to notice, commenting that it was good I had company as he was late home too. 'Anything could have happened to me,' I told him as he followed me up the stairs to bed, his hands on my hips to steady me. He laughed, said he trusted me to be sensible, but I probably shouldn't have driven, even on two glasses of wine, and to prove his point I stumbled, his quick reflexes righting me as I tipped back towards him.

I check my phone again whilst Rob is in the bathroom, but there's still no reply from Sash. I've messaged her twice now, once last night and once this morning; any more and I'll definitely arouse her suspicion. I must be patient, but it's so hard. I just need to hear something normal from her, something that tells me she has no idea I was at the bar last night. I discard the phone on the bed, but snatch it up straight away as Sash's reply comes. She has a hangover, was out late last night with 'The Girls'; she's in Thomas's bad books because she forgot to take her keys so got a lecture from him as he'd had to leave the doors unlocked, then on top of that she threw up when she got in. She has to go; she'll be late for work. I exhale and close my eyes, snapping them open when Rob's head appears from behind the bathroom door.

'Are you due to be a good person again today?' he asks.

'Yes, but . . .' I wait as the whir of Rob's electric toothbrush interrupts our conversation. 'I've been thinking maybe I go there a bit too much . . .' I falter, waiting for Rob's reaction.

'I told you . . .' he says, his words thick with toothpaste '. . . once they get their hooks into you . . .'

I sit up, leaning forwards to pull my nightdress from the

floor and then standing to slip it over my head, the dampness between my legs running down my inner thighs. Then I run towards the bathroom, pushing Rob out of the ensuite just in time, the tears flowing over my burning cheeks as soon as I close the door.

I stood in the shower for ages last night, allowing the water to run down me, my thoughts loud in my head until Rob banged on the door, startling me with his imperious tone, joking that I'd drown if I didn't come out soon. The shower made no difference of course; no amount of hot water and scented shower gel could have changed how dreadful I felt as I crawled into bed beside my unsuspecting husband. The guilt-sex I initiated this morning didn't make any difference either; but why would it?

'You okay?' he asks from the other side of the door.

'I'm fine,' I call back, flushing the toilet. 'Out in a minute.' I wipe my eyes with a torn-off sheet of toilet paper and splash my face with water as I wash my hands, catching sight of myself in the mirror; shocked at how normal I look.

'Not that I mind . . .' Rob is saying through the door. 'You know I've never been that keen on you volunteering, but I thought you were enjoying it?'

'Not any more,' I tell him, opening the door, head down as our paths cross.

'Has something happened?' he asks, spitting toothpaste into the sink. 'No one's upset you, have they?'

'No,' I reply, pausing to watch as he gargles and rinses. 'Why would you ask that?'

Images of last night appear, so vivid I'm certain Rob must

notice a change in my expression as he looks back at me, something that will give me away. I climb back into bed and pull
the duvet up to my chest.

'No reason. But you love your volunteering,' Rob is saying.
'There all the time. And now you want to leave.' He dries his
mouth on the white hand towel as he walks back into the
bedroom. 'Something must have happened to change your
mind.'

'Rob, you've stained the towel.' I point at the blue drool he's
left behind. 'Look at it!'

Rob inspects the damage. 'It's fine.'

'It's not,' I tell him, grateful for the distraction the towel has
provided. 'I'll have to wash it.'

'So you think you'll give it up?' he asks, tossing the white
hand towel into the laundry basket on the landing. 'Volunteering,
I mean.'

'Yes, I think so. For the time being.'

'You know what they say?' Rob asks, still entirely naked as
he wanders back from the landing. 'No good deed goes unpun-
ished.' He laughs at his own joke; oblivious it seems to my
desperation. 'But it's not like you to give up quite so soon,
you've only been there a few months.'

'Three,' I tell him, as I try to return his smile. 'I've given it
a good go.'

I watch him dress, wondering if this is a taste of my life from
this point on; always covering up, lying, fearful, over-compensating
with Rob to somehow atone for what I did. Perhaps I should
tell him now, throw myself on his mercy, cite the many years
I was completely faithful, as if they would somehow outweigh

the awfulness of last night. I think of Nick and me, half dressed and fumbling with one another in his office, then Thomas, entirely naked, pulling back the covers to invite me into his bed, Sash's bed—

'Jo!'

'Sorry, what?'

Rob laughs, teases me again about my hangover. 'All joking apart, I think volunteering's been a good thing for you,' he says, fastening his cufflinks. 'I've been so busy at work . . .' He stands up to shrug on his suit jacket. 'I'm sorry if I've been neglecting you. You know I'd spend every waking moment with you if I could.' He smiles at me. 'Especially if morning sex is now on the menu.'

'You look very handsome,' I say, seeing him properly for the first time in ages. Or is it that I now view him entirely differently, my perspective altered by the risk I've taken with our marriage?

He frowns at me, his expression quizzical. 'You sure everything's okay?

'Everything's fine.' I smile, my voice sounding unnatural. 'Can't I be nice to you without you wondering what's wrong?'

'Sorry,' he says, bending down to kiss me lightly on the lips. 'Of course you can. I appreciate it's been hard for you, with the kids, and me not being here much, but I'm hoping that will change soon. Once all this craziness at work is done with. Okay?'

I tell him I don't mind, I understand. I appreciate his commitment, the way he provides for us all; always has. Then I force myself to stop talking, to simply smile at Rob as I would have before; certain of our roles. Rob looks at me directly, a question on his parted lips. I panic, afraid he may have noticed something, a change in me, as if my thoughts were projected across my face, a flickering image of my spectacular fall from grace last night, but then he says, 'Did you get that email yesterday?'

'Which one was that?' I ask, a crack in my voice.

'The one about the leaving do at work,' he says, turning away. 'Don't even know why Colin asked you, years since you worked there, bloody decades in fact. God knows how he got your email address.'

The invite arrived yesterday, sent to Rob and copying me in. I wondered too how Colin had found me; it had been a very long time and our paths hadn't crossed since I'd worked with him and Rob.

'I thought it was bit odd,' I reply. 'I barely remember him.'

'Maybe he guessed your email from mine, thought it would be nice to include you?' Rob suggests. 'He's a bit of a strange character.'

'You think I should go?' I ask.

'God, no! Man's a complete bore. Thought I might pop in for an hour myself, if that's okay with you?' Rob says, waiting for my reaction.

'Yes, whatever you think,' I reply, the unimportance of it irritating me. 'I really don't care either way.'

'I don't have to go.'

'No, it's fine,' I tell him, side-tracked now with thoughts of Rose and how I'll explain my decision to leave the drop-in centre. 'I've got a few things to sort out today. Just let me know what time you'll be home.'

'Quite late,' Rob says, kissing me again, this time on the cheek. 'Sorry sweetheart. I promise it won't be *too* late. And like I said, as soon as this busy period is out of the way I'll be back to normal, nine-to-five, again. We can go out more together in the evenings, cinema and stuff. Okay?'

'Sounds good,' I reply as brightly as I can.

I'm already composing my text message to Rose as I hear Rob's tyres cutting through the gravel. The excuse I use may be unoriginal, but aren't the best lies also the least complicated? Besides, I do feel unwell; it could be flu for all I know. I pull the duvet over my head and close my eyes tight shut, but I know I won't sleep.

The Limes looks entirely different in the daylight, not benign, but much less threatening than it did last night, although as soon as I walk in and see Thomas perched on a stool on the wrong side of the bar, my fear returns. He's slumped forward, his back to me, resting his head on the solid slab of mahogany. He turns to look at me over his shoulder, his eyes heavy, his chin stubbly. The Thomas I'd admired last night has now gone, replaced by this degraded version, a jeer on his face to shame me further.

'I thought it might be you,' he says, only his right eye open to peer at me. He wipes the drool from the corner of his mouth and pushes his hair back from his face. 'Fuck, you look rough,' he says, as I take the stool beside him.

Perhaps I should retaliate, tell him he surely looks ten times worse than me, but I know I must look terrible, I haven't even tried to make myself presentable. 'Is Sash here?'

He shakes his head, then lays it down on the bar again. I look around, but there's no one else in the place. It's far too early for even the most hardened of drinkers and Sash will be at work.

'If you've come here to give me a lecture, I'm not in the mood,' he mutters. 'Your daughter's already got that covered.'

'What do you mean?' He doesn't answer, throwing himself forwards across the bar to grab a beer, loosening the cap with his teeth and draining half of it before he sits back down.

'What did Sash say?' I ask, grabbing his arm. 'Tell me!'

He smiles, shakes me off as his swagger returns, perhaps because of the beer, or maybe because he senses there may be some advantage to be gained from my desperation.

'You haven't spoken to her?' he asks, draining his beer and slamming the bottle down on the bar.

I jump at the loud sound. 'No, just texts. What have you told her? Did you say I was here, that I saw you—'

'Of course not,' he says, leaning in so his mouth is an inch from mine, stale beer-breath finding my nostrils as I turn away. 'Why would I do that?'

'Good. That's good.' I take a deep breath to deliver my rehearsed speech. 'I came here to ask you to leave my daughter, end it now,' I tell him, holding eye contact. 'I think it's best after . . . and anyway . . .'

He laughs, rocks back and forth on his barstool. 'Yeah, I guessed as much. So much easier for you if I'm out the picture.'

'Please, Thomas. I'm begging you.'

237

'*Begging?* Oh this gets better and better.' He laughs again, pushing his hair back from his face to reveal bloodshot eyes and grey skin. '*What?*' he demands, making me jump again. I shake my head. 'You think it's that easy, Jo? That I'll just disappear?'

'I just thought—'

'You thought you could come here and sort things out. Make everything perfect again for your perfect family in your fucking perfect house?'

'I don't know what you—'

'Sash has told me what you're like. Living in your own little bubble, pretending everything's fine.' He spits the words in my face, a single spot of spittle landing on my cheek. 'Well I have news for you, Jo. It isn't! It's all fucked up, just like everyone else's life.'

'I was drunk. I was looking for Sash.'

'Tell yourself that if you like,' he says, smiling to himself.

I stand up and walk towards the door, but Thomas shouts my name, the single syllable slicing through me. I pause, then decide to ignore him, the door slamming shut behind me.

14

Ten Days After The Fall

The meal is almost ready; just reheated Bolognese sauce from the freezer, but it smells delicious, evocative of better times. I stir the sauce again, freeing it from the bottom of the pan, melancholic thoughts rising up with the steam as I drop dried spaghetti into the pan of boiling water: *Could I really have been unfaithful? Risked my marriage?*

Rob should be home any minute now. He sounded weary when he called from the car, but I'm hoping he's not too tired to talk, although what I might say to him is still hard to antici-pate. I hear tyres on the gravel outside, the sound of a car door opening and closing. I glance at the table, topped with the candles I'd lit; force of habit perhaps. They're almost burned away, their flames shooting shadows across the walls as Rob opens the door and calls out my name. I expect it's the cold air rushing in that causes me to shiver, but I say nothing by way of reply, wrapping my cardigan across me as I walk towards the hall to meet him.

'Hey, what's all this?' Rob asks, looking past me into the kitchen. 'Special occasion?'

'Just a meal,' I tell him as I bend to pick up his overnight bag which he's dropped on to the floor. 'How was the conference?'

'Leave that!' he says, holding his hand out. 'It's heavy.'

I pass the bag back to him, although it wasn't heavy at all. He says he'll just get changed before dinner, but then he stops, turns back and asks, 'Have you remembered anything else while I've been away?'

I shake my head and watch as he takes the stairs two at a time. 'I'm fine, Rob,' I say under my breath. 'Thanks for asking.'

Rob's smiling when he returns, his work clothes replaced with a casual shirt and jeans. 'This is nice,' he says, picking up the bottle of red I've placed on the kitchen island with two glasses beside it. 'Like old times.'

'Is it?' I ask, glancing over my shoulder. He smiles at me and I turn back to the food. 'The sauce is almost ruined.' I stir the bubbling liquid, which has dried out again. 'Can you see to the wine?'

'You shouldn't drink alcohol with those strong painkillers,' he says, pouring himself a large glass.

'I've stopped taking them,' I call across, steam engulfing me as I drain the pasta over the sink. 'My head's clear now; thanks for asking.'

'That's great news,' he replies, filling my glass and taking them both to the table. 'I was about to ask, sweetheart. Honestly.'

He tells me how tired he is, what a nightmare the weekend

was. How much he's missed me. Worried about me all the time. I present him with his bowl of pasta and sit down opposite him, watching as he virtually inhales his food.

'I've been using the time to work out why I might have lost my footing on the stairs,' I say, twirling strands of spaghetti on my fork. Rob doesn't reply; his mouth full, although he's looking directly at me. 'Was I carrying the washing down? Or looking back up at you? Or . . .'

'No,' he replies, taking a sip of his wine to help swallow down the food. 'You were just walking ahead of me. Maybe . . .'

'Yes?'

'I think you were looking at the photos; perhaps that's what distracted you.'

I was looking at the photos and I tripped, missed a stair. It's entirely plausible, except . . .

'I thought we might have been arguing,' I say.

Rob shrugs, but he's stopped eating, his fork mid-air. 'Arguing about what?'

'I don't know. Maybe the drop-in centre?'

Rob drops his cutlery, a length of spaghetti spilling on to the place mat. He picks up the starchy strand and wipes at the crimson residue left behind, a dampened finger to the table before dropping the spaghetti back into his bowl.

'Rose emailed me. Do you know who I mean?' I demand. 'She volunteers there.' He looks away, still no reply. 'And Sash did, met Thomas there I think. Quite the family affair.' I raise my glass to him. 'Because I did too. Did you know that?' I feel belligerent now, on a collision course with the truth. 'I was a regular volunteer, probably still would be if I'd known about it.'

He looks straight at me. 'Have you been back to the drop-in centre while I've been away?'

I shake my head. 'Why didn't you tell me, Rob?'

'I didn't think it was important.'

'Oh come on!' I pick up my wine again and take a mouthful, waiting for him to react, to tell me he knows about Nick and me. To explain why he would so deliberately keep that from me.

'I wanted you to get better first, that's all.' He drains his glass and pours another. 'They always put pressure on you to do more and more.'

I lean back in my chair and look at my wine glass in my hand, swirling the red liquid in front of the candlelight. The fight has gone out of me and yet there's so much more to unpick.

'The thing is . . .' I take another sip of my wine. 'Sash said something quite odd to me about you.'

Rob looks up from his food, asks me what I mean.

'Apparently you said it might be better if I didn't remember what's happened in the last year. Is that true?'

Rob's face is stricken. I think he's about to explain it all away, maybe he intended to, but then he blurts out, 'It was stupid, I know it was, but when you said that the last thing you remembered was taking Fin to university . . .' He looks away, his eyes closing for a moment. 'I wanted some time to . . .' He looks across at me. 'It's been such an awful year, Jo. I wanted to protect you from it for as long as I could. Is that so wrong? We've both done things we'd rather forget. But you and I, we're worth so much more than that.'

He looks much older than the year I've lost. I can't believe I hadn't noticed until now, but perhaps I wasn't looking. His skin is sallow, dark circles under his sagging eyes and his hair is greyer, hardly any of its original colour left. He's a man who's always thrived on routine and order. The sudden chaos of the children's lives, and then mine, must have been unbearable for him, but he's lied to me, deliberately kept me from the truth. Even if it was to protect me from myself, it's still wrong. *Isn't it?*

'Jo, I don't want you to think I planned this, that it's what I wanted,' he says, staring at me across the table. 'Everything is for you, Jo. Always has been; always will be. You're my whole world.'

'You lied to me, Rob.'

'No, not lied. I would have told you about the drop-in centre. I promise.' He smiles, tries to take my hand but I stand up, throw my bowl into the sink where it smashes. I don't know whether I'm angry with him or me or both. My pity has turned into rage and I can't bear to even look at him.

'Where are you going?' he calls after me as I leave the kitchen.

'I'm going to bed,' I tell him, then more quietly, 'I've had enough.'

When sleep comes it is deep and dark, all-encompassing, but when I wake it's sudden and violent, as though I've been shaken, dragged to the surface to take deep gulps of air. Rob's arm is thrown across me, placed there without my knowledge, although I'd turned my back to his side of the bed. Outside, the wind is talking to me in hushed tones, rippling the fallen leaves, encircling our beleaguered home. I'd been dreaming of

Rob, his face contorted with anger as we argued, but it wasn't that which woke me, it was the look on his face as I fell; he was laughing, raucous vicious laughter. I listen to Rob, his slow steady breaths, his rest undisturbed by such nightmares.

March – This Year

The drop-in centre is quiet today. It's a sunny early-spring afternoon, one which no one wants to spend in a dusty dark room, least of all me; not when I have bad news to deliver. Rose is hunched over a rather suspect-looking stain which she's scrubbing from the carpet, or trying to. She looks up as I approach, a wide smile greeting me.

'Hey stranger!' she says, an obvious reference to my absence over the last couple of weeks, a bout of imaginary flu my excuse.

'Where is everyone?' I ask, removing my coat, the room overheated as always, but I don't bring it to Nick's office as I usually would, instead draping it over my arm.

'Nick's shut himself away, masses of phone calls apparently,' she says, getting up from the floor one knee at a time. 'Funding issues, I think. The lottery stuff didn't pan out unfortunately. Plus . . .' She draws breath. 'I've sent Sue home; she's neither use nor ornament these days, so you are a sight for sore eyes. Feeling better?' She smiles that wide gummy smile of hers again and my resolve almost fails me, the perspective my time away has afforded now threatening a change of heart. I've been listless and lonely at home and I've missed this place, but I've decided I must make a clean break. It's for the best.

'Yes, much better thanks, but I was hoping to have a word with you.'

'Oh yes?' She looks at me properly. 'Not bad news, I hope?'

Rose and I find a quiet corner, not difficult today, and we sit down, my fingers tracing the profanities carved into the sticky table top. I explain I'm not certain I can spare the time to help any longer. It's been great, very rewarding, but I need to concentrate on my family at the moment; Sash still refuses to speak to her father, Fin seems entirely directionless now he's given up on university and . . . I run out of words, looking at Rose for her reaction.

'Everything okay between you and Rob?' Rose asks, affecting a casual tone.

'Yes, of course,' I reply. 'It's been difficult, you know, with the kids gone. Takes a bit of adjustment on both sides, but we're good now.'

From Rob's point of view, I imagine things do appear improved; as though we've watered a dying plant just in time. I've been entirely focused on my husband's needs, waiting for his late returns with home-cooked meals and an anticipation he has clearly appreciated.

Rose looks unconvinced and I find myself losing patience

with her. 'You know some people do have happy marriages.' It's unkind of me, but I'm not in the mood for Rose's psycho-analysis.

'Yes, of course,' she replies, apparently unfazed.

'Like I said, it's the kids; you know how it's been.' I glance across at Nick's office door, still closed, keen to make my escape before he emerges. I've ignored his 'Get Well Soon' messages, hoping he'll take the hint. 'I just need to put the kids and my marriage first for a while.'

'I get the impression Rob hasn't been that supportive of your work here,' Rose responds. 'I hope he hasn't suggested that you—'

'He's actually been trying to persuade me to rethink,' I tell her. 'Said it's been good for me coming here.' I glance at Nick's door again.

'Have you fallen out with Nick?' Rose asks, her eye for trouble as astute as always.

'No, not at all.' I smile at her. 'It's just a bad time for me to be away from home a lot. When I started I said two hours and now it's much more than that, which I don't mind, but—'

'I'll get Nick,' Rose says, interrupting. 'He should hear this.' She stands up.

'No!' I say, grabbing her arm as I stand too.

Rose spins around to face me, her usual smile replaced with an uncharacteristic frown. 'What's going on, Jo?'

'Nothing,' I reply too quickly. 'Honestly, nothing. Give me another week or two, maybe a month and I'll probably be back. Maybe just do my two hours a week when you're here on your own.'

Nick's door opens and we both stop talking, staring at him as he looks back at us, not a flicker of emotion in his eyes, nothing but his usual straight-talking slightly stressed tone as he says, 'Okay, ladies?' Then, with less certainty, 'You got a minute, Jo?'

'I was just saying to Rose . . .' I reply, but Nick's already turned his back, expecting me to follow.

He tells me to close the door behind me as I walk in. I hesitate and he tells me again to shut the door. 'Jo, please. I'm not going to try anything.'

I close the door and we sit, the replication of our previous tryst uncomfortable to say the least. Nick speaks first. 'Feeling better? Flu was it?' He raises an eyebrow.

'Yes, much better now,' I say, tight-lipped.

'Look, I understand why you've stayed away and I'm really sorry if I overstepped the mark. We'd both had a lot to drink that night, and I—'

'No, it wasn't your fault,' I reply. 'It was me who . . .' I look away, feeling the blush rise in me. 'Like you said; we'd both had a lot to drink.'

Nick laughs. 'I had a humdinger of a headache.'

'Me too,' I say, not smiling.

'So we're okay?' Nick asks.

I hesitate, feeling hot from the claustrophobia of the room, and Nick so close again, just us two. 'I still think it's best if I leave,' I say, looking away. 'I don't want things to be awkward between us.'

'They won't be. I promise,' he replies.

I look back and he's so serious, sad almost. I'd been certain

I should leave. It seemed the obvious thing to do. But now Nick and I have cleared the air I wonder if I might be able to stay. I look around the room at the piles of files, at least half of which contain a story that would break your heart. I love my work here, it's sustained me through the weeks and months when sometimes I've had literally nothing else to do, and perversely I finally have Rob's blessing. I've missed this place over the last couple of weeks, more than I'd thought I would. And I could do with the distraction. Despite his promises, Rob is still working long hours.

'As long as we're agreed it will never happen again,' I tell Nick. 'I'm married, I can't—' The words stick in my throat and I cough.

'No, absolutely not.' He smiles back. 'It was a mistake,' he says, finishing my thought. 'Never to be repeated.'

I open the door to look out at the late-comers who've wandered in, recognising a few faces. I turn back to Nick. 'I should get back.'

'Yes, good to have that sorted,' Nick says. 'I thought we might have lost you, after . . .'

'I'm here, aren't I?' I reply, smiling across at him.

Nick smiles back, a familiar warmth returning to his eyes. 'Close the door after you, would you, Jo?'

Tired from a morning's work, but happy to have reinstated my role at the drop-in centre, I rush towards Sash's office. Relieved to find she's also late for our hastily arranged lunch, no sign of her in our usual spot opposite the revolving doors, I pause to catch my breath and am startled by a tap on my shoulder.

She laughs as I turn to face her. 'Mum, you walked straight past me!'

'Oh my god, Sash!' I reply, my hand to my mouth. 'What on earth have you done to your hair?'

The café is quiet, so my voice is hushed, although it's hard to keep an even tone as I apologise again and attempt to convince Sash it will just take a bit of getting used to, that's all.

'You hate it!' she pronounces, throwing her menu on to the place mat before her. 'I can tell.'

'No. I don't hate it. It's just so different, darling.' I reach out to pat the short choppy layers that now end by her chin, silently mourning the long silky strands of blonde that for some reason she's seen fit to eradicate. 'Where did you get it done?'

'Guy at the bar used to be a barber. He does tatts too.'

'You haven't got a tattoo?' I ask, my voice now raised.

'Not yet,' she tells me, picking up her menu to hide behind as she slides down in her chair. 'Can't decide what I'd like.'

The waitress approaches and takes our sandwich order, a welcome distraction from our conversation.

'What does Thomas think?' I ask, sipping my tea.

Sash shrugs, and for a moment I hope I've found the silver lining to this rather unfortunate situation; but no, apparently he loves the new haircut and was instrumental in this latest element of my daughter's radical transformation.

'So everything's okay between you two?'

'Yes, great.' Sash looks up at me from her hot chocolate. 'I really think he's the one, Mum. I feel like a grown-up at last, and I love him so much. He's everything to me. Like Dad is to you. My whole life.'

After the revolving doors have taken Sash away from me, I wait for the tears, of shame or anger, but I find there's nothing, only a cold numbness as I walk back to my car. I think of Thomas, how much he means to her, and my guilt burns deep within me, a stone in my heart.

15

Thirteen Days After The Fall

It's been almost two weeks since my fall; thirteen days of waiting for the lost year to return. I think I've begun to accept maybe it won't, not entirely. Rob keeps talking about a fresh start, how I should forget the last year, the drop-in centre, everything, just move on, but it's not as simple as that. The images of Rob and I arguing have stayed with me, and they've become clearer, Rob's angry words as we fought at the top of the stairs now audible. 'It's always been you and me. Everything I did was to keep us together, I can't lose you, Jo. I won't allow it!' Sometimes I see Nick, flashes of recollection running through my mind when I least expect them: *a drink shared, a kiss, me running from the drop-in centre, the door slamming behind me. Then I'm outside The Limes, pushing open the door to the bar.* Sometimes I'll see the naked man, his back turned, his smile as he turns towards me, Thomas's face always wrenching me from sleep or my daydream, back to the harsh reality of this life, so much poorer than the one I thought I had.

Sash is waiting outside her office when I arrive, a light wind tugging at her loose shirt to bend it to her curves, revealing what I've suspected since the night I came home from the hospital. I'd been shocked by her appearance, the short hair, the dark make-up, but they were mere distractions from the most profound change: her fingers swollen, her jumper baggy and shapeless, her thin face rounded out. Was I too ill, too confused, or too preoccupied with my own troubles to face up to hers? I assume Rob knows, another secret he's kept from me. I could have challenged him, but he would have told me he was only protecting me until I was strong enough to deal with it, and in a sense I think that's what I was doing too; unable to admit it to myself until now.

The sign for the drop-in centre catches my eye as I walk towards Sash, but I ignore it. Sash is waving to me, wrapping her coat around her as I approach.

'Hey, Mum,' she says, careful not to press her stomach too close to mine as we hug. 'You're looking better today.'

'Yes, I feel it,' I say, stepping back to take in Sash's appearance. She has the same high colour in her cheeks I had when I was carrying her. 'You look well; are you feeling well?'

'Yes, I'm fine,' she replies, looking away. 'Shall we get some lunch? I'm starving and I only have half an hour.'

'Yes, sorry I'm late, I couldn't find a space. Had to go to the multistorey in the end,' I tell her, my head now pounding.

She smiles, links her arm through mine. 'Where are we going, the usual?'

'No. I know a nice place much closer; just over there, in fact.' I point to the café where I met Rose.

'Not your usual style,' Sash observes, looking around as she takes her seat. 'Dad always says you should never eat anywhere with wipe-clean menus.'

'I came here with a friend; thought it would be quiet.' I smile at my daughter, glancing across at the table by the window, then quickly back to Sash, whose lip is curling as she brushes crumbs from her place. I pop a couple of painkillers in my mouth and swallow them down with the glass of tap water I'd asked for as we walked in.

'You okay?' Sash looks up at me. 'You were quite insistent we should meet today.'

'Oh, yes. I'm fine,' I tell her, turning my attention to the laminated menu.

The waitress arrives and we order jacket potatoes with tuna mayonnaise. 'You're eating fish again?' I ask Sash. 'I thought you were vegan?'

'Just fish,' she replies, smiling in a dismissive way at the waitress, the mannerism so reminiscent of her father. 'I feel I need it,' she says. 'The protein.'

A dare? To see if I'll say something? But I want Sash to tell me herself. I glance across at the window and for a split second I imagine Thomas outside again, his coat billowing at his back, the smile there as he notices me. I close my eyes, willing the image away.

'Mum, you okay?' Sash asks. I open my eyes and smile at her. 'You're being really weird; you can't just zone out like that.'

'Sorry,' I reply, but she frowns back.

I notice she's fiddling with the largest ring on her right hand and I comment on how pretty it is, much nicer than the rest.

'I love it.' Sash smiles, twisting the ring forwards again, then holding her hand up to show me. 'You bought it for my birthday, you don't remember?'

'Horrible to have missed it,' I say. 'First one.'

'You didn't,' she says, looking at the ring again. 'You just don't remember. March the—'

'I know when your birthday is,' I tell her, but then I fall silent again, trying to recall not only her birthday in March, but Fin's in July.

'It doesn't matter, Mum.' She smiles. 'I had a nice time.'

I smile and we talk about me, how I'm feeling so much better, and she asks if I've remembered anything since she last saw me. I make vague references to how some things are coming back and I study her expression, looking for any sign of the huge secret she still refuses to give up.

Sash sips her sugary drink through a straw, her dark lips puckered, her eyes thickly lined, but nevertheless looking very much like the child she still is. Our food arrives and is eaten, devoured in Sash's case. It's almost time for her to return to work and I haven't mentioned the thing I came here to discuss.

'Is there something you want to tell me?' I ask, leaving the correct money plus a tip on the table. 'Something important?'

Sash is putting on her coat, still seated. 'Like what?' she asks, feigning distraction.

I sigh, disappointed she has made me say it. It's insulting; her bump there, between us. 'I know you're pregnant, Sash.'

I wish I'd spoken sooner, for we only have a few minutes together before I'm watching the revolving doors to her office, imagining her within, perhaps rushing to the toilet to wash her tear-stained face. She said it's wanted, was planned. She's happy; *please* be happy for her. I saw the desperation in her eyes, felt the worry in her swollen fingers as she'd reached across the table and laced them through mine. But there's no way of returning her to the days when Rob or I could swoop in and take over, fixing a problem she had created. It's just not an option. She's almost five months pregnant; the neat bump much bigger than I'd expected when she'd lifted her shirt to show me the stretched skin beneath; the sight of it both shocking and needed, tangible and irrefutable. I asked if her father knows and she hung her head, then nodded, said he asked her not to say anything until I was feeling a bit stronger.

I watch the spinning door which took her away from me, wrapping my arms around myself, the endless parade of office workers in and out strangely soothing in its perpetual motion. The days are a little colder now it's mid-September. This time last year Rob and I had just taken Fin to university and soon after we'd gone away on holiday together. Rob said we were happy, getting on with our lives. We looked away for a moment and tragedies unfolded; as I'd always feared they might.

April – This Year

Rose arrives at the drop-in centre after me; at one time a rare occurrence, but less so these days since I've taken to getting in early and leaving later too. Spotting me from the far side of the room she shoots me a quizzical glance, beckoning me to join her.

'Okay if I leave you to it?' I ask the young lady at my side. She nods and continues to tap the keyboard two-handed and at great speed.

'Hey!' I say to Rose, catching up with her in Nick's office. 'Everything okay?'

She's slipped off her rainproof jacket and is folding it back into its own pocket, depositing it in her bag-for-life. 'Where's His Nibs today?' she asks.

Sometimes he's Nick, sometimes 'His Lordship' or 'His Nibs'. Presumably in reference to his private education; the upper-class accent was dropped long ago, along with the corporate suits and flash cars, though Rose did tell me he has a 'swanky apartment' overlooking the park.

'He's gone to meet with Anderson's, to discuss redundancy and pensions,' I tell her. 'There's so many of them losing out, they're thinking of mediation.'

I'm summarising the briefest of conversations I had with Nick. He was rushing out as I was arriving, although he paused to tell me my hair looked nice. I'd thought to reprimand him, the warning look I'd given him seemingly ignored as he'd returned it with a cheeky grin, but in the end I thanked him for noticing my trip to the hairdresser when no one else had. It's been two months since that night in his office; we both know where we stand.

'Let's hope Nick can do some good over there,' Rose says, stuffing her belongings into a corner of the office behind a pile of papers. 'The pensions should be protected, but redundancy packages have been disappointing, much less than expected. I can't see they'll change them, though. There's no money for it.'

Nick's previous experience in corporate finance has allowed him to act as a mediator between the ailing firm and their ex-employees; a self-appointed role. It's strange, because although he speaks evangelically of his passion for charitable work, he still behaves like a corporate man, drawn to high-level meetings and finance plans. I've sometimes wondered if he's angling for a role back in that world, although I know he'd deny it, citing his love of the Third Sector.

'Did you want me for anything in particular?' I ask Rose.

'Not really, just a chat,' Rose says, pouring herself a coffee.

'Second time this week you've been in early.' She smiles, gums on show. 'Couldn't help but notice.'

'Is that a problem?' I ask, almost adding a sardonic, 'Didn't know you were counting.'

'No. Just an observation.'

'I'm still not as committed as you,' I reply, refusing her offer to pour me a cup too. I may have taken to the work, but the coffee is virtually undrinkable; especially when it's stewed. 'You're practically wedded to this place,' I say, wishing immediately I could take back the less-than-tactful comment.

'You know . . .' she says, glancing past me to the room beyond. 'This is a place people come to face up to their problems.' She looks me directly in the eye. 'Not run away from them.'

Rose's bluntness always shocks me, although it shouldn't; we've known each other for five months now and I've come to think of her as a friend – an unlikely one, but a loyal one too.

'Are you talking about them or me?' I ask, looking behind me to the early-comers; most of them regulars whom I recognise.

'I'm talking about you,' Rose replies, unrepentant.

'I should get back,' I say, but Rose walks past me and closes the door.

'That lot can wait,' she tells me. 'I think we need a chat.'

Rose has noticed over the last few weeks, she says, facing me across the small room, that I'm at the drop-in-centre more often, arriving earlier and earlier, and I stay for longer too. She tells me I'm very good at what I do, so I'm not to take this the wrong way, but if there's anything I'd like to share, she's always there for me. 'You can't shock me, Jo. I've heard it all before.'

Rose and I have discussed many things as we've wiped tables and hoovered carpet tiles caked with mud, or worse. I've confided my worries for the children, how detached I feel from their lives and how rarely I see them, but I'm circumspect in what I choose to tell her and I think she's aware of that.

'You know everything there is to know about me, Rose,' I reply. 'I'm really very boring.'

'That's not true at all,' she says, looking straight at me, and for a heart-stopping moment I panic she may have guessed what happened between Nick and me in this very spot, but then she goes on to say, 'You're the least boring person I know. Anyway, no one's boring, not when you get to know them properly. This place has taught me that if nothing else.'

I smile, thank her for the compliment, if that's how it was meant. Rose sips her coffee then rests the mug on a thick reference book left open on Nick's desk, some kind of legal tome, then balances one of her wide hips on the corner of the cluttered desk. 'I'm concerned about you, Jo. You seem withdrawn lately, and if there's anything I can help you with, then I'd like to.'

'There's nothing,' I reply, smiling at Rose to reassure her all is well. 'I should probably get back.'

'I know you think I'm interfering, Jo. But I worry for you. I worry a lot.' She reaches out and touches my arm. 'You're looking for something, always searching, but just be careful, okay? Make sure it's what you really want.'

'I don't know what you mean,' I say, turning to the door so she's forced to relinquish her hold on me.

I return to the young lady I'd abandoned earlier, although

my thoughts remain with Rose and our conversation in Nick's office. I've considered confiding in her more than once, the burden too much at times to shoulder alone, but it would seem more real if I told her what happened between Nick and me. Even if I could get past the humiliation of saying out loud what I constantly try to silence in my head, I don't think it would help, the shame doubling if shared, reflected back at me in her pitying eyes. And I know I will never be able to share with her how I'd run to the bar looking for Sash and found Thomas instead. She wouldn't judge me, but I would judge myself, and life is slowly returning to something akin to normal now Rob and Sash are finally speaking to one another. I can't risk undoing that. Thomas seems to be keeping our secret and so must I.

'How's it going?' I ask, sliding on my glasses to read the covering letter the girl typing away beside me has composed in my absence.

'Yeah, no problems,' she replies.

Distracted by the atrocious grammar and proliferation of emoticons and text-speak, I don't notice Rose approach.

'Sorry,' she says, crouching down beside me. 'I think I may have overstepped the mark back there.'

I lean back from her breathy apology. 'It's fine, I know you meant well, but honestly everything is good. I promise.' I smile at my companion too, directing her attention to the red words on the screen.

'So we're okay?' Rose asks, hauling herself up with a hand to the back of my chair.

'Of course.' I smile up at her.

I watch Rose as she moves around the room, the instinctive way she spots anyone struggling, just as she did with me. The only difference is they came here to ask for help, not give it. But she was right, I am here to get away from my problems. I suppose it's much the same with Rob, sinking himself into his work, spending more and more time away from our empty nest, crawling into bed long after I've fallen asleep. We used to be a couple, but now we run in parallel, our paths rarely crossing; and more than anything, I feel alone.

16

Thirteen Days After The Fall

I contemplate walking straight back out; the drop-in centre is so busy it seems the wrong time to talk to Rose, and I'm still upset after my lunch with Sash, but then Rose spots me standing by the entrance and comes over.

'Jo, how are you?' She places a hand on my arm. 'I was going to contact you if I hadn't heard from you.'

'Yes, I'm sorry, I meant to get back to you but—'

'Did you sort things out with Nick? He wouldn't tell me what you'd discussed, but I guess it was a bit of shock seeing him again like that? You looked upset when you left!'

'A shock, how do you mean?' I ask, looking around the crowded room for him. 'Is he here?'

'You two were such good friends, must be odd not remembering him; or have you?'

'No, not really,' I tell her, glancing across at the closed door, the familiar feeling of dread returning. 'Is he in?'

'Locked away as usual,' she says. 'So you're feeling better I hope; up to joining us again?'

'Not really,' I tell her, ignoring her concerned expression. 'Sash is pregnant.' Rose doesn't seem particularly surprised at the news.

'You knew?' I ask. 'Why didn't you say anything?'

'Sorry, I assumed you remembered, or that—'

'Someone would have told me?' I say and she nods. 'Rob wanted to wait until I was stronger,' I tell her, although neither of us seem convinced.

'Well he's told you now,' she says, smiling back, but her lips are closed over the gums.

'Yes, all sorted,' I reply, glossing over the facts, anxious to leave before Nick emerges from behind that closed door. 'The thing is, what with the situation with Sash and my fall . . .'

'You're leaving?' she asks. 'God, Jo. I just get you back, then you're off again.'

I explain how I've decided to give up my volunteer role, but only for the time being, just until Sash has the baby, or maybe for a few months after. As I speak I begin to look ahead, wonder what the next year may bring. Sash may well need to go back to work; there's a limit to how much we can support her financially, babies are expensive and Thomas can't earn much. Besides, her career is too important to abandon at this early stage, and we have Fin to support as well. Perhaps Sash will want some practical help with the baby, especially if Thomas proves as useless as I suspect he will be. Panic grips me at the thought of Thomas's continuing presence in our lives. It's stupid, but I hadn't considered that before. I'd been too wrapped up in Sash, the implications for her. The realisation hits me hard. *I will never be free of him. He will always be the father of her child, my grandchild.* But of course, he won't stay. He's unreliable. He will tire of her; the realities of parenthood will find him out. It's little consolation, and any it does provide wracks me with guilt; for he will leave my child, and his, of that I have no doubt. 'How could it be planned?' I'd asked her. 'Why on earth would this be what you want?'

Rose reaches out to touch my arm. 'Jo, you okay?'

'Yes, sorry. What did you say?'

'Just that you don't have to leave us. Keep something for yourself.'

'I can't, Rose. I have to—' Nick's door has opened. He looks across the crowded room to Rose and me and raises his hand in a wave.

I'd told myself I need to leave because of Sash, to free myself up for her entirely, but the sight of Nick distils in me a thought I had barely acknowledged. I don't ever want to see him again.

'Jo?' Rose asks, her voice fading away, just her mouth moving, dulled out of focus.

I look at Nick and the sight of him fills me with such a sense of shame. For surely that is what I feel, my insides turning to water as he wrinkles his brow at me, then smiles and begins to walk towards us.

'Look.' Rose grabs my attention with her imperative tone. 'We're having a bit of a do for everyone a week Friday. Just a few of the regulars. A little thank-you for everyone's hard work. Come back for that. Say goodbye properly.'

265

'I don't know, Rose,' I reply, backing away as Nick draws closer.

'Any time after lunch, okay?' she says, undeterred.

'I'll think about it,' I call back to her as I head towards the door.

May – This Year

It's late when I leave the drop-in-centre, Rose behind me locking up. With Rob away overnight – some kind of 'networking opportunity', whatever that may be – I'd stayed as long as I could, chucked out with the other malingerers, nowhere better to go than a tired community centre with bad coffee and a strange smell leaching from the stain on the carpet which refuses to be either removed or identified. Rose thinks it was probably Badger, the dreadlocked *Big Issue* seller who needs delousing and a good shower. I call out a goodnight to Badger and Rose who are now debating her selfless proposal to lend him her bath. I think of Rob, probably eating steak at the five-star luxury hotel where he's staying. The cost of the bottle of wine he'll have ordered would probably turn around Badger's fortunes for several nights to come.

'Come with me,' Rob had offered as he packed his overnight bag. I wrinkled my nose, knowing he wouldn't have much time for me between his jam-packed itinerary of client meetings, even over dinner. 'Another time then. A romantic night away just the two of us,' he said, bending to kiss me on the lips as we said goodbye on the front doorstep. He touched my cheek, his hand cold as he whispered, 'I need to spoil you a bit more, I think.'

My car is parked a few streets away, opposite Thomas's bar, the sight of The Limes both repellent and somehow magnetising to me. I tell myself I park there because it's free, an anomaly which is bound to be rectified with double-yellow lines when someone at the council notices, but maybe there are other reasons too, as though I have to keep an eye on Sash, still living above the bar with Thomas despite my hopes one of them would have tired of the other by now. I looked over this morning, imagined Sash still asleep in her bed, her soft pout, the flush in her cheeks. Then Thomas's face intruded into my thoughts and I turned and walked towards the drop-in centre at speed.

I survey the bar again now, my car key in my hand as my focus travels up to the flat above, the red curtains gaping. It's not dark outside, but it still seems odd that there are no lights on at all behind the grubby windows. Sash should be home from work by now. It's usually a comfort to me to see the lights on or the curtains drawn, as if I were part of her routine. It feels strange that the flat is apparently empty and although I can think of a number of reasons why she may not be home, something feels off. She's told me she rarely drinks in the bar these days, or goes out much, preferring to 'play house' as she puts it.

As I approach, thoughts of that night in February return, flashes of Thomas naked, turning back the covers and inviting me into his bed, Sash's bed. I falter, my concerns about Sash's whereabouts only just overriding my reluctance to push open the door and walk inside.

Thomas is propping up the wrong side of the bar, his words brash and incoherent. He's loud, everyone's his friend, but those he's corralled seem anxious to get away, using my approach to make their exit.

'Jo, come over here!' Thomas calls out, his welcome as if we'd seen one another only the other day, when it's actually been three months.

The thought burns my cheeks as it always does, but especially now; the shabby beer-swilled room a painful reminder of that night when I'd stumbled across it in the darkness.

'You're drunk,' I tell him, sitting on the barstool next to his, although I pull mine away, leaving a decent amount of space between us.

'Shame you're not,' he says as he swivels around to face me, almost falling off his seat in the process, his large hand grabbing my arm to save himself. 'You're much more fun when you are.'

'You haven't said anything to Sash?' I ask, throwing off his hold on me. The barman, who has obviously been listening to his boss from the other side of the bar, catches my eye and I look away.

Thomas laughs, then shakes his head. 'Course I haven't. And I'm not drunk.' He smiles at me. 'Been too long, Jo. You're looking very—'

'Where's my daughter?' I ask. 'Is she asleep?'

Thomas looks at his watch for a long time then says, 'Too early to be asleep.'

'There's no lights on in the flat, I assumed . . .'

Thomas leans in, breathing alcohol in my face. 'We don't live up there any more.' He laughs, pointing to the ceiling. 'We've gone up in the world; hasn't anyone told you?'

'*What?*' I push him away. 'Where's Sash?'

Thomas leans back, sways a little, rights himself, then beckons to the barman who had been serving the few remaining customers.

'Yay!' the barman says to Thomas, pulling at an already stretched hole in his ear.

'Tell her!' Thomas says, waggling a finger in my direction. 'Tell her where Sash and I live.'

'Oh yeah, they have one of those flats near the park,' he tells me, smiling. 'You know those expensive new ones near the college? Her *daddy* pays the rent.'

He says the word *daddy* in a salacious way, as though it were a different kind of arrangement; although . . . what is the arrangement?

'What does he mean?' I ask Thomas, wishing the barman would leave us alone to talk.

'Rob pays,' Thomas whispers to me, his breath hot and beery, then he turns to the barman and explains that *daddy* is 'her husband', pointing at me again, his finger too close to my face. I swipe it away, frowning at him.

'You know . . .' the barman says, looking over at me. 'You do look a lot like your daughter.'

Thomas laughs loudly. 'Yeah, like mother like—'

'Don't you dare!' I warn him, standing up.

The barman finally moves away, a smirk on his face. Thomas

sits up straighter, and assumes a serious expression. 'You didn't know about the move?'

'Clearly not,' I say, sitting back down as I try to process the information. 'When did this happen?'

'Few weeks ago,' Thomas says, then he laughs again and asks, 'Things not great between you and Rob?'

'Things are fine, thank you.'

Thomas leans forwards. 'You know if you ever feel like—'

I push him away and walk fast towards the door, ignoring his calls after me: 'Fuck you, Jo! Fuck you! I wasn't bloody interested anyway!'

I've already opened the door, but I turn back, blinkered to the stares I must surely attract as I tell him, 'If you EVER do anything to hurt my daughter . . .' Then I walk out.

17

Thirteen Days After The Fall

I reach the multistorey car park after a brisk walk, breathless but grateful to be away from the drop-in centre, and in particular to have escaped another confrontation with Nick. He'd called after me, but I'd ignored his pleas to wait as we 'need to talk'. I don't know why exactly, but his words had seemed familiar.

I hadn't found a parking space opposite the bar today, perhaps a good thing given my confused state, but in my haste to get away I drop the coins I'm feeding into the pay machine; chasing them down as they roll across the dirty concrete floor. I thank the strangers who help me pick them up, at least the ones who don't huff with impatience, and then I rush off in search of my car. I have no recollection which floor I parked on, walking up and down until I finally spot my Mini tucked behind a longer car.

Calming myself enough to begin the drive home, I thump the steering wheel with the heel of my hand, frustration and anger giving way to regret and fear as the tenderness of my wrist reminds me again of my fall down the stairs. Since I woke on the hall floor I've been presented with too many edited-down and economical versions of the last year, snippets at best: from Rob, Nick, Thomas, even Sash. I rewind Sash's words in my head, so reminiscent of her father's when I confronted him about the deliberate deceit they had co-managed. Neither of them appears to regret concealing her pregnancy from me, citing my recuperation as their rationale for so many lies. Is there no one I can trust? No one truly on my side? Then I think of Fin. *My boy*.

'Mum, hi.' His voice is edged with doubt, although it's difficult to be sure as the signal fades in and out, filtered via Bluetooth through the car's speakers. I can hear voices and a guitar being strummed, the music retreating as he walks away from the source of the background noise. 'Are you okay?' he asks. 'You sound upset.'

'Yes, I'm fine,' I reply, hoping I'm not over-compensating as I try to keep the emotion from my voice. 'Just leaving town, wondered if I could see you.'

'Now?'

'If you're free. I'm a bit—' I bite back the tears. 'Just at a bit of a loose end.'

'Yeah, I guess. Can you give me twenty minutes?'

It takes me longer than that to find Ryan's house. I'd typed the address Fin texted me into my satnav but, like me, the technology hasn't caught up with the new layout of this part of town; all one-way streets and no-through roads, the priorities constantly changing. It's not an area I know well; mainly student lets, which is ironic given Fin's rejection of that life. The drive has given me time to compose myself, and I'm calmer as I park my car in the nearest gap and walk towards Fin's choice of home; a scruffy terrace in a run-down street. I shan't ask him anything, I tell myself; just enjoy his company.

'Hey, Mum,' Fin says as he opens the door. 'You found us.'

The use of *us* strikes me first, then the overpowering smell as Fin steps back to allow me into the small front room. It's dark inside, the curtains still closed although it's mid-afternoon, and the air is smoky; the scent not acrid like tobacco smoke, more herbal and organic than that.

'Ryan not here?' I ask as I watch my son close the door.

'No, he's still at rehearsal,' Fin replies, turning to face me. He's wearing his coat, the shoulders of it loose about his narrow frame, revealing an angular collar bone and a printed tee-shirt.

'Rehearsal?' I ask, kissing him lightly on the cheek.

'Yeah, band practice. We've lined up a few more pub gigs.'

'Ooh, sounds promising.' I smile. 'You're on guitar, I assume?'

'Yeah, and vocals,' he replies, looking around him. 'Sorry about the mess.'

The sofa is covered with a grimy terracotta sheet which presumably hides greater misdemeanours, the carpet tacky with grit and stains beneath my shoes.

'I just wanted to see you,' I say, trying not to look too carefully as I take a seat. 'Maybe I shouldn't have come; it was short notice.'

'Yeah, it's just . . .' He looks around him. 'This place is a bit of a disappointment to you, I guess.' He sits at the other end of the sofa and looks across at me. 'Like me.'

'You could never, ever disappoint me, darling,' I say, reaching across to place a hand on his lap. 'You're my son and I love you, I just want you to be happy.'

'Not sure Dad feels the same,' he replies, edging away.

I will myself not to cry, knowing how much he hates it. I'd wanted to see him, to hold him, to be comforted by him, but now I'm here I'm only reminded of the distance between us. 'Your father's giving you money,' I point out, looking back at Fin. 'That must show you he cares.'

Fin looks up at me from beneath his fringe then he shakes his head and laughs. 'You know, Mum, whatever happens you always just keep on going, don't you? Keeping it together, pretending everything's fine. You really have no idea, do you?'

'I don't understand,' I say, stung by his words. I'd come here to find an ally, but Fin has changed too. 'What do you mean?'

'It just seems like you all take the money and shut up and maybe just once—' Fin stops himself and flicks his fringe out of his eyes. 'Doesn't matter; think what you like.'

'Is that what you think I did? Took the money and shut up?' I ask and he shrugs. 'No, Fin. You can't make accusations like that and then say nothing. Isn't that what you've done anyway, taking your father's money for this place?'

'Nice to know you have such a high opinion of me,' he says, standing up and walking towards the window to stare out into the street. 'At least with Dad I know where I stand. Absolutely nowhere.'

'That's just not true, he loves you so much! We both do!'

'Can we please drop it, Mum? I shouldn't have said anything, just leave it. Okay?'

'Are you trying to tell me something, Fin? Are you and Ryan . . . together?'

He continues staring at the view of the narrow street, punctuated by the sound of a car as it passes by, then he shakes his head, not in denial, more disappointment. 'It would be so much simpler if this was about whether I'm gay or not, wouldn't it? Why do I have define it for you? Why does it even matter?'

I tell him it doesn't, not at all. I'm just trying to make sense of what's happened, what I've forgotten. He turns to me and says he should probably get back; they've only got the rehearsal room for a couple of hours.

I stand too and try to hug him but he stiffens, pulling away as soon as he can. I wave goodbye as I drive off, Fin at the door, his slender figure still shrouded by his oversized parka. I bought him that coat, a surprise for university; thought he'd look the part in it. He'd filled it out back then, shoulders up, straight back, for once proud of his height, but by the time we'd got him there he was already defeated, his head slumped down again. Why hadn't I listened, or at least noticed how little he wanted to go, how it wasn't right for him? Maybe I could have saved him from all this quiet rebellion. Saved myself from his obvious resentment.

June – This Year

Nick and I were locking up when he picked up on my reluctance to go home, asking if maybe it was a good time for a catch-up? If Rose had been around I might have confided in her, but she's with her father at the care home as he's had a 'funny turn', so Nick was the only option. That or go home to an empty house. So I nodded and he unlocked the door again. It was only then I thought to warn him, half joking, that there was to be no funny-business. We both laughed, Nick teasing me he was sure we could be in the same room without ripping each other's clothes off; besides it had been months since, well, you know. He switched the entrance light on and led the way across the hollow-sounding room, the darkened space somehow feeling much bigger now it was empty.

That was an hour ago, maybe more. Nick is sitting with his back up against the wall of his messy office, mirroring my position on the opposite side of the small room. He smiles at me, listening without interruption; as he has been for most of that time.

'So let me get this straight . . .' Nick says, shifting his position from one buttock to the other. 'Rob rented this new flat for Sash in April?' I nod. 'Without mentioning anything to you at all, even after she'd moved in?' I nod again. 'You know how much the rent is on those places?' He kicks over a pile of files with his heavy boot as he adjusts his position again. 'One down-stairs from me just went for twelve hundred a month, but that's a two-bed.'

'Hers is a two-bed,' I reply, recalling Rob's description of the apartment. 'Apparently it has the best view of the park.'

Rob didn't apologise for keeping it a secret from me, even when I'd described how humiliating it was to hear the news from Thomas of all people, a drunk belligerent Thomas who took great pleasure in telling me *Daddy* pays the rent. 'I told you I'd do anything to sort it, Jo, and I have,' he replied. But he hadn't sorted it, not entirely. It might have ended the rift between father and daughter, but Thomas is still very much on the scene, despite Sash's promises to Rob that she wouldn't move her boyfriend in with her.

'What did you expect?' I asked Rob. 'She's besotted with him.'

'And that kind of told-you-so response is precisely why I didn't tell you,' he replied, walking out of the lounge and up the stairs to slam the bedroom door behind him.

'Wow! No expense spared then,' Nick observes, wriggling again.

'Apparently not. *What Sash wants, Sash gets,*' I say, more to myself than him.

278

'She's a piece of work,' Nick says, then catching my eye he says, 'Sorry.'

'She's still my daughter, and she's only twenty-two,' I reply, looking away. 'Anyway, if she is, it's my fault.'

'Not true,' he tells me. 'Have you spoken to her about the new flat?'

'We've exchanged a few texts, but I'm not ready to go there yet. She and Rob have always been like this, cooking up their little schemes, well this time I'm not . . .' I stop talking as I notice Nick is now edging forward, an awkward move that involves walking on his buttocks. 'What are you doing?' I ask, amused by his clumsiness then concerned at his intention.

'I'm trying to get near enough to put my arms around you.'

'Nick, no.' I stand up, almost colliding with him as he does the same. 'We agreed.'

'I was only going to give you a friendly hug,' Nick says, holding out his arms. 'Because you looked so sad.'

I allow him to embrace me, at first out of politeness, but then I begin to imagine how it would feel to kiss him again, to feel the weight of him against me as he guided me back towards the wall. He smells of cologne and hair products, and this place. He's such a different man to Rob – socially minded, principled, thoughtful – and I'm so angry with Rob for going behind my back. It takes me a moment, almost too long, but I pull away, already concerned he may have misread the signals, picking up on my thoughts and extrapolating them to mean something they really don't; for I don't want Nick, although I may want the notion of him. I tell him I should go. He hesitates, then nods, asks me to take care. I close the door, my grasp remaining on the handle for a moment, then I march with purpose across the dark and silent room, back towards the entrance light and then my car.

The barn is in shadow as I let myself in, calling out to Rob although I already know he's not home; his car isn't in the drive. With no inclination to eat, I go upstairs and lie fully clothed on the bed. Nick's concerns, so similar to mine, have reignited the anger I felt when I first found out about Sash's new flat. It was totally unacceptable of Rob to take such a huge decision without consulting me. All he's achieved is to give Sash somewhere nicer to live; with Thomas. And more than that he lied to me and asked Sash to do the same. It wasn't just about the flat and the ridiculous expense of it; it was about our marriage and trust.

The phone rings, Rob's voice tired at the other end.

'Where are you?' I ask.

'At work of course.'

'It's late, Rob. Come home.'

There's a beat of silence, then Rob says, 'Everything okay?'

'I don't know. You tell me. You're never here. You always have an excuse. Should I be worried?'

'What's that supposed to mean?'

'Are you having an affair?' As soon as the words are out, I regret them. My anger is about Sash's new living arrangements, resurrected by my discussion with Nick earlier. Rob has never given me any cause to doubt his fidelity. Not once. If anything, I'm the one not to be trusted.

'For god's sake, Jo. We have a huge mortgage, and now I'm paying most of the rent on a very expensive flat. And I give

Fin money. I work long hours to keep my job; I thought you knew that.'

'Yes, of course. I'm sorry. Drive safely.'

'Jo, don't go. You really thought that I was cheating on you?'

'No, not really,' I reply. 'It's just sometimes I'm afraid of what's happening to us. We're growing apart, almost leading separate lives.'

'I'll leave now, be home in ten, okay? Jo, you still there?'

'Yes, of course I'm still here.' I can hear Rob at the other end, deep breaths in and out, and I imagine how he must feel, or try to. 'I'm sorry, Rob. I do trust you. Of course I do.'

18

Fourteen Days After The Fall

I'm washing up the breakfast things when I hear Rob's large feet coming down the stairs, the sound of his descent creating a picture in my mind of the two of us somewhere close to the top. The memory I have of the moments pre-fall is fairly consistent now. *We were arguing, Rob was angry, begging me not to leave.* After that, I'm less secure in my recollections, although sometimes I see my foot slip, a hand outstretched to save myself as the tiles on the hall floor hurtle towards me. Rob comes into the kitchen and plants a peck on my cheek, undeterred it would seem by my frosty silence.

I turn to face him, my soapy hands dripping on to the floor. 'You lied to me, Rob. About the drop-in centre, Sash's pregnancy, and probably a hundred other things. How am I supposed to trust anything you say any more?'

Rob sighs and places his laptop case on the kitchen island.

'I thought you understood, Jo. We talked about this last night, or have you forgotten that too?'

'That's a cheap shot, even for you,' I tell him, turning back to look out of the window.

'I'm sorry,' he says, wrapping his long arms around my waist. 'That was uncalled for and I apologise.'

I shrug him off and move away, drying my hands on a tea towel and switching on the coffee machine.

Of course I remember last night. I tackled Rob as soon as he came home from work, the shock of seeing Sash's swollen belly far too big a secret to remain unspoken for a moment longer than necessary.

'You just can't leave well alone,' Rob said, accusing me of going behind his back, which seemed rich as he'd kept Sash's pregnancy from me for the last two weeks. I'd anticipated his excuses, some regret, an apology, but I got none of those, just a hard-faced vindication of his decision to protect me from the awful news. 'Look, Jo. This may seem harsh, but telling you wouldn't have made any difference,' he said, rubbing his hands across his tired face. 'You've forgotten a lot of the last year, which must be incredibly frustrating, I understand that, and maybe I should have told you sooner, but I was thinking of you. I wanted you to get better first.'

'You know, Rob,' I said much later, as I went up to bed, 'there was a time when you and I knew everything about one another. *Everything.*'

I sip my coffee and turn back to look across at Rob, typing into his phone, oblivious to me it would seem. This morning is a new day for him, a line drawn under last night's argument. 'I thought you were going to work?' I ask him.

He looks up. 'Sorry?'

'Are you going to work now?'

'Yes.' He picks up his laptop case and smiles at me distract-edly as he slings the strap on to his shoulder. 'We'll talk more later, okay?'

I follow him into the hallway. 'I saw Fin yesterday too; went to his house,' I tell him.

'You didn't say,' he says, turning back to me.

I wait, expecting a lecture about overdoing it, a lunch with Sash then seeing Fin – he doesn't even know I also visited the drop-in centre – but Rob's surveillance of me seems to have slackened off of late, and he's again distracted by his phone, frowning at the screen as he types. 'How was he?' he asks.

'You know, same old Fin, except . . .' I reply, trailing off.

Rob glances up. 'Look, I'm sorry, but I should really go—'

'He said something quite strange . . .'

Rob looks up again and this time I have his attention. 'What do you mean?'

'Something about taking the money and shutting up,' I tell him, returning his stare. 'Do you know what he meant?'

'I have no idea,' Rob says, but makes no attempt to leave. 'Did you ask him?'

'I did, but he didn't give me a straight answer. He was quite angry though. Upset me.'

'I'll speak to him. Leave it with me.'

'No, don't. I just wondered what he meant, can't seem to get it out of my head.'

'I told you, I don't think he's that happy taking the rent money I give him; best not mention it again.' He smiles at me. 'I should really get going. Talk later, okay?' He walks to the door, then turns back and tries to kiss me goodbye, sighing when I look away. 'Fin is struggling, Jo. Don't make things worse by stirring it all up again.'

I step forward and slam the door, walking back into the kitchen and throwing my cold coffee into the sink to produce a satisfying dark stain on the cream enamel. I look up to see Rob's car turn out of the drive as I rinse away the coffee dregs with a jet of cold water. How dare he tell me not to speak to Fin, as if I'm the one stirring things up. I take a fresh coffee into the den and stare at my open laptop, waiting as my emails download, but as before I find nothing of note. What was I doing with myself all day? I was at the drop-in-centre a fair bit, probably met Sash for lunch occasionally, but what else? The obvious conclusion is an affair, the ultimate distraction from this endless solitude and boredom. I think of Nick in his office, embarrassed when I'd pressed him for details. Is it his naked back I recall, or Thomas's? My thoughts wear me out, the questions a constant dizzying soundtrack. I need to obliterate them, find some peace, even if it is only some temporary respite from this god-awful loneliness.

Rob's headlights track across the glass of the front door, then the kitchen window, as he reverses his huge car into its usual position. I haven't closed the blinds, or switched on any lights. The whole day has evaporated into nothingness, the evening the same. I lift my head from the dining table and wipe the dampness from my mouth, closing it on a yawn. The empty bottle of wine at my side speaks to me of the wasted hours, slipping from one glass to the other. It was a gradual process, which didn't really start in earnest until mid-afternoon, an ingrained sense of decorum prevailing until then. I run my fingers through my hair, the bump on my scalp now almost gone, but the tenderness is still there. I listen for Rob's key in the door, but the room spins around me. I close my eyes and grip on to the table, trying to recall my day. I definitely went upstairs after the first bottle because I remember I was looking for my phone to send a message to Rob, demanding to know why he wasn't home in time for dinner.

I open my eyes, the room still spinning as I try to recall what happened next. I know I had the phone in my hand, checking it as I came back down, which was probably why I stumbled; not because of the drink, because I wasn't completely drunk by then. It wasn't even the same stair I fell from before. I was almost at the bottom, just a missed step, not even a fall, but it had jolted me out of my stupor, my free hand going to my chest, heart pounding, and with the shock came another memory of the night I fell.

Rob was so angry, angrier than I've ever seen him and I was trying to get away from him at the top of the stairs, but I needed to do something first, something important. I'd wanted a photo to take with me. One from the wall. One of the kids. One without Rob in it.

'Jo? Where are you?' Rob calls out from the hallway, the light now switched on out there.

I tuck the empty wine bottle behind my back and turn on the kitchen lights as I walk through to the utility room, throwing the bottle into the recycling bin next to the first one. The sound of smashing glass unsteadies me further and I collide with the edge of the worktop, gripping on to it for support, a bag of clothes pegs spilling on to the floor at my feet.

'Jo, where are you?'

'I'm in here,' I call out, a little less articulately than I'd hoped, bending over to pick up some of the pegs and then righting myself as a wave of nausea and dizziness hits me. 'In the utility room.'

'Hey,' Rob says. 'How you doing?' He looks across at me as I join him in the kitchen, my hand to the wall for support. 'Before you say anything; you're right,' he tells me, placing his laptop case on the island. 'I should have reminded you Sash was pregnant straight away. I'm really sorry.'

'Yes, you should have,' I say, steadying myself with my other hand on the door frame. 'What time is it?'

'Late,' Rob replies. 'Bloody audit.' He pulls a beer from the fridge and opens a drawer, rummaging around noisily until he finds the bottle opener.

'Seems strange,' I say, my words slurring despite my best efforts to form them correctly.

'What did you say?' he asks, then he frowns and tells me work should settle down soon; a few more weeks at most. He opens the beer, takes a mouthful, then he purses his mouth in a tight line, his eyes narrowing as he looks across at me. I'm now leaning, or perhaps slumping, against the worktop beneath the kitchen window. 'Have you been drinking, Jo?'

Maybe it's the second bottle of wine I threw back, glass after glass in quick succession, the first not really hitting the mark after that jolt on the stairs, but I hear myself say, 'Long hours for a fucking actuary.'

287

He looks at me again and sighs, then removes his jacket and drapes it on the back of a stool, sitting at the island to drink his beer. 'How many glasses have you had?' he asks, pointing to the empty wine glass on the dining table.

I walk towards it and rub at a dark ring left on the wood. He watches me over his shoulder and I shrug, walking up behind him to drape my arms on to his shoulders. I notice the shirt he wears is unironed, the collar stained with more than one wear. 'Maybe I have had too much to drink, but you should have a clean shirt. I'm a bad wife, aren't I?'

'You're not making any sense,' he says, trying to shrug me off.

I laugh, then dance as I did earlier when I'd turned the music to full volume to fill up the emptiness of the barn. I'd sung along too, as loud as I could with no one to hear me. This time the music is all in my head as I sway around the kitchen then circle the island, not particularly elegantly as my foot catches on the leg of one of the stools. At first Rob laughs as I twist and sing, the room swaying with me even if he won't, but then he tires of my performance.

'Stop it, Jo!' he says as my hand lifts his from his beer, trying in vain to coax him from his seat.

'Why not have some fun?' I ask, pulling all my weight against his as I grab his hand again. 'Dance with me!'

He stands up and pushes me away, my footing lost for a second as I stagger backwards. We look at one another, neither of us speaking, then he looks away.

'You know, you have a nasty temper, Rob,' I say, straightening my hair with flattened hands as I steady myself, my clumsy efforts knocking a magnet from the fridge to the floor. I stare for too long at the place where it lies, smashed into four or five pieces, then I kneel down on the cold tile to pick them up, sun, sea and sand melding in my hand. 'You pushed me,' I say, looking up to meet Rob's gaze.

'Get up, Jo,' he says, holding out a hand.

I tell him no, I'll see to myself, a hand to the floor, the other holding the broken pieces. I walk unsteadily across the kitchen, throwing them from an exaggerated height into the bin.

Rob has his hands to the sides of his head in exasperation, watching me. 'You've had too much to drink, it's not good for you, not after—'

'After what, Rob?' I lean against the bin for support and the lid pings open again, my hand slipping from under me. '*My fall?*'

'Yes, after your fall.' He tries to take my arm as I pass, but I shrug him off.

'Get off me!' I stumble again and save myself against a kitchen cupboard.

'Jo, you're being ridiculous.' He reaches out, but I bat away his hands. 'How much have you had?' he asks.

'Enough to remember,' I tell him, standing up straight again.

'Remember what?' he asks, stepping back.

'I remember you and me at the top of the stairs. You were angry, weren't you? *Really angry.* And you were shouting at me, and I'm trying to remember what I was doing, but I fucking can't!'

Rob stares at me. 'I can't talk to you when you're this drunk.' He pushes past me to the door and starts to walk upstairs, but I haven't finished with him yet, follow him out.

'Why were you so angry, Rob?' I call up after him, my bare foot kicking at the head-shaped hole at the bottom of the stairs. 'Did you push me then too?'

'*What?*' He turns around and runs back down. 'What are you talking about?' He grabs my arm and holds it, shaking me. 'Tell me!'

'Get off me!' He lets go and we stare at one another. 'I don't know what I'm saying, that's the point, isn't it?' I reply. 'I need you to tell me what happened that night.'

I step back and almost fall again.

'For god's sake, Jo. Sit down in the lounge.'

Rob brings me a mug of black coffee, which I take without thanks.

'Sip it,' he tells me, asking if I'm sober enough to have a proper discussion.

I tell him of course I am, but when I look up I see two very grumpy Robs staring back at me from the other end of the sofa. I close one eye to bring him back into focus, asking, '*What?*'

He raises an eyebrow to me, then he takes an audible breath and exhales. 'What do you want of me, Jo? I'm trying my best here.'

'I want to know . . .' I shake my head to try to clear it and Rob takes the mug from my hands. 'I want to know exactly what happened before I fell. And don't tell me we weren't arguing because I know we were.'

He passes me the coffee again and leans back against the sofa, his eyes almost closed. 'Yes, we argued that night, of course we did, we were both angry. That's what happens when you're married.'

'What were we arguing about?' I ask, sipping my coffee again to stem the nausea.

'You were always at the drop-in-centre and I was at work too much,' he says, rubbing his eyes. 'We'd neglected one another, I suppose—'

'Yes, but—'

'Let me finish!' he says, sitting up straighter.

'No, you let me speak!' I tell him, sloshing the coffee into my lap, but I ignore the mess and Rob's efforts to help me as I need to say something before I forget, before Rob explains everything away, because a fragment of a memory has crept back into my consciousness.

We were in the bedroom when the argument began. Rob had been talking about work, how busy it was getting, how he might have to pull an all-nighter again, and I was screaming at him, telling him he must think I'm stupid.

'I accused you of having an affair,' I tell him, daring him to contradict me, because I know I'm right. I know the memory is real.

'No,' Rob replies, holding my gaze. 'You're confused.'

'*Am I?*' I am confused, but not by the memory. I wish I hadn't drunk so much; I feel sick and my head is still spinning.

'Yes, you are,' he replies. 'Completely confused. You were angry, understandably so. I was working long hours. We'd neglected one another; both of us. But—'

'So you weren't?' I ask, the effects of the wine slowing down my thinking. 'You weren't having an affair?'

'I can't believe we're having this conversation,' he responds. 'Do you have any idea of the amount of pressure I'm under?' He frowns, shakes his head. 'Sash's flat, Fin's handouts, they've put a huge strain on our finances. I can't afford to sit back, just expect to have a job if I don't adapt. They're talking about cut-backs, more redundancies. I have to make contacts, be prepared to change roles . . .' He looks away, moves one hand to his eyes and rubs them. 'I can't believe you'd think that I would . . .' He looks at me again. 'You know I'd never do anything to hurt you; you're my world. God if you and I . . . if I ever thought we were over . . .'

I don't reply, my thoughts disordered by the wine. The memory I thought I'd recovered is now unreliable, his explanation feasible; muddying my recollections with the certainty of his clarification. I feel nauseous again, wondering if I'm the one at fault.

'Come on,' Rob says, standing up. 'I think you need to go to bed.'

'I'll sit here a while, sober up,' I tell him, holding up my half-drunk coffee. 'Feel a bit sick.'

'Want me to stay up with you?'

'No, you look tired,' I tell him; wanting to be alone.

I listen as Rob climbs the stairs, his long feet taking them two at a time and then I lay my head on the sofa and close my eyes, trying to make sense of it all, but my head spins even more and the nausea gets worse. I open my eyes and run to the downstairs cloakroom, only just making it in time.

July – This Year

Maybe I'm jealous; although it feels like anger which is building inside me. There's certainly a trace of envy, for at her age I didn't have a white-washed apartment with a picture window showcasing an amazing view of the park. I look around the spacious sitting room, filled with beautiful furniture, dominated by two squashy pastel sofas, one of which I'm sitting on, pale carpet beneath my feet. As usual, everything has landed in my daughter's lap, and although I don't begrudge her a better place to live, maybe I resent the indulgence of it; just a little. Rob's told me the apartments usually sell to parents of the privately educated children at the college down the road. It was by pure chance he saw this one was available to rent, fully furnished. Someone at work was looking to move and Rob had been trawling through the rental properties with them.

'Did he find somewhere?' I asked as we drove here for

Saturday-morning coffee at our daughter's apartment; a surreal and somewhat daunting prospect.

Rob turned the car into the underground car park and entered a code into a keypad before replying, 'Sorry, did *who* find somewhere?'

'The guy at work who was looking for a rental when you spotted this place?' I said, checking my reflection in the mirrored sun visor. 'You said that's how you found it.'

'Oh yes, I think they did. On the new estate near where we used to live,' he told me, reversing into a visitors' space next to Sash's blue Fiat, then opening my door to guide me towards the rear entrance to the flats.

'The new estate?' I asked as we'd waited for the lift to the top floor.

'Yes, there's a new development beyond our old house,' he replied as the doors opened.

Our daughter greeted us very much as I'd imagined she would, a big smile on her face, and no trace of embarrassment. 'Mum! Dad! Welcome!'

Sash has been desperate for me to see the apartment ever since I told her I knew about it. She said if I could see it, how beautiful it is, then I'd understand why her father had decided to help her out. But I knew why he'd done it, and so did she. It was a bribe; one Rob knew would win her back. Thomas's continuing presence wasn't mentioned either, there seemed little to be gained by poking at that particular bear. I'd refused her previous invitations, but I couldn't avoid a visit forever; both Sash and Rob wrongly assuming my reluctance has been a protest against the cost, which I suppose it was in part, but mainly I've been terrified at the thought of seeing Thomas again. Who's to say what he might do when the four of us are thrown together again? Last time it had ended in a fight, Sash storming out of our lives. This time it could be so much worse.

I look across at Rob and Sash, seated on the other sofa, facing each other, Sash's bare feet tucked up beneath her. She's deep in conversation with her father, something about the landlord refusing to fix the broken fan in the bathroom. I allow their voices to drift on in the background as I take in my daughter's good fortune, casting my eyes around the large bright space. The appliances in the kitchen look expensive, a chrome designer kettle and toaster and a complicated-looking coffee machine resting on the oiled wooden counters, and the corner of a very large bed is visible through an open bedroom door. It all seems so excessive. Am I a bad mother to think she might have struggled a bit longer, paid her own way before this? But it's a moot point as clearly I'm the worst kind of mother for other reasons entirely. I pick up my phone, illuminated by a rare message from Fin, a photo in fact. He's standing in front of an undulating field, rows of crops behind him; strawberries, I think. I enlarge the image. The caption reads **Backbreaking work!** but he's grinning at the photographer, presumably Ryan. I look across at Sash, still engrossed in discussion with her father. It was Fin's birthday last week, we sent him money for a new guitar, but I don't think Sash will have remembered to send her brother a card.

'Well you can open the window,' Rob is telling Sash, his long legs stretched out in front of him, crossed at the ankles. 'Or use the ensuite.'

'There's only a shower in there. You know I like a bath.'

My scream isn't loud; although I wish it was, more of a gritted-teeth inward exclamation of fury, but it draws immediate attention.

'Mum, what is wrong with you?' Sash asks, her eyes wide with alarm. 'You're acting crazy.'

'This!' I stand up and look around the apartment. 'You have two bathrooms?!'

'Jo,' Rob warns me, sitting on the edge of the sofa as if he might spring up at any moment. 'Not now.'

I stare at them both, my palms raised to the ceiling, waiting for some recognition of the falsity we're all perpetuating. 'You can't just pretend that everything's normal,' I tell them. 'You didn't speak to one another for months.' I look at Rob. 'She's living here with *him*, have you forgotten that?'

'Mum, don't,' Sash says, close to tears. 'Just don't.'

'It would be funny if it wasn't a fucking tragedy,' I tell her.

'Mum! You never swear!' Sash looks more shocked by the swear word than the scream. 'I didn't want to move again,' she says, sitting up too, although she stretches her feet out before her in the air, admiring the darkly lacquered toenails. 'Three moves in less than a year is not ideal, but this place is amazing. Do you want me to go back to living over a noisy bar, or that shitty bedsit?'

The temptation to challenge Sash on her willingness to set aside her independence, taking the easy option once the novelty of roughing it wore thin, is hard to suppress.

'And what does Thomas think of it all?' I ask, the sound of

his name unnatural in my mouth, as if I shouldn't use it, only hers to mention, but this is our reality, with him at the centre of it.

'He likes it.' She must catch my expression, just a twitch but she knows me too well. 'Don't raise your eyebrows at me, it's been difficult for him too. He's very principled, but—'

'Not too principled to take your father's rent money,' I tell her, catching Rob's eye, a warning in his expression. I sit down, my leg bouncing up and down. 'When will he be here?' I ask her.

'Any minute,' Sash says, smiling at the thought. 'And it's really important to me that everyone tries to—'

We all look at the door, the sound of the key sliding into the lock echoing in the silence. I look away, aware of the heat in my face at the sound of Thomas's voice as he calls out to Sash, and the prickles that break out across my skin as the air around me is disturbed by his presence. I shouldn't have come, this is far too dangerous a situation, but when my curiosity can be contained no longer I take a chance and glance up at him.

Thomas's demeanour surprises me, such a change, his eyes cast down, away from not only me, but Rob and Sash too. Rob moves to sit beside me, Thomas taking his place next to Sash. I avert my eyes to look at my husband, but Rob is staring at his phone. He must sense my irritation for he pockets it, studying his fingernails instead.

'Have you told them?' Thomas asks Sash.

I look over at them and notice that Thomas's ever-present smile, always at someone else's expense, is surprisingly missing.

'Of course not, I was waiting for you,' Sash replies, grinning as she reaches for Thomas's hand.

Until that moment, I'd been consumed by my own selfish thoughts. Analysing Thomas's every nuance, every gesture, afraid to look and yet fascinated by him, but now a warning siren is ringing somewhere in my head, distracting me. I look at my daughter, everything else in the room out of focus, even Thomas. She's so happy, parading him in front of us, presenting a united front when even she would know it would be wise to be more circumspect on our first joint visit. And Thomas, why has he agreed to this? Surely under any other circumstances he would have stayed away.

'You're pregnant,' I tell her, the world up until that point falling away from me as the words leave my mouth. 'You're fucking pregnant.'

Then I laugh, stupid raucous laughter, because it's so ridiculous. This cannot be true, but it is. Of course it is. We're all being punished. This will never, ever, end. And although it's my actions I abhor, then Sash's, and of course Thomas's, I choose to blame Rob, because he gave them this place. A home to make a baby in.

'Mum, don't!' Sash says, tears in her eyes. She looks at Thomas, but he looks straight at me, and although I'm not certain of it, I think he shrugs, a half-apology.

'Is this true?' Rob asks, a crack in his voice.

'Be happy for us,' Sash says.

'Happy?' I'm shouting now. 'You seriously think we'll be happy about this? What about your job, your future?' I push Rob away as he tries to reason with me. 'This is a living nightmare!' I tell her, standing up. Then I look at Rob, his hand reaching out to me. 'This is your fault!' I scream as I push him away.

I'm striding out across the park, blinded by tears, attracting the stares of concerned bystanders when I hear Rob's voice, calling my name over and over. I turn around, making fists to punch his chest, his arms, his head, but he grabs my wrists, restraining me and then supporting me as I fall to my knees, sobbing into the sun-warmed grass.

'Look what you've done!' I tell him. He's kneeling at my side, bearing witness to my desolation. 'You gave her a place to make a family; a fucking family, Rob! With that awful man. That terrible, terrible man.'

'Jo, stop it!' Rob tells me. 'You have to pull yourself out of this. She needs you. We have to be there for her.'

'Why would she do this?' I ask him, sobs taking away half the words. '*Why?* She's beautiful and clever and he's . . . nothing.'

'I don't know why,' Rob replies. 'I just don't know.'

We go back inside and we try to be grown-ups, because that's what we must do. And we tell her we'll support her; ignoring Thomas. We even force a smile at the thought that we're going to be grandparents, and won't Fin be pleased, he's always wanted to be an uncle? It's very early days she says, but it was planned. I want to scream again, this time the words that shout so loudly in my head, *Planned? You planned to make Thomas the father of your child? A man who has no ambition, no morals, who is fifteen years older than you. You stupid, stupid, girl.* But I say nothing, and Thomas is silent too, staring out of the window at the view below, the cocksure attitude dropped, in its place quiet mistrust, as though we three are once again a unit and he is an unwilling adjunct, co-opted into a family he never meant to be a part of. But there's small victory in his defeat, because he will leave our baby, and his. It's just a matter of time. I look at him and see his fear, and I smile at him as he once smiled at me, a wide grin at his expense, and Sash is happy when she notices, because she must assume I'm making the effort, but she knows nothing of that smile, the hate it contains, and the warning.

And when it's all over, when the emotion wears us all out, Rob and I leave, and once we're back home we piece back together a semblance of normality. We eat dinner, even pour a glass of wine, to steady our nerves, and when we tire of the endless discussion, only one subject on our minds, we watch television. I see nothing beyond blurred images and Rob just stares at his phone, tapping out a message, to someone at work he says when I ask, about something which feels unimportant to me; but what would I know? Then we dovetail our use of the bathroom, and we climb into bed and say our goodnights and there is resentment in mine and he must hear it, but he chooses to say nothing in his defence. We are done talking, there is nothing left to say; except now the initial shock is subsiding I feel something other than the pain and bitterness of before. I feel remorse for how I dealt with the shocking news.

'Rob.' I lean across. 'Please, wake up,' I tell him, shaking his arm. 'I need to tell you something.'

'*What?*' he says, rolling towards me in the darkness. 'I'm too tired to argue any more, Jo.'

'I don't want to either,' I say, reaching out to touch him, his skin warm beneath the pads of my fingers, his broad shoulder, then an arm, lean and strong. 'I need to say I'm sorry. I blamed you for renting the flat, but I think I understand now.' I sit up and switch on my bedside lamp. Rob shields his eyes with his arm, then he sits up too. 'You did it for me, you did it all for me,' I tell him. 'You promised me you'd do whatever it takes to sort out the situation with Sash and that's why you did it. I understand.'

Rob turns to me, his face slack with tiredness, his eyes still adjusting to the light, and in them I see tears. 'Doesn't matter, though, does it? I've ruined everything,' he says, covering his face with his hands. 'Sash pregnant; it's too awful. The way you looked at me, Jo. I know you hate me.'

'No, that's not true. It doesn't have to be so awful. Only if we let it.' I hold him to me as he cries and I tell him I'm so sorry, over and over.

'I thought you were going to say you'd finally remembered,' he says, pulling away from me. I'm about to ask him what I've forgotten when he opens the drawer beside him and removes a gift-wrapped box. 'Happy anniversary, Jo.' He hands it to me, a sad laugh at the irony of his comment. 'Twenty-four years. Most of them pretty good, I think.'

I open the box and find a bracelet coiled inside, delicate gold filigree. I tell him I love it, such a thoughtful gift, and I say I'm sorry again, this time for forgetting our anniversary, and we kiss and say we will get through this together, and Rob goes to sleep, his world once more settled into a neat order, or at least as much as it ever will be after today. Soon

I hear his even breaths, but I am far from sleep. The light is switched off, the darkness enveloping, but something is still wrong; as though we've broken something, and although we have all the pieces and we're saying we can put it back together, it's already too late.

19

Seventeen Days After The Fall

I suffered for my over-consumption of wine on Friday, the next day a complete write-off. Rob had seemed keen it should be 'just us two' over the weekend, telling the kids I needed to rest, which I guess was true, although the claustrophobia of the barn, with him in it, felt at times too much, the garden my only real escape. If he noticed my animosity or distrust, then he chose not to comment, and I too have kept my thoughts to myself; deeply troubling thoughts. Thoughts of the men in my life who all seem to control me. Thoughts which have kept me from sleep in those dark waking hours. My husband's slow breaths counting themselves in and out of my subconscious whilst I have travelled to other places, recesses which repel and attract me in equal measure. I have seen terrible things. *Nick and I behind that door to his office, so close to one another, his face almost touching mine, my back against the wall. Thomas's smile, so secretive, dangerous even. Rob screaming at me at the top of the stairs before I fell, his anger enough to wrench me from sleep and drive me from our bed.* The relief I'd felt when Rob went back to work this morning was exhaled in a long-held breath. Alone at last.

I sit at my laptop with my coffee and look up at the window above my desk, the view of the back garden brightening my spirits, just a little. It's a sunny day, a late-summer treat, and I decide I should go outside, make the most of this rare day of calm, weather-wise at least.

The wind has dropped, but I notice signs of previous weather damage which have beaten the late-flowering plants to the ground. It's as I step on to a flower bed to pick up a crushed rose that my shin knocks hard against a low branch; the familiar pain precipitating a memory. *I'd run.* I look down at my shin and rub at it, allowing the memory to form, detached at first and then more settled, an unravelling narrative. *I'd run and I'd caught my shin on something, a table I think. I was running from Nick's office.* But when? And where to? Think, Jo! Think! I straighten up and close my eyes, the wind in my face now, once again gathering force. *It was cold outside, and dark, I had my coat; so it must have been months ago, before the summer; that first time when I was drunk and I kissed Nick. February, was it he said? I made the first move, he told me, then I ran away. But where to? The drop-in centre was in darkness, the door slammed behind me. I ran out into the street, disorientated, upset, just running, until I looked up and saw the flat above the bar. I'd wanted my daughter, but she wasn't there; Thomas was.* I look down at my shin, a bruise already blooming and I know I will have to go back to the bar. Now. Before my courage fails me.

*

The Limes is quiet, only three people to greet me as I walk in, their faces swivelling towards the door. There's the barman with alarmingly large holes in his ears, and a couple seated in the corner with empty glasses between them. It's early, Thomas and the regular clientele will be in later, or maybe not until tonight. I should have waited; but I was desperate for answers and afraid my resolve may desert me as before.

'Hey!' the young barman says, pulling on a distended lobe. 'What can I get you?'

'I'm looking for Thomas, is he here?' The barman shrugs, says he's in and out, hard to say when he might turn up. I notice a weariness in his response. I ask for a coffee and sit up at the bar as he prepares it. He keeps glancing over at me, asks if he knows me then he says, 'Oh yes, you're the sexy mum.' He laughs. 'Like mother; like daughter.'

'*Excuse me?*' I ask, using my seniority to wipe the smile from his face, but he's cheeky, still smirking to himself. The coffee burns my lips as I finish it quickly, wishing I hadn't ordered it in the first place as there's still no sign of Thomas.

'Thanks,' the barman says, eyeing the ten-pound note I've handed over.

'Will Thomas be in later?' I ask, picking up my change and returning it all to my purse.

'Who knows?' he replies. 'Shall I tell him you were asking after him?'

'No,' I answer. 'I'll find him myself, thank you.'

I emerge into the bright sunshine, flushed at the thought of the barman's innuendo. He can't know anything, can he? Surely Thomas wouldn't have . . . boasted about us? My memory of that night is nothing more than a disjointed picture of a drunken pass at Nick and my run from him to the bar. If only I could remember exactly what happened after that. The image of Thomas naked reappears and I glance at my watch, then back at the barman who is looking at me through the door as I turn away and walk off at speed.

The apartments are impressive slabs of glass and steel, three storeys high and surrounded by manicured lawns and regimented flower beds. I wonder how much the maintenance payments are costing Rob; let alone the rent. It only took me a few minutes to walk here from the bar, but the change in tempo is marked; this area gentrified and genteel. I try to recall Sash's address, the flat number Rob told me changing and muddling in my head as I rewind the many conversations we've had since I came home from hospital. I take a seat at a bench in the park opposite and watch the entrance doors. There are three in total, one for each block. When I tire of that, I look up at the tinted windows, wondering if Thomas is looking out at me; the thought galvanising me into action once more.

I plan to work methodically, reading each of the names next to the entry buzzers, but as I approach the first building I spot Nick – maybe a hundred yards from me, descending the flight of steps which lead down from the furthest block of flats – his distinctive spiked hair and leather jacket unmistakable. He must live here too, in one of these expensive apartments, a world away from the lives of the people he helps at the drop-in centre. His squat legs are taking him away from me towards the park, but the sight of his receding figure still causes me to shelter in the shadows of the nearest door, my back pressed against the cold stone wall. There's a loud buzz and the door opens, a woman roughly my age emerging. She pauses to ask if I need any help; her expression haughty rather than helpful. 'Oh no, sorry. I don't live here. I was looking for someone.'

'Who's that?' she asks, letting the door swing shut behind her and hunting in her handbag for something. 'Ah, there it is!' she says, holding up her phone.

'My daughter, Sasha Harding. She lives in one of the flats with her boyfriend, Thomas . . .' I can feel the colour rising in my cheeks. 'Sorry, I don't know his last name.'

'And you don't know which flat?' she replies. 'Oh dear, then I'm sorry I can't help you.'

It takes me ages to check every resident's name, some of the labels handwritten, some neatly typed, some blank. My heart rate speeds up when I spot Nick's name, my backward glances temporarily slowing the process of scanning every entry buzzer for anything familiar. I reach the last door and realise my search will not be rewarded. Sash has clearly not had the presence of mind to change the name plate to hers or Thomas's names.

I turn to go and jump at the sight of Thomas, cigarette in hand, observing me from the bottom of the steps. 'You looking for me?' he asks, pausing to relight the half-smoked dog-end.

'No, no. I was—'

He smiles, blows smoke out of both nostrils. 'You were at the bar, Jo. You've obviously been trying to find me.'

'No, it was nothing. I wanted Sash,' I say, turning away; my face burning.

'Bye, Jo!' he calls after me and I can hear the smile in his voice, no doubt at my expense.

I should have done as I'd intended and asked him what happened that night. Maybe he could have reassured me, but I doubt it, he clearly derives pleasure from my pain. Caught out in a lie, as I so obviously was, had wrong-footed me yet again. Each time I have the chance to find out the truth something holds me back, something too awful to make real by uttering the question I know I must one day ask. What did we do that night, Thomas? What did we do?

August – This Year

I imagine many of life's tragedies occur at three o'clock on a weekday afternoon, when no one is paying much attention. You spend your whole life expecting the worst; even when life is good, worrying it will all be taken away from you. And then, on a seemingly innocuous day much like any other, when everything you thought you knew and trusted is without warning snatched from you, you realise you were always looking the other way, were never ready for disaster, never would have pre-empted it, however hard you tried.

Rose and I had spent the morning tidying Nick's office, or attempting to, and I suppose I'd been reasonably content, chatting with her about Sash's scan, how they think it's almost certainly a boy. Rose may have frowned a little when I'd assured her I was fine, may have noticed how I talk less about Rob these days, how Fin has all but dropped out of my life, but it was a day like most others, unremarkable. We'd swept piles of papers into drawers and cupboards and I may have even laughed as Rose called me Granny, which seems ridiculous now, given what was to come. Then I drove home, perhaps listening to the radio, I don't recall. I was probably thinking of Sash, or Fin – I often do – or wondering how to kill the empty hours until Rob's late return, but nothing sticks in my mind before that phone call.

It was a dull voice, suited to him, I thought afterwards, although I suppose he's as much a victim as I am, but there's a part of me that blames him too. The landline rang maybe thirty minutes after I got home. I think I'd been at my laptop with a coffee before that, but I was upstairs when the phone rang. My hands shook for a long time afterwards, but they're steady again now, resting on my lap.

'You don't know me,' he'd said. 'At least, you might remember me, I'm not sure. My name's Colin; we were colleagues, many years ago. I work with your husband, well, I used to until recently. My wife, Anna, is his assistant. Do you remember either of us?'

I'd only a vague recollection of him. It's been over two decades since we were colleagues and we were never particularly close ones, but I've met Anna a few times; a dumpy woman, unmemorable, the kind you don't want to be seated next to at a dinner party. Then I remembered the rather odd email invitation to Colin's leaving do, arriving out of nowhere and immediately disregarded. I offered an apology for not attending; the only possible reason I could think he might be calling. But the invitation had been months ago. I couldn't understand why he was contacting me now. 'I'm sorry, is it Rob you want to speak to?'

He laughed without mirth and said no, he'd tried talking to my husband. It hadn't worked. It was me he wanted to warn. There was a trace of pity in his voice, but the overriding tone was bitterness. He said he'd tried to save us both this awkwardness, that's why he'd emailed me when he'd found out, hoped I'd contact him, open up the conversation.

'How did you get my email address?' I asked, the message now taking on new meaning.

He laughed, said it was a long shot, but he'd simply substituted Joanne for Robert and hoped it would work. It was a kind of intervention, he said. A last-ditch attempt to confront them head-on and put a stop to it. He'd thought with both of us at the party they might see sense. Rob had gone alone, and they'd promised, and he'd believed them. I told him he was a liar before I hung up. Swore at him as I stared at the phone, thrown on to the bed beside me.

I pace the bedroom, muttering to myself that it was a bloody cheek. Rob will be livid when I tell him, but Colin's words loop in my head; an unwanted soundtrack. 'Jo, you have a right to know. It's been going on months. And that's not all—'

I ignore the other calls, running downstairs to disconnect the answer machine, deleting his voice as he begins to leave a message, stabbing again and again at the button until the machine tips sideways and falls from the hall table.

It's quite some time before I do anything practical, staring out of the windows and pacing the barn as I cry angry and then sad tears. Then I'm frenetic, rifling through Rob's hideous macho study; but the desk is tidy, the drawers empty. I run into our bedroom, pulling open his wardrobe door to remove his overnight bag, unzipping it to see the price tag still attached inside, a half-emptied bottle of cologne lying at the bottom, the lining pristine. Then I open his bedside drawers and the cupboard beneath the sink, and every drawer and cupboard in the kitchen, until I reach the den, my haven, and that's when I cry again, fearful tears, then wracking sobs of utter despair.

It's an hour later when I'm closing the front door behind me, calmer now, order restored to the barn. Steely, my mother would have called my mood, and the thought bolsters me. Then Fin's message flashes up on my phone, a picture of him and Ryan, both smiling, the backdrop a huge festival site. They look so happy I think I may turn back, go into the barn and convince myself that it's not true, but then I hear Colin's voice, and Sash's and Fin's, telling me I can't always ignore things and carry on as if nothing were wrong. I start my car and drive down the hill, adrenalin making me slick; fast gear changes and my foot hard to the pedal. Rob told me he would be late home tonight, I wasn't to wait up for him, could even be an all-nighter, the connotations of the phrase only now resonating. I've been a fool. He's not a doctor or a fireman. He crunches numbers. Head in the fucking sand, Jo.

It's after five when I arrive; reversing into a visitors' parking space opposite the long flight of steps every employee must descend on their way out. I used to work here, and for a while after I'd left to have Sash I'd drop Rob at work every day, but that was many years ago when we'd had to manage with one car. The building is much the same, looking a bit tired perhaps, and the grass is in need of a cut. I watch the crowded steps leading up to the entrance, a central atrium flanked by rows and rows of green-glass windows three storeys high. Putting on my glasses, I study each man who descends, assuming they are returning to a calmer scene than the one I fear may unfold for me. More suits appear and begin to merge, a homogenous corporate grey, so it's not his attire which distinguishes my husband to me, but the familiar gait, his height causing his shoulders to round, the long legs lithe and quick as he sprints towards his car. I start the engine and follow him out of the car park, allowing two cars to slide between us, the scene quite surreal, although there's no amusement or sport in it for me, quite the opposite.

Rob's car is heading away from home. A shock. Although perhaps I shouldn't be quite so surprised, he told me he'd be late. He's taking the main arterial road which bisects the new estates. The roads are busy with rush hour traffic, but I still worry he may notice me. My Mini is distinctive if not unique. I slow, ignoring the car tailgating me as I see Rob's brake lights flash red. He indicates and then turns right. We drive past our old house, Rob now a hundred yards ahead of me, speeding as always. I allow a gap to open up between us as I pass our previous home, glancing across at the colourful blooms which fill the front garden. The couple who bought it from us were new to the area. They had two small children, boys I think. Rob has driven further into the estate. I follow, past the park where we'd push Sash and Fin on the swings, or twirl them on the roundabout until their faces were animated with frenzied excitement. I hang back now, watching as he slows and turns into a cul-de-sac, before I turn too and then pull into the side of the road. I'll walk from here.

At first I'm afraid I might have lost him, but then I see Rob's car parked in one of the drives on the left, about ten houses away from where I now stand. He's still sitting in the driver seat, the doors closed. I can just see the blue of his work shirt; the one I ironed last night along with five others, my back aching. I lean against the wooden fence next to the path, a drooping bush growing over the top of it, my limbs now heavy, my head light. I could turn back; pretend I haven't seen what I've already witnessed. It's not too late, I tell myself, although I know in my heart it is.

The houses are small, staggered modern terraces, imitation stone and no garages, just drives. They weren't here when we lived on the estate, but there are tens of them now, all the same, a sprawling mass of starter homes around a triangle of undulating grass. Young families live in this road, children playing on bikes up and down the grassy slopes. Rob climbs out of his car and locks it. The double-blip scours through me, an incongruously familiar sound which usually alerts me to his arrival home. But he's parked in another drive and now he's using a key to let himself in. I stagger a pace or two, afraid he may see me, almost falling, my hand to the rough fence beside me. He has a key? I can't bear it, I look away, the tendrils of the flowering bush above me tapping at my head and shoulders, as if they want to attract my attention. They release a scent of summer, too beloved, too happy, and glancing up I see slender drooping cones of deep purple flowers with orange eyes, each stem smothered in butterflies. He has a key? I close my eyes, the flapping of a thousand tiny wings loud in my ears.

It feels too long before I can open my eyes, as if by waiting it will no longer be true, shutting out the hurt, and yet it must only be a second or two. The door is closed. Glossy red. Rob behind it. I have no frame of reference for what just happened and no idea what to do next. He's my husband of twenty-four years, I thought I knew everything about him. It's like an out-of-body experience, as though Rob will emerge at any moment and walk towards me, laughing at some perverse joke he's playing, an entirely reasonable account to hand. Or the door will open and it won't be Rob, but someone who looks like him, who has borrowed his car. Rob will have an explanation, he always does, but he had a key, he let himself in. This isn't the affair I'd so feared; it's much worse than that. This is a whole other life. He's made me the fool I thought I'd never be. I'd publicly mourned the loss of friends' marriages, privately certain that Rob and I would never do that to one another. Complacency: the death of everything. Neglect by another name. But I am not culpable, this is not my doing. I turn away, guide my feet back to my car, each step laboured, and yet hurried by the horror of discovery, as if I am the one at fault. But he had a key.

20

Nineteen Days After The Fall

Rose throws open the door, the sight of her gummy smile so welcome. It's been almost a week since I rushed out of the drop-in centre, away from Nick and whatever he may have wanted of me, but by default also leaving Rose behind. Her email yesterday had brightened my day. Her invitation readily accepted.

'I wasn't sure you'd come,' Rose says. 'I always got the impression you'd rather keep our friendship to our chats over coffee in Nick's office.'

'Haven't I been here before?' I ask, and she shakes her head, stepping back to let me in.

Rose tells me to go through, following me along the narrow entrance hall. The front room is much lighter and surprisingly spacious, although the décor is firmly seated in the past, floral chintz fabrics covering every surface, the carpets and walls competing in different prints, swirls and fleurs-de-lys creating a dizzying sensation. Rose disappears to make tea and I look out of the net-curtained window to my car below, nervous of where I've left it on the side of the road. The view of the other blocks of flats and the green spaces surrounding them is entirely different to the manicured common areas which surround Sash's pristine flat. The abandoned cars and shopping trollies which litter Rose's view a stark contrast to the beautiful park those flats adjoin.

'This is nice,' I say, turning from the window to see Rose place a tea-tray on the lace tablecloth covering the coffee table. 'You been here long?'

'My whole life,' Rose says, patting the sofa cushion next to her then straightening the crocheted antimacassar draped over the back. 'It was Mum and Dad's and I was lucky enough to keep the tenancy.'

'Thanks.' I take the teacup and saucer she's holding for me.

'Mum passed two years ago, only sixty-two, and Dad's been in a care home for five months. He's almost eighty,' she explains. 'I visit every day.' She looks at me and smiles the saddest of smiles. 'I just couldn't cope, Jo. Even if I'd have given up the drop-in-centre. There's only me, you see.'

'I'm sure you did everything you could,' I tell her, sipping my hot tea. She reveals her gums again, but there's still sadness in her eyes. 'I'm an only child too,' I tell her, although I'm sure she must know.

'Kindred spirits,' she says and unlikely though it is, I smile and agree, finding such comfort in the thought that despite everything I have found a true friend in the last year.

'Have you told your husband about Nick?' she asks, direct as always.

I look up at her. 'I don't know what you mean.'

'Come on, Jo. It's pretty obvious something was going on between you two. I don't blame you, he's a good-looking guy.'

'I don't remember,' I reply, my cheeks burning, but grateful for the excuse my memory loss has provided.

She smiles back. 'It was obvious he liked you,' Rose says. 'Late-night drinks and always sending me out of the office. I didn't like to say, hoped you'd tell me yourself. Did Nick tell you?'

There seems little point in keeping up the pretence. 'He said we'd agreed to just be friends,' I reply. 'You really think we were lovers?'

Rose offers me a biscuit from a worn-looking tin which bears a faded portrait of Princess Diana and Prince Charles. I chew my custard cream and study the barrel, now facing away from me on the table, the ill-fated couple curved around it.

'Can I be honest?' Rose asks.

'Are you ever anything else?' I reply, forcing a smile.

She smiles back, but there's a note of caution in her voice. 'You didn't say, not exactly, in fact you did your best to cover it up, but if I had to guess why you were leaving Rob, I think it was because you'd found out *he* was having an affair.' Rose reaches for my hand, even her perennially direct manner challenged on this occasion. 'I'm so sorry, Jo. You said it was because of the kids, but I didn't believe you. Why suddenly decide to leave your beautiful home, your twenty-odd-year marriage? I thought maybe Rob was violent towards you, but you've always said not. There had to be a more compelling reason and discovering an affair seemed the obvious conclusion.'

'Maybe it was me.' I say. 'Nick said-'

'I think that was always pretty one-way. Nick's way, not yours.'

My gut feeling is she's right about Nick being keener than I was, but there's still that memory of Thomas naked, my desire for him. I can't bring myself to share that with Rose, and anyway, even if something did happen between us, he's unimportant, he wouldn't be a reason to leave. But Rob having an affair, that's ridiculous, isn't it? As ridiculous as him deliberately hurting me.

'If I was leaving Rob . . .' I say. 'If!' I tell her before she speaks again. 'It was because we'd drifted apart after the kids left home, found we had nothing in common beyond them.'

'That's what you said,' Rose replies, smiling at me. 'But I got the impression—'

'He works long hours,' I say, cutting across her again. 'It puts a lot of strain on us both.'

But even as I speak my mind is elsewhere, an image of Rob and me returning. *Rob is talking about work, how busy it's getting, how he might have to pull an all-nighter and every thought and emotion held within me explodes in a tirade of abuse and recriminations. 'Do you think I'm stupid? I saw you!'*

'He does seem to be away a lot,' Rose is saying. 'He's an actuary, isn't he?' she asks, looking straight at me.

'Yes, he is,' I answer.

'I'm no expert, but . . .' Rose hesitates and places a hand to my trembling cup. 'Let me take that for you.' She smiles at me, places the cup and saucer back on the tray and tells me she's so sorry, but don't actuaries tend to be office-based, not away all the time at conferences and seeing clients?

I look at her and I know she's right, the signs have all been there; the excuses, clumsy, ridiculous even, but I've chosen to accept them and yet still felt dissatisfied afterwards, as if I'd known deep down he was lying. He's covered up so much of the past, he said to protect me, but maybe he was protecting himself.

'It all makes sense, doesn't it?' I say, a stone falling from my heart to my stomach. 'Oh my god, I've been such a fool.'

'No, not a fool.' She takes my hand. 'You trusted him.'

'What should I do?' I ask her, holding her hand as if it will stop me from falling into the black void which awaits, her tight grip the only thing keeping me safe.

'Talk to him, Jo,' she says, her words as directions, clear and distinct. 'Ask him. You still don't *know* anything.'

'No.' I shake my head, releasing her grip on my hand. 'You're right. I don't. But I need to before I make any decisions. Can I come here, if I need to?'

'Of course, you don't even have to ask.' She places her hand on my arm. 'Anything you need, I'm here. Anything at all.'

Even after I leave, the subject turned over and over with Rose, I'm still not sure I should be thinking this way. Rob's always been a faithful husband, why change now? He's devoted to me, cloyingly so at times. I've never once thought he might stray. And yet . . .

I start the car, glancing up at Rose's window to return her wave. She'd wanted to come with me, worried what I might do, but I'd needed time to think. I thump the steering wheel as I drive off, muttering to myself, 'Even his bloody overnight bag was empty when I'd picked it up! Fool! Damn fool!'

I stop the car at a red traffic light, braking sharply, then something comes back to me. *A flash of colour. The house where we used to live. Rob's car parked in the drive. No, it was a different drive, and there was a door. A red door. I'd followed him there, I'd driven to his work and followed him there.* And with that image comes another. *A woman's face, crumpled with grief or fear.*

The car behind me overtakes and races through the now green light, the driver shouting obscenities at me from the open window, but I remain stationary, trying to remember where that house was. All I can recall is driving past the house where we used to live and then leaning against a fence, a bush growing over it. There were flowers, big bold purple blooms, and butterflies, masses of butterflies.

August – This Year

I've put off coming here for the last few days, my loyalty to the drop-in centre the last thing on my mind. My life has divided itself into Before and After. I close my eyes and I see him; my husband. Opening another door. He had a key. And then I look at him: sleeping beside me, smiling across our dining table, dozing next to me on the sofa. And I want to kill him. But today I felt strong enough to come here, to offer some kind of explanation. Because this place has been a refuge for me, a place where I was wanted, even loved, and maybe one day I will want to return. Rose sees out the last of the day's patrons and locks the door behind them, ushering me towards Nick's office to continue our discussion.

'No, I told you. Nothing's happened,' I reply. 'It's just some stuff at home, not something I really want to get into now, but—'

'Look, if it's anything I've said or done. I know I can be a

322

bit direct at times. Or Nick?' She leaves the words hanging between us as she closes the door.

I tell her I'm hoping to be back here soon, but I have a few things to sort out first. Rose asks if it's to do with Sash and I shake my head. She looks at me for more of an explanation and I take a deep breath and tell her my marriage is over. The first time I've admitted it to anyone, including myself.

'You're leaving him? Really?' Rose sits down in Nick's chair, a solid descent which causes the chair to groan beneath her. 'Where will you go? Oh my god, Jo. Are you okay? Is there someone else involved?'

I don't answer her questions, instead reassuring her I'm fine, which in a sense I am, if numbness interspersed with moments of white-hot anger and then panic equates to being fine. I mutter something about the kids, how it's sad, but we've grown apart, Rob and me. I'll find somewhere to rent, maybe a hotel room at first, or perhaps Rob will move out. I don't know yet. I haven't worked out the details.

'You haven't told him then?' she asks and I shake my head, grateful she doesn't press me further.

I didn't wait to see him emerge from behind that glossy red door. Big scenes aren't my style and I'd seen all I needed to. I cried as I drove away, the realisation he'd virtually told me where she lived, finding his mistress a house at the same time as he'd also looked for an apartment for our daughter, only adding to my despair. I cried again in our bedroom, waiting for Rob to come home, desperate to confront him then and there. But of course he was with *her*, so it was much later when he turned a key in *our* door. And I'd had more time by then.

Time to consider what I should do. He called out my name, just as he's done every time he's returned to me from his other life, and then he ran up the stairs to find me, ready with excuses, but this time I could see his duplicitousness; compounded and confirmed with more lies about his whereabouts. He was working late, of course. He had a key and I was a fool. But even then I knew I would wait, use the time and knowledge to my advantage. And now I've had many days to think, to plan, to knock the edge off the rawness of my discovery.

Rose nods as if she's worked out what's happened and I suppose it's the natural conclusion to draw when someone tells you they're leaving their husband. Part of me would like to confide in her that I followed Rob, that he had a key, but then it would seem too real. Whilst it's inside me I can contain it, at least for now.

'It hasn't been the same since the kids left home,' I tell her again, the only detail I'm willing to share at this stage. 'I'm in practical mode now: money, somewhere to stay, that kind of thing. Sash will need my help with the baby, so I want to be close by.'

'Stay with me,' Rose offers. 'I've got a spare room.'

'You're very kind, but I think I'd rather be on my own. I'll book into a hotel for a few days probably, somewhere neutral where I can explain to the kids.' I think of Rob, wonder again how he'll react. Whether he will be angry or show some contrition. For a moment, a spark of fear ignites and then I dismiss it. He's never hurt me, not once.

'Sash has got a spare room, hasn't she?' Rose asks. 'You could go there.'

'No, that wouldn't work,' I say and thankfully she again doesn't push it.

'Will you keep in touch?' Rose asks, the sadness in her voice so touching, although my emotions are very close to the surface these days; if Rob were ever around, or even a little bit perceptive, he would surely have noticed the change in me.

'Of course I will,' I tell her, brushing biscuit crumbs from the low chair so I can sit down, exhausted now by the reality of it all.

She smiles. 'I knew you were keeping something back.'

'It's not you, Rose. I'm a very private person.'

She leans forwards and regards me across the desk. 'He hasn't hurt you, has he, I mean physically?'

'No, of course not,' I tell her, shocked at the level of her misunderstanding, but I guess she's heard many such stories, it's not such a leap for her. 'Rob's not a violent man, Rose. We've neglected one another, grown apart. Maybe it was just the kids that kept us together and now they're gone . . .' In a way I think this is true, but then the words return again: *he had a key*. Rob's other life has taken me over, an obsession that obscures all others.

'Nick will be so—' she begins, but her words are interrupted when the door is flung open.

'Talking about me?' Nick asks, bursting in with such force he almost demolishes a newly ordered pile of files, a wide grin for me and a jerk of his head to Rose to indicate she needs to move out of his chair.

'Jo's unfortunately leaving us,' Rose tells him, standing up. 'Personal reasons.'

325

Nick looks across at me from the door, his face stricken. 'You can't,' he says. 'I won't allow it.'

Rose walks to the door, the looks exchanged between Nick and me more than enough to signal her departure, although before she goes she asks me if she should wait outside the door so we can leave at the same time. I shake my head and tell her she'll miss the last bus. 'I'll be fine, honestly.'

'What's going on, Jo?' Nick asks the second Rose has left, resting a hand on my arm as he walks past me to take his chair.

'God, where to start,' I tell him.

He listens, his eyes downcast, as though the shame were his not Rob's.

'Have you confronted him?' Nick asks.

'Not my style, not yet anyway. It's been difficult, knowing and not saying.'

'My god, Jo! Difficult? How long have you been married, twenty-five years?'

'Twenty-four,' I correct him. Nick's bluster isn't helping; I'm barely holding it together as it is. 'I needed to ensure everything is in place before I leave. Rob's . . . *persuasive.*'

'I can't believe you didn't tell me,' Nick says. 'I should have noticed.'

'I don't see how.'

Nick admonishes me again for keeping this to myself, he would have helped. He's neglected me lately, he should have spent more time with me, checked I was okay. Then he looks up, as though a thought had just occurred to him. 'Stay with me! Just as friends, of course. I'll sleep on the sofa, you'll be near Sash and the baby when the time comes, it's walking distance from here, it'll—'

'You know I can't,' I say, edging forward in my seat. I lay a hand on his, looking down at his square palm pressed flat against the desk beneath mine. 'It wouldn't be fair on you.'

'Please, Jo,' he says, standing up, his hand grabbing mine. 'Stay with me.'

'Nick, don't . . .' I say, standing too, but he's already around the desk, holding on to me, his arms around my waist, his face up to mine. 'Nick, I said don't,' I tell him, freeing my arms to push back against his chest, gently at first, my feet slipping on papers and folders which have tumbled from the precarious piles, the low chair finding the backs of my legs. 'Nick, stop!' I shout, pushing harder, panic taking over as I stare at the closed door. Rose will be long gone, the place deserted.

His mouth is all over mine now, his chin rough against my face. I pull away, more forcefully this time, pushing my palms against his shoulders, no longer mindful of his feelings or maintaining any pretence of politeness, but he lunges towards me again, his right arm raised, slamming me hard against the wall; the force of his body holding me there. I reach out, trying to turn his face towards me, to make him look into my eyes, one last chance to end this with some dignity, to make him see sense, but he shoves my hand away, grasping my wrist to dig his fingers hard into the skin and then the veins beneath, his rapid breaths hot against my neck. I cry out in pain, looking down at my wrist where he's drawn blood with his fingernails, then again at the door, but beyond it there is silence. I close my eyes to shut him out, his hand beneath my skirt, searching and searching. He smells of sweat, a sickly scent thick with salt. I'm sinking, losing grip, but then I free my hand for a second from his clenched fist, burying my nails deep in his arm.

'Jo, don't! You know you want this; we both do.' His voice is different, guttural.

Insistent and urgent he holds me there, pinned to the wall and when I think it will be too late, that he will force himself inside me and I can do nothing to stop him, I scream. A pure primal scream I know only he will hear, but I cannot suppress, and at last he releases me.

He steps back, raises his hands to the top of his head, half-moons of sweat darkening the pits of his shirt. 'Oh my god. Jo, I'm so sorry.' He recovers quickly, starts to excuse what he's done, demanding I take some of the blame, it was both of us, I led him on. 'Come on, Jo. Speak to me. Say something!'

I pull down my skirt, find my bag, a lost shoe, lick the blood from the cuts on my wrist. I do not speak. I cannot. I turn to leave, open the door and look out. Beyond is emptiness and I run towards it, the darkness engulfing me, providing protection. I reach the door to the street and unlock it, flinging it open to enter the safety of the outside world, deep gulps of air into my lungs, but this time my screams are silent, inside my head.

21

Nineteen Days After The Fall

I know I must drive past our old house, but beyond that I have no idea where I'm headed, other than a recollection of a bush draping over a fence, smothered in purple blooms and butterflies. Except it might not be flowering now; the march of time relentless despite my attachment to the past. Maybe the purple blooms will have turned brown in the last few weeks, the butterflies flown.

I turn into the familiar road and feel another tug from the past. Our previous home is relatively unchanged, although the present occupants have filled the front garden with colour, the summer blooms fading, but still gaudy. I slow the car as I pass, recalling the couple who bought it from us; younger than Rob and me, maybe by five or ten years, and with two boys I think. I wonder if they still live there and resent their occupation, as if they stole the house and its happiness from us. I glance over at the park where I used to take Sash and

Fin, remembering that's where the road used to end, but now there's a new estate.

When I reach the end of yet another cul-de-sac I turn my car around once more, all the time looking for the fence and the tumbling purple flowers, doubting more and more the accuracy of my memory. Then I spot tiny splashes of purple lingering amongst brown over-ripe blooms. I pull into the side of the road beside a fence and look across at the long row of identical houses, the sheer number of them overwhelming. I take a deep breath to clear my head, hoping I will be able to recreate the memory.

It's chilly as I climb out of my car; I shiver before I pull my jacket around me. The bush is large, maybe six feet across and seven or eight high, growing over the fence from the garden behind, just as I'd recalled. I lean against the wooden panels allowing the tumbling tendrils to conceal me from view, imagining how I must have done the same the last time I stood here.

The houses are small, staggered modern terraces, imitation stone with no garages, just drives; a sprawling mass of starter homes around a triangle of grass, but it's the ones directly ahead I'm interested in. The desiccated blooms are disturbed by a gust of wind and shed brown confetti on to my hair and clothes, but I am transfixed by a glossy red front door; the feeling of déjà vu overwhelming now. I want to be wrong, but know I'm not, the memories revealing themselves frame by frame as I relive that awful moment. He parked his car in the drive and then . . . oh my god . . . he let himself in with a key.

I cross the road and lean against the wall beside the red door, my head aching, my legs now weak, my thoughts spinning away from me. He had a key, given to him by whoever is inside, whoever is going to answer the red door. This isn't a drunken one-night stand, this isn't even an affair, this is a whole other life. I lift my hand to knock, my fingers trembling as I press the bell too. I hear her approach, the heavy footsteps, her fingers turning the latch.

'Jo!' she says, stepping forward to catch me as I fall towards her.

I wake on the floor of the hallway; a space so confined I'm amazed I appear unhurt, although as Anna coaxes me towards the small front room I feel jarred, like the ache of an oncoming illness. 'I'm sorry,' I tell her; not the first words I'd expected to say.

The shock when she'd opened the door, her face smooth and round, her belly so distended, had lifted me up, detaching me from the awful reality to send me down towards the floor.

'You fainted,' she says. 'I'll make you some sweet tea.'

The front room is tiny: a feature wall behind the fireplace papered in a bright bouncy pattern of mauve and pink. The other walls are painted in a saccharine shade of pale baby pink. I lean back against the sofa, my head still woozy, and it strikes me how Rob will have to adapt his very different taste to hers, a moment of cruel clarity cutting through the fog of my thoughts. Anna places a neat cup and saucer, china and floral, on the side table, then she lowers herself into the armchair facing me, a glass of water in her hand.

'How many months gone are you?' I ask.

331

'Six,' she tells me, her hands circling the huge domed bump.

'*Six*? You were together in March.' The thought swamps me, threatens to drag me under again, but I fight the light-headedness and when I speak my words are cold and emotionless. 'When did it start?'

'Just before Christmas. We tried to end it,' she replies. 'Rob and I feel terrible about it, but—'

'Who tried?' I demand, pushing away the tea. 'Who?'

'Both of us. After Christmas, then again in February, March time.'

'So you trapped him with a pregnancy?'

'No, that's not—' She coughs, takes a sip of water. 'I know this must be awful for you, Jo. But we both need to calm down. Neither of us is well.'

'You know about my memory loss?'

Anna nods, looks away to readjust herself in the chair and place her water back down. She tries to sit up straighter then gives up and slumps back, her knees apart, clad in leggings under a tunic top. She's a chubby woman, must be in her forties; too old you'd think.

'How did you find me?' she asks, then before I can reply she leans forward. 'Did Rob tell you?'

'No, he doesn't know I'm here.' She visibly relaxes; the news still hers to tell, unless I get there first. 'So, how . . . ?' she asks.

'It doesn't take a genius,' I reply. 'I know my husband better than anyone.'

Anna looks away, bites down on a response.

'So I'm guessing I didn't come in when I was last here?' I ask her and when she looks up I can tell she had no idea I'd known before.

'When?' she asks.

'Not sure. At a guess a few days before my fall.'

She strokes her bump, looks away. I imagine her in ten years, twenty even. Her child an adult, her in her sixties, Rob in his late seventies; an old man. Maybe dead. I should feel something. Such terrible thoughts. Anna is pregnant and alone, perhaps fearful the father of her child may yet desert her, which he may well have done if I hadn't found out. A pitiable creature and yet I feel nothing, not even resentment at her part in this. Just an aching numbness in my chest when I think of what the man I've loved for all these years has put me through. To discover his infidelity not once, but twice. He could have saved me all this, but he chose not to. He told me he loved me, that there was no one else, lied again and again, deliberately concealing the past for his own ends. He wanted to reinvent history, keep me and his pristine home, that bloody empty barn at the top of the hill, with me in it, splendid fucking isolation, rejecting all this mess, this big pink mess.

'Why are you here, Jo?' she asks, her voice quiet. 'I mean apart from the obvious, what do you want from me?'

'Just the truth,' I tell her.

I ask where her husband is, does he think the child's his? Could it be? I hate myself for the bubble of hope that thought supplies, but no. It's definitely Rob's, her husband is in their marital home on the other side of town. 'So who pays for this place?' I ask, already knowing the answer.

'Rob,' she says, having the decency to look away. 'And me. I have my sick pay.'

'Jesus, he keeps you, me, Sash, Fin. No wonder my son blames us all for taking Rob's money.'

'*Fin?*' she asks, looking back. 'Of course. That's why you're here. He told you.'

'Told me what?' I feel my stomach clench. No, please god no, not my boy, not just for his father's money, not that. I clutch the arm of the chair, willing myself to rally. I cannot pass out again.

Anna hesitates, the inner deliberations revealing themselves in her expression, at once decided and then diffident again. 'Are you sure you want to hear this?'

'I think we're beyond the niceties, don't you?' I say, a defiance in my voice that belies the awful sense of betrayal I feel.

'Your son . . .' Anna says, glancing across at me as she begins. 'He was playing in a band, in a country pub miles from here, the middle of nowhere. We didn't notice him at first, we were seated in a far corner and Fin was stood at the back. They were very good, have you seen them?' I shake my head, treacherous tears released. Anna looks away, towards the front window. She must be able to see my car, parked opposite. 'It's not your son's fault, Jo. Rob told him we were over and he meant it at the time.'

If Anna is trying to save my feelings, then there's no point putting myself through this. 'Tell me the truth!' I say, my strength returning.

'I am, Jo. It was early on, not long after Christmas. Rob spoke to him; swore he would end it.'

'Well he didn't,' I say, pointing to her stomach. 'Just tell me the truth, Anna. Everything. I need to know.'

Anna spares me no details, and at times I wonder if she's reminiscing, my presence temporarily discounted. She says they tried to stay away from each other, but they work together, very closely in fact; it was impossible. Rob was so unhappy; she couldn't bear to see him like that. I balk at that, the inference being our marriage was somehow deficient, that I wasn't enough for him. She loves my husband, that much is clear, but it's hard not to point out that he's stayed with me, and that he is still with me now. This clearly means more to her than it does to him. I remember when I was pregnant with Sash and Fin, the feeling of connection to Rob, pride that we'd made something together, just us two, but also terror at the thought I might lose him and be left to fend alone; a single parent. But I can't allow myself to feel sorry for her.

'We didn't mean for it to be anything serious, not at first.' She speaks so quietly I have to lean towards her to hear the terrible words. 'But we were both unhappy. Colin and I have never wanted children. I thought it was enough, you see; my marriage and my work. It was, for many years.'

'So you trapped my husband with a pregnancy?'

'No, I said. It wasn't like that. Not at all.' She looks flustered, sips her water again, takes a few deep breaths. 'Sorry, I have to be careful, my blood pressure's up.' I wait for her to continue. 'I didn't think I could still have children,' she explains. 'I assumed, at my age . . . stupid of me, but—'

'Yes, very stupid of you,' I say. 'Both of you.'

'It was a shock, but Rob wants to do the right thing.' She

looks up at me. 'For both of us, Jo. You, me and this little one. And your kids. He's a decent man. You know that.'

'You still believe that? He was cheating on us both, Anna.' Her loyalty is exasperating. I throw myself back into the sofa, my head finally clear. 'He had the chance to leave, so many times. He could have told me, confessed the affair, but he didn't.'

She's saying no, shaking her head, barely listening although I still try to convince her.

'He took the opportunity my fall gave him to save our marriage,' I say, softening my tone just a little as she's obviously distressed. 'I'm sorry but he doesn't want you, Anna. He only wants me. He might have wanted you, for a while, you clearly adore him and Rob thrives on that, but no, not long term, not instead.'

'No!' she says, standing up. 'That's not right. He told you he was leaving you, but you took it badly and you fell. He was only staying because you were so ill. He even spoke to the doctors, asked when he could break the news. He said it would be soon. He told me he was leaving you soon! He told me!' Her face is contorted with denial, her body shaking. I think of the woman I'd recalled, her face contorted with fear. I hadn't challanged Anna when I came here before, but I'd clearly imagined this scene playing out.

'But he didn't tell me, did he Anna? I found out. He was never going to leave me; I was leaving him.'

It takes me a while to calm Anna down. I tuck her up in bed and bring her phone to her. She has the number of my newer phone if she needs me and I take a note of hers. We will talk soon. We've agreed. The hatred I briefly felt for her is now redirected. She's a minor player in all this. I look back at the house, pitying her the next twenty years raising a child alone. It was hard enough with Rob, but at least we did it together. For that much, I'm grateful. Now I just need to plan my exit from a man I have come to realise is prepared to do almost anything to keep hold of me.

September – This Year (The Day of The Fall)

I sit on the bed and wait for my husband to come home, knowing this is the last time I will do this. The last time I shall wait for him, and the last time I shall refer to him as my husband without adding a prefix. It's quite simple to unravel a life, to pull at the threads and separate the weft from the warp. A new credit card in my purse and my passport tucked into the zippered pocket of my overnight bag, just in case. Simpler than excusing Nick's behaviour in his office. I told him no. Whatever happened between us in the past did not give him a mandate to force himself on me. My email to the charity who run the drop-in centre has been drafted and redrafted, but remains unsent, the latest draft deleted as were all the others. I hear Sash's words in my head, 'Head in the fucking sand as usual, Mum.' To compound my dilemma, I've heard from Nick many times, as I knew I would. I've ignored his voicemails and emails, none of them listened to or read; all his calls rejected.

I couldn't bear to hear his voice, to think of him in any way. Rose has tried to contact me too, and I feel guilty for cutting her out, but the thought of the drop-in centre, even her, is too much for me right now. It's all too much: Rob, Nick, Fin, Sash, Thomas; so many betrayals.

I'm still sitting on the bed when I hear Rob's car in the drive. He's not late tonight, no trips to his other life. I wonder what he tells her. What excuse he makes for coming home to me? I make a mental note to ask him, although I may not bother. It shouldn't matter to me any more, but somehow it still does. Twenty-four years of marriage and all that provides: protection, companionship, love, sex. I thought we knew every single thing about each other; all that shared history wiped away with a key in a door.

He comes up the stairs two at a time and he's so sure of himself, and me, that he doesn't notice my expression, just assumes I'm the same, telling me of his day, asking how mine was, but he doesn't speak the truth, or truly care about my answers; because he's a liar. I observe all his movements as if for the first time, but they are so familiar; achingly so. He changes into his jeans and a casual shirt, the Ralph Lauren one he bought for our holiday in the Caribbean, and something shifts inside me, a rage building, but I remain mute and motionless.

That holiday was almost a year ago now; the year in which we broke, and I wonder again when the affair began, maybe after that holiday, although I suspect later, maybe Christmas, or January after Fin left, or was it even later than that? There's no point to this, I've been over it in my head a thousand times.

Rob goes into the bathroom, uses the toilet, then I can hear his electric toothbrush. He comes out, waves a palm in front of my face. 'Jo, I asked you what's for dinner.'

He laughs, bends to where I'm seated on the bed, kisses me on the cheek, asks shall we go out, it's been ages since we've had a date night? He hasn't noticed my preparations to leave because there's nothing to see. I'm not taking much with me. I thought about it, but I don't want anything we jointly own, it's all his taste, not mine. Just a couple of photographs which I shall pull from the wall as I leave, and a few essentials in my overnight bag which is already stowed in the boot of my car: jeans, tee-shirts, nightclothes. I'm ready to go. I have a hotel room booked, my passport just in case, and rehearsed conversations in my head for when I tell the kids, and yet . . . I look up at him, wonder if he should be the one to leave. But I never wanted this barn, it's all his choices; his dream.

Rob is talking about work, how busy it's getting, how he might have to pull an all-nighter, and every thought and emotion held within me now explodes. 'Do you think I'm stupid?' I scream at him. 'That you can make up more and more ridiculous lies and I'll just believe them?'

'What?' Rob is half-laughing, his shock evident despite the smile. 'Have you been drinking?'

'I know,' I tell him. 'I saw you.'

'Saw me?'

He turns away, a dismissive move, and something inside me gives. It's such a small tug, so insignificant, and yet with it comes everything, as if the plug had been removed to an ocean of recriminations.

'I know about her! I saw you! You have a fucking key!' And

I'm on my feet now, and he's covering his head, protecting his face as I lash out. I want to do harm, seeking out the flesh on his cheeks, his hands, his neck, but he grabs my hands, pushes me away, tearing two of my nails as I wrench my hand free.

'Jo, listen to me! You need to calm down.'

I ignore him, striding out of our bedroom, past the empty rooms where our children once slept, away from the man who took everything I ever loved. My home, my kids, my self-respect, my marriage.

'Jo, wait!' he calls after me as he comes out of our bedroom. 'You can't just walk out. At least let me explain.'

'I don't want to hear it, Rob. I saw you. You had a key. Colin rang me. I followed you there. I know about you and Anna.'

He's behind me on the landing now, too close, his long strides outpacing me. I run, afraid of him, afraid of us both; what we might do to one another. His hand is on my arm, spinning me round to look at him.

'Just look at me, Jo! Twenty-four years. They're worth a few minutes more aren't they?'

'No more lies, Rob. No more!'

Rob is crying now, and although I know I should feel something, there's nothing but coldness within me, a shocking feeling of separateness, then distaste as he pleads with me to stay. We're by the window on the landing now, the beautiful view bleak and grey as I look out.

'I've been such an idiot.' He sobs, his nose running, eyes streaming, and yet he does nothing to clear up the disgusting mess of it all. 'Jo, listen to me!' He grabs my arm again. 'It was nothing, just a stupid one-time thing.'

'Oh for god's sake, Rob. It's a whole other life. You let yourself in with a key. I saw you.'

'No, it wasn't another life, Jo. It wasn't, you have to believe me. It was never meant to be, but then this baby . . .' He looks at me, his face filled with grief and shame.

'What?' I ask, spitting the words in his face. 'She's pregnant?'

'I thought you knew. You said you'd been there. I thought you must know.' He looks away, his face crumpled, his hands covering it. 'Oh god, forgive me, Jo. I was trapped, I didn't know what to do.'

The wind is tapping a branch against the window, a beat which works its way into my brain as my husband tells me his mistress is pregnant with his child.

'I couldn't leave her, Jo. Not after she'd told me she was pregnant. She begged me to stay, Jo. She begged me.'

I imagine Anna pleading with Rob, her face contorted with terror at the thought of losing *my* husband. I push away the pathetic image of her in my head. 'You weren't hers to keep, Rob! You were mine! My husband!'

'I know that, Jo. You're my world. But I couldn't tell her, not yet, not until—'

'Until what? At what point would this have all worked out for you?' I stare at him, but he says nothing. 'I'm leaving, Rob.' I turn towards the stairs, but he grabs my arm again, pulls me back.

'I don't want her, I want you,' he says, his voice wired with desperation. 'It's always been you. Everything I did was to keep us together. I can't lose you, Jo. I won't allow it!'

'It's over,' I tell him. 'Let me go!'

But he won't. I struggle from his grasp and manage to reach the top stair. I want a photo of each of the children, not Rob, just them, but I have no time to choose, and each one I try resists my attempts to remove it. I should have done this before, but I'd been afraid he'd notice, guess I was leaving before I'd confronted him. I couldn't risk it, but now my frustration hampers the task and Rob is behind me, taking each step down as I do, begging me again not to leave, he'll do anything, his hand reaching out to me. I step away from him. He can't stop me now, he can't.

22

Twenty-One Days After The Fall

A s I succumb to sleep the memories come, but I know they are unreliable; broken and unpredictable. The harder I search the further they retreat, but then something breaks through, at once unbidden and yet desperately wanted, and as much as I crave the past, I fear it too.

He lunges, his right arm raised, slamming me hard against the wall; the force of his body holding me there. In his eyes I recognise passion, but of what nature and from what emotion it's derived I cannot tell. I reach out again to the memory, my hand touching his face, turning him towards me to read something in his expression, to look into his eyes, begging him to stop. He pushes me away, grasping my wrist to dig his fingers hard into the pale skin and then the veins beneath, his rapid breaths hot against my neck. Insistent and urgent he holds me there, pinned to the wall. I fought him, of that I'm certain; my nails deep in his skin until he cried out.

I concentrate, searching for honest answers, knowing if I force it, the memory will not come. As before it recedes, becomes an invention of the present rather than a recounting of the past. I must be patient, wait for the triggers, because they're true and reliable. But the memories are like flashes of colour, constantly alluring, I cannot resist them, a moment of technicolour which evaporates before me as I reach for the truth; a burst of sun shrouded by the rain.

I open my eyes; traces of early morning sunlight warming the room, creating patterns on the ceiling. I watch the rise and fall of my husband's chest; the gentle sound of his breathing. Then he wakes too, turns to me and smiles, an easy smile, no trace of deceit; as though the last year had never happened.

'Jo, are you okay?' Rob's voice is thick with sleep as he rubs his eyes.

'No, Rob. I'm not okay,' I reply, climbing out of bed. 'Just go back to sleep.'

Downstairs the barn is quiet, almost ghostly, as if it waits too, a hushed anticipation. I open up my laptop and type an email to Rose. Her reply comes back immediately, although perhaps I shouldn't be surprised, she's been my sole confidante since I found out about Anna two days ago. Is that all it's been? Forty-eight hours. I look up at the ceiling, listening for Rob, imagining him turning over in his sleep, but today isn't about Rob. For now, he can wait. Today is about Nick, although poor Rose doesn't know that yet, her response that she 'can't wait to see me for the get-together' stabbing at my conscience. I look at the tiny cuts inside my wrist, running my left thumb across them. They've almost healed over, but not quite.

The drop-in centre is already alive with activity when I walk in, Rose spotting me from across the room, a length of paper towel draped across her forearm. 'Jo! Jo! Over here!'

I negotiate a rowdy table of young men, who call out to me by name as I walk by, and beyond that a subdued collection of mature volunteers who barely acknowledge me.

'How you doing?' Rose asks, frowning with concern. 'Have you confronted Rob yet?'

'Is Nick here?' I ask her, returning her kiss on the cheek and ignoring her questions. She smells fresh and floral, like talcum powder.

'On a call,' she says, passing me a tray of brightly coloured biscuits to add to the buffet table she's arranging. 'But he's promised he will join us soon. I think he's keen to see you.'

'Oh?' I ask, taking a deep breath to calm myself.

She's fanning sheets of paper towels next to the stack of plates. 'You know how much he likes you,' she replies, turning away.

Rose is the main organiser of this 'get-together' it would seem, me her co-opted helper. 'I can't stay long,' I tell her again, opening the bag of crisps she's handed me and tipping them into a bowl. 'Just a few minutes.'

'Well at least have a glass of elderflower,' she replies, pouring some of the warm fizz into a plastic cup. 'And don't go before you see Nick; he'll kill me if you do.' She laughs. 'Oh here he is.'

The office door has opened and Nick is walking towards us, calling ahead, 'Jo! Great to see you.'

The sight of him now, in context, is too much, all the muddled pieces beginning to fall into place. I thought I knew what had happened in his office, but I wasn't certain, not until now, his hand raised to wave at me. I place the drink down before I drop it and back away from Rose. 'Excuse me. Sorry,' I say as I push past the two filled tables.

'Jo?' Rose calls after me. 'Where are you going?'

'I have to leave,' I tell her, not turning around.

'Jo!' Nick shouts. 'Wait! Don't go. We need to talk.'

I speed up, stumbling into the table by the entrance, knocking the neat piles of leaflets into one another, and then Rose is rushing to my side, holding me up as though I might faint and for a moment I wonder if I will, the blackness fogging my thoughts as I hear Nick, repeating my name over and over as he approaches. I shake Rose off, frantic to escape, but then something leaps out, an image on a leaflet, familiar to me: a woman's face covered in bruises, the word 'No!' emblazoned across her raised palm. I snatch it up, turning around just in time to hold it up to Nick's startled expression.

'This!' I shout at him, the background noise dying away. 'This!'

'Jo.' Nick reaches out to grasp my wrist, but I back away, recoiling at his touch and sheltering in Rose's abundant embrace as she gathers me to her. 'You're upset,' Nick says, 'Come into my office, we can talk. Sort this out.'

I look up, aware now of the silence which has fallen on the room, all eyes turned to us. People have got up and are moving closer, whispering to one another.

'You want me to go in *there*?' I ask him, waving the leaflet in the direction of his office. 'So you can close the door again? Just us two? No means no, Nick!' My hand shakes as I hold the leaflet up for all to see. 'No means NO!!!' I scream at him.

He stares back, his blue-grey eyes cold, anger deep within now resurfacing. I remember that look, know what it meant, and I grasp Rose's hand in mine.

'Watch what you're saying, Jo,' he warns me. 'That's tantamount to slander.'

'You said it was a misunderstanding, that you'd got the wrong end of the stick. But it wasn't a misunderstanding, was it?' I tell him, stepping forward and shaking my hand free of Rose's. 'We'd agreed to be friends, but you didn't want that. You wouldn't take no for an answer. You forced yourself on me, Nick.'

'Jo?' Rose moves between us, her arm around me again. 'Can you tell me what's going on?'

'Ask him!' I tell her. 'Ask him!'

Everyone waits for his response, but it never comes; he simply turns away and walks back across the room, pushing his way through the parting throng and then slams the door to his office.

The moment the door closes everyone speaks; the young lads encircling us, the older volunteers too, so many voices, questions. Someone is even banging on Nick's door, demanding he come out or they will go in.

'Jo, go next door to the café,' Rose says, pushing away Badger who is trying to comfort me. 'Just go, okay?' I nod. 'I'll be there in ten minutes. Alright?'

I pick up my bag from the floor and try to walk out, the

voices blending into a chorus of a thousand questions around me, barring my way.

'Out of her way!' I hear Rose shout as I try to push my way through.

I just need to get outside, to breathe in fresh air. I stagger to the door and open it, almost falling outside.

Rose arrives at the café as promised, within ten minutes. She checks on me, then orders us both a syrupy glass of frothed milk to replace the pot of untouched tea in front of me. I cannot stomach anything, not even the glass of water she presses into my trembling hands.

'What about Nick? The drop-in centre?' I ask as she sits down, the table rocking dangerously as she shifts herself into position.

'Nick's gone home and Sue has the keys to lock up, don't worry about that.'

'What did he say?' I ask, sipping the tepid water. It tastes metallic and I place it carefully back down.

Rose is scant with the details, but tells me she instructed Nick to leave at once, his protests met with her insistence that if he didn't she'd report him to the police then and there. I smile weakly back.

'Maybe I encouraged him,' I tell her. 'There was a previous time when I instigated something; a kiss, maybe more . . .'

'This is not your fault, Jo. Trust your instincts. If you didn't consent, then it's . . .' She stops herself. 'You've had quite a time of it,' she says, covering my hands with hers. 'If I'd known, Jo. If only I'd known. I wish you'd told me at the time. When did it happen?'

'I'm not sure, but not that long ago.' I squeeze her hands but then withdraw mine, her touch, anyone's in fact, unwanted right now. 'We have to do something, Rose. We have to stop him doing this again.'

'And we will,' Rose says, stilling me with a gentle hand on mine as I try to get up. 'Sit down, Jo. Tell me everything.'

I look down at our clasped hands as I tell Rose what I can recall of that moment in Nick's office, only glancing up once I've got to the part where I'm running away from him. Her face is stricken, her free hand wiping her dampened cheeks, the tears still falling. 'I got away in time,' I reassure her. 'I'm okay.'

'I remember that night,' she says. 'You'd just told me you were leaving Rob. I was trying to persuade you not to give up the drop-in-centre and Nick arrived, said you couldn't leave, he wouldn't let you. He told me to go, leave you two alone in his office, and you said it was okay. I knew something was wrong,' she says. 'I'm so sorry, Jo. I didn't trust my instincts. Nick was so charismatic, so in-charge all the time. I think I was a bit overawed by him.'

'This truly isn't your fault, Rose. He was clever. He fooled us all.'

'Do you know if you reported him to anyone at the time?' she asks, gathering herself. 'The police? Head office?'

'I don't think so,' I tell her. 'Surely the police would have contacted me . . .' I wonder again if Rob might have deleted any emails relating to the drop-in centre, but it seems more likely I chose to ignore what had happened with Nick; so much else to contend with. 'I'd remember if I did,' I reply. 'Wouldn't I?'

As Rose talks about contacting the charity who run the drop-in centre, to see if there's any record of my complaint, she tells me how Nick seems to have no friends left in the City, no one who would donate to his good causes.

'I wonder now if something happened there too,' she says, apologising to me again. She's clearly upset that her intuition let her down. 'He's been offered a role at Anderson's, some sort of troubleshooter he called it; don't suppose they'll want him once this comes out. You can still report him to the police, you know?'

'I can't deal with this now, Rose. I have so much else to sort out. Do you understand what I mean?'

'Of course,' she says. 'Leave it with me and I'll find out what's going on. If you did report him then Head Office will have a record of that, but like you said, it seems unlikely; he'd have been removed before now. They're very hot on this kind of thing; zero tolerance, and too right!' She smiles at me. 'Don't worry. I'll get him bloody suspended at the very least,' she says, flashing those pink gums at me. 'Never liked him, stupid spiked-up hair and leather jacket.' She attempts a smile through more tears.

'I'm leaving Rob this Sunday,' I tell her. 'Can I come to yours afterwards, around lunchtime?'

'Of course,' she replies. 'You don't even need to ask. Stay as long as you need to.' She squeezes my hand again and wipes a single tear as it runs down my cheek.

'It's his birthday,' I say, looking out of the window.

23

Twenty-Three Days After The Fall

The rain is lashing against the landing window, a storm rolling in off the hills. I stand at the top of the stairs and look down, listening to the voices in the kitchen below. I can hear Rob's voice above the others, garrulous, no trace of regret or shame. He's happy, despite everything. Oblivious to the truth which has returned. He has squared away the deceit within himself, absolved by the days which have passed since my fall. Surety has come and he thinks he's got away with it. But the last year happened. It cannot be changed.

Maybe on some level I chose, as he did, to bury the parts of the past which had broken us apart, but the memories were always inside us, a few recovered, many not. Even as I woke up on the hallway floor, Rob's voice in my ear, I think I sensed something wasn't right, a dissonance between the life I imagined we still had and the one we'd led for the last year. We have destroyed one another; there's no going back. And yet . . . I hesitate, my foot on the top stair, listening to the voices below me again, Sash's excitable tone melding with her father's, then Fin's, much quieter so I have to strain to hear him. They sound so normal, as if I could walk into the kitchen and join them at the dining table, enjoy their company, still live that life. Then I hear Thomas's reply to Rob, the barely concealed disdain in their exchange. Sash's laughter, placating them both, and Fin's soft tone in response. Could I have found a better way? Taken the kids aside, a lunch for the three of us? Warned them. Somehow explained. But they both colluded with their father, kept secrets for him. I couldn't take that chance. Not this time.

I take another step down; the point from which I fell? I look back up to where we'd argued, my grip now tight on the bannister, the stairs below vertiginous, as though I might fall once again, but this time I won't be able to get up. Would that be better? Some kind of release? I steady myself, take a deep breath as I look behind me again, imagining Rob reaching out as I fell. Could he have saved me, if he'd tried harder? I close my eyes, will the images to return, and for the first time since my fall I am able to conjure the memory I've been waiting for: the missing piece of the puzzle.

Rob is behind me, begging me not to leave, he'll do anything, he says, his hand reaching out to me. I step away from him. He can't stop me now, he can't. There's no excuse. I don't want him any more, there's nothing left. Nothing worth fighting for. I abandon the photos I'd been trying to remove from the wall. I just need to get away from here, from him. My foot slips, just a little, an inch too far from the tread. I reach out to Rob, my hand outstretched.

I open my eyes and stare at the top of the stairs. He was

there, right behind me. He was close enough to take my hand and save me from falling.

Rob smiles at me as I walk into the kitchen and I almost pity him his lack of guile, except of course he's only innocent of the fact he's been caught, not the crimes themselves. He's seated at the dining table; our guests too, Sash and Thomas, Fin and Ryan. The sight of the kids defeats me. I'm so close now, the wait finally over, but I feel myself losing my resolve. Rob's opening a bottle of Prosecco. Our family tradition. His birthday. He calls me across to join them. I shake my head, say I need to check on the food. Thomas catches my eye, a smile spreading across his mouth, the lips curled around our secret.

I lean against the island for support and turn away, opening the oven door to stab the roast beef with a meat thermometer. Sash is talking to me now, calling across that she will have some meat, for the baby, but Thomas won't, not even the gravy. Panic is welling inside me, threatening to escape. I close the oven door, inhale and exhale as the memories come back once more.

I'd run from Nick, from that drunken kiss I'd initiated, run until I reached the bar. I'd wanted to see Sash, sober up, a friendly face, but she wasn't there.

'Jo!' Rob is at my side, supporting me as I lean against the island again. 'You look so pale, sweetheart. This is too much for you. Sit down.'

'No!' I tell him, shrugging him off. 'I need to go to my car, get your present.'

I hadn't realised the storm had gathered such force, the rain heavy now, the wind knocking the breath from my lungs as I run to my car and open the boot, feeling around in my overnight bag until my new phone is in my palm. I hold it up, the metallic pink incongruous against the grey sky, sheltering the screen as I press Anna's name on the short list of contacts. Come on, Anna. Pick up! Please pick up! The phone pressed tight to my ear I look across at Ryan's car, rusting bright orange, then Sash's beside it, pale blue, then next to that Rob's, a beast of a car which had contained another secret.

I couldn't have known for sure, not until I had the opportunity to check, but Rob's car was the only place I hadn't looked. My chance came yesterday just as I'd begun to wonder if it ever would, time running out. Rob was going to the wine merchant's, buying Prosecco for today, so I suggested he take my car, so much easier to park a small car in town. I watched him go, waved him off in fact. It was early, the sun hadn't burnt the mist from the hills, the gravel crunchy beneath my bare feet, the metal of the car door icy to my touch. As if to issue a warning show of strength, the wind had taken the heavy door from my hand and wrenched it free of my grasp, snapping another nail on my right hand, bloodied where it had torn. I sucked on that finger as I sat in the passenger seat of my husband's car, a taste of blood on my tongue, and a memory of how I'd tried to claw at Rob's face and hands when I'd attempted to leave him before came back. It would not be like that this time; I would protect myself.

The supposedly broken phone had been hidden behind a stack of CDs, barely a mark on it, nothing more than surface scratches. I wasn't surprised, but it was still a disappointment to be proved right. I wondered if it was even in my hand as I fell, trying and failing to recall where it was that night; probably in my handbag or next to our bed, forgotten as we argued and easily retrieved when Rob returned from the hospital alone. Maybe he'd meant to give it to me and changed his mind, or perhaps even then, as I lay alone and confused in my hospital bed, the idea of concealing my past, and his, had begun to form. I switched it on, relieved when the screen lit up, and checked through the messages; some from Rose, and of course Nick, his texts increasingly aggressive in tone. I erased them, eager to get to the saved voicemails, but Nick's voice had sent a chill through me as I'd shivered in Rob's car. Knowing Rob must have heard the messages had left me breathless. He would have assumed Nick and I were lovers, and yet he still wanted me to stay, and had done everything he could to save our marriage. In some ways his single-mindedness and quick-thinking, deleting emails from the web and hiding my phone, was impressive; but of course it wasn't, it was opportunistic and despicable; an appalling breach of trust. Unforgivable.

I hold my pink phone to my other ear, away from worst of the wind, begging Anna one last time to please pick up before I end the call. Anna's either ignoring me, or already on her way. I close my car boot and something catches my eye at the far end of the drive, a dumpy woman, her gait ungainly. She must have left her car in the lane as we'd planned. She's dripping wet, the rain a deluge now.

'Jo!' she calls across to me. 'I'm here! I made it!'

'Anna, you have to go back,' I tell her, running across the drive to meet her, then grabbing her arm when she refuses to stop. 'This is all wrong. My kids are in there; they've brought their partners.' I flick my wet hair from my face to see her better. She looks terrible, her eyes red, her hands trembling, her fine hair flattened with the torrential rain.

'You asked me to come,' she replies breathlessly. 'We agreed. You wanted me here. And the kids. You said he'd change your mind, poison theirs. You can't go back on this, Jo. I can't—'

'Anna, listen to me! I haven't changed my mind, not about leaving him, of course not. But not like this, Anna. Not in front of my kids.'

'He knows what to say, Jo.' She tries to push past me, then speaks through the torrential downpour, our faces close to one another. 'He'll convince me if I don't do this, and you. He'll stop you, you said so. The kids will take his side. You said it had to be like this, for all our sakes. I have to do this, Jo. Even if you can't.'

'Let me handle this my way, please, Anna—' But she's shrugging me off, marching towards the front door. I implore her not to, pulling her back, but she's much bigger than me and my grasp is slippery against the wet sleeve of her raincoat.

The front door is open, the wind sending it away from her into the empty hallway. She walks in and looks around her; first to her left, towards the deserted sitting room, then right to follow the voices in the kitchen.

'Anna, please don't' I say, catching her up, but she has no time for me.

She's told me she hates him for what he's done to us, but love and hate are twin souls, both fuelled by passion, and Anna is an unstoppable force.

The conversation at the table is at once silenced by our entrance. Rob, his glass half-drained and held aloft to toast my return, looks up to see Anna, tearful and soaked through, me at her heels. At first he is slack-jawed, then he stands up, as if compelled to do so. Ryan and Fin have their backs to us, but their heads swivel to see who has arrived. Sash is smiling, eyes wide, as though I'm about to introduce my closest friend.

'Anna!' Rob rushes towards us. 'Don't do this!'

He's between us now, trying to steer Anna from the room, but she refuses to move, shaking her head and releasing beads of water from her hair and clothes as she grabs on to the kitchen island for support. Rob looks at me, leaning in to whisper, 'Please, Jo. Not like this. Let's talk. I can explain.'

I glance across at Fin. His head is bowed but he's watching his father, then he catches my eye and looks away. I was deeply hurt, betrayed by my son's decision to keep what he knew from me, but I should never have been this cruel. What was I thinking? But I wasn't, I was acting. Trying to save myself from Rob's lies, his manipulation of the truth. I'd wanted Fin and Sash to see this for themselves, bear witness, but now I couldn't want anything less.

'Fin, darling.' I move towards him. 'I'm so sorry, I know you didn't mean it, he told you it was over. You believed him. This is all our fault; you are not to blame.'

Fin turns away from me towards Ryan, speaking quietly so I can't hear. I think Fin won't say anything, that his head will remain down and he will simply stand up from the table and leave. He does stand, his chair scraping noisily on the hard floor, but then his eyes meet mine, an intensity behind them, and although his voice is measured, the words are not.

'Couldn't you see it, Mum? Everyone could, surely?' He looks around him to his sister, then his father, then back to me. 'Was it easier to pretend? Like you did with me? All those years I was struggling, begging you to notice that I needed help. That all the money in the world couldn't make me happy. You ignored it all, told yourself I was fine, that sending me to university would make everything better somehow. I'm not like you, Mum, not like any of you. I can't stick a plaster over everything and just imagine it's better than it is.'

I reach out to him. 'Why didn't you tell me you were unhappy?'

'You're the parent! Why didn't you ask?'

'I did ask you. I asked you all the time. Are you trying to tell me that this is my punishment, that I deserve this?'

'Mum? Dad?' Sash asks. 'What's going on?'

Ryan speaks for Fin now; says they should leave, but Fin pauses next to me as Ryan walks out. 'Dad did promise me it was over.' He looks at his father who meets his eye then looks away. 'I never took a penny of his money, so if he said I did then he was lying.'

I pull Fin to me. 'I'm so sorry. I shouldn't have—'

'No, you shouldn't,' Fin says, pulling away. 'You should have had more faith in me.' Fin follows Ryan out and the door slams behind him.

'You pleased with yourself?' Rob asks, turning on me. 'Is this what you wanted?'

'This isn't my doing! This is your mess, Rob!' I scream in his face. 'Your mess!'

Anna is backing away from both of us to lean over the sink, running the tap as she splashes water on to her bright red face.

'Are you okay?' I ask her, placing a palm on her back which she shrugs off.

'Can someone please tell me what the fuck is going on?' Sash demands, standing up from the table, her burgeoning bump proudly displayed beneath a tightly stretched floral dress.

Thomas turns to her, whispers something in her ear as he pulls her to sit back down. 'What the . . . ?' she says, looking at her father. 'You're having sex with *that*?' She points a darkly painted nail at Anna who is now leaning with her back to the sink, her face still crimson. 'When you're married to that.' She points at me.

Sash's incredulity at her father's poor choice is fiercely loyal and I love her for it – at last someone on my side – but it is at Anna's cost and she is a wretched creature. I look behind me to where Anna's holding her ground against Rob's renewed efforts to persuade her away from the unfolding carnage. He's got her as far as the kitchen door, but no further. He lets go of her raincoat which falls open to reveal a very prominent stomach.

'Oh my god,' Sash says. 'Is that your baby in there?' she asks her father, pointing at Anna's midriff. 'Or is she just really fat and old?' Sash walks towards me now, pulling me into a fierce hug, the mass of her baby bump squashed between us, pushing her father away as he tries to comfort her.

Rob returns to Anna, coaxing her out of the kitchen and into the hallway; she's hysterical now, Sash's punishing jibes pushing her over the edge. I remove myself from Sash's protection to follow them, watching from the door as he drags Anna across the drive. Anna is resisting, turning away from him, then she walks off and he runs after her, both disappearing around the hedge into the lane, the storm taking them quickly away.

'Mum?' I look back at Sash, her hand to my arm, Thomas at her shoulder. 'Did you know?' She asks me.

'I'm sorry, there's so much I should have told you.' I look up at Thomas. 'I should have told you everything,' I say. 'Everything.'

Sash's eyes blaze once more and she shakes herself free of Thomas and runs outside screaming for her father to come back. I move to follow her, but Thomas grabs my arm and pulls me back into the hall, slamming the front door.

'Thomas, no! Let go of me!' I try to shake him off, his grasp on my upper arm tight enough to be painful.

'I need you to listen,' he says, 'Before Sash comes back.' He releases me and steps back. 'Nothing happened between you and I that night you came to the bar. Nothing! I should have told you at first, but . . .' He glances towards the closed door. 'I'm a shit, Jo. But I'm telling you the truth. You have to believe me: nothing happened.'

'I don't believe you. I remember being there. I know what happened, and Sash has a right to know.' I push him away as I walk towards the door. I can see Sash coming back up the drive, framed in the glass panel, her floral dress inadequate protection from the awful weather. I try to open the door, but Thomas's hand covers mine as I reach for the latch, preventing me from unlocking it.

'Wait!' he says. 'Think back to that night. Try to remember. Please. You know what happened, Jo. It's in there somewhere. Just think!'

I try to focus, to trace my way back to what I already know, but it's so muddled, so incomplete. I close my eyes, shutting everything else out: Thomas, the storm beyond the closed door, even Sash.

I was drunk, running from Nick, and from myself, from a drunken liaison, and from what had almost happened between us in that office, what I'd thought I wanted. I was looking for Sash. If I could just get to my daughter, sober up. Dazed, I wandered towards the darkened bar. The door was unlocked, no lights on inside, but there had been a light in the flat above. I just had to find my way up to it. There were so many doors, cupboards, a stock room, the stinking gents' toilet, but then a flight of stairs, a sliver of light at the top from an open door. I stumbled as I climbed, cried out. I thought how careless it was, leaving the place unlocked. Anyone could have wandered in. I pushed on the open door at the top of the stairs, peering in, expecting to find a hallway, or a sitting room, and instead finding just one room, a bed at its centre.

Sash knocks loudly on the front door and peers in, calling out when she spots me and Thomas the other side. 'Mum, let me in! I can't find Dad, he's gone! Mum! Thomas!'

Thomas calls back that the door is stuck, hang on. He pretends to wiggle the lock and turns back to me, his voice a low but insistent whisper. 'You remember, don't you? What really happened. You have to, Jo. Sash is pregnant, she needs us, both of us. Don't make her choose.'

I close my eyes again, ignoring Sash's pleas and Thomas's attempts to convince her he's trying to unlock the door.

I stepped back into the shadows, afraid they might have been in that bed together, my daughter, with him, but then I saw it was only one prone figure, Thomas, a naked back illuminated by the lamp at his side. A smooth curve of taut skin, muscles beneath, a thigh, a leg, a foot, a face as he turned towards me, his wide mouth drawing me in, his smile making me complicit in his treachery as he said my name, turning back the sheet to invite me in. I wanted him, to be next to him in that bed, to feel him within me; the same desire that has looped in my memory day and night. I wanted him more than anything, to make me feel alive, to desire me as I desired him.

'Mum! Thomas! What's going on in there?'

'I wanted you,' I say, opening my eyes to Thomas again. 'I'm ashamed, but I did want you, Thomas,' I tell him. I'm whispering, but I know he can hear me, even above Sash's knocks and calls, our faces close together as I look up at him. 'You asked me into your bed. You—'

'I didn't mean it, Jo. I wanted to see how far I could push you. I would have said no, but you ran out first. You know I wouldn't have—'

I stare at him and he shakes his head again. 'Nothing happened, I promise.'

Yes, I ran out. I ran away. I'd wanted him, desired him for that moment. To my shame. I'd wanted to feel something; passion, youth, desire. But I ran out. Nothing happened. Thank goodness. Nothing happened.

'You bastard!' I tell Thomas as he opens the door and Sash steps in, soaked through.

'What's going on?' she asks, her voice pleading, her eyes filling with tears as she glances up at Thomas.

'Everything's fine. I promise,' he says, smiling down at her. 'Did you find him? Your dad.'

'No, he must have already left with that woman.' She looks across at me. 'You two are hiding something. What is it?'

'For fuck's sake, Sash. The door slammed and the lock got stuck. That's it!' Thomas turns away from her.

'I have to go, Sash,' I tell her, unable to meet her eye.

'Go? Where to?' she says, grabbing my arm. 'Dad's gone. You can stay here. This is his fault, not yours. This is your home. Stay here!'

'I don't want to. I'm going to be staying with a friend, Rose, from the drop-in centre, but I'll be in touch. Okay, my darling?'

'I need you, Mum,' she says, pulling away from Thomas who has taken her hand and is telling her to let me leave now. She rushes at me, her arms around my waist, her tears wet against my cheek, her body cold and damp pressed tight to me, their child between us as she sobs. 'I need my mum.'

I tell her I love her; I'll always be there for her. *I promise*. Then I hand her over to Thomas, the bastard who took pleasure in taunting me, letting me think the worst of myself and him, and I pick up my keys from the hall table and walk outside into the squall, lifting my tear-stained face to the elements, as if the rain can wash away the hurt, the pain, the guilt.

'Jo, where are you going?' Rob is coming towards me, his long strides pulling him up the drive, Anna already collateral damage I presume, on her way back to her pink sitting room. 'You can't leave!' he shouts, running towards me. 'I won't let you!'

'Get off me!' I scream, shrugging off his grasp, his large hands pulling at me as I try to unlock my car. My hands are trembling and I drop the keys on to the wet gravel, Rob snatching them up before I do.

'Give them to me!' I shout.

'Not until we've talked about this. There are things I know about you. This is not just my fault, is it?'

I make a grab for the keys, but Rob holds them above his head. 'Come inside, Jo. We can sort this out.'

'You can't *make* me stay like you did last time,' I tell him, spitting out my words. 'You didn't even try to save me, did you? Did you want me to fall?'

'No!' Rob screams.

We both stop shouting, staring at one another instead, and maybe it hasn't, but it feels as though the storm has died down too.

'I remember what happened, Rob,' I tell him, my voice quiet and still. 'I reached out to you as I slipped.'

'You're wrong,' he says. 'Come inside, Jo.'

I tell him there's no point and I think he's going to deny it again, try to convince me, to lie his way out of it, but his voice is steely when he replies, 'I knew about Nick and I forgave you. But you won't do the same for me?' He laughs. 'Bloody price-less.'

'You know nothing of what happened between Nick and me; you have no idea.' I step away from him, my car solid and cold behind me, the rainwater soaking into my clothes as I look up at my husband, towering above me. 'The sad thing is you know less about the last year than I do,' I say, my voice calm. 'You've bent the past to fit your needs, lied to everyone, including yourself. This isn't about blame, Rob. It isn't about

Nick or Anna. It's about you and me; what we've done to one another. Go to her, Rob! She's pregnant with your child and she's not well. She needs you. Do the right thing!'

Rob's face crumples and he sobs, 'I want you, Jo. It's all been because I love you. I can't see a future without you, I'm begging you—'

'Give up, Rob. There's nothing to save any more. Just give up.'

He steps back, then he throws the keys on to the gravel between us and walks towards the barn, pushing past Sash and Thomas, who are emerging from the open door. I hear Sash shriek at her father that she hates him and they all go inside, the door slamming behind them.

I grab the keys from the wet stones and get into my car, distraught now, as my unsteady hand fumbles with the key. I open the window to allow the rain in, cool on my skin as I press down on the accelerator to drive away.

The hunched figure emerges slowly through the driving rain, a dark mass seeping into the edge of my consciousness as the wipers clear the windscreen. I'm aware of her before I act, the distance between us slipping away as I slam on the brakes, stopping just short of her, her arms raised in a silent surrender as I hear my voice scream, 'Anna!'

I throw open the car door, running towards her as her hands fall to her sides. Cradling the mass of her stomach she stumbles backwards, her face contorted with pain. She screams and drops down heavily on to the gravel, her legs landing in an ungainly manner, a shoe lost, reaching out for me to save her although I'm still yards away. I lunge forwards, losing my footing too, the stones skinning my knees as I desperately scrabble towards her. I see the blood now, her tights soaked with it as I try to comfort her. She's moaning, writhing in pain.

'I'm losing the baby, Jo. I'm losing it, aren't I?' She grabs my hand. 'Don't leave me, Jo. Stay close. Please stay close.'

'Anna, I have to get help. I'll be quick, I promise.'

I run towards the house, shouting ahead for someone to please open the door, banging my fist against the wood, the rain beating at my back as I scream my husband's name, then my daughter's, over and over.

24

Three Months After The Fall

The barn looks much the same as I pull into my usual spot on the drive, the wind greeting me as I open the car door; my hair lifted from my scalp then slapped back in my face. I look up at the darkened windows as I clear the wet strands from my view, the sky dirty white above bare-limbed trees, their branches silhouetted against the oppressive blanket of cloud, shivering in the gloom of a December day. I lock my car and then pause as I turn back to the house, a light now on in the kitchen. I worry if I should use my key or knock instead, but as I approach I see the front door is ajar, the wind rattling it back and forth. Three months since my fall and two months since I left the barn, and only now have I felt able to return, my belongings collected by Sash as I'd needed them, the thought of coming here before now always proving too much.

'Hello!' I call out, my heels echoing against the tiled floor of the hall. It feels colder inside, although it can't be, the bite of winter always harsher up here at the top of the hill. I spot the head-shaped hole at the bottom of the stairs and it still surprises me, as though I'd expected it to have disappeared, or never have been there at all.

'Jo? Is that you?'

Rob's voice comes from the kitchen, the room bright with antiseptic light as I walk in, the polished granite surfaces dusty with the weeks they've waited here for us. I always imagined he'd stay, but he left within a matter of days. The place empty ever since.

He has his back to me, the coffee machine blinking a red light as he watches the slow funnel of cream dripping into a mug, then he looks around and smiles, asks if I'd like a cup too. I reach out to steady myself against the island, a hard knot of emotion welling in my throat, the force of it so unexpected.

'You okay?' he asks, handing me the mug.

He's added milk, but I try to drink it anyway. 'I'm good,' I say, keeping my voice level. 'You?'

He frowns by way of reply and I note the signs of damage: his eyelids drooping over his pale eyes, lending them a hooded appearance, his face that of an old man, and his hair much thinner, although it's longer, in need of a cut.

'Not great,' he responds as he turns back to the coffee machine.

I look for the tanned strip of skin above his shirt, the familiar sight of it suddenly so needed, but the longer hair covers it. 'And Anna?' I ask.

He shakes his head.

'Sash told me she saw her at the hospital,' I say. 'It must have been so hard for her, seeing Sash like that.'

369

'It was a girl,' he says, and he turns back to me. 'Didn't think I wanted her.' He tries to laugh. 'Fucked up or what?'

'I'm so sorry,' I say and I truly am. 'I know that baby would have been loved and wanted.'

He nods, then says, 'Sash says she barely sees you other than the hospital appointments.'

'I try to avoid seeing Thomas,' I reply, turning away. I cannot forgive him for what he put me through, or maybe I cannot forgive myself for that moment of temptation. 'I give it a few more months.' I say, glancing back at Rob, and he nods.

We walk into the garden, despite the sharp air and the sodden grass which leaches dampness into the cherry suede of my new boots, a tidemark of dull burgundy. I mind that the boots may be ruined, but it's easier to be out here, walking side by side, our words caught and tugged at by the stiff chilled wind. Rob tells me he's asked Sash and Thomas to take over the rent on their flat. I laugh, say he'll be lucky, but I agree they do need to stand on their own feet; like Fin. Rob doesn't take the bait, he knows how heinous it was to blame Fin for the hand-outs which were actually going to Anna. Fin was angry with me too, only recently agreeing to see me, and I know he has little contact with his father.

I hang back, feigning interest in a holly bush, the bright red berries the only stabs of colour in the neglected garden. Rob waits for me to catch up, says the sale of the barn seems to be going well and I agree, tell him it was a good price, we were lucky. *Lucky*. The word dances between us, sneering before it evaporates on our breath, white puffs ahead of us as we walk.

'What do you do with yourself?' he asks, looking at me directly as the sky releases its first flakes of snow, catching on our eyelashes and settling on our shoulders and hair.

'What do you mean?' I ask, wrapping my coat more tightly around me.

'How do you fill your days?' He pauses, reaching out to brush something from my face.

'Don't!' I tell him, but we remain still, facing one another, fat snowflakes now falling fast.

'Do you see Nick?' he asks. 'Is he still your lover?'

'Don't,' I tell him again as I walk ahead, back towards the house. 'Just don't!'

If there were a time when I would have told Rob what really happened between Nick and me, then that moment has long passed. He believes Nick was my lover, and perhaps in a sense it's easier that he does. It's none of his business any more, he has no right to the truth and I have no desire to share it with him. There are questions I could ask him too, about deleted emails, a deliberately concealed phone, all the lies, but what would be the point? I have my answers already.

Rob calls after me, 'What do you do every day, Jo?'

I stop, turn around, open my mouth to speak, but then I'm unsure what to say. What would I tell him? That I attend my weekly meeting at the brain injury group, eat Rose's home-cooked meals, sleep in the single bed that was once hers whilst she sleeps in her parents' room next door, that we talk endlessly about Nick's disappearance and our work at the drop-in centre, and how I'm thinner, or more tired, or how many weeks until Sash's baby arrives, as though that were the great hope; a new year and a new baby all it takes to mend a broken heart. Or would I want to share with him how sometimes when I'm behind Nick's desk – now tidy – updating the new paperless system that Rose and me, but mainly me, have grappled with for weeks and almost completed, I can feel almost content. How I forget the room was once the source of such fear and pain, and I lose myself in my work. Would I brag how the charity has offered me Nick's job at Rose's insistence, and I'm taking my time to think about it, although I'm almost certain I will? How I have moments when I feel in control at last, worthy of respect. Or how when I leave the centre with Rose, I imagine myself, once this place is sold, walking to an apartment or small house of my own, filled with everything I have chosen, everything I will learn to love, and closing the door on the rest of the world.

'It doesn't concern you any more, what I do,' I reply as I go back inside the empty barn.

The forms are on the dining table, neatly laid out with a pen at their side. I sign first. Rob pauses, looks up at me and I hand him the pen. He takes it then says to me as he signs, 'Anna wants to try for a baby again, but if it would make any difference, if there were even a small chance that—' He looks up at me.

'There isn't,' I tell him.

After I hear his car drive away I go upstairs and switch on the bedroom light, pulling the blind against the near darkness. The snow has stopped, but the lane will be dark and slippery. I need to go soon, before it's too treacherous. The suitcase is on the bed, taken down from the loft as promised. He's even unzipped it. I open my wardrobe doors and begin packing my remaining clothes, every dress or jacket taken from its hanger and folded neatly. Then I do the same with the contents of each drawer, picking up a book, half read, still resting on my bedside table. I glance at the cover then I throw it in too, closing the zip around the tangled mess inside. I wheel it along the hallway, past the empty rooms until I reach the top of the stairs where I push the handle down and lift the heavy case on to the first stair, almost losing my balance as I reach out to save it from falling. I steady myself, adjusting my technique to go down backwards, the weight of the case above me now as I bump it from tread to tread. I've only tackled two stairs when the image rears up, a perfect picture, fully formed and clear. I stop, supporting the suitcase as I look up.

Rob is behind me, begging me not to leave, he'll do anything, he says, his hand reaching out to stop me. I step away from him. He can't stop me now, he can't. There's no excuse. I don't want him any more, there's nothing left. Nothing worth fighting for. I abandon the photos I'd been trying to remove from the wall. I just need to get away from here, from him. My foot slips, just a little, an inch too far from the tread. I reach out to Rob and he hesitates, but then he grabs my wrist, his reflexes quick as his firm hold tethers me there; safe. I feel such relief, the protection of his hand on mine, the tightness of it, squeezing so hard around my wrist I think the pain may slice straight through the bone.

My tears are falling hard now, my chest heaving as I feel that same relief again. He'd held me there; safe, his grip so tight it had bruised my wrist.

But I still fell.

My hands cover my mouth, suppressing a scream as I see Rob's expression change, his eyes clouding over, the frown deep.

He releases his grasp on my wrist all at once, an opening of his palm, a stretch of the long fingers, my body tilting back as I scream, 'Rob. No!'

The heavy suitcase slides towards me, its weight knocking me off balance. I step back, losing my footing, but this time I manage to grab the bannister and save myself, watching as the case falls, two heavy thuds as it hits first the wall, then the tiled floor below. I sink down on to the stair beneath me, my hands shaking, my eyes closed; but the image of Rob is still there, his hand opening to let me fall, the cold hard tiles of the hall floor hurtling towards me; the first lie already forming on my husband's lips.

Acknowledgements

Without Sarah Williams, my wonderful agent, this book would not be in your hands. Sarah's patience and tenacity have always equalled and often exceeded my own as we walked this path together. She spotted something in my writing and held her nerve. For that, and her skill and intelligence, I owe her everything. And to Sophie Hicks, who always offers the best and most down-to-earth advice, and Morag O'Brien, who has taken *Close To Me* to places I could never have dreamed it would go. I am forever grateful.

Thanks also to everyone at Headline who has been involved in the many aspects of publishing *Close To Me*. I am so fortunate to have found such an amazing publisher. Aside from their expertise, the team at Wildfire – Alex Clarke, Kate Stephenson and Ella Gordon – are also the loveliest people you could hope to meet. A special thank you is reserved for Kate Stephenson whose editorial skill has brought my book to life. I have loved working with you, Kate, every minute of it. Also thanks to Katie Brown for her superlative PR, Jo Liddiard for her creative marketing, and Siobhan Hooper for my beautiful cover.

To my Mum and Dad, who inspired me to always follow

my dreams and instilled in me a belief that I could achieve anything if I wanted to, I am so grateful. And to my wonderful husband Chris, who has put up with the strange and volatile world I inhabit as I write. You have always believed in me; thank you so much. And for my children, Beth and Dan. You are my world and I am so proud of you both.

To my extended family and friends, thanks for knowing when to ask, 'How's the book going?' and when to talk about something else. The support from you all has been such a source of strength. To George, Val, Clare, David, Hannah, Morgan, Olivia, Tony, Kim, Gayle, Caroline, and all my family and friends, thanks for caring about something that matters so much to me.

A huge debt of thanks is also owed to my writer friends, Hayley Hoskins, Kate Riordan and Helen Maslin, who have understood this journey in ways no one else can. It's a long road and without them it would have been so much harder. For their thoughtfulness, loyalty, fun, laughter, and all the hours spent reading on my behalf, I thank them endlessly. Thanks also go to Henri, an early supporter of my writing.

To all the members of Cotswold Creative Writing, thank you for sharing your beautiful stories with me each week; they have entertained and moved me and it has been a pleasure and a privilege to get to know you all.

No one writes a book alone, so to everyone who has helped, thanks, thanks, and more thanks. It's never too late to dream. Never.